Return to Sycamore Hill

VOLUME 2

STACEY WEEKS

Praise for Stacey Weeks

One of the things I enjoy about Stacey Weeks' writing is her ability to present a powerful & touching gospel message organic to the story, without it feeling forced or preachy. Instead of stopping an entertaining story for a sermon, Weeks uses the faith-centered elements to enhance the characters' journeys on the page and point to the Source of peace, strength, and courage.

— CARRIE ~ BOOK REVIEWER, READING IS MY SUPERPOWER

Weeks is a writer I count on for sweet contemporary romances with faith messages to make me think. She combines sympathetic characters with heartening take-aways about the freedom of living in grace and the power of community.

— AUTHOR EMILY CONRAD

The town of Sycamore Hill is warm and welcoming. The heart of God shines throughout the story.

— JULIA - BOOK REVIEWER, CHRISTIAN BOOKAHOLIC

More Fiction by Stacey Weeks

SYCAMORE HILL

MISTLETOE MEADOWS

STAND ALONE TITLES

Contents

THE SYCAMORE SLOPES

ONE SYCAMORE SUNDAY

A SYCAMORE SECRET

Free Short Story

Download at StaceyWeeks.com

When sweet peppers and jalapeño mix,
anything can happen.

Addison avoids visiting the city. He hates the crowds, traffic, and pace. He especially hates the compact vehicle the rental company insists he'd reserved. But then he runs into Sarah. Or, more accurately, she runs into him, mixing sweet peppers and jalapeño with burnt metal, petrol, hot pavement, and her desperation to not merely survive life in the city but find a place to thrive. Addison isn't looking for a weekend thrill or a romantic entanglement anymore than she is. They both want to go home. Maybe, together, they'll find their way.

To God, who has done far more for me than I could ask for or imagine.

So, whether you eat or drink, or whatever you do,
do all to the glory of God.

1 Corinthians 10:31

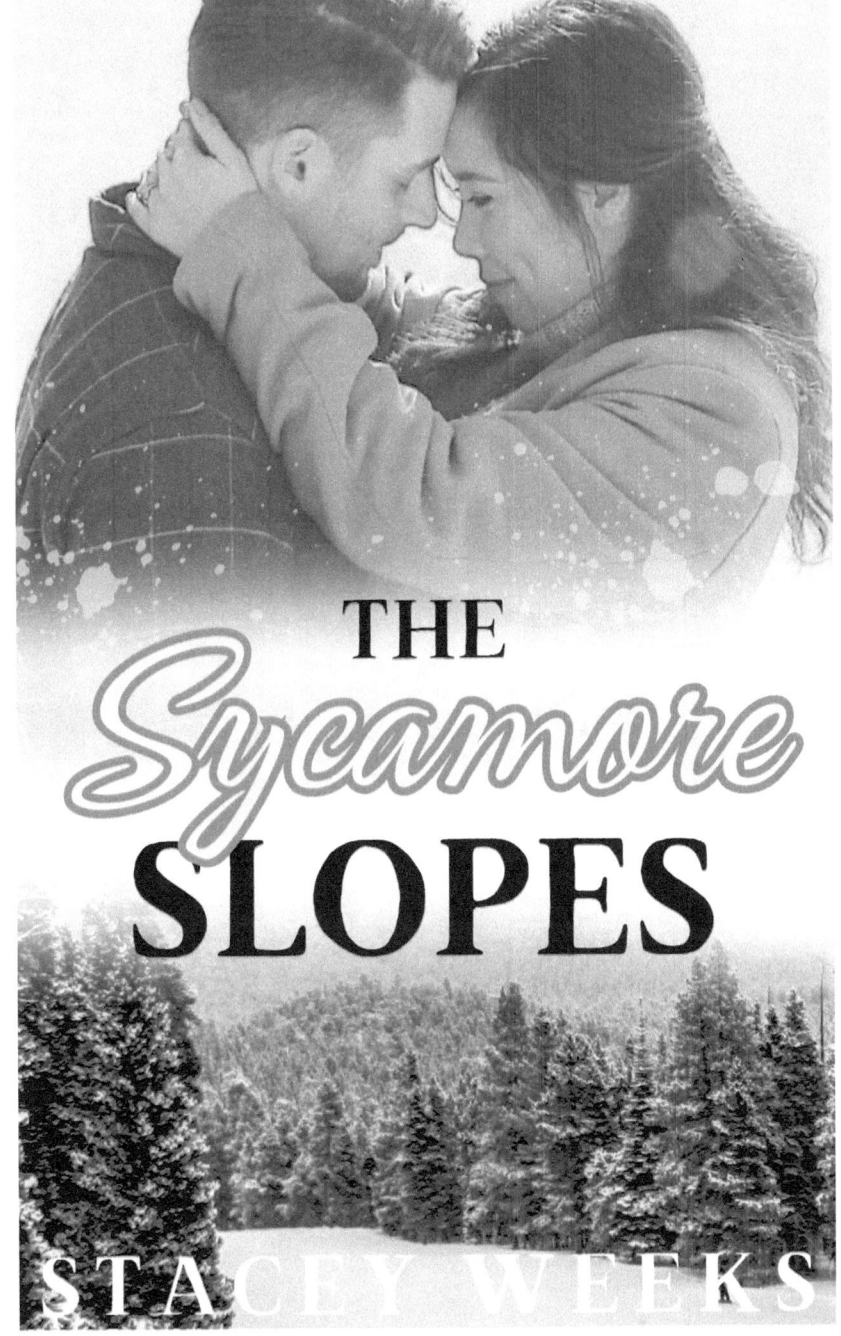

THE
Sycamore
SLOPES

STACEY WEEKS

The Sycamore Slopes

Ben Sawyer gives the vulnerable a voice and strives to protect them, but he can't stop the avalanche of trouble descending on his nephew. His strongest opponent isn't the grumpy Grinch sowing discord in the community, but the one person he believed would always be by his side, Nurse Practitioner Emma Powles.

Emma Powles is busy in her newly established medical clinic as the fallout from sledding and skating accidents inundates her clinic. She treats the suspicious injuries of a local child and she's forced to intervene for the girl's safety. Her actions rouse traumatic memories in Ben, testing the foundation of their relationship. Will the echoes of Ben's past shatter their future?

The Sycamore Slopes is an enthralling romance that seamlessly weaves together family drama, small-town politics, and powerful themes of resilience.

One

A bloodcurdling shriek sliced through the air. Ben Sawyer didn't flinch. He merely lifted his camera, peered through the lens, and rotated the focusing ring. He concentrated on Sycamore Hill's ice-covered pond, the origin of the happy squeals. Skaters glided into the frame, and he held down the shutter release to utilize the camera's continuous shooting mode—a trick a fellow reporter taught him. Small-town newspapers didn't have the budget for photographers. The reporters pulled double duty.

Local Kids Glide Toward Better Health. Not the best headline, but it'd have to do. The assignment editor threw this at Ben last minute. He thought an article on the town's outdoor activities paired well with Ben's exposé on the rising statistics of childhood obesity. Ben captured another cluster of images. The story wasn't a lead. Not even a shocker. It might as well be printed in the classifieds.

A chilly breeze pushed the scent of hot chocolate and corn

dogs from a cluster of nearby food trucks. The sweet aroma dominated over sweaty bodies stuffed into winter snow suits. *Pop Up Food Vendors. Who Moderates Them?* Still boring, but he committed the potential headline to memory anyway.

Ben adjusted the camera lens again. The nip in the air reddened noses and chapped cheeks, but it colored no one more adorably than little Oliver, Kim Jansen's son. Kim had only recently regained custody of Oliver after her ex had spirited him out of the country. Ben covered the mother/son reunion for the paper, which was spearheaded by Oliver's Uncle Jackson.

Kim and Jackson sandwiched Oliver, clutching his mittened hands and supporting him on his skates. The average person would never guess all they had endured to get to this happy spot. But that's the way it often was. People only saw the outside. Scars lived underneath.

The blades slipped and slid beneath the boy. Oliver's face scrunched as if he were trying to climb Mount Everest. "I do it! I do it!"

Ben snapped another picture. *Local Boy Learns to Skate.* Cute kids dominated the front pages of Sycamore Hill's paper. This one was sure to score Ben a place above the fold, but it was hardly the exclusive that jump-started a career. He'd already written that exclusive, and it had gotten him nowhere.

A rope of kids linked hands to play crack the whip on the far side of the pond. Janelle Holmes, his neighbors' kid, squealed. The momentum of the skaters pulled the unfortunate tail over the surface of the ice.

Ben pivoted again. He zoomed in on the adjacent slope. Calling it a slope was a bit of a stretch, but it was the closest thing to a sledding hill the town could offer. Children slogged up the gentle incline, dragging sleds and plastic carpets behind them.

Their friends zipped down the steep side in a strange conveyer belt of activity. He captured another grouping of images. *Fun on the Sycamore Slopes.* That should be enough.

But not Pulitzer Prize enough.

He navigated through the pictures, zooming in on faces, deleting the ones with closed eyes or unflattering angles. People liked seeing their photos in the paper, but only if their likeness complimented them. And parents loved seeing their children in print. He had enough shots of delighted youngsters for his bland assignment. Done with a capital D.

He repacked his satchel and squinted against the early pangs of a headache. The boughs of a frost-dusted pine tree blurred as he rubbed the butt of his palm in circles on his forehead. Could a career reporting for Sycamore News make him happy? Just the idea of covering common occurrences for the rest of his life made his limbs heavy. Everything required an astronomical effort. Even his lungs resisted inflating.

"Uncle Ben!" Nico waved as he raced toward the hill. A long blue sled attached to a thin yellow rope bounced behind him.

The iceberg in his chest liquified. This was why he stayed. He wanted to watch his nephew grow up. He wanted to help his sister, Claire. He wanted to be here for his parents. But mostly, he wanted to make things permanent with Emma. He had the ring hidden in his bedside table. All he needed now was a plan. Nobody *just proposed* anymore.

"Look out!"

The panicked cry lifted the head of every adult. Ben swung, fumbling for his camera. Never pack the camera! Rookie mistake.

Powerful momentum sent Janelle on a trajectory toward Oliver. The ten-year-old girl's impact forced Oliver from Jackson and Kim's grip in seemingly slow motion. The boy catapulted into the air like a bull's prey and came down even harder with a thwack.

Silence fell just as spectacularly. Too quiet. Oliver should be crying.

No, no, no. No. NO.

This kind of quiet screamed everything was not okay. It roared in Ben's ears. Everything was not fine. Everything might never be fine again. His cold fingers fumbled for his phone. Emma was the top of his favorites. He stabbed the screen.

Emma didn't answer.

Come on. He tried again.

Still no answer.

He called a third time, knowing three calls in quick succession would override her silence feature.

"Hello?"

"Come to the slopes! There's been an accident."

That's all she needed. She promised to hurry.

Ben pushed through the cluster of people. He stuffed the phone into his zippered pocket. His fat fingers couldn't pull the tab to close the teeth.

Jackson's hands roamed each of Oliver's limbs, and Kim cradled Oliver's head, not moving his neck.

Janelle had crumpled onto the ice off to the side. Her elbows pressed into her body. "I'm sorry! I'm sorry!"

"Emma's on her way." Ben dropped to a knee beside Jackson. "She'll be here any second."

The tendons in Jackson's neck popped out as he nodded. "Keep his head stabilized, Kim."

As the only police presence in town, Jackson, with his emergency training, was the next best thing to Emma. And as the only nurse practitioner in a town with no doctors, Emma was the next best thing to a paramedic or hospital. Ben's fisted hand bounced against his thigh. She should be here by now.

Oliver roused. He tried to move.

Ben craned his neck to scan the line of parked cars on the side road, looking for Emma's familiar hatchback. *Come on.*

Kim leaned over Oliver so he could see her face. "Stay still, baby. You'll be okay." Oliver's knitted red hat absorbed Kim's tears.

Ben smeared the sweat beading on his lips across his cheeks. Traumas that involved children— They changed you. He sucked in and held his breath.

Stop thinking about that.

Kim pressed her lips to Oliver's forehead, still stabilizing him and murmuring soft words.

She sounded just like his mother had.

Emma's medical bag thudded onto the ice beside Ben, jolting him from the past. He didn't even remember kneeling beside the boy, but his pant legs were soaked through. Emma checked Oliver's vitals. Her slender fingers moved his body. A long auburn braid fell over one shoulder, and her knitted toque had been knocked askew. The bright striped pattern of blue and red contrasted with her creamy skin. Her clear eyes fixed on Oliver. "How long was he out?"

Kim's features pinched. "Just a few minutes."

Seemingly satisfied that nothing was broken, Emma flicked a tiny penlight across Oliver's eyes. What she saw must have pleased her. As the stiffness in her posture loosened, Ben's relief shot out like a bullet.

Emma held Kim's gaze. "I think he'll be fine, but I'd like to take him to the clinic for a more thorough check up."

Kim wiped her eyes and reached for Jackson with a shaky hand. "Thank you."

"Can I carry him?" Jackson hovered, ready to scoop the boy up but unwilling to move him until Emma gave the okay.

She nodded.

Jackson tenderly carried the child to Kim's van. Jackson was one of the good guys. The kind of police officer children could trust. Like the one that returned Ben to his parents when he was lost as a child.

Not like the other officer. Not like the one that took him away. Ben stretched his cramped fingers, flexing them at his sides.

Ben caught words and phrases like *champ*, *be brave*, *you'll be okay*, and *I've got you*. Jackson's optimistic tone and word choices contrasted with his sickly white complexion. The man loved that kid like a father.

"What took so long?" Ben shuffled closer to Emma as her attention shifted to Janelle.

Janelle's hands jammed into her armpits, and she rocked back and forth. Shallow breath sounds. Catatonic gaze.

Emma flicked her gaze to Ben, but instead of bouncing back to Janelle, she lingered. "I couldn't find a place to park." Her chin lifted to the right, and her head tilted. "Are you okay? You look pale."

Ben flattened his lips. The parking situation had become ridiculous. The pond and the slope jetted off a dead-end street. Vehicles filled the nearby side roads, many of them blocking the resident's driveways. "I'll be fine. But Janelle's not looking so good."

Emma knelt in front of Janelle. She patiently waited for Janelle to lift her head. The circumference of the dark circle growing over Emma's denim-clad knees increased. She kept her hands still.

Finally, Janelle made eye contact.

"Are you hurt?"

Janelle shook her head. "Is Oliver gonna be okay?"

"I think so. How are you?"

Janelle blinked. At some point, her hat had fallen off, and static electricity lifted strands of her dark hair.

"I'm fine." Janelle cut her eyes to Ben. "Is this going to be in the paper?"

He started to say no but stopped. He'd been sent to report on the activities. The editor might divert to winter safety once he heard of the accident. "I don't know. But I won't take your picture unless you want me to." That, he could promise.

"I don't."

Ben patted his satchel. "Then my camera stays put."

"Can I check you over?" Emma placed a gentle hand on Janelle's shoulder.

Emma's soft mannerisms had a calming effect. Ben's erratic pulse normalized. Emma was not the doctor that made a terrible mistake. Jackson was not the police officer that took Ben away from his parents. Everything was going to be fine.

Janelle tugged her jacket sleeves down over her gloved hands. "I'm okay."

"I expect you are, but I'd like to be sure. Sometimes shock stops us from feeling everything."

Janelle nodded a curt consent.

Emma completed a basic examination and then sat back on her heels. "You're right. You seem fine. But I'll call your parents so they can keep an eye on you."

Janelle diverted her gaze.

Interesting. Was she afraid they'd be angry at her? Ben had never seen or heard anything concerning from his neighbor's house.

Emma repacked her emergency medical kit and hoisted herself to her feet. Her damp knees didn't seem to bother her. "I better get to the clinic. Oliver will be waiting."

Ben clutched the top of his satchel to camouflage the shakiness in his hands. "You have to fill out an incident report, right?"

She nodded.

"I saw the accident. It wasn't Kim or Jackson's fault. I want to add my testimony to the paperwork."

A tiny laugh bubbled from Emma. Not a laugh of mockery. She wasn't the type to poke fun. It was more like a chuckle of relief. She started to walk toward the side road where she must have parked, although he still couldn't see her vehicle. "That's not necessary. I'll make a note it was an ice-skating accident. It's no big deal."

Ben didn't remember the doctor's exact words to his mother, but they were probably similar and spoken in the same casual tone. The doctor had no idea that his belief in the system would rip Ben's family apart. Emma stood at the edge of the same cliff, and another family teetered on the precipice. "It's a big deal for me. I want to be sure everything is noted. You know, for later, if necessary."

Emma stopped and faced Ben, fisting her hands on her hips. Her eyebrows pulled together, and her nose wrinkled adorably. "Did something happen that you're not telling me?"

He avoided her eyes. He wasn't ready. He might never be ready. "If you have legal responsibilities to report certain types of injuries, I just want to be there."

She studied him for a second longer before conceding. "You're a sweet man for caring so much." She lifted onto her tiptoes and pressed a chaste kiss to his lips.

An unexpected release of tension loosened the knots in Ben's neck. He wasn't sure whether it was relief over not needing to explain why this mattered so much or her yielding to his request. But either way, justice would prevail.

"Thank you. I'll be there as soon as I can." He lightly squeezed her hands as she pulled away.

She gave him a playful wink. "Don't be long."

Now the excitement was over, skaters had returned to the ice. They twirled and held hands. Blades scraped the frozen surface, mixing with laughter and innocent squealing. Life went on.

Someone pressed play on their winter playlist, but it couldn't quite smother the songs of childhood. Ben wanted this for his kids. A community. A place to belong. A place that stood together.

His future kids.

An increasing warmth in his chest warred with his cold toes. Emma had reached her car, tucked between two vans. She turned for a final wave, disappeared inside, and drove off. He and Emma hadn't discussed children yet. They discussed marriage. That was where their track headed. At least it was where he hoped it was headed. They'd reached what his mom called "the ripe age of early thirties," and according to her, their train raced to the tick of a biological clock.

His career ran alongside that train on a parallel track. At least, it was parallel until Grander City Daily News offered him a job. It wasn't the hard-hitting journalism he once dreamed of, but it was a step up from Sycamore Hill. The only catch was they required him to move to the city. Emma had worked too hard to become a nurse practitioner and open her medical clinic to follow him to the city. He'd have to choose.

He'd worked his whole life for an opportunity to report at a big city paper and stir the poisonous pots the government had its hands in. But now that a paper had reached out, his feet got cold. Ben stomped his boots, and they sunk into the snow. A frosty tingle crept toward his ankles.

He couldn't think about that right now. Protecting Oliver was all that mattered. The poor kid had already suffered enough in his young life. Ben would write an article that mentioned the incident. It ensured the truth was officially recorded somewhere. It was an accident. And someone other than the doctor and police needed to know.

Accidents happened. This wasn't anybody's fault.

Two

"I'll be a few more minutes with Oliver, then I'll take a closer look at Janelle."

Janelle's mother, Kellie Holmes, nodded her head. Her mousy brown hair fell forward. "Thank you."

Kellie's words, tone, and facial expression conveyed appropriate emotion, but her demeanor didn't quite match. Emma's belly somersaulted. Something was amiss. She made a short note on the appointment chart at her reception desk.

The clinic's exterior door slammed against the door stopper. Ben stumbled in, and the door bounced back into place. His spectacular entrance drew every eye, but it was Janelle's wince that made her curious.

Ben's gaze roamed the reception area as he tugged off his cap. Short tufts of dark hair sprung to attention. "Is Oliver okay? Have you signed off on his injuries?" His words huffed with each rise and fall of his chest.

Did the man run all the way here?

"He's fine." Emma walked around the desk. "Kim and Jackson

are with him now. Are you okay?" She squinted as she stared into his eyes. She always loved Ben's dark eyes, but this moment had nothing to do with romance. His pupils constricted. It was probably due to the brightly-lit waiting room. She led Ben to the nearest chair.

"I had to run here. My car was blocked in."

That explained his heaving chest and flushed complexion. But what explained the panic? She dispensed some cooler water into a tiny paper cup and handed it to him.

Ben looked like he was about to say something more, but he closed his mouth and accepted the cup.

She let his erratic behavior go. She had a patient in the room, another in the queue, and a receptionist who'd called in sick.

"Is Oliver really okay?" Ben studied her as if trying to read her non-verbal cues.

"Kim and Jackson can fill you in." She wouldn't divulge detailed patient information. Ben's concern might be genuine, but the ethical line existed for a reason.

Jackson poked his head out from the examination area. "Is that Ben?" When his gaze landed on his friend, he briefly disappeared behind the door before popping out again, pulling the door closed behind him. He extended his hand to Ben. "Kim and Oliver are fine. We really appreciate your concern. Emma told us how important it was to you that everything was documented properly."

Ben shook Jackson's hand.

"I'll wait here with you." Jackson claimed the empty seat next to Ben. "Did you catch the game last night?"

Emma threw Jackson a thankful nod and then hurried back to her patient.

"Ben sure is sweet." Kim stroked her fingers through Oliver's hair. It was still baby fine, and her movements sent several strands to attention.

Emma closed the door behind her.

Sweet. That was one way to describe it. Another word was relentless. A dog with a bone. His tenacity was what made him a good reporter.

"I'm going to test your reflexes, Oliver. Is that okay?"

The boy's eyes expanded when she pulled her reflex hammer from her pocket. He burrowed his face into Kim's side.

Emma chuckled. She tapped the hammer. "It's got a soft head. Want to feel it?"

Oliver peeked from behind a fold of fabric and nodded. Oliver was one month shy of his third birthday.

Emma extended the hammer, and he reached out a tentative hand and stroked its head.

"I'll tap your knee, and it should bounce. See?" Emma tested Oliver's deep tendon reflex, and the boy giggled as his leg gave an involuntary kick.

"I didn't know Ben cared so much about the kids in the community." Kim rubbed small circles into Oliver's back. "It's kind."

Sure. They'd use that word. Kind.

Not overbearing.

Not disproportionate.

"Now, we'll check your coordination. First, I'd like you to put your hands on your thighs."

Oliver looked at his mom.

"These are your thighs." Kim tapped Oliver's quadriceps.

He complied.

"Turn your hands over and lift them up." Emma modelled the action.

Oliver completed the task. "This is silly."

Emma grinned. "If you think this is silly, try doing it over and over as fast as you can."

A belly laugh rumbled deep within Oliver, and the sound made Emma's heart swell. He was going to be just fine.

"You're great with kids."

Emma thanked the Lord Kim's eyes stayed on Oliver. Judging from the temperature in her cheeks, they had to be blazing red. "Thanks."

"How long have you and Ben been dating?"

Emma bounced her gaze back to Oliver. "About a year."

"Hmmmm." The sound wasn't even a word, yet it carried a punch.

"We had our first date at last year's Life House banquet."

Kim perked up at the mention of the gala. She'd organized the annual fundraiser that brought in enough money to support Life House and its ministries for the following year.

Emma twisted her lips to the side. "Did I ever tell you how we ended up attending together?" She lifted Oliver from the examination table and set his feet on the floor.

Oliver reached out as if he were about to touch the stethoscope slung around Emma's neck. Kim wagged a finger at him, and he retracted his hand.

"It's a funny story. Ben literally broke through my skylight the night before your event."

"You're kidding."

"Right through the ceiling and onto my kitchen floor." She shifted her gaze back to Kim's son. "Now I want you to touch your nose. Can you do that?"

"How come *that* never made the paper?"

"It did, in a way. He was chasing a lead for the Emergence story. That's how I got involved. By the time we cleaned up the mess the broken skylight had created, he'd invited me to attend the gala with him."

Oliver pressed his index fingertip to his nose. One digit slipped inside, and Kim gently tugged his arm to pull it out. She made a face at him. "That's gross."

Emma had been about to ask Oliver if he could touch her fingertip with his, but she twisted around and grabbed a hand wipe from the back counter instead. She disinfected Oliver's fingers and tossed the wipe in the trash. She stretched out her index finger. "Now, touch my finger with your fingertip."

Oliver pressed his fingertip to hers.

"Now touch your nose."

He obeyed.

"And my finger. And your nose. Keep doing this."

As Oliver alternated between touching his nose and Emma's finger, Kim peppered Emma with questions. "Is Ben always this intense around kids? Did he ask for your help in the Emergence trial? Why is he so wound up about Oliver's skating accident? I appreciate his concern for Oliver, but . . ." her voice trailed off.

"That's good, Oliver," Emma deflected. "Now close your eyes and see if you can keep touching your nose and my finger. No peeking."

The boy giggled.

Emma didn't know how to answer Kim. The way Ben pressed Emma to document everything was a bit offensive. Emma knew how to do her job, but she sensed there was more to the story.

"Good job, Oliver. Open your eyes. Now, let's see if you can repeat the experiment with the other hand."

Ben's restlessness concerned her. He was overreacting, that was for sure. Kids get hurt. And despite Ben's assurance that he knew that, his actions told a different story.

"One more test, Oliver, then we'll be all done. You're doing great."

"Do you ever think about having kids?"

Kim's question twanged Emma's heart. She tried to set her thoughts aside, but they fought back. She used to assume she would have kids, and then school took up all her time, then starting the clinic. But once she'd met Ben, and she began to hope that maybe, one day, the Lord would answer her prayer for a family.

Kim must have read something in her expression because she pulled back. "I'm sorry. That was nosy of me."

Emma smiled. "It's okay. Oliver, can you walk from this trolley cart to the edge of the curtain and back again?"

"What are you checking for?"

"Gait. How he walks and swings his arms tells me a lot." Emma had Oliver repeat the test on his toes, walking heel to toe, on his heels, and finally, she had him hop in place.

"Oliver will be fine. If he has a headache, over the counter pain medication should be sufficient. If you have any other concerns, or anything new develops, just give me a call." She retrieved Oliver's jacket from the wall hook and handed it to Kim, placing the matching snow pants on the examination table.

"Thanks, Emma. I'm really thankful you opened your clinic. Sycamore Hill needed local medical care." Kim stuffed one little, wiggly arm into the puffy coat and started wrestling with the other.

Emma was thankful, too. Running her own clinic was a dream come true. She opened a cupboard and pulled out a small trunk shaped like a treasure box. She'd stuffed it with all sorts of goodies. Emma opened the lid and held it out to Oliver. "You did such a great job. Why don't you pick a prize from my prize box?"

Oliver freed his arm from the jacket sleeve as he reached for the box. His gaze flicked to his mom's, and she nodded. He dipped his hand into the treasure and rooted around, removing several options to examine them.

"He doesn't need any imaging?" Kim asked.

"It's not necessary, but if you'd feel better, I can order some."

"No, that's okay. If you're satisfied, so am I."

Oliver still debated his prize choice.

"It's a tough decision, isn't it?"

His lips puckered. He scrunched his forehead. "I want the bubbles."

"Good choice," Kim affirmed.

After wiping down the equipment and changing the paper that covered the examination table, Emma followed Kim and Oliver to the waiting room. How Oliver tucked his hand into his mother's and looked up at her with such adoration intensified Emma's longing for a family of her own. Kim fought hard to get here—to get Oliver back from her ex. Hayden might have gotten away with the parental abduction had his twin brother, Jackson, not intervened.

And now Jackson was here with Kim, and they made a beautiful family.

One day, Lord willing, she'd have one too. A family. Her eyes sought Ben. If she kept saying one day, would she eventually run out of days?

Ben was just as career-driven as she was, especially after breaking the Emergence story. When no immediate offers came from the big papers after the exclusive hit the news, he deflated. She loved Ben, and she wanted good things for him. But if an offer came in from a larger paper, he'd have to move. And her clinic was here, in Sycamore Hill. She bit the inside of her cheek. What if she wasn't enough reason for him to stay?

Oliver tugged free of his mother and darted into Jackson's outstretched arms. "Look, Unca Jackson. Bubbles!"

"We'll have fun with those."

Jackson, Kim, and Oliver left, and Emma wondered how long it would be before they announced wedding plans. Oliver's biological dad might be Jackson's deadbeat brother, but it was obvious to anyone who saw the threesome that they made a perfect family. But they had baggage.

But who didn't? She and Ben lugged an entire luggage set.

Ben slumped in his chair.

"Janelle can go into the examination room," Emma said to Kellie. "I'll be right there."

Kellie motioned for Janelle to move, and the girl hopped to her feet.

Emma frowned. Janelle moved more gingerly than she had at the pond. Had she missed something in her initial examination? Was it a simple case of the aches settling in?

"You wrote everything down, right?"

Ben's fixation made her jaw tense. A bee was having a fit in his bonnet. "Of course, I wrote everything down."

Their gazes held for a long minute. There was something Ben wasn't telling her. Before she could probe deeper, Ben's sister, Claire, burst through the clinic doors with Ben's nephew, Nico. "Help!"

Three

en bolted to his sister and slipped his arm under Nico to help support his weight. Claire transferred Nico's weight to Ben. How did she get the boy this far on her own? The ten-year-old was solid. Built like a linebacker. A tank. At the moment, a very wobbly tank with bones of jelly.

"Lay him down." Emma directed them to a second examination room with a table.

Ben scooped Nico under his knees and arms and carried him to the bed. The white sheets amplified the paleness of Nico's usually warm skin tone.

"He was on the hill." Claire wrapped her arms around her middle. "His sled hit a tree."

Nico was conscious but groggy. "Uncle Ben?" His eyelids fluttered.

Ben's knees weakened. "That's a good sign, right?"

"Did he lose consciousness?" Emma's tone had shifted from the slightly irritated woman bothered by Ben's questions to a focused, in-command professional.

Ben sagged. *Thank you, God, for Emma.*

"Briefly." Claire's voice caught. She pressed a fist into her mouth. His sister. His only sister. A sister he might not have known had things played out differently. The trickle-down effect of the possible paths his life could have taken hit like a sledgehammer. If he didn't know Claire, he wouldn't know his brother-in-law. He'd have never met Nico.

Stop.

Ben wrapped an arm around Claire's shoulder and pulled her into a side hug. She slumped into him. "He'll be okay. Emma will take care of him."

Claire turned into him. A quiet sob rippled down her frame. "It was awful. He wouldn't open his eyes. I keep seeing it over and over in slow motion, and there is nothing I can do to stop it."

Lord, have mercy.

"Nico, can you tell me where you are?" Emma hovered over Nico so they were eyeball to eyeball. Her intensity iced Ben's veins. She was probably checking to see if his pupils responded the same or if they were unequal, but fear nearly took him out at the knees.

"Doctor's."

"That's good." Emma smiled. "Who am I?"

"Auntie Emma."

Ben melted. Lord willing, one day, she'd *really* be Nico's Auntie Emma, and the title would be more than an endearment.

Emma flicked a glance at her watch and refocused on Nico. She was secretly taking his pulse. Ben had been around her long enough to recognize her tricks for monitoring her patients. "Do you have a headache?"

Nico peeked at Emma through tightly squeezed lids. Ben usually joked about the boy's stocky build, but right now, all he could think was how fragile God had made the human body. How delicate life was. How quickly it could be gone.

Changed.

His throat narrowed. He swallowed, but thickness made it nearly impossible.

"A little."

"That's to be expected. You have quite the bump starting. Are you dizzy?"

"Not anymore."

"Is the light bothering you?" Emma gestured to the bright overhead fluorescents.

"No."

Emma was running through a checklist, looking for clues as to whether Nico had a concussion. Each question landed with the force of a fist on his gut. This wasn't just any kid. This was Nico. His nephew. His responsibility.

And Ben didn't take that lightly.

While Claire's husband was deployed overseas, protecting the family fell to Ben. He and Matt had an arrangement. Matt defended the country, and Ben supported the family.

Emma started running Nico through the same drill she imposed upon every patient who presented with a possible head injury.

Notes. He should be taking notes. Ben pulled out his phone and opened the note app. "Claire, tell me exactly what happened."

"I don't know. I was chatting with Gloria, and one of Nico's friends came to get me."

Ben groaned. That wouldn't be sufficient for the courts. Without details, history might repeat itself. God wouldn't allow something so cruel.

Except maybe He would.

Because He had.

Nothing occurred that God hadn't allowed. Not even this. The theology of God's sovereignty during tragedy rose like a hurdle Ben wasn't sure he could clear. Not when it involved Nico. Not when he knew how bad things could get. "Think!"

"Ben," Emma cut in like a fresh breeze in the desert. Ben's internal temperature had doubled since Claire arrived with Nico in her arms, but Emma's calm tone and clear-headedness fell like sweet spring rain.

"Take a breath before I have to stop treating Nico and come treat you." Her busy hands had stilled. They all stared at him, but it was Emma's gaze he held onto.

Her forehead puckered. It drew her eyebrows together in a question. His expression? He wasn't sure. But based on her reaction and how hot his face felt, he'd have to guess wild-eyed.

Ben closed his eyes and forced himself to inhale deeply. *Whatever the day holds, Lord, I want to trust you.*

Ben wasn't some fair-weather Christian that only accepted good from God's hand. He was realistic. God owed them nothing. But he also knew the real injuries could hit long after the body healed, coming from nowhere. A man could do everything right and still have everything go wrong at the hands of the very people dedicated to protecting life and health.

He knew because he'd lived it.

So had Claire, but she didn't remember as he did. She'd been too young.

Seemingly satisfied with Ben's response, Emma pivoted to Claire. "Nico seems to be okay. I want to keep him here for a bit. In ten minutes, I'll run through the tests again, and then one more time in thirty minutes, just to be sure. Assuming everything comes back fine, I'll send you home with some concussion protocols."

"Protocols?"

"Basic stuff. His brain needs to rest."

"If he falls asleep, do I wake him up?"

"No, not if I determine he's fine. Over-the-counter pain

medications for the headache and complete rest for the first twenty-four hours should be sufficient as long as nothing new surfaces. If he doesn't rest like he needs to, the recovery is much longer." Emma rested a gentle hand on Claire's upper arm. "I'll print it all out for you. And I promise you, I'll take good care of him."

"I know you will." Claire's eyes dampened as she shuffled closer to Nico.

Ben locked eyes with Emma. Emma loved them. She wouldn't put anything on that chart to jeopardize his family. He believed that with everything in him. But sometimes, that didn't matter. Sometimes a person higher up made a decision you could do nothing about.

He believed that, too.

Hours later, after Ben had settled Nico at home and Claire had assured him that she was okay, Ben headed to the office. He still had a deadline to meet.

"Ben, I need you to swing by the condo site this week and speak with Franklin Cooper about the delays." Thomas leaned his hip against the side of Ben's desk.

"Did we get another complaint?"

"Another letter to the editor. Seems like the neighborhood folk are getting tired of staring at mounds of dirt all day."

Ben wasn't surprised. New Horizon Properties tore down the only four houses in Sycamore Hill's historic area that were not historic homes. They started work on the condos in the summer. Their design plan indicated the new builds would match the neighborhood, but there were a lot of unhappy people when it first hit the news. "I thought we'd milked that cow already?"

"We did, but my contact in Grander City said that Cooper's

taken a financial hit on a few other builds that will delay finishing this one. Take a look at this." He handed Ben a printout.

Ben scanned it. This was not going to go over well with the community. They could be staring at a mound of dirt downtown for months.

Thomas handed him another piece of paper. Thomas was probably the only person on earth that still preferred actual paper to electronic notes.

"What's this?"

"It's another letter about the slopes. I think it's referring to Nico."

Nico? Ben snapped the page in his hand. Thomas had printed an email that came through shortly after Nico's accident.

The children's use of our town's slopes and pond has become quite a nuisance for our neighborhood. I understand kids need to play, but recent injuries have compelled me to speak up.

Two children were injured today, one skating and one sledding. I understand accidents happen, and children can't grow up in a protective bubble, but the slopes and pond are dangerous and relatively unsupervised. We are lucky the injuries weren't worse.

The town needs to close access to the slopes and pond for the sake of our children or invest in moderating them better. It's high time the authorities stepped up to protect our children.

A Concerned Citizen.

Conflicting emotions tore through Ben, but he fought to keep them off his face. Local parents should be able to decide whether their kids could skate or sled. There was no way Ben wanted the authorities poking their noses in where they didn't belong. Parents parented, not the government. And he knew better than anyone what happened when someone on a power trip took on the role of protector.

But a small part of him, a tiny voice that he couldn't seem to shut off, agreed with the anonymous writer. Or at least he saw the person's point. The slopes were dangerous. Nico did get hurt. And it could have been much worse. Closing the slopes meant no injuries, which meant there was no need for the authorities to investigate individual families. Was it possible that allowing over-reach in one area would protect them from a deeper and more dangerous reach in another?

"What do you think?" Thomas folded his arms across his chest. "Is this inviting the authorities to exercise power they shouldn't have? Who gets to decide what kids do on public land? Who knows what's best for kids, parents, or the community? This is your wheelhouse."

Ben's passion to cut overreaching arms at the elbows and expose corrupt authorities should have dusted this assignment in catnip, but it hit too close to home. He'd debate any other topic. He'd write about anything else. But not this. Not this time. Not when it had the potential to blow back on his family.

"I'm running the letter." Thomas eyed him carefully.

Ben dropped it on his desk. If Thomas caught a whiff of Ben's internal struggle, he'd give the story to someone else. Someone who might not do it justice. Someone who'd make things worse. "How can you run it without his name?" He kept his voice non-committal. Neutral. Switzerland.

Thomas snickered. "He might have signed it that way, but he sent it from his personal email. The letter came from Hank Sinclair. I already spoke with Hank, and he admitted to writing it and agreed to have his name attached to it. I want you to follow up with Hank."

The liquid in Ben's veins froze. This was headed for disaster. He could feel it, like a cold hand on his spine. Good ol' Hank.

Older than Moses and impossible to please. The man stirred the pot at so many church meetings that Ben would have stopped attending them if the paper didn't require his presence. The guy was a hornet, willing to sting unprovoked.

"What letter?" A waft of rosewater drifted from behind.

Emma.

She dropped a sweet kiss on Ben's cheek. "Sorry I'm late. I wanted to finish up the paperwork while things were still fresh. Then, Kathryn called to confirm our plans for lunch later this week."

Right. He and Emma scheduled a double date with Kathryn and Ethan. Emma and Kathryn had gotten to know each other better when Kathryn interviewed Emma on her internet morning show for Emma's part in exposing the scoundrels at Emergence Pharmaceutical. The two had become fast friends.

"Hank Sinclair wrote the paper." Thomas answered. "He wants to shut down the slopes and the pond because of the incidents this morning."

"Really?" Emma's eyes widened. Her mouth curved into a smile. Not a disrespectful one, because despite how quick-witted Emma could be, she never mocked people. It was more of a shocked smile. Incredulous. A can-you-believe-some-people sort of smile. But when she turned to him, the smile died. "Do you agree with him, Ben?"

Shoot. His brain might not know how he felt, but his face did. He re-schooled his features into what he hoped was a more open expression. "I'm the press, so that makes me neutral. Just call me Switzerland."

"But you see how ridiculous this is, don't you?" Emma's head vacillated between Ben and Thomas, her long braid swinging with her. "They were accidents. Accidents can happen anywhere. If he wanted to log a legitimate complaint, it should be about the parking situation. I had to park more than a block away to get to the slopes."

Ben inhaled deeply through his nose. She was so innocent. It was one of the things he loved about her. The world hadn't jaded her yet. When his lips started to tingle, he unclenched his jaw. "Like I said, neutral."

Four

"Thanks for coming back in today." Emma welcomed Claire, Ben, and Nico from behind the clinic's reception desk. With her receptionist still out sick, Emma pulled triple duty, greeting and treating patients while answering the phones. She had been tempted to take Kathryn up on her offer to pinch hit as a receptionist, but thankfully, Nico was her last patient for the day.

Before they could respond, the shrill of the phone interrupted. Emma raised her index finger, indicating she needed a minute. "Emma Powles, Nurse Practitioner." While she made several notes in her calendar, adjusting an appointment for the caller, she watched the threesome covertly. They stood at reception, stiff, pale, and pinned under an elephant of unknowns. Interesting.

"Thank you for calling. I'll see you then." She disconnected and circled the desk. Claire's short dark hair, recently cut into a pixie style that flattered her heart-shaped face, usually made her blue eyes pop, but right now, concern darkened them. Emma wished she could alleviate Claire's deep-set anxiety, but Claire and Ben had circled the wagons and left Emma on the outside.

Claire wrung her hands.

Ben stood behind his sister, holding Nico's hand. His grip tightened when their gazes met, and the moisture in Emma's mouth evaporated. Every time Ben filled in for Matt as a stand-in parent, her midsection flip-flopped. This peek at the kind of father Ben could be, if the Lord blessed them with a future, threatened her heart. The more she hoped, the greater the risk of disappointment. The pessimistic route was safer. Yet, her cheeks warmed. She couldn't stop the lurch in her heart. Her thumb rubbed against the backside of the fourth digit on her ringless left hand. Nothing good came from running ahead of God.

Emma ruffled Nico's hair, but the boy pulled away, surly. The rejection landed like a blow. Wow, oh for three. She straightened, stiffened her lips, and slipped into her nurse persona. Professional. Detached. Safe.

"This is just a follow-up. Nothing concerning." She motioned for them to enter the examination room. Did Nico's sullenness stem from being unwell or being a preteen? She cut a glance to Ben. What was his excuse? She tugged on a thick curtain, and the metal rollers moved around the track, revealing an examination table. "Hop up, Nico."

He shrugged out of his winter coat and handed it to his mother. He jumped onto the table. His movements presented as normal and fluid. "How are you feeling?"

"Bored."

Preteen for the win.

Ben chuckled. With the laugh, his entire body relaxed, and the tight lines on his face eased. Whoever said laughter was the best medicine wasn't far from the truth. "This is the longest break he's ever had from his gaming system."

"Mom won't let me on *any* screen." Nico dragged the word *any* over three syllables and folded his arms across his chest.

"And yet, you've lived to tell the tale. A-ma-zing," Ben dead-panned, copying Nico's whiny tone.

Emma suppressed a smile. "Head injuries are tricky. It's better to be extra safe and do nothing for one whole day than do too much and then be off screens for months." Emma wiggled her eyebrows as if the possibility of such a long time without screens would be the worst thing in the world. Which it probably would be to a boy Nico's age.

Nico mumbled what sounded like agreement.

Emma picked up her tablet and opened her notes on Nico. "You had a headache yesterday. How is your head today?"

Nico shrugged.

"I gave him pain medication every six hours yesterday, but he hasn't had any since bedtime last night." Claire's constant hand twisting projected more alarm than the situation warranted.

"Is your headache gone now, Nico?" His pupils looked good. Emma didn't see any indicators that rang an alarm.

"It don't hurt no more."

Emma made another note and then studied her would-be nephew. Would-be if Ben ever proposed.

"You can't be this upset about one day without your games." *And your mom can't be this upset about a simple fall.* "What gives?"

Nico flicked his gaze away.

Emma turned to Claire, who shrugged. "Got me. I've been asking all morning, and that's all I get."

"Nico, if something else is going on, you have to tell me." Emma rolled the stool from the computer terminal to the edge of the examination table and sat down. Nico perched on the edge of the bed, swinging his legs. She placed a hand near his knee, and his swinging stopped. "Nico?"

Their eyes met briefly. He turned away, but not before she saw the dampness in them. "The kids at school are mad."

A tiny crack in the circled wagons opened. "Mad you got hurt?"

"Mad that the slope and pond might get closed because I got hurt."

Emma bit the inside of her cheek. She and Ben hadn't discussed their opposing positions on this debate since their lunch date yesterday, where Ben finally confessed that he wasn't as neutral as he had claimed. Switzerland, her foot.

Ben had leaned toward closing things down *for the sake of the kids.* If they could do something to ensure the children's safety, why wouldn't they?

Emma hated that a stupid hill could divide them and trickle down to split others. All the way to a fifth grade classroom.

"Kathryn Withers was talking about it on her show this morning." Claire smoothed Nico's hair, but he pulled away. She dropped her hand to his shoulder.

Ben shot Nico a trenchant look.

Emma had worked too late finishing up paperwork to catch her friend's *Sycamore Hill at Sunrise* program. Kathryn often had the local scoop before the paper went to print. Most townfolk tuned in to catch her spin on resident gossip.

Claire squeezed Nico's shoulder. "Hank Sinclair is pushing pretty hard for the pond and slopes to close. Kathryn interviewed him. He cited the accidents yesterday as proof they weren't safe and said even if parents were present, they weren't watching their kids."

Claire's cheeks reddened, and Emma recalled her admittance

that she didn't see the accident that caused Nico's injury because she was visiting with Gloria Sycamore.

"Kathryn's camera panned the side road, rolling footage from a previous day. The parking situation looked horrible. Especially with the food trucks taking up so much space. It was chaos."

"And everyone at school blames me," Nico grunted.

Emma narrowed her eyes. "How do you know if you didn't go back to school?"

A pink flush crept past the collar of his shirt.

"Did you use your phone?" Claire's voice rose.

The pink turned red, reaching his cheeks.

Emma clucked her tongue. "That wasn't a bright move, buddy. No screens means no screens."

Claire glared at her son. "We'll talk about this more at home." Her hardness softened when she shifted her gaze to Emma. "Hank started a petition to close off access to the area for the rest of the winter. It's gaining some traction, especially with the people who live in that neighborhood."

"And the kids blame you?" Ben, who'd remained quiet until now, squatted in front of Nico.

Nico stared at his feet, avoiding his uncle. "It's my fault for getting hurt."

"You didn't carve the path that led to the tree. It could have happened to any one of your friends."

Ben's logic wouldn't work on fifth graders.

"Besides, the controversy is probably more about the chaos the area brings to the neighborhood than it is about you. Emma couldn't find a spot to park anywhere close to the slopes. I had to walk here after the accident because my car was blocked. If the town clears that up, this problem all goes away."

Walk here? Emma snorted. Try sprint.

"Doesn't matter," Nico grumbled.

"What about Janelle?" Claire pressed. "Are they blaming her as well?"

He shrugged.

Emma gave her head a slight shake, and Claire dropped it, despite her hackles getting all mamma bearish.

Emma ran Nico through the same tests as yesterday, updating her notes on her tablet as they went along. "Nico seems to be recovering well."

Claire's stiffness relaxed. "His dad'll be relieved. It's hard to be away when things like this happen."

Matt was a sergeant with the Canadian Armed Forces. He had been tasked to help with training at Camp Aldershot in Nova Scotia, where he'd remain for another two months at least. Emma couldn't imagine Claire's life. It must be hard to have a husband on deployment and function as a single parent for many months, carrying the weight of every decision and managing the house. That's why Ben's presence mattered so much.

"Nico can gradually return to normal activities, starting slow and going to the next more active and mentally taxing activity if there continue to be no symptoms."

"That means no hockey tonight, buddy." Ben nudged his shoulder.

"Awwwwww." If Nico slumped any further, he'd turn himself inside out. He folded his arms across his chest, and his bottom lip jutted out.

Ben tapped Nico's shoulder with a soft fist. "Why don't I pick you up after school, and you can come with me to interview Franklin Cooper."

Nico harrumphed. Double whammy. No screens or hockey, but well enough to go back to school. Poor kid.

"See if you can get Frank to tell you when the condos will be done." Claire handed Nico his jacket. "I'm tired of the dirt blowing from the build site. I had to clean my windows once a week until the cold finally came and froze it in place."

Emma's lips twitched at Nico's souring expression. He shoved his arms into his coat with the force of a torpedo. Interviewing a builder was not the carrot that would entice this horse.

"Afterward, I'll take you for chili cheese nachos."

Nico lifted his face.

There's the carrot.

"You know, Nico." Emma straightened some folders that didn't need straightening. "You could start your own petition. Something to challenge the grinch's position."

"The grinch?" Nico's voice lightened.

"Sounds like a grinch to me." Emma lifted a shoulder. Was that the beginning of a tiny smile?

It mattered to her that the kids had a place to play outside. Every winter, more and more children reverted to virtual activities instead of fresh air and exercise. They had more interaction with two-dimensional people than three. She wanted better for Nico. "Maybe you could seek the support of the Sycamore family? They are pretty invested in the town."

"I don't know," Claire interjected. "Hank already feels like that family gets preferential treatment."

"They do have a lot of influence on the council, but what's wrong with that? Hank's trying to influence the council. Besides, this is about the kids, not who's running the town."

"It's always about who's running the town," Ben added dryly. "But I don't know how wise it is to stir this pot. Hank wrote a second letter to the paper. Thomas didn't print it out of respect for us."

"Us?" Emma's eyes stretched.

"Claire and I."

The other us. Emma's cheeks burned. "What did he say?"

Ben's eyes shuttered. "Something about unexplainable injuries and protecting families from similar investigations to ours."

Claire's face drained of color. "How does he know?"

Unexplainable injuries? Investigations? Emma's mouth sagged. What injuries? How long ago were these injuries? Why would Hank bring this up as a defense for his position? She had so many questions. But as her head swirled from Ben to Claire, she snapped her jaw closed. Claire's sickly complexion and glassy eyes catapulted a new priority to the forefront.

"Sit here." Emma pushed a chair into the back of Claire's knees to force her to sit before she fell over. She pressed a cup of cold water into her hand. Emma counted the pulse throbbing in her neck. "Drink this."

Claire's eyes cleared. "That's ancient history. We didn't even live here then. The charges were dropped." She lifted her chin, but it trembled. She spoke with more bravado than she projected. "What do you say, kiddo? Should we stop by the Sycamores' house and see what they think about this kerfuffle?"

"Yes!" Nico jumped from the examination table and punched a fist in the air.

"You still need to take it easy." Emma grinned.

Ben raked his fingers through his hair, the only one not sucked into the celebration. "I don't like this. If you go that route, the town will take sides, and this could blow up into a big deal. More than skating and sledding. And you'll be at the center."

"Seems to me like they are already at the center." Emma kept her eyes on Claire as she spoke.

Ben's frown deepened.

Did he really think that something as trivial as a sledding hill could divide a town, or was this somehow more connected to whatever happened to his family in the past? Nico's injury triggered something. Something Ben hadn't told her. Something he needed to tell her.

Ben's scowl constricted until his lips nearly disappeared.

"Emma's right," Claire said. "I bet Hank wants the place shut down because of the parking, noise, hot chocolate, and vendors. Their quiet cul-de-sac has become a carnival for half the year. That is what he wants to stop. If we address that, it all goes away."

Emma was right.

Ben glared at her.

She should have stayed neutral and claimed Switzerland.

Five

Ben picked up his pace. Being late for an interview screamed unprofessional, and a guy never knew when a scout watched. Sloppy little league players never got called to the majors. As he stepped off the curb, a car trying to squeeze into a space far too small leaned on the horn. He made a show of glancing at the no parking sign before making eye contact with the driver. *That's right. I see the sign you're ignoring.*

Vehicle congestion forced Ben to park more than a block away from Hank's house. By the time he'd slid into a spot and hoofed it there on foot, it would have been quicker for him to walk from the office.

Ben took the porch steps two at a time, noting how the back end of a compact vehicle blocked half of Hank's driveway. Ben could have pulled his car into the driveway if that one had not been illegally parked.

Hank swung open the front door before Ben could knock and barked, "You're late."

Ben shuffled back a step or two. The glare in the angry man's eyes told Ben all he needed to know about the straw that broke Hank's back. Or, to be more precise, the Honda Civic out front.

Noise from a television spilled from another room. Hank slashed his hand in a downward motion. "Let's get this over with."

Ben followed the man through the small entryway. Considering Hank's goal to sway people to his point of view, Ben expected a more cordial greeting.

But Hank was rarely cordial.

Hank jerked a thumb toward an armchair across from a worn recliner, and Ben sat down. "What prompted you to write that letter to the paper?" Ben had to practically yell to be heard over the news program.

"I already told you—" Hank stabbed a button on a remote control, and the TV went dark, "—those kids got hurt. It's about the kids."

A high-pitched carnival song replaced the newscast. The melody reminded Ben of the blare from an ice cream truck that got stuck in your head. It leaked through the seams of the closed windows on Hank's modest house and polluted the living room. Ben knew without looking that the music spilled from the hot chocolate and pretzel vendors near the middle of the expanse between the pond and the slopes. Their portable businesses left every night at dusk and set up again as soon as school let out on the weekdays and all day on Saturday. Sunday was the only day the vendors remained quiet.

But that wasn't likely to last much longer.

Ben had heard the song a thousand times while Nico sped down the slope, but he had never once considered how it fell on the people who lived here.

Nails on a chalkboard.

No. That's not quite right.

Psychological warfare to break the community's will.

Torture.

The Sycamore Slopes and Psychological Suffering. The alliteration pleased him. He forced his full attention onto Hank. "It's about more than the kids. You have skin in this game."

Or ears.

Hank turned away, and Ben followed his gaze out the window.

Shrieks and laughter echoed in the valley as community children played and enjoyed the fresh air. This was the exercise Emma insisted they needed. But at what cost? Was it fair their healthy lifestyle cost Hank his solitude? But it wasn't the kids' fault either. The park had never been this busy until some businesses started setting up these pop-up stores. Now people could stay longer, warm up and fuel up, and head back out to skate and sled some more.

"Is it possible that part of the reason you wrote the letter and started the petition against the slopes was because you've had it with the noise and the rudeness?"

"Wouldn't you?" Hank snapped. He launched himself across the room and disappeared into the front entrance. The click of the door latch, a waft of cold air, and bellowing followed. "Read the sign! It says stay off my property!"

The door slammed so hard the window near Ben rattled in its frame.

A cluster of teens hurried down a track that cut right across Hank's yard.

"I should booby-trap the place. That'll teach those hooligans." Hank slumped into a recliner with more wrinkles than him.

Emma was right. Hank's concern was for his property and peace of mind, not the community. Not that he blamed the man. But small-town grievances made for boring articles. Emma called him a grinch. *The Grinch that Stole Sledding.*

Too harsh. He trashed it.

Hank flipped up the footrest on his chair. He could probably police the front yard and the trail from this vantage point. A steamy mug rested on the stained wood side table. A folded newspaper with the crossword facing up and a large remote control with only four buttons rested beside it. Was this how the man spent his days? Looking for reasons to get angry?

"Lois planted bulbs in that corner." Hank tipped his head in the direction the kids had trekked. He shifted his weight to his left hip and dug knuckle-deep into his pants pocket to retrieve a handkerchief. He dabbed his eyes, wiped his nose, and balled up the fabric, stuffing it back into his pocket when he was done. "If they keep trampling the spot, the flowers might not come back."

That wasn't how perennials worked, but now wasn't the time to correct Hank's understanding of gardening. This wasn't about the flowers. It was rooted deeper than that.

"What was this neighborhood like before the slopes and the pond became so busy?"

The hard lines in Hank's weathered skin eased. An almost-serene expression rose from somewhere deep inside. "When Lois was alive, we'd walk the trail that circled the park every day. We'd see about twenty different birds, depending on the season and the occasional deer. We even picked enough wild raspberries to make a small batch of jam." His eyes glazed over and drifted to a framed picture on the wall.

Hank and Lois.

Lois, with her head tipped back and laughing, and Hank, looking down at her, smiling. A rare candid from an era that favored formal pictures.

"It was simpler."

A shriek cut into the moment, and Ben winced. "Quieter, too. I'd bet."

"Pfft."

"I'm starting to see the problem. Or, maybe I should say, *hear* the problem."

The wordplay pulled a smile from the man. Ben and Hank both attended Sycamore Hill Community Church. The man was a bit of a grouch, for sure. He liked to be in charge and enjoyed stirring the pot, always taking the opposing point of view and playing devil's advocate. But somewhere, deep inside, beat a soft heart that missed his wife and wanted the flowers she planted to return every spring.

And those desires were valid and, for the most part, being ignored by the town. Maybe there was more to this article than he thought. *Grieving Man Forced to Sacrifice Wife's Memories.*

Ben had caught glimpses of Hank's softer side in the past. It showed up when the older man taught the youngest in their congregation how to make paper airplanes from old bulletins and then held a contest for the kids, measuring the distance flown and acting as the final judge. But a camel could only carry so much on its back before breaking.

Another shriek.

Hank's chest heaved, and he looked away, but not before Ben saw the dampness in his eyes.

"I think I have what I need for the article. Do you mind if I come back or call on you again to follow-up?"

"Do what you want," he said gruffly. "It won't change anything." His attention lingered on Lois's photo. After several quiet minutes, Hank stabbed a button on the remote control, and the television screamed to life.

No one should be forced to live his final days like this. Ben had his story, but it wasn't the story he'd assumed he'd be writing when he arrived.

After saying goodbye, Ben retraced his path to his car, when a little action down a side road caught his attention.

Some pushing and shoving between boys.

"It's your fault." One of the Desmount boys shoved a smaller kid, who stumbled, but picked himself up again. The bigger one shoved the kid from behind, knocking him back down. The Desmount boys were a tough bunch. This could go south fast.

"Hey," Ben called out as the largest kid lifted his fist and brought it down hard.

Oomph. The boy staggered and dropped to his knees.

Ben broke into a run. "Hey!"

"Lucky for you, your uncle's here!" The oldest brother tossed a snowball at the body curled on the ground.

Uncle? *Nico!*

Ben slid on his knees to Nico's side. "Nico, are you okay?"

Nico rolled onto his back and squinted. "Uncle Ben?"

Ben sagged. No slurred speech. Nico recognized him. What were the other things Emma had checked for?

Nico pushed himself up until he was sitting, keeping a hand over his eye.

"Let me see." Ben pried his hand off. "That's going to leave a mark."

"It'll be fine." Nico shrugged as if it was no big deal. "It's always fine."

Ben stiffened. "Always? This has happened before?"

Nico looked at the brick on the building behind Ben as if it had become the most fascinating piece of art the world had ever known.

"Nico—"

"Only since the talk about shutting down the slopes. It's my fault for getting hurt."

"You know that's not true."

He shrugged again. "No big deal. I can fix this."

Ben frowned. "This isn't something you should have to fix."

Nico avoided meeting Ben's eyes. "I need to get home before Mom wonders where I am."

Claire.

His sister carried enough stress with Matt on deployment. She didn't need this. "After your head injury, a fist to the face isn't something we brush off. You're coming with me to see Emma. I'll call your mom once we know you're okay."

Ben held out a hand and pulled Nico to his feet. Nico swayed a bit, then stabilized. "I can feel my heartbeat in my eye."

"I don't think that's something to be proud of." Ben slung an arm around Nico's shoulder and led him toward his car. They were walking through the clinic doors in less than ten minutes.

Janelle sat in the waiting room with her mother. She gingerly held her left wrist with her right hand.

Ben's gut hardened. Were the boys beating on Janelle, too? It was bad enough that Nico took a hit, but he was bigger. Stronger. The idea of a girl being victimized did something to his insides. It wasn't that girls were weaker. He'd tussled with Emma the night they'd met, and she showed him a thing or two about a woman's power. It was more that they deserved to be protected. It was how God had designed it. Men were to honor women. Not harm them.

"Nico? What happened?" Emma's concern cut through Ben's thoughts. She'd exited the examination room. "You can take Janelle back now," she said to Kellie.

Emma knelt in front of Nico, and with the most tender of touches, she prodded his face, all around the fast-growing bruise. They may be on opposite sides of the debate about the slopes, but they both loved Nico. Would that be enough when his sympathetic article on Hank hit the stands?

Six

"**A**bout how many injuries a year do you see from the slopes and the pond?" Mr. Sycamore slid his reading glasses down his nose and peered at Emma over the top of them. She resisted the urge to squirm. If he was on her side, the side of keeping the slopes open, why were all his questions so prickly?

The town council requested her presence at the meeting tonight, and she was happy to oblige. But she didn't expect to be dropped in the hot seat. Had they been upfront with her regarding the information they sought, she would have pulled files and come prepared with stats. As it was, she could only estimate. "I don't have my charts in front of me, but it is safe to estimate that I see one to two bone injuries, be it bruises or breaks, and several possible concussions each year connected to the slopes or pond."

Mr. Sycamore frowned, and a murmur rippled through the meeting room in Sycamore Hill Community Church's packed sanctuary. There was no separation between church and state in a town this size. Not when the authorities needed a larger space than usual due to the volume of people who expressed a desire to speak.

"Is this year more than usual, or has that been consistent over the years?" It was Mr. Martin's turn to stare her down, and she could guess where his questions were headed. The man was a shark in the courtroom. Aggressive, sometimes unreasonable, and willing to fight. When convinced of his position, he rarely backed down.

"As the winter activities have increased, so have the incidences requiring my care."

He nodded and made a note.

She, of course, was just telling the truth in answer to a question, but these honest answers were tanking her cause because no one was asking the right questions. Sure, there were more injuries, but it was a proportional increase. "Can I say something?"

Mr. Sycamore and Mr. Martin looked to Pastor Owen, who nodded his approval as the moderator of the town meeting.

"Before the winter activity in town increased, child obesity was on the rise. I frequently saw kids as young as ten struggling with depression that I linked to not getting outside enough. I saw kids with what medical professionals call gaming-posture. It's when the curve in their neck and spine is more pronounced as a result of excessive use of their gaming systems. Bad posture leads to headaches and spine alignment issues. But nobody was concerned about those stats. Nobody called me into a meeting to ask how the town could intervene for the sake of the kids." Emma's attention moved around the room, landing on parents, teachers, and the people she expected to support her argument.

She avoided Ben.

He gathered at the back of the room with a handful of other reporters from nearby newspapers. Grander News had picked up his coverage of the debate splitting the town. Kathryn sat near him, furiously taking notes for her morning show. Emma swallowed the hurt that rose in her throat. *Reporters are neutral.*

"So yes, there have been an increase in injuries since the slopes and the ponds increased in activity, but there has been a decrease in those other conditions. It's my professional opinion that the benefits outweigh the risks."

Ben drew her gaze like a magnet that she was powerless to resist. She tried not to evaluate his reaction to her position, but she couldn't help it. He didn't agree with her. They tip-toed around the issue when they were together, but she followed the coverage, even going as far as to pick up the paper in Grander when they carried the story. She got that Ben couldn't control what assignments landed on his desk, but he could control the tone of his articles. He might claim to be neutral—like every journalist did—but he filtered events through his worldview. It was impossible not to. And there was a way to report the truth and still slant it toward a personal bias. She'd seen it in some of his colleagues, but she never thought she'd see it in him.

Her stomach churned. What were the odds that tomorrow's headline would read, *Local Nurse Admits to an Uptick in Injuries?* She pressed a hand to her midsection. After all, they'd been through together, fighting Emergence and cheering for the underdog, she'd thought he was the one person who would always have her back. She hated that she no longer knew for sure where his loyalties lay.

They locked eyes. His chin dipped into his chest, and he pulled his ball cap lower.

A deep and painful breath filled her lungs. She'd lived this debate as a kid and knew what it was to have parents that wouldn't allow her to do anything that came with potential risk. She pretty much spent her childhood with her nose in a book, living vicariously through the characters. Ben's experience differed. One he had yet to share with her fully but was clearly steering his ship. If they couldn't find common ground on something as simple as whether or not children should be allowed to play outdoors, how could they have a future together? Was this God's way of showing her that Ben wasn't the man for her?

"Thank you, Ms. Powles. If no one has further questions for Ms. Powles, we'll move onto the next speaker."

Emma followed Pastor Owen's gaze as it moved down the line of seven people representing Sycamore Hill's town council. They stretched across the church's stage and included the influential Mr. Martin, Mr. Sycamore, and several other local men and women. When no one objected to her dismissal, he cleared his throat. "Next, we'll hear from the community. Mr. Kovak, you're first."

Emma returned to her seat.

Mr. Kovak approached a microphone standing in the center aisle and briefly rubbed his hands together before pulling off his cap and smoothing his hand over his hair. "Most of you know our family's been having a rough go."

Mrs. Kovak had been into the clinic to see Emma about an issue with her feet. She delivered the mail in town and had been forced into a medical leave while awaiting surgery in the city. The last time Emma had seen her, she'd shared that the financial hit had been hard.

"My wife's off work, and the family ice cream business is struggling. We are barely making ends meet. Who eats ice cream in the dead of winter? But then I opened a pop-up store near the rink and slopes on the weekends, and the hot chocolate and pretzels I sold were enough to make up for the dip in our budget. I'm able to pay my mortgage and even have a bit of a cushion. Closing the slopes will impact my family negatively."

Mr. Sycamore nodded along as Mr. Kovak spoke. Mr. Kovak jammed his hands into his pockets and returned to his seat.

"Please remember to pray for the Kovak family. Mrs. Kovak's surgery is scheduled for next week," Pastor Owen added. He glanced at the paper in front of him. "Hank Sinclair."

Emma groaned.

Hank strode to the microphone like a man on a mission. "Most of you already know my position. It's been all over the papers."

Emma cut her eyes to Ben again. He pulled his gaze away, but what she saw in it before the shift jolted her heart. Genuine concern. Sympathy. And maybe even a hint of fear. But of what? What could possibly stir fear in him about sledding and skating?

"It's hard to sit at my window and watch reckless kids fly down that hill." Hank jabbed his finger in the direction of a crew of teenagers that filled an entire pew. "Honestly, it's a miracle any of them are still living. It's enough to give an old man a stroke."

A small chuckle rippled through the room.

"Our little dead-end road used to be a quiet place. A happy spot to raise a family. Lois and I had many wonderful years there." His eyes clouded over briefly as if the memory momentarily swept him away. "We chose that spot because it was on the edge of town, yet in town. Farther from the downtown hustle than most neighborhoods. But it feels like downtown has come to us. To me," he corrected. "With all the pop-up businesses—"

"I need that income!" Mr. Kovak shot to his feet.

"And I deserve a little peace and quiet!" Hank retorted.

"Order please," Pastor Owen interjected. "Remember to speak with kindness, even when we disagree."

Especially when we disagree.

"It's Hank's turn to speak. You had your turn."

Mr. Kovak sat back down.

Emma chuckled. A word from Pastor Owen carried more weight than a correction from any town council member, as if the man had a direct line to God's ear. The council knew what it was doing by asking the pastor to moderate.

"Like I was saying, all the little businesses have made parking dangerous. I'm afraid to back out of my own driveway in fear of hitting some kid running ahead of their parents. I just want my neighborhood back."

"Communities change, Hank."

Emma's heart thundered in her chest. She twisted to look behind her. *Ben?*

No, not Ben. It was the guy next to him. Owen gave the press a bit more liberty than the town.

"Neighborhoods change as the needs of the community change."

"At what cost?" Hank's eyes flashed. "What sort of injury does a kid need to get to convince you it's not safe?"

"You can pretend this is about the kids, but we know what it's really about. You're afraid your house value will tank if the park activity grows."

Hank's face turned such a deep shade of red that Emma tensed, ready to intervene if this became a medical emergency. She gripped the handles of her medical bag. She'd taken to carrying it with her at all times.

"Lay off," Ben cut in gruffly.

Nico's head snapped at the sound of his uncle coming to Hank's defense. The utter betrayal in his eyes broke Emma's heart. Claire wrapped an arm around his shoulder. She leaned in and whispered something into his ear. Nico nodded, and he got up and left.

Ben rubbed the heel of his palm against his chest as if it ached.

"That's enough," Pastor Owen's authoritative command cut

through the increasing tension. He didn't have an official place on the town council, but his position as the moderator and his role as the pastor gave him a bit of room. "If we're not careful, this issue will divide the town, the church, and our relationships."

Emma cut her eyes back to Ben and found him already looking at her. Had it already divided them?

"We're better than this," Owen said. "We have to be."

But were they? Meg and Eli Martin, soon to be married, sat on the side of the room that wanted to close the slopes down, probably because Eli's dad had been running numbers and statistics of cases where families sued the town for injuries. Emma had certainly heard enough of that from him.

On the other side of the room, Gloria, Pastor Owen's fiancée, sat with the Sycamores, clearly supportive of keeping the slopes open. She and Pastor Owen were busy planning their wedding, and Emma and Meg had been helping. So far, the tension hadn't seeped into their friendship, but how long could that last?

"The council will take a few days to deliberate, and then we'll announce our decision. For the safety of all concerned, the slopes and the pond will be temporarily closed until we make our decision."

Hank smiled, and the Martin side of the room gave a little cheer.

Who cheers when the children lose?

Emma tapped a loose fist against her heart. At least Nico had left before the devastating announcement. Janelle, sandwiched between her parents, winced. Her hands fluttered like they'd lost track of what they were supposed to be doing. No one appeared to consider how closing the rink would impact the two children the younger population blamed.

Kathryn threaded her way to Emma. "Would you be open to

an interview on location? I know you want to keep the slopes open, and I'd like to give you a voice."

"I don't know." Emma rolled her lip into her mouth. Publicly taking a stand against Ben felt wrong. Like she was dishonoring him somehow. But she was allowed to have her own opinion. And he didn't seem to be concerned that his articles opposed her wishes.

Kathryn squeezed Emma's upper arm in a gesture of support. "No pressure. But call me if you change your mind."

The milling crowd swallowed Kathryn and spit out Ben. He gently moved his gaze over her as if looking for injuries, but emotional wounds didn't present the same way as physical ones. Still, her heart softened at his concern. They might be on opposing sides, but he cared enough to check in. "How are you?"

"Depends. Are you asking for the paper or as my boyfriend?"

Brief hurt flashed across his face, and she immediately regretted her words.

"I'm sorry. I don't know how I feel. It's not what I wanted, and somehow, I feel like my testimony contributed to the outcome."

"You had to be honest. Now, we trust God for the results."

Claire tapped Ben's shoulder from behind. "I'm going to head home. Nico is pretty upset. He's already left. He's sure the kids will all blame him."

Ben's face colored.

"Did you make a decision about Grander News?"

"What decision?" Emma's heart jolted.

"You didn't tell her?" Claire looked at her brother curiously.

Ben rubbed the back of his neck and bit down on his bottom lip. "The newspaper in Grander reached out to me. They might make me a job offer."

"Ah, I gotta go." Claire backed away, her gaze bouncing between them. *Sorry*, she mouthed to her brother.

"The offer you've been waiting for finally came. Congratulations." An emptiness hollowed her stomach. A million questions pushed to the surface, but she refused to voice any of them. If he had wanted to discuss this with her, she wouldn't have learned about it from his sister. She locked a smile on her face. But her insides swirled.

"I was going to tell you. I was trying to sort it out for myself first." He scraped a hand through his hair, ruffling it.

Emma's fingers twitched to smooth it.

"You might become a big-name reporter yet. It's what you've always wanted. I'm happy for you."

She detached from the moment in the same way she protected herself in medical emergencies. She created emotional distance.

"Emma—" Ben's voice broke.

Those who love greatly risk great hurt. She didn't remember who said it first, but that didn't lessen its truth—this hurt.

Seven

Ben stuffed his hands into the pockets of his coat and turtled down so the collar covered the lobes of his ears. He avoided eye contact with the people bustling on the street. The shock and disappointment in Emma's expression had burned into his mind. That was not how he had wanted her to find out about his job offer.

He kicked at a chunk of ice in the middle of the sidewalk. He hadn't meant to keep the job offer from Emma. He'd planned to tell her as soon as he figured out how he felt about it. But a day turned into a week, and then he asked Claire for her opinion. And that ring still sat in the box in his bedside table.

Agh. He dragged a gloved hand down his face. He should have told Emma right away. Just like he should tell her about—

His gait hitched. Could he?

How would he start that kind of conversation? *The people who were supposed to protect me took my sister and me away from my parents when I was a kid. They had no right.*

Ben avoided an icy patch of sidewalk in front of the Muffin

Man. He couldn't tell her like that. Detached, as if he were reporting on someone else's life. When he put his history into words, it resurrected the pain, which squeezed his lungs until he could hardly choke out understandable sounds.

Ethan nodded hello as he salted the slick area under his gilded sign. Emma thought Ben's opposition to the slopes flowed from a hard heart instead of a broken and fearful one. She deserved to know the truth. Maybe she'd understand.

My parents did nothing wrong. But the authorities set a chain of events into motion that they couldn't easily reverse.

The door to the Muffin Man opened, and Meg exited the bakery on the arm of Eli. The two lovebirds were only days away from their wedding. Ben and Emma were attending together. Assuming she'd still want to go with him.

"I forgot my textbook." Meg spun on her heel and dashed back inside. Meg's troubled past had followed her to Sycamore Hill, but she and Eli had overcome it.

Lord, if it would help, provide an opening for me to ask them how they did it, how they moved beyond a painful history.

The wind stirred a funnel of loose snow. Eli met Ben's gaze. "You look like you're carrying a heavy load. Anything I can help you with?"

Shock muddled his thoughts. This was his window. The Lord didn't let any dust settle under his prayer.

Ben swallowed, and a painful lump moved down his throat. "At what point did Meg tell you everything about her past?"

Eli leaned his right shoulder against the red brick exterior of the bakery. The building offered a tiny bit of protection against the wind. "If you mean all the nitty-gritty details, she still hasn't shared it all, and I don't expect her to unless she wants to. But if you mean the general information, the fact she came from abuse, had a daughter that she gave up for adoption, and an ex willing to extort her, she told me in bits and pieces over the first six months we dated."

Ben rolled that over in his mind. He and Emma had been dating longer than six months, and he still hadn't told her. She needed to know.

"Is there something Emma's not telling you?"

"No." Ben shook his head. "It's about me. My past."

Eli nodded. He didn't know the story, so he couldn't comment. Ben's family moved to Sycamore Hill after the *event*. His parents needed a fresh start. They needed a place that didn't know, neighbours who weren't playing out a scene in their mind about what might have happened. They needed people around them that weren't trying to fill in the blanks withheld from the newspaper articles.

Yet, despite those needs, Hank Sinclair knew. Ben's parents confided in the wrong person.

"I'm here for you if you need to talk." Eli's offer pulled Ben back into the present moment.

Meg whooshed out the door, her cheeks rosy and bright and her textbook clutched to her chest.

Ben lifted his chin to acknowledge Eli's offer, and Eli gave a slight nod. They'd chat later. Alone.

If Meg could find acceptance in Sycamore Hill, if her story could be well-received, his would be, too. Ben knew that. But it wasn't just his story to tell. It involved his parents and sister, and they deserved their privacy. Or was that just a convenient excuse? He and Emma weren't married. Not even engaged. His gut heaved. Lame justifications. Especially when the piece of jewelry that would represent her permanent link to him sat in his drawer.

Despite his inability to ascertain his motives, Ben's feet found their way to Emma's clinic. *Lord, help me find the words to share this burden. Prepare her to hear it. Prepare me to tell it in a way that respects and honors the rest of my family.*

He turned up the walkway that led to the clinic's main door as Jackson McGregor jerked his cruiser into the tiny parking lot and jumped from the vehicle. His alert gaze and strong posture, combined with his fast-paced stride, increased Ben's heart palpitations.

Ben broke into a run.

Inside the clinic, Emma stood nose-to-nose with Kellie Holmes. Kellie's gaze moved past Ben, then to Jackson. When she recognized the officer, she lunged at Emma. "You can't do this!"

Ben dove. It was pure instinct that hurtled him between Kellie and Emma. He latched onto Kellie's arm. If he'd been a few seconds later, she would have struck Emma. Instead, her nails raked down Ben's face. Kellie fought him as Jackson worked quickly to subdue her.

Jackson yanked the woman off Ben, and Ben repositioned himself to keep his body between Emma and Kellie.

"Stop, or I'll cuff you." Jackson's threat bounced off the woman.

"She's my daughter. You can't do this." Kellie thrashed against Jackson. Her bright red complexion and her raw terror touched that place inside Ben that he fought to keep buried.

She looked just like his mom.

And just like that, he was back in time. Back to a day when his mom's eyes grew big, and her lips wobbled. She looked scared, but she was never scared. She squished the spiders in his room and cuddled him after a nightmare. She told Ben everything would be okay when he got sick. But she wasn't saying those words. Whatever the doctor had said, it wasn't okay. It was never going to be okay again.

His mom didn't move toward the police officer. She stepped

back, pulling him with her. He stumbled and twisted to look at her face. Fear. Raw terror that he didn't need explained to understand. This wasn't going to have a happy ending. This wasn't going to be a good day.

"Mom?" His voice cracked.

The strange woman knelt to one knee. She held out a hand. "I need you to come with me."

He moved further away. Mom's fingers tightened on his hand. "What's happening?" He looked to the officer. He'd help. He had to. That's what they did.

But he didn't. He said, "Let the boy go. It'll be easier for him if you cooperate."

Let him go? Go where? Ben didn't want to go anywhere. He didn't want to leave his mom. The officer stepped between Mom and him and the strange woman scooped up his hand. He yanked it away. He threw himself at Mom, but the officer caught him.

He reached for her while authorities pulled him away—her clawing the air, trying to touch him. A door closed between them, but it couldn't stop her wailing from assaulting his ears.

"Janelle!" Kellie's screams blended with his mother's.

Ben's eyes found the closed examination room door. Was Janelle hidden back there? Were her hands over her ears? Was she rocking in place, trying to keep back the darkness? Was she crying? Confused? Scared? Was anyone with her?

"My hands were tied." Emma dragged him back into the present scene. That's what the doctor had said to his mother.

Emma's expression paused Ben's inner trauma. There was no anger or judgment. Just sadness. Profound sadness.

She met and held Jackson's gaze. "The slopes and the rink are closed. When I pressed Janelle for the reason for her new bruises, she froze."

Ben's middle flipped.

"Family and Children services are on their way from Grander."

Jackson led Kellie to a nearby chair. "We need to have a conversation, and escalating things isn't going to help your case."

Janelle peeked out the doorway, tears streaming down her face. "Mom?"

Kellie lunged toward her daughter, and Jackson made good on his previous threat. He pulled out his cuffs and restrained her.

The guilt laced through Janelle's one syllable stabbed Ben right through the heart.

Emma locked her focus on him. "You can't put this in the paper."

"I'd never do that." He choked on the thick words, barely able to force them out.

Emma's white lips and tight features softened. She cautiously approached Janelle. Her posture reminded Ben of how a person might approach a wild animal that needed help but didn't know it. "It'll be okay," she said. "We'll sort everything out. You've done nothing wrong."

She sounded just like the woman with the kind eyes and soft hands who pried him from his mom's arms as she wailed. The keening filled his mind as clearly as if his mom was right here, grieving, pleading, and desperate.

His stomach heaved. Ben lurched toward the nearest trash bin. It took several deep breaths before the feeling of nausea passed. It wasn't twenty-five years ago. It was the present day, and the wails poured from Kellie, not his mom.

"You can't take her away. You can't. Janelle, tell them it was a lie. That you were wrong. Tell them!"

Emma held onto Janelle, who tried to pull out of her arms and run to her mom. "I'm sorry!" Damp lines tracked down her dirty face. She fought against Emma. Her sleeves pulled up, and Ben could see fresh bruising. "It's not true. It's not." Janelle hiccupped and snorted the words.

Bruises were inconclusive. Accidents happened. Injuries didn't equal abuse. Not always. The system didn't always work. It was broken.

He was broken.

He'd sat beside Janelle in the waiting room a few days ago. He chatted with her over the shared fence separating their backyards. How did he miss this? How did he not see? How did the entire town not see it?

He shoved the trash bin away, sank to the floor, and pressed his back against the wall. Was there anything to see? Was it abuse, or was this a horrible repeat of history? He heaved himself up. Wooziness made his head spin. He sat on the nearest chair. He shrank.

Jackson spoke to Kellie, and Emma murmured to Janelle, who'd twisted herself into Emma's arms. Workers from Children's Aid soon added chaos to the scene, asked questions, and made notes. Jackson led Kellie away, and the workers took Janelle. All the while, Ben sat in the farthest chair, away from the chaos, trapped in a memory.

The officer had handed Ben to the woman, and he'd knocked her glasses off her face. She didn't stop to pick them up. A nurse opened the door, and they whisked him through it.

"MOM!"

He couldn't see her anymore, but he could hear her. Her keening filled the corridor, getting softer and softer as the woman hurried.

"MOM!"

The door flung open, and Mom darted into the hall. She ran toward him, and he reached for her. But before she could reach him, the officer intercepted her. Mom collapsed to the ground, sobbing.

Ben made eye contact with the policeman. His face hardened. It was the first time he ever hated a person.

"Ben?" Emma's palm on his hand jolted him.

How could she do this? How could she take a child from her mother without being sure, one hundred percent sure? A slight defensive shift in her demeanor amplified the questions in his head.

"Ben," she tried again. She stared into his eyes. Probably measuring his pupils.

A shuddering breath shook his body. He'd become a reporter to right wrongs. To give the mute a voice. To prevent injustice and people in power from overreaching and causing more damage than good. But that world just collided with Emma. The woman he thought he might marry. The woman he had hoped might mother his children had just taken a child from her mother. Emma was the over-reaching power. Emma was the one who ripped a family apart. Emma.

But these weren't Janelle's first bruises. He'd seen them before. He'd seen her. The times she sat on the sidelines, her arm in a sling or a tensor on her wrist, all explained away by a clumsy girl. But if Emma was right, Ben had never seen Janelle. He'd seen what he wanted to see. Janelle was the one in need of a voice, not Kellie. But his mind couldn't handle it. Couldn't comprehend. His body shut down.

"Ben, I need you to look at me." Emma's tone commanded attention.

Her face pinched. It was as if what she saw in his eyes hurt her. But she didn't look away. She searched his expression for assurances that he couldn't give.

"What's going on?" Her question slammed Ben with the force

of a tidal wave. He pressed his lips together. If he cracked them even the tiniest bit, vomit would spew everywhere. The bile of his past contaminating his present.

Emma slipped her hands into his and pressed on the webbing between his fingers. The roar in his head lessened. The darkness creeping into his field of vision lightened. His vision cleared. New awareness tightened his senses. Sweat dampened his shirt under his jacket. His cheeks felt wet. Yet Emma didn't pull away. She squeezed his hand, anchoring him to this moment. To her.

"When Claire and I were young," he started, "I got hurt. Nothing serious. Happened on an ice rink."

She held his gaze as if he were the only person in the room.

"My mom monitored it. We had a doctor's appointment the following day, so she didn't take me to the hospital. I was fine."

Emma's hand tightened around his. Did she guess where this headed? Did some part of her intuitively know?

"Our doctor was great. Affirmed that I was likely okay, but referred us to Grander Hospital for some x-rays to make sure." The pressure she put on his hand was the only thing tethering him. If she let go and pulled away, he wasn't sure he'd be able to find his way back. "They thought my mom had abused me."

When it was all over and Ben was back home, they told him he needed counselling. They told him he wasn't okay, and one day his body would force him to deal with the trauma of his past. The body remembered. It always remembered. What wasn't dealt with proactively would be forced to the surface passively.

Nothing about this moment felt passive.

"An unfounded accusation against your parents must have been awful, but this is different. You see that, right?"

Was it?

He felt her breath on his face. "Janelle told me. She told me what has been happening ever since her dad left. Without the easy excuse of the slopes and rink, it all tumbled out of her."

Emma acted on information, not suspicion. But if that was true, why did his insides spin?

Because he still hadn't told Emma the worst. What happened after the accusations. He couldn't. If his mind went there, it might never come back.

Ben inhaled deeply, feeling the expansion in his lungs and holding it. "I know that here." He tapped his temple. "It's just going to take some time to get that here." He patted his chest.

Time, he feared, he didn't have.

Eight

"I'm so glad you changed your mind." Kathryn grinned widely from where she waited for Emma at the base of the slopes. To the right of Kathryn's booted feet were two over-the-shoulder, waterproof bags, probably to cart her filming equipment around.

Emma rubbed her gloved hands up and down the arms of her puffy jacket. The friction of knitted fabric against the water-resistant shell made a satisfying zipping sound. It distracted her from overthinking. Was her impulsive decision to let Kathryn interview her foolish or wise? After Ben fell apart in her office, her reservations about the slopes and second-guessing her position melted away. His opposing position was not rooted in logic. It was rooted in the trauma of the past. As awful and horrific as that was, the children in the community shouldn't pay the price.

Emma's heart ached for Ben and all he endured, but it also ached for the local children, whose physical health she was called to care for. Ben had blinders on, falling into "my kingdom come, my will be done" prayers, and his kingdom clashed with what the community needed. The kids needed an adult to step in and say enough was enough. They wouldn't grow into strong adults if they were continually forced to live in a protective bubble.

At least, that was her medical opinion.

Her chest constricted. A tiny prick of guilt stabbed. She wasn't upset Ben's prayers seem to clash with God's will. She was upset his prayers clashed with *her* will.

The snow fell steadily, adding a fresh layer nearly three inches deep to the previous accumulation. Several flakes clung to Kathryn's eyelashes before melting. She wore those fake lashes when filming. They looked great on television, but they were wildly distracting up close. "Have you been waiting long?"

Kathryn shook her head. "I've been here for about an hour filming B roll for the show. I was at the pond for a bit first."

An hour? The sun had only been up that long. Emma couldn't imagine the time of day that Kathryn rose to prepare her face and hair for her morning show. The next time a middle-of-the-night emergency tempted Emma to complain, she'd count her blessings those came infrequently. Kathryn did this every day.

Yellow caution tape blocked the area to the slopes, and another string prevented access to the pond. Would they get into trouble for crossing the line? It wasn't like they were contaminating a crime scene or anything.

"What changed your mind?" Kathryn removed a smaller camera from her bag and slung it over her shoulder. She tilted her head to the left to indicate Emma should follow her.

A million things impacted her decision to meet Kathryn. But mostly, Ben's confession about the authorities investigating his parents for abuse tipped the last domino. But she couldn't say that. She'd never say that. It wasn't her story to tell. He vowed that he'd never let a corrupt authority abuse another kid, but he was too close to see that was happening right now. Not in the same way he faced it as a child, but still valid—still an overreach. A higher power was stealing their childhood.

"I want to help the kids have access to healthy, outdoor fun." Emma skirted around the real motivation. Calling out the leaders in the community for overstepping their bounds and making an arbitrary decision that the children had to pay for would only make matters worse. She only hoped that Ben would understand why she'd done this when he saw the morning show. Why she spoke out publicly.

And she hoped their relationship would be able to withstand the tension.

"And you think the slopes and pond are the best way for kids to maintain a healthy lifestyle?"

"Without outdoor options, they're forced to an indoor alternative. It's not reasonable to expect kids to pack away the remotes when the sun comes out after playing on electronics all winter. They'll be conditioned to favor electronic play by then."

When Ben's head was clear, he'd see they'd always been on the same side. The side that wanted what was best for the kids. He had to.

"Say that again," Kathryn lifted her camera. "Just like that."

Emma was just warming up. "And what's next? Close the pond to swimming because someone might dive into the shallow area? Outlaw bicycles because a child could fall and break a limb? Life is not safe. We can't raise the next generation in a bubble and expect strong children to emerge."

Kathryn's grin widened with each sentence. She pulled her camera back, rewound the film and viewed it. "I got it. Passionate. Outraged. Perfect."

Kathryn lifted the camera again and motioned for Emma to continue.

Emma stiffened. Passionate? Sure. But outraged? Was there

ever a place for outrage? Was believing righteous anger filled her a sign of wisdom or pride? Her morning Bible reading plan had taken her to the book of James. What was it that James wrote? You quarrel because you want what you don't have, or something like that. The real root of dispute was selfish desires.

Had her desire for a good thing grown larger than her desire for God's glory and eternal purposes? Had her good desires turned into evil desires? Every person was just a decision away from allowing desire to push them over the edge.

But it wasn't selfish. It was for the kids. Her heart wanted this for the kids. That's why she was fighting for it. That's why it mattered. She pushed her hesitations aside. Her desires had not become sinfully exalted. The fact she was willing to go to war with the town didn't mean she was wrong.

"I have an idea." The thought had hardly formed in her mind before she presented it. The slope in the background beckoned her. "I'll go down the hill and show everyone that if I can toboggan at my age, then there is no need to fear the kids sledding."

Kathryn laughed. The camera shook in her hands. "Love it. Action shots are the money shots. I left a plastic carpet for you at the top of the hill." Kathryn pulled her face out from behind the camera and winked. "Great minds think alike."

Emma hiked up the gentle incline. By the one-quarter mark, her insides had heated enough that there was a distinct difference between the temperature of her booted feet submerged in the fresh snow and her screaming thighs. This aerobic exercise was what the kids needed. She slapped her thighs as they burned. The frosty air coated her lungs. Less screen time and more fresh air.

It felt good. Healthy.

The toe of her boot caught something, and Emma stumbled. She landed on her hands and knees with an oomph. The snow shot up around her and reached her elbows. Her fingers tingled. The thin, knitted gloves were not enough protection from the elements. Emma pushed herself up with a laugh and brushed the snow away, revealing a small rock.

She glanced over at the run the kids took down the slope. No footprints or animal tracks. The steady snowfall made sure of that. But it also meant she couldn't see what was underneath. Her stomach hopscotched. The kids raced down this hill all the time.

When she reached the peak, her breath came faster and puffed in front of her face in clouds of white exhalation. She fisted her hands on her hips and looked down. Not a single mark marred the covering of white.

Though your sins are like scarlet, they shall be as white as snow.

A clean covering to erase a lifetime of stain.

Kathryn gave her a thumbs up from the base. Just behind Kathryn, the rays of early morning light cast hues of gold, pink, and orange over the glistening ice topping the pond. It momentarily took Emma's breath away.

The heavens declare the glory of God, and the sky above proclaims his handiwork.

The wind caught the tips of the trees, and they swayed. Their heavy, snow-laden tops rocked like a church choir.

Then shall all the trees of the forest sing for joy before the Lord, for he comes, for he comes to judge the earth.

What would the Lord find if He came today to judge Sycamore Hill? Would he be pleased? Would they be found like a bride eagerly awaiting her groom?

"You ready?" Kathryn shouted.

Emma found the plastic carpet wedged between two trees, exactly where Kathryn had said it would be. She rolled it out and positioned herself at the top of the slope. She gave Kathryn a thumbs up. Her stomach flipped again. It looked steeper from this position, and she wasn't as young as she used to be. She inhaled through her nose. *Lord, this is for the kids.*

She pushed off.

For several glorious seconds, she flew down the hill. The wind stung her cheeks. Her hair billowed out behind her. She couldn't help it. A shriek of joy ripped from her body at a volume that probably woke the entire neighborhood. The speed. The wildness. The freedom.

She saw it too late. She yanked left, but momentum wouldn't allow her to change the trajectory. The seemingly innocent tip of a stone poked through the upper crust of the snow. Her mouth twisted in horror.

In reality, it happened in seconds. Milliseconds. But in her body and mind, it slowed down. It moved excruciatingly slowly. Painfully inching through time as her shriek turned from joy to panic. Her body twisted away from the impact. She pinched her eyes, instinctively protecting her core as the rock broke her descent.

The next thing Emma knew, she was on her side, cradling her arm, writhing. Her arm burned. White-hot stars seared her eyes. Nausea tore through her midsection. She turned her head to the side and vomited. Every movement sent molten pain coursing through her.

Kathryn's face hovered over her. "Don't move. I've already called for help."

Emma opened her eyes and tried to speak, but a jarring blast of lightning stole her words. She pinched her eyes closed. She nodded. It sent another wave through her.

Shock. She must be in shock.

She wanted Kathryn to put a blanket or something around her, but then she realized Kathryn already had.

Good.

Her right hand cradled her left arm. She tried to move, and white clouded her eyes. Nope. Not doing that again.

"I've got you."

Ben. How did he get here so fast?

The warmth of his voice took the edge off the chill deep in her bones. Ben would take care of her. Ben would make sure she was okay. Ben loved her. He wouldn't let anything bad happen to her.

She felt hands probing her body. She caught a few words like stick. Splint. Careful. Followed by the sensation that someone was preparing to lift her and the realization that this would hurt.

Brightness exploded behind her eyelids. Then, it all went dark.

Emma roused to the rocking of a vehicle. The hum of an engine vibrated in her head. But she was no longer cold. That was nice.

Voices mixed. Sounds, not words. Urgent.

Darkness again.

Then lights. Bright, blinding lights that she could see even though her eyes were closed.

"It's Emma." A voice shook.

She should know that voice. She tried to open her eyes, but a stickiness held them together. Despite extraordinary effort, she couldn't let in a sliver of light.

"You'll be okay, Emma," the same voice assured her.

She felt the softness of a mattress under her and lost track of the words trying to sort themselves into an understandable format.

Where was Ben? Was he here?

Emma moaned. Something poked through her skin, and warmth crawled up her arm. It spread through her middle with increasingly thickening tentacles and inched down to her toes. A weight compressed her body. She nearly sighed with relief.

Like a weighted blanket. She didn't have a weighted blanket.

She must be at the hospital.

Her brain strained, connecting fuzzy dots. Medicine. They must have given her med—

Her head rolled to the side. Someone turned the volume down. They dimmed the lights.

Everything went black.

Nine

Ben couldn't slow the panic galloping through his chest despite the nurses assuring that Emma was okay, and it was normal for her to still be out from the pain medication. Even with massive doses, her features occasionally tightened. Her eyes pinched. Her head rolled to the side. Small moans escaped. Emma hadn't opened her eyes in a long time. She looked so fragile.

Had his pigheadedness caused this? Why had he been so consumed with getting his way? He should have led her to love and enjoy God more deeply, not pushed her to impulsive decisions. The boa constrictor around his gut tightened further.

Anger sparred with guilt. His blood heated, the emotions as equally strong as his love. What had she been thinking?

"Is she awake yet?" Kathryn set a to-go coffee cup on the wheeled tray that Ben pushed up against the wall.

"No."

"How was her night?"

"Painful, but the nurses insist that's normal, which is good. I guess." He dragged a hand down his face. The stubble on his jaw scratched his palm. "They think she should wake up soon."

Kathryn's gaze lingered on Emma's face. "I guess this is it for the slopes, then. You win."

Out of all the words Ben could use to describe what had transpired, win wasn't one of them. As much as he wanted to keep the kids and Nico safe, sadness darkened the victory. This wasn't what he wanted. Not by a long shot.

"Hank will exploit the accident to prove the slopes should be banned for good." Her gaze never left Emma's face.

Hank. Ben slumped in his chair.

The man arrived on the scene almost as quickly as Ben. He'd been so distraught. Ben had briefly wondered if he'd require medical attention. Maybe he cared more about the community than they had given him credit for.

Kathryn pulled a chair to the other side of the bed. "Something about the way Emma fell seemed off to me."

Her thoughtful expression piqued his interest. "What do you mean?"

"I can't put my finger on it. I've watched the video—"

Ben straightened. "You have video footage?"

"I was recording for the morning show."

"Can I see it?"

Kathryn pulled out her phone. "It automatically syncs with the cloud, so I can access it anywhere." She scrolled through the selection. "Here it is." She handed the phone to Ben.

Emma trudged up the slope, slowing a bit as the incline steepened. She looked so full of life. Full of joy. How had they let things escalate to the point of hospitalization? In the video, Emma's sincerity shone. She cheerfully served her community using her gift and abilities on the platform God had given her. Her expression held none of the contempt that filled Hank's face when Ben interviewed him.

When Emma reached the top, she stopped to appreciate the view. Was she thinking of the Lord and His glorious handiwork? She plucked a sled from between two trees and positioned herself on the plastic carpet.

An internal snake constricted his intestines. His lips tingled, knowing what was coming.

Emma pushed off.

Kathryn had zoomed in, and she followed Emma's descent with a steady hand. Midway down the hill, Emma launched into the air before her body crumpled into a heap. Even in the video, he could tell from how her body automatically accommodated her clavicle that the injury was severe.

His stomach rolled, but he slid the video back until right before the launch and watched it again.

And again.

And again.

Something was off.

"What do you see?" Kathryn lifted her chin.

"I'm not sure. Something seems—"

Emma moaned.

Ben hurriedly handed the phone back to Kathryn and scooped up Emma's good hand. "Emma? Are you awake? Open your eyes, Emma."

Her head lolled to the side.

Kathryn hurried into the hall, calling for a nurse.

"Come on, Emma. You can do it. Open your eyes." An iron fist clutched his lungs. He couldn't breathe. Not until she opened her eyes.

She blinked.

Relief uncoiled his stomach. "That's my girl." Ben tenderly pushed her hair off her forehead. Why did it take an accident to realize how much he loved her? Why was that blasted ring still in his bedside table? It should be on her finger, declaring his undying love.

He'd strayed. He'd become consumed by fear and what-ifs. But the soul consumed with God was less easily offended. That's who he wanted to be. Who Emma needed him to be—consumed with God.

She turned toward his voice, and his insides leaped.

"Do you feel pain?"

Emma's tongue poked out and bumped along her lips. "Water?"

Ben lifted a cup of water and put the straw in Emma's mouth. "Take a sip."

"Thank you." Her eyes drifted closed again.

"Do you remember what happened?"

She rolled her lips for a second. Before she could answer, a nurse bustled in with Kathryn on her heels.

"Emma, it's good to see you awake." The nurse checked Emma's vitals and made a note on her chart. "Are you in much pain? What number are you on the pain scale?"

"Seven." Her eyes stayed shut.

"I'll see what I can do for that. You've broken your clavicle."

Emma's eyes popped open. The whites glowed brightly at the nurse's words. Did she forget what happened? She sought Ben, and he leaned forward so she could easily see him. "I'm here."

The panic in her gaze lessened.

"You broke it when you fell off the sled."

"It's a non-displaced fracture," the nurse said. "An X-ray showed no movement."

The panic in Emma's eyes lifted.

"That means the bone is broken, but it remained in place," the nurse explained for Ben's benefit. "I'll see if I can find the doctor. He'll want to know that you're awake." The nurse hurried off.

Emma's gaze stuck to Ben. "What happened?"

He didn't like Emma's confusion. She should remember. She didn't hit her head. At least, he didn't think she hit her head. The angle of the video didn't provide a definitive answer.

"What do you remember?" Ben carefully touched Emma's hand, so he didn't disturb the IV line.

She squeezed her eyes shut. "I remember walking to the top of the hill." Her lids popped open. "I was sledding. Kathryn was there."

"She's still here." Ben gave a shaky laugh.

"Hi, Emma." Kathryn leaned into Emma's field of vision.

She turned toward Kathryn's voice. "Sorry to ruin your morning show."

"Don't worry about that. You just focus on getting better." Kathryn made it sound like no big deal that her show ran a repeat, but Ben knew better; Kathryn didn't run repeats. He loved that she prioritized her friend over her career.

"What else do you remember?" Ben prodded.

Emma pulled her lower lip into her mouth. Ben hated the tiny indicators of pain in the corners of her eyes. Whatever meds they were giving her, they weren't enough.

Her eyes opened fully. "The sled hit something. Something hard."

That would explain the odd angle that Emma shot into the air. She had sledded down the middle of the slopes. It was the same run the kids had used hundreds of times. If something had been buried there, it would have been discovered by now. "We noticed something was off in the video."

Kathryn stood up and slipped her arms into her jacket. She slung her purse strap over her shoulder. "There shouldn't be anything under the snow on the hill. I've recorded video several times. I'm heading back to take a look around. I want to see if I can find whatever it was that Emma hit."

Emma lifted her good hand to Kathryn. "Don't let anyone else go down."

Kathryn's features softened, and she squeezed Emma's fingers. "You don't have to worry about that. Hank saw the accident, and he's taken it upon himself to sit outside at the base of the slopes and ensure no one uses it."

Emma turned her face away, but not before Ben noted her sadness. He caught Kathryn's eye. "Let me know what you find?"

She nodded. Kathryn leaned over the bed and looked tenderly at her friend. "I'll call you later, okay?"

The corners of Emma's lips turned up slightly.

Kathryn passed the doctor as she exited.

"It's good to see you awake, Emma."

"Hi, Dr. Blake."

"You were pretty banged up. Maybe you should leave the sledding to the kids. Their bones are more forgiving."

She chuckled, then winced.

The doctor explained her injury and treatment with medical jargon that Ben didn't quite follow, but Emma tracked, which dissolved any lingering fears she might have suffered from a head injury.

"You've passed the twenty-four-hour mark, and you're doing well. We'll likely discharge you later today."

"Today?" Ben massaged the back of his neck. That seemed a bit fast.

Dr. Blake flicked his gaze to Ben briefly. "Yes. She'll heal quite well with conservative management. She runs no risk of damaging the blood vessels, since bone fragments were not created. All she needs now is pain management and rest." He turned back to Emma. "How's the clinic going?"

Right. Emma would know the doctor. She worked at this hospital before opening the clinic in Sycamore Hill.

The mention of the clinic made Emma try to push herself upright, but her face pinched, and she let herself down gently. Ben held up an extra pillow, and Emma nodded. She supported her arm that was in a sling as he slipped an extra pillow behind her. "What does Emma's injury mean for the clinic?"

Dr. Blake sighed deeply. The sound made Ben's heart lurch.

"You'll have to temporarily shut down."

Emma's eyes filled with tears. The clinic meant everything to her. "What about my patients?"

"They'll have to come here like they did before the clinic opened."

Emma took in a sharp breath. She blinked quickly.

Ben would give anything to take the disappointment from Emma. If he could go back in time, he'd—

Well, he didn't know what he'd do. They still fundamentally disagreed on what was best for the community. But at the very least, he'd stop her from going down that hill.

"I know this is disappointing, Emma. But it won't be for long. Just until you are off the strongest of the pain medications. Maybe a week, then you'll be able to manage with acetaminophen or ibuprofen." Ben appreciated the way Dr. Blake gave Emma his full attention. He wasn't taking notes or itching to move on to the next patient. He gave every appearance of having all the time in the world.

"What if I refused to take the meds? Could I work then?"

She'd do that? Ben started to object, but Dr. Blake cut in. "You still wouldn't be able to practice. Without the meds, the pain would prohibit you from working. I'm sorry."

A single tear slipped down her cheek.

The doctor patted the bedsheets. "I know, it's disappointing, but the clinic will still be there when you've recovered. You need time to heal, and that's not going to happen if you're moving your arm, neck, and head. Just stay still. Rest." He glanced at Ben. "Are you staying for a while?"

They'd have to drag him away.

Ben nodded.

"I'll check in again later. And I mean it. Try to get some rest."

"What's the total recovery time?" Ben asked before Dr. Blake could leave.

"Two to three months."

"Months?" Ben blurted.

"Our bodies are amazing things, but healing from something like this takes time. There is no way to speed the process of a bone knitting itself back together."

The silence that followed Dr. Blake's departure lay heavier than one of the hospital's weighted blankets. "I'm sorry, Emma."

"I was trying to prove the slopes were harmless fun. Instead, I made the opposition's case." She blew out her cheeks. "You're welcome."

His stomach plummeted. She lumped him in with the opposition? Sure, things had been tense between them since they'd landed on opposing sides of the debate, but she had to know that he was always for her. He wanted good things for her. "This isn't what I wanted."

She focused on the wall behind his right shoulder. She looked past him. Not at him.

"Emma?" His voice cracked. He leaned his weight onto the edge of the mattress. She couldn't believe he'd be happy with this. None of this is what he wanted.

What did he want?

Yesterday, he might have said he wanted the slopes closed and a guarantee that everyone he loved would be safe. That was what he'd been fighting for, but he'd reaped the opposite. Today, he wanted Emma to be healthy. He wanted to give her back her clinic. He wanted the debate about the slopes to be settled, and it surprised him to realize he didn't care how the vote swayed anymore. Today, he wanted whatever would make Emma happy.

She looked at him. Finally. His heart sank. She still saw him as the enemy. His phone vibrated in his pocket.

Emma turned away. "Are you going to get that?"

He withdrew his phone, fully intending to silence it until he saw the display. "It's Claire. Someone must have told her what happened."

He tapped the speaker icon on the phone. Before he could assure Claire that Emma was okay, Claire blurted, "Nico's missing."

Ten

Emma gritted her teeth as she carefully folded herself into Ben's vehicle. Hot waves rolled through her, muddying her mind even with the pain meds. She forced her expression to stay neutral and relaxed, but inside, she slogged through sludge. If Ben caught even a whiff of her fog, he'd force her to stay in the hospital. But she'd checked out earlier than planned because Nico needed her.

The car rocked as Ben slammed her door closed, and she clamped her teeth against an ambush of pain. Emma fumbled one-handedly with the seatbelt to cover her discomfort. The sling and swathe setup restricted her gross movement. She was right-handed and could grab the strap and stretch it over her body, but she couldn't click the latch plate into the buckle.

The tightness in her chest advanced to her neck, shrinking her windpipe and bleeding into jaw pain. Burning increased the ache in her injuries. She bit back a scream. *She was useless!* It would be weeks before she could lift or shift her affected arm. Months before she was back to normal. She ground her teeth together, and the ache in her jaw crept to her ear.

Ben connected his phone to Bluetooth and got his sister back on the line before helping Emma with her seatbelt and clicking his own. His movements were simple, seamless, and second nature. She couldn't even fasten her seatbelt.

"What's happening?" Ben barked as soon as Claire picked up the call.

"The school phoned. Nico never showed today."

Ben's jaw moved back and forth. A muscle near the hinge twitched. Emma braced herself against the lunge of the vehicle as Ben thrust it into gear and tore out of the parking spot. The clock on the dash changed by one minute, and Emma started counting that twitch in his jaw. When she'd reached one hundred and twenty before the minute number changed again, she stopped counting and began to pray.

"Are the Desmount boys at school?"

The cell connection crackled. "I don't know. Why?"

The car lurched at the lot's pay station. Ben swiped his credit card to pay for parking, and the vehicle jerked again. Sharpness exploded in her shoulder. She bit back a cry, turning her face toward the window. Weight pushed against her eyes and sinuses. The meds should kick in at any moment. She just needed to hold on until then.

"I caught them giving Nico a hard time." Ben's ejected words seeped through his clenched teeth.

"When?" Claire's voice sharpened.

Nico had failed to tell his mom about the shouting match on the street that led to his black eye. Emma snorted. Of course, Nico didn't tell his mom. He wouldn't have said anything to Ben except Ben stumbled upon the fight in progress. Every kid that graced her clinic abided by some unspoken honor code that refused to snitch.

"A few days ago." The sharp lines of Ben's jaw dominated his features despite the scruff filling his neck and cheeks. There was something primal about him all unshaven, natural, and intense. He was ready to stand in the gap and fight for his family.

An odd noise gurgled from his throat. Ben was a fighter, but could he manage this? Could he manage when the hits landed this close to home?

"What can we do, Claire?" Emma cut in.

"Emma? What are you doing out of the hospital?"

"They released me."

"You left against the doctor's orders," Ben cut in. "He was going to release you later tonight."

"You didn't need to do that," Claire's words thickened.

"Yes, I did." Emma's reply nearly stuck in her swollen throat. Ben may not have put a ring on her finger, but she loved Claire like a sister and Nico like a nephew. She'd face an invading army for them.

Claire's shuddering breath said enough.

Ben's gaze hijacked Emma's attention. It hung on her face, assessing her pain. "Why don't I drop Emma with you? Then I'll go help search."

"Sounds good."

They disconnected.

"What were the Desmount boys beating on Nico for?" Emma hoped her grimace might be interpreted as concern. She screwed her lips to the left and compressed them.

"They blamed him for the slopes being closed."

Emma reached her good hand across her body and over the center console. She gently touched Ben's leg. "It's not your fault. You don't even know if it's connected."

His lips twitched as if he was trying to find the right words. "I pushed so hard. I thought I knew what was best. I thought I could protect him." His voice cracked.

"We can't protect the people we love from life."

He flinched. "No, but we should be able to protect kids from harm." Ben scrubbed a hand down his face and shook his head like he needed to clear it.

"Tell me more about the Desmount boys." The pain medication Dr. Blake administered ambushed her faculties like a burst dam. Emma sighed at the rush of relief. She channeled her energy into sharpening her thoughts. Agony faded to a dull throb, but relief made everything fuzz around the edges.

"Nico kept muttering something about fixing it."

"Fixing it." She let her lids close and rolled the phrase in her mind. "If you were a kid, how would you fix a closed sledding hill?"

Her eyes snapped open. They spoke simultaneously. "Find a new one."

Ben's Adam's apple bobbed. "This is good." He poked his tongue into his cheek.

"Where else can kids toboggan?" Her muddied thoughts refused to cooperate.

"Grander. But if Nico was trying to appease classmates, he'd stay local." Ben drummed the pads of his fingertips on the steering wheel.

"We don't have other hills."

"Are there short runs that lead into drainage ditches?"

The hair on her nape and arms lifted. Nico was smarter than that. He had to be. "He'd want something equal or better than the old hill. That would be the only way to stop the bullying."

They fell silent. Ben changed lanes to pass a Grander City garbage truck headed toward Sycamore Hill.

"Grander City brings its garbage to a Sycamore Hill landfill, right?" Emma asked.

"They have been using our landfill for a while now. It's how Sycamore got the funds to revamp parts of the downtown."

"And we had a fresh snowfall, right?" Emma fought hard against wooziness.

"That would transform a mountain of garbage into a pristine sledding hill." Ben shook his hand and waved her suggestion off. "But the landfill isn't open to the public. It's not like he can waltz in there and start playing around and have nobody notice."

Sure, she didn't know Nico like Ben, but she knew boys. And she never met a boy that a chain-link fence could stop.

Ben changed lanes again. A car horn blared behind them as Ben cut across the highway and took the exit ramp.

Emma's mouth dried up. She supported her aching arm as the momentum pressed her body against the sling, pain working almost as well as adrenaline to revive her. "Where are you going?"

"There's one more man-made hill we haven't considered."

Every location in town scrolled through her mind, and she discarded each one as it popped up. Ben's gaze slammed into hers as if he just realized how his impulsive driving might impact her body. "How's the pain?"

Higher than it should be, but she'd never tell him that. Never. The only thing that mattered was finding Nico before he got hurt. She ground her teeth. "I'll be fine."

They neared the historic residential area of Sycamore Hill, and Ben slowed the vehicle until they inched along.

Understanding dawned. The construction site!

"Maybe I'm crazy, but when Nico and I were here, he commented on the hill the excavator created. It was twice the size of the slope."

And it was only protected by that flimsy orange construction fencing. "The angle of that hill—" Her voice cracked. There was no way Nico tobogganed down that hill without sustaining an injury. There wasn't enough space at the bottom. He'd collide into whatever equipment stood there, shoot out into the street, or— She forced herself to stop. Catastrophizing wasn't going to help.

Just seconds ago, Emma had scoffed at the idea of a fence being a strong enough barrier to stop a boy. Now, she desperately needed to believe it could hold back Nico's determination.

Ben's knuckles whitened as he gripped the steering wheel.

Lord, please, keep Nico safe. They wove through the streets of Sycamore Hill. *Have mercy, God. Please.*

Ben parked the car across from the building site. Bright orange temporary fencing wrapped the entire block. "You stay here. I'll take a quick look."

Emma's imagination raced. There were a million places and ways Nico could be hurt. If she was seriously wounded from a rock under the snow on a slope with a reasonably gentle descent, how much worse could it be for Nico on a hill angled to launch him like a rocket?

Ben disappeared around the corner.

Lord, please. Emma scanned the area in the opposite direction, looking for any hint of the boy. Her breath hitched in her throat. A backhoe, wooden pallets, lumber with a tarp covering it.

Where was he? Were they wasting time? Nico didn't have time. This made sense. It was the only logical place for him to go. But boys were not always rational.

Front-load tractor. A skid steer. A forklift. All powered down, waiting for the finances to start up again.

Blue. Bright blue. She backtracked. One ice-cold moment of incomprehension and then she knew—the same blue as Nico's jacket.

Amongst the piles of lumber was an out-of-place blue lump. A burst of clarity revived her mind. Adrenaline-induced hyper-alertness only lasted a few minutes, so she moved quickly. She pressed the button to release her seatbelt, and it retracted automatically. Cold air blasted her face as she pushed open the car door, and as carefully as possible, so as not to bump her injury, she exited. Every step shot fresh agony through her gut. She glanced in the direction Ben had gone. He'd come around the other side soon enough once he circled the block. She started toward the lump of blue.

The closer she got, the more her heart hammered in her chest. Her stomach somersaulted when she spied the hole cut into the mesh fencing.

At the bottom of a dirt pile capped with snow lay a body.

"Ben!" Time slipped sideways.

Emma's slow progress forward shot stabbing pain through her body. She fought a wave of light-headedness as she contorted her body to fit through the broken fencing. *She was not passing out. She was not passing out.* Sweat beaded on her forehead.

The footsteps pounding behind her increased, but she kept her eyes forward. Nico. She had to get to Nico.

Lord, help. Help me help Nico. Clear my thoughts. Make me able. She steeled herself. In her peripheral vision, she registered Ben surpassing her, hurdling a pallet, and dropping to his knees. Her scream brought the residents out of their homes. Someone had to have called an ambulance already.

She limped, her gait slowed by pain.

Finally.

There.

At the sight of his white, still face, another dose of adrenaline rocketed through her.

Nico's chest rose and fell.

"His airway is clear, and he's breathing." Emma carefully

lowered herself to her knees and swallowed bile threatening to escape her throat. She turned and gagged, only to have nausea amplified by the pharyngeal reflex. It was like a twisted merry-go-round with no place to get off and find her bearings.

She pressed the fingertips of her good hand to Nico's wrist. "Pulse is good."

Every movement sent hot streaks through her body. She couldn't pass out.

Nico's eyes fluttered. "Uncle Ben?"

Emma leaned in. "Nico, what hurts?"

"My head." His eyes drifted closed again, then his body convulsed.

"Roll him onto his side." Emma fumbled the automatic response to adjust Nico's positioning, and the pain crumpled her.

Ben supported Nico, but his eyes latched on hers. "Are you okay?"

She ground her molars and fought fresh waves of nausea. One curt nod was all Ben needed to refocus on Nico.

Lord, help.

Ben held Nico on his side, eyes continually darting from her to Nico. The last she needed was to be a distraction.

"I'm fine," she barked. "Focus on him."

But she wasn't fine. She wasn't even close to fine.

Eleven

The paramedics loaded Nico into the back of the ambulance. His body filled three-quarters of the adult-sized stretcher, and his pale skin faded even more against the white sheets.

"We'll follow in the car." Ben squeezed his sister's shoulder. Ben had been on the phone with Claire when Emma had screamed. He'd shouted his location and disconnected. Claire arrived on the scene before the paramedics. The medics had to come from Grander city.

Claire climbed into the back of the ambulance and perched beside Nico. The weariness carved into her expression sent currents of guilt ripping through Ben. All he wanted was to keep Nico safe. But Ben brought him to the building site that day he'd interviewed Franklin Cooper. Ben might as well have shoved the boy off the peak of dirt himself.

Emma stepped shoulder to shoulder with Ben, cradling her arm. A warm sensation expanded his chest. She'd pushed through her pain, denying it at every turn, prioritizing Nico. She was the hero of this story.

Before Ben could comment on the darkening circles under her eyes or her pained, watery gaze, a medic joined them. His brows furrowed, and his lips pursed as he carefully looked Emma up and down. Slowly. In a way that indicated they knew each other. That inner warmth in Ben's chest started to burn. He shifted closer to Emma, so they were viewed as together, not merely standing side by side.

"Are you okay?" The medic's question was appropriate considering the circumstances, but it came across as personal— even familiar.

"I will be," Emma deflected. She tossed a sidelong glance Ben's way. Pinched features contradicted her words.

"I'll take her to the hospital, Ryan." Ben read the name stitched onto the medic's uniform. "I'll make sure she gets looked at again."

Ryan scrutinized Ben, and Ben lifted his chin. A powerful urge to be found sufficient rushed through his veins. Ryan jutted his chin in Emma's direction. "Don't let her bully you into believing she's okay when she's not."

Yeah, the man knew Emma, all right. Ben couldn't help but smile, but the second his features shifted into one, guilt landed like an anvil. How could he smile while an ambulance carted away his nephew and while Emma was battered and bruised?

A second paramedic that had been busily hooking Nico up to all sorts of machines called out the open bay doors. "Ready."

Ben sought Claire. "He'll be okay," he promised. That wasn't a promise within Ben's power to keep. He knew it, and she knew it, but he said it anyway because he had to believe it was true.

Lord, please.

Claire curled over Nico's body, her face close to her son's as she whispered to him. She carried so much weight, usually with an appearance of ease, always with grace. Her husband was deployed more than he was home. She didn't need this crisis. Not on her home turf. Not where she was supposed to feel safe and secure.

Not when Ben was supposed to carry the weight for her.

A boulder of guilt snowballed larger and larger as it rolled downhill. He'd failed to recognize Janelle needed help. He'd failed Nico. He'd failed Claire. He failed. The two words repeated in his mind over and over until they were all he heard.

After a quiet word with Emma, Ryan closed the ambulance's bay doors and slipped into the front. It pulled onto the street. No siren. No lights. That was a good sign. It had to be. Neighbours that had emerged from the chaos and noise slowly made their way back into their homes.

Ben slipped his arm around Emma's waist loosely, careful not to touch any part of the sling and swathe. She slumped into his side. Her head turned, and she rested her cheek on his shoulder. Her entire body shuddered. The strength she'd projected since they'd found Nico drained. He pressed a kiss against the top of her sweaty head. At some point, she'd lost her hat. He aided her back to his car.

The ginger way she compensated for the left side of her body, combined with her lack of conversation, told him all he needed to know. He didn't push her. She'd pushed herself far enough already. She didn't complain, but pain laced every step, movement, and expression. She could say she was okay as much as she wanted, but she wasn't.

Still, she did what she had to do. The adrenaline carried her, but the crash was imminent. After Emma had briefed the para-medics and released Nico to their care, it was as if someone had pulled the plug on her energy.

All because she loved Nico more than she cared about her recovery.

He helped Emma settle in the front seat and latched her seat-belt. They headed back in the direction they'd come. She still hadn't said anything beyond a simple *thank you* and *yes, please* to his offer to help. Her silence afforded him time. Too much. How did they end up here? How did a ridiculous sledding hill lead them to this spot, with Emma post-surgery and Nico in an ambu-lance? Ben scrubbed a hand down his face. His whiskers scraped his palms.

"I'll be okay." Her words came out rougher than his bristled chin.

He ground his teeth. She should be saving energy, not wasting it on a pep talk.

"Nico has seen the growing dirt pile every day, just like the rest of us."

A vein along his jaw started to throb. But Ben was the one who'd taken him there. Ben was the one who'd brought Nico with him to hear that Franklin Cooper had paused the build indefi-nitely, which meant there was no one on the grounds. Ben was the one that championed the closing of the old hill and practically pushed Nico toward this one.

But he couldn't say that. Saying it out loud would make it true, and he couldn't let it be true. He wanted to protect the vulnerable, but all he'd done was increase their trouble.

"Nico would have gone there whether he went with you to that interview or not. And he'll be fine," she assured him.

Ben finally looked at Emma. He realized that he believed her. Emma was good at her job. Better than he'd ever known. She barked commands so Ben could be the hands treating Nico. Emma was the woman he wanted to spend the rest of his life with. She was the woman he wanted to mother his children. She was the woman that he wanted to love and cherish forever. She was the one. She was always the one. He only hoped he hadn't realized it too late.

He forced the corners of his lips to turn up. The tightness in his throat only allowed two words to escape. "Thank you."

The thirty-minute drive stretched for an eternity. An eternity of self-examination. Judgment. Guilt. Shame.

Would the slope have stayed open if Ben hadn't taken Hank's side? If Ben had published his suspicions—that Hank's sourness sprouted from displeasure and inconvenience and not a concern for the well-being of the kids—could this have been avoided? Had Ben allowed his personal bias to influence his handling of the story? Had he committed the unforgivable sin for a reporter? A grunt came from the back of his throat.

"It's okay to be angry."

Ben stared straight ahead. He flexed his grip on the steering wheel, and the throbbing ache in his jaw stretched to the base of his ear. Was it okay to be angry at God? He didn't dare look her way. If he did, she might see the wreckage of his soul. He could feel her gaze boring a hole into his profile.

"It's possible to be angry and not sin."

He swallowed, but it refused to go down.

Emma's eyes drifted closed, and her head tilted back against the seat, but she continued to speak. "You're hardwired to know some things are just wrong. I love that about you. You give a voice to the weak. But—" Her eyes opened and found his. "You don't need to fight God on this. You're angry, so be angry. But take it to God. Cry out for help and comfort. He'll fight for Nico."

Deep inside, Ben knew she was right. He was angry at God because God was the only one powerful enough to impart any kind of change, and it felt like He wasn't doing anything. God *allowed* this trial. Chose it. Ordained it. None of it was outside his control. In a way that Ben couldn't understand, this was part of God's plan. That knowledge didn't sit well because it wasn't what Ben would have chosen. How did a person accept hardship and sorrow from God's hand? It wasn't possible.

Except his parents had.

Not only did they accept it, but they forgave the doctor who, in a moment of haste, made a decision that nearly destroyed their family.

Ben's stomach rolled. Was his faith strong enough to love and forgive like that? What if the path grew so hard and lonely that he stopped walking? He gave Emma a side glance. Her eyes remained closed, but her presence beside him was proof he didn't need to walk any path alone.

Ben steered the vehicle into the hospital parking lot. He stopped at the guardrail to push the button for a parking ticket. It gave him something to do besides look at Emma. She was so sure about God. So confident in her faith. But she didn't experience what he did. She didn't know what it was like to pray and pray and pray and pray for God to fix something gone terribly wrong and for Him to delay. She didn't know that God could, but He sometimes didn't. And Ben refused to voice his deepest fear. What if God didn't? Could Ben survive?

Instead of asking his questions, he parked the car. "I'm getting you a wheelchair." When Emma didn't argue, his heart hammered against his ribs. He hurried back, helped her into the chair, and pushed her through the emergency doors.

"Nico will be in the children's department by now," Emma said.

Ben's gait hitched. The children's department. He hadn't set foot in that wing of the hospital in over fifteen years. The morbid plot twist soured his stomach. God placed the fate of Nico in the same department that destroyed Ben and Claire's childhood.

"Ben?" Emma's tone lifted in a question.

She didn't know. He hadn't told her the rest of the story. He hadn't told her how the hospital had made everything worse. He pointed her chair in the right direction and started walking. It was time to face his demons.

Twelve

E mma squinted at the person hurrying down the corridor. She remembered that authoritative strut from when she worked at the hospital. *Thank you, Lord!* Reuben would tell her what was going on. "Reuben!"

Dr. Reuben O'Neil stopped in his tracks so suddenly that Ben yanked back on the wheelchair to prevent ramming the back of the man's heels. The motion set a wave of pain through her.

"Emma?" The whites of Reuben's eyes popped against his dark skin. "What happened to you?"

"I had a run-in with a sledding hill." She tried to laugh, but it fell flat.

"Are you okay?" Reuben's attention flicked behind her.

Right. Ben. Where were her manners? "I'll be fine once I get another dose of painkillers. Reuben, this is Ben. Ben, Reuben and I worked together when I nursed here."

Reuben's eyes widened further at Ben's name. Emma's cheeks heated. He must remember her gushing about Ben. She had hoped he'd forgotten, or at least wouldn't have made the connection until after she and Ben had moved on. The men shook hands, sizing each other up. One to see if Ben was worthy of Emma's affections and the other to see if Reuben posed a romantic threat. Any other time, she might find their posturing amusing.

"Do you happen to know where Nico Privett was brought? He just came in."

"The boy in the sledding accident? They took him to get a CT scan."

"And his mom?"

"Went with him." Reuben raised a brow.

"Nico is Ben's nephew."

Understanding softened Reuben's features. He'd always been a compassionate doctor with a warm bedside manner. "For what it's worth, he was alert and talking when they brought him through here. I think he'll be okay."

Ben didn't respond.

Emma twisted around to see his face. The movement shot heat through her shoulder. "Ben?"

The cloudiness in his eyes lifted, and he tried to cover his discomfort with a quick smile.

Reuben watched Ben with the eye of a doctor, assessing, evaluating, and drawing conclusions. He opened his mouth, hesitated, and seemed to reconsider. He turned back to Emma. "I just finished the paperwork on the case you referred. That was a good call, Emma. It couldn't have been an easy one."

"I'm glad she is able to get the help that she needs," she said.

Ben's crazy ring tone shook him from his frozen state. "It's the paper." He excused himself, walking a few steps down the hall.

"The paper? So, he *is* the reporter guy you told me about!" Reuben wiggled his eyebrows.

The warmth in Emma's cheeks intensified until her face felt like it was on fire. When Ben literally fell into her life, the staff at

Grander Hospital got an earful when she relayed the story of how he was chasing the Emergence rumors and found her. They practically swooned when Ben and Emma started dating. They'd created a pool on how long it would take to make their romance official. The winner got free coffee for a week.

A page blared over the hospital's loudspeakers.

"That's me." Reuben glanced to where Ben had wandered. "Tell him it was nice to meet him. Hopefully, you and I'll have a chance to catch up soon."

Ben rejoined her just as Reuben disappeared around a corner. "Did he have any more information on Nico?"

"No, but if you wheel me in the direction of imaging, I bet we'll find your sister in the waiting area." Emma pointed the way they needed to go.

The florescent lighting bounced off the pale walls, making her head hurt. They passed a nurses' station. Behind the desk was a whiteboard loaded with specific patient information. A box of latex gloves sat off to the side, and a metal IV stand with an empty saline bag hanging from the hook stood abandoned. No one manned the station. A phone rang, and two call light buttons were flashing.

It was just as she remembered it.

"He was talking about Janelle Holmes, wasn't he?" The tiniest whisper of Ben's breath caressed her earlobe.

Emma didn't have the energy to fight him on this again, not after everything that had happened today. Ben's tone landed like a fresh blow. This was personal for him. It reminded him of the accusations his parents had faced. She knew that now. But reporting suspected cases of abuse was part of her job. An essential part of her job.

"You sent her here," he pressed. "To this hospital?"

She rubbed her right hand gently over her left arm, which she cinched tightly to her body. The tension in her muscles only seemed to amplify the deep ache in her bones. She wrinkled her forehead against a wave of discomfort. Had a nurse been at the station, she might have asked Ben to stop so they could look for more medication.

"All cases come through here. They actually opened a new wing. Dr. Troy Alister runs it. Reuben works for him."

Ben stopped pushing the chair. He spun her chair around and backed it next to a bench. She clenched her teeth against the momentum. Ben sat, planted his elbows on his knees, and leaned into her space, finally voicing what was really bothering him. "What if you were wrong?"

A family walked by. The little boy skipped, holding his mother's hand, and clutched a stuffed giraffe under his arm. The whoosh of the automatic doors that separated the children's wing from the rest of the hospital opened and closed. On just the other side of the doors, an alarm dinged. Patients walked the halls. Snippets of conversations bled through forced tones of cheer set to the background music of adjusting beds, side rails snapping into place, running water, and the blare of a television.

"I've been trained to look for it. I don't make those calls lightly." Her mind whirled, but she kept her voice as tender as possible. They trod on thin ice, and she didn't want to be the one who broke it from underneath him.

"Why did you have to send her here? Why couldn't it be handled in Sycamore Hill by the people who knew her and care about her?"

Emma puckered her lips. She got enough pushback from outsiders. She didn't need it from him as well. "We couldn't manage it alone. She wasn't fine. She confessed to me. I had a legal obligation to report it. They'll follow her family closely from here. She'll be okay."

Something in Ben cracked as if the ice gave way and plunged him into the freezing water. His features slackened. He disconnected from the moment, forcing her offended feelings to melt into the background. He was going into shock. "Ben." She spoke loudly and with authority. She squeezed his hands. He needed to make a connection. He needed something solid to ground him.

He blinked several times. His eyes sharpened. He was back.

"This department was created specifically for cases like Janelle's. They are good at what they do here. The people in charge care."

"Like God cares?" It came out all scratchy and hoarse. "If God is all-powerful, this only confirms that all power is corrupted." He squeezed his eyes shut and gripped his knees so hard his knuckles whitened. Emma couldn't make sense of his struggle. Ben cheered for the underdog and gave a voice to the voiceless. This was his wheelhouse. Championing a department that gave children a voice should be a no-brainer for him. But something had triggered him, and he didn't want to talk about it.

Couldn't talk about it might be more accurate.

Not even with the woman he said he loved.

"Ben?"

He drew back slightly. Not far enough to be rude, but enough to communicate that he was done talking. For now, anyway.

So instead of pressing him, she deflected. "What did the paper want?"

He relaxed as if he understood her redirection was a gift to pause the conversation they needed. His fists loosened.

"Some kids came forward. They claimed that Hank relocated some of his garden gnomes near the slopes."

Her good hand went to her throat. Hank did this on purpose? Her stomach turned over. "Why?" It came out all rough and whispery.

Ben shrugged. "To make sledding difficult, I'd guess. To cause an accident that forced their closure. But this seems extreme, even for him."

"I should feel thankful I was the only one to get hurt." Better her than a child.

"Your arm!" Ben jumped to his feet. "You need stronger pain meds."

"Let's find your sister first."

Ben walked at a faster clip, and they followed the yellow footprints on the linoleum floor to the imaging department waiting room. Claire lifted her head as they came in. A cry ripped from her throat. She launched herself across the room and threw her arms around her brother.

"I'm so glad you're here." She pressed her face into his shoulder and muffled the words.

Ben wrapped his arms around her and pulled her in. His body swayed slightly as he held his sister as tenderly as he would a scared child. There was something beautiful about their relationship that made Emma love Ben even more. He was the kind of guy that was all-in, forever.

"What did the doctor say?"

Claire wiped her eyes. "They think he's going to be fine. They are just making sure there is nothing going on under the surface."

"That's good." Ben kissed her forehead. "I'm so sorry."

"Sorry?" Claire's expression registered shock. She completely untangled herself from him. "For what? For finding him? For helping Emma stabilize him while we waited for the ambulance? For being here with me now? What are you sorry for?" She punctuated her questions by ticking off her statements on the fingers of her left hand.

"I'm sorry that you had to come back to this place with Nico. After all we went through, this can't be easy."

It was Claire's turn to hug her brother.

Come back to this place? Emma struggled to connect the dots, but they were spaced too far apart.

"I think this has been harder on you," Claire said. "I don't remember that time as well as you do. And the doctors have been nothing but good to us. It's okay, Ben. It's going to be okay."

"That's what Mom thought."

Claire paled.

Remember that time? That's what Mom thought? Emma pulled from her memory snippets of phrases, conversations, and history, but the pain made it hard to think clearly. Ben's mom never referenced a poor experience with the hospital, and since Emma worked here for the first several months she and Ben dated, there had been plenty of time and opportunities. "I think someone needs to fill me in."

Thirteen

It was time. Ben could see it as clear as day. Emma needed to know. And maybe he needed to say it. Deal with it. Finally, and fully.

Ben focused beyond Emma, on the ugly landscape painting hanging on the wall. It'd be easier if he didn't watch her reaction. He detached from the present in a way that made him feel like an observer of the conversation rather than a participant. "When Claire and I were little, I had that fall on the ice. Claire and I were taken into protective custody."

His peripheral vision noted Emma's nodding head. She remembered.

Ben chewed the inside of his cheek. He didn't know if he could do this. He hadn't spoken of this, ever. Not even afterward, when everything wrong was corrected. As corrected as something like this could be. Not to his parents, who tried their best to make him talk about it. Not to Claire, who didn't really remember. Not to the counsellor that his mom made him go to for months. The only way Ben could cope was to stuff it so deep inside that he couldn't feel it anymore.

Except the body and mind didn't work that way. Even if he forced his brain to reject the memories, the body remembered the trauma. The body reacted instinctively. Ben inhaled deeply. Emma waited. Watched. Not pressing or hurrying him along. Just waiting.

"We were taken into protective custody because of the doctor who treated us at this hospital."

Emma pressed the fingertips of her good hand to her lips.

"He was in a hurry. He didn't ask the right questions. And we were separated from our parents for almost a year."

She gasped.

"I was a lot younger," Claire added. She curled herself into her brother's side. "Only a baby, really. So, I don't remember much. Just flashes of visits with Ben."

"Visits? You weren't placed together or with family members?"

"No. But we had scheduled visits."

Emma's lower lip trembled.

"And I remember everything," Ben said.

Emma's blinks got faster and faster. The color drained from her face as she put the puzzle pieces together.

Ben sucked in a grateful breath. He wasn't sure he'd be able to handle her tears on top of all that raged under his skin.

"That's why this place triggered you."

"The doctors didn't listen to me. I told them what happened. But they didn't believe me."

"Tell me." She reached for him. "I'm listening."

Tears he should have cried years ago finally released. Cleansing tears. Healing tears.

"I'd hurt myself on the ice. Cracked my head pretty hard. But my aunt Grace was visiting, and she's a nurse. She looked me over and told my mom I looked fine. We had a regular check-up scheduled in a few days, so she told my mom what to watch for and advised her to loop in the doctor at the check-up."

Emma's head bobbed. She'd heard this part already. The medical community's understandings of concussions had changed so much in the last decade. Things would have been different had it happened today.

"By the time we went to the doctor, the bruises were ugly, but he knew our family. He checked me over and agreed with Aunt Grace. I was fine. But Mom was worried, so he referred us here for a CT scan just to be on the safe side."

Emma rolled her bottom lip between her teeth. Her eyes widened, but she remained silent, letting him get this out.

"The doctors here didn't know us. By the time I saw them, a bruise had formed on my arm from where my mom grabbed me when I fell. It bothered them."

"A handprint bruise," Emma murmured.

He nodded. She got it. "They reported my injuries as suspicious to Children's Aid, and despite Aunt Grace and the family doctor, things spun out of control. We were taken into care."

Care. He spat the word. Care was the last word he'd use to describe that season of life.

Emma's expression morphed from soft to hard. "Their highest priority is keeping families together. How could something like this happen?"

She'd moved from denial to anger. She'd get to acceptance eventually. If he and Claire could, she would, too. "Mom and Dad had to fight it in court. We had supervised visits with them. Our lawyer kept saying the decision would be reversed. They didn't have a strong case, but it dragged on."

"This should have been a quick fix." Emma's jaw twitched angrily.

Claire wiped her eyes with the back of her hand. "Except no one would own it. Jobs were on the line. Case workers dug into their positions instead of humbly admitting the error."

"They spoke with people who said they saw Mom grab my arm roughly. It got taken out of context, and once certain things had been set into motion, it was nearly impossible to reverse the train. Rulings went against us, and Mom and Dad kept appealing. They nearly went bankrupt. Finally, a judge at the highest level looked over the case, the testimonies given, and my statement, and threw the entire case out of court with sincere apologies to my parents."

Emma exhaled her words. "That's awful."

"Awful doesn't even begin to describe it."

"Afterward," Claire interjected, "Mom struggled to get an appointment with the head of this department to discuss what went wrong. She didn't want this to happen to anyone else."

"They kept refusing to meet," Ben said. "They put her off for months. They were sure she was going to ambush them with some sort of civil suit."

"But Mom forgave them." Claire's eyes shone. "She laid out exactly how the series of bad decisions impacted our family. She placed the blame with them, acknowledging that at any point they could have humbly realized their error and turned the tide, but they dug in. And she forgave them, saying she had to because if she didn't, the resentment would kill her. This is where Ben got his passion for helping the powerless and exposing corruption."

Ben dipped his head at his sister's praise.

"I need to introduce you to Dr. Troy."

His mouth slackened. After spilling his guts out, all she could think about was introducing him to the head of the department that destroyed his life?

"Claire," Emma asked. "Can you roll me to the desk?"

Claire pushed Emma toward reception. Ben cradled his head in his hands. He curled inward. Heat prickled his chest. It was too much.

A page requesting Dr. Troy to imaging sounded over the loud-speakers.

Lord, I don't know if I can do this.

But his parents did it. In fact, what they did was even harder.

I need you, Lord.

A clean-shaven man in his mid to late forties approached the desk. The receptionist pointed at the threesome.

"Emma?" Surprise colored his voice. "What happened?"

She gave a succinct summary of her accident.

"You look like you're in pain."

"I am," she admitted.

Yet she insisted on doing this first. Helping him before addressing her needs.

Dr. Troy returned to the reception desk, said a few words to the nurse, and then returned. "They are pulling your chart. I've asked them to bring you more pain meds."

"Thank you."

"What can I do for you? I'm sure that's not why you called me to imaging."

"I want you to meet Ben."

Dr. Troy tilted his head slightly to the side. "It's nice to meet you, Ben."

"Ben Sawyer," Emma added softly. "And his sister, Claire."

Dr. Troy did a double take. Understanding fell over him that Ben didn't get. Why was his name so significant to this man? The doctor straightened to his full height and offered Ben his hand.

Ben saw nothing but sincerity in the man's gaze. He stood to accept his offered handshake hesitantly, not sure what was happening.

"Your family is legend here."

His family?

"The hospital was determined to learn from its mistakes. To be what your mother suggested, humble and teachable."

"You know my mother?"

"Not personally, but she had a key role in shaping the job description for my position at the hospital."

"My mom?" Claire appeared just as flabbergasted as he felt.

"My job is to investigate suspected cases of abuse. I still have to report to Family and Children Services, but this policy ensures a fuller report that includes family history and hospital visits from neighboring communities or a lack of hospital visits to neighboring communities. It came into effect after your family's crisis and because of your family's experience."

Because, like junkies looking for a fix, abusers spread out their care to avoid detection.

"We are determined to never put a family through what you endured again."

"Why wouldn't Mom tell us this?" Claire whispered.

"I think she might have tried." Ben's face felt slack. Memories of his mom trying to talk with him about that time in their life filled him. "I always shut her down. I couldn't talk about it. I couldn't go there."

Regret slammed against his ribs. Could he have found the peace he needed long ago if he'd just been brave enough to have the conversation? He not only refused to talk about that trauma with his parents, but he also insisted on moving forward as if nothing had happened.

"You're treating Janelle?"

"I can't talk about a patient, but children like Janelle are why these services are still needed. *You* are why these services need checkpoints and real people reviewing the documents."

Ben's head swam. He sank onto the bench, and the vinyl seat whooshed. He could hardly think. His mom, probably scarred just as deeply as he was, came back to the hospital, to the same people that nearly destroyed their family, and worked alongside them to better their policies.

Because that was who she was.

"Sometimes the system fails, but it's doing its best." Dr. Troy held out his hand again to Ben. But this time, it wasn't in greeting. This time, Ben knew, without a doubt, it was an apology and a promise. An apology for all his family endured and a commitment to never again let something like that happen on his watch.

Ben accepted his offering, and as he did, the rock that had been permanently lodged in his gut dissolved. Instead of leaving Ben empty, it made him feel whole. Complete. And hopeful.

Fourteen

Kathryn zipped up the back of Emma's dress, and Emma's cheeks burned. She couldn't believe the number of things she could not do one-handed—intimate things that required her friends to step up and be the hands and feet of Jesus. But Emma was home now, and she was so grateful to be in her condo, even if it meant giving up her independence for a time.

Lola, her cat, curled up and warmed her feet most nights, making everything feel almost normal. As per the doctor's orders, Emma had taken it easy since leaving the hospital. Kathryn, Claire, Meg, Gloria, and a few other women from the community created a schedule and rotated staying with her. But today was Meg and Eli's wedding, and nothing was going to stop Emma from standing with her friend.

Kathryn turned Emma around and looked her over from top to bottom. "Perfect."

Emma grinned as she moved to sit on the bed. "As perfect as a gown accessorized by a sling can be."

Kathryn rifled through Emma's closet, talking over her shoulder. "I made an interesting discovery when sorting through my videos of the slopes."

"Something better than my blooper reel?"

Kathryn held out a pair of close-toed strappy heels. "These ones?"

"Yes."

"Better isn't the word I would use." Kathryn pulled out a newspaper and handed it to Emma before kneeling at her feet to fiddle with the ankle straps. "It's folded open to the right place. Read Ben's article."

Emma ran her gaze over the page. Her pulse hiccupped. "They charged Hank?"

"With mischief." Kathryn sat back on her heels after buckling the shoes. "Now, what purse would you like?"

Emma couldn't think about purses. All she could think about were the snippets of memory starting to come back about the day of the accident. Hank bent over her, crying. Hank, telling her to stay strong. That help was coming. That he was sorry.

She never heard the apology as a confession. No one did until they discovered Hank's actions. She'd seen him as a compassionate man grieving the actuality of a catastrophe that he'd predicted would happen.

Kathryn held up two purses.

"The black one, please." Emma motioned to the black purse with a gold chain strap, and Kathryn returned the brown one to the shelf in the closet.

"The rumor was Hank moved the garden gnomes to the slope to make parents think it was too dangerous for their kids. His plan was to be out there first thing in the morning to discover them." Kathryn put air quotes around the word discover. "He wanted to find them in front of an audience before anyone went down and got hurt."

"But we arrived early—"

"—for my morning show," Kathryn finished. "I hope it helps a little to know that he didn't intend to hurt anyone." Kathryn slipped an arm around Emma's waist and aided her to her feet. "What about your hair? Up or down?"

"Down is fine. It's easier." Emma followed Kathryn into the bathroom, where a hot curling iron waited. "You said video. What video?"

"I had arrived at the slopes long before you to film the sunrise and some B reel. Turns out, I caught Hank in the background without knowing it."

"I still can't believe it," Emma murmured. Hank was a bit grizzly at church, but he wasn't malicious. But when a person wanted something badly enough, most were willing to sin to achieve it. Hank was no different.

What a troubling idea.

She continued to scan the article. "The town is reopening the slopes?"

"Yes, but with some changes." Kathryn ran the iron through Emma's hair, creating a cascade of curls down her back. "They're discussing a dedicated parking lot and vendor area to relocate the chaos away from the homes on the cul-de-sac. They are also putting in an outdoor ice rink."

Emma had just reached that part in Ben's article. "Why? We have the pond."

"Since our winter temps fluctuate so much, they wanted a space they could guarantee was safe to skate on. Plus, they can run an outdoor ice hockey league in the winter and ball hockey in the summer."

"I feel like I've been laid up forever to have missed all of this."

But really, it wasn't that long. It only felt that way because Ben had been so busy with the paper that they hadn't had the chance for a long and lingering visit. They hadn't even unpacked all the emotions he must be feeling about the hospital.

About her.

Them.

A part of her still feared she had pushed the only man she ever loved away. But tonight, they were going to the wedding. Tonight, they would chat. Finally. About the things that mattered.

"You haven't read to the end yet, have you?" Kathryn's eyes twinkled.

Emma's gaze hopped to the last paragraph. "It says part one of two."

Kathryn had that look that meant she knew something Emma didn't. Before Emma could ask, the doorbell rang. Kathryn hurried out of the room.

The heavy footfalls in the hallway were not the light step of her friend. The stride was all wrong. "Kathryn?"

"Try again." Ben's chuckle settled over Emma like hot fudge on a sundae. Delicious, comfortable, and warm.

"You're early!" She jumped up from her perch on the edge of the bed. She looked past Ben and down the empty hallway. "Where's Kathryn?"

"She said something about taking Lola out front."

Emma was probably the only person in the world that walked her cat on a leash.

"What do you think?" Emma spun for Ben as he let out a low, appreciative whistle. Heat filled her cheeks.

"First, you look amazing. Second, do you need help with anything?" Ben leaned a shoulder against her bedroom doorframe, keeping both feet firmly in the hallway.

Pleasure over his compliment rippled through her body. "I'll be out in a minute." She was ready now, but she needed a minute to compose herself. Something about Ben standing in her hall, looking at her the way he was looking at her, made her feel dizzy inside.

She found Ben in the kitchen, settled on one of her horribly uncomfortable barstools. Uncomfortable but stylish. A newspaper was spread out on the island.

"What's this?" She nodded toward the paper.

"Part two of that article series. It goes to press tomorrow, but I got an early copy for you."

She wrinkled her forehead.

"Read it." He nudged it closer to her.

Emma slid onto the stool beside Ben. His eagerness aroused nervousness and excitement equally. The weight of Ben's gaze on her profile never lifted as she moved her eyes over the article. Her heart thumped in her chest. Her eyes moved slowly over the words, taking in each phrase. Somehow, she knew deep in her bones that this moment was special. Important. Worthy of her time.

"Read it aloud," he prompted. A notch between his eyes deepened.

Gooseflesh crept across her arms. She cleared her throat. "Normally, you read my article above the fold. I report on breaking news, local news, and everything that impacts our town. But today, I'm in a new section of the paper, the letter to the editor section, because what I have to say is not just facts from a neutral reporter. It's about my heart, which holds a definite bias.

"When a man reaches a fork in the road, he has to decide. Will he follow his heart or follow the job? For as long as I can remember, I wanted to be a journalist at a big paper. I wanted to be a voice for the voiceless. I wanted to right wrongs and fight injustice. This deeply-rooted need drove every decision until the day I fell (literally) for Emma Powles." Her swollen throat pinched off her words.

Emma cleared her throat, but it didn't help. She tried again, but the frog remained. Ben gently took the paper from her hand and continued the narration. The pages trembled. "Emma showed me what it meant to release my burden to the Lord. She showed me that my worth wasn't tied to my performance. She showed me that the only One able to right the wrongs we face on the earth had to die in order to do it and rose to new life to secure eternity for those who believe."

Her eyes filled. Her voice turned husky, "If you make my makeup run—"

Ben's smile was delicious and slow, creeping across his features a millimeter at a time. She willed her focus from his lips to his words. "I was offered my dream job as a result of my coverage on Emergence and the town battle for the Sycamore Slopes. But in a strange moment of clarity, I realized I already had everything I had ever dreamed of right here in Sycamore Hill. In this community. In Emma Powles. In my faith in the Lord."

Now Ben's voice hitched. As his words thickened and grew rougher, Emma wiped the dampness from her cheeks. No wonder Kathryn insisted on waterproof mascara. Emma's fragile grip broke when Ben slid off the stool and bent one knee to the floor. Her belly quivered, and she pressed her hand against it. She couldn't breathe.

Ben continued to read from his position at her feet. "Emma Powles is my best friend, and today, I hope that I can say, my soon-to-be-wife. Emma Powles, will you marry me?"

Emma's tears dampened her upper lip. Her gaze moved over this man who had stolen her heart from the day he landed in a heap in the middle of her living room. She loved his compassion for the lost, his strong sense of justice, and his willingness to do anything for the people he loved. It was a privilege to love him.

She slid from the stool and stooped over, threading the fingers of one hand through the back of his hair. She pressed their foreheads together.

He cupped her cheek with his palm, and she leaned into his warmth. Her eyes fell closed, and she whispered one word. "Yes."

One Month Later

Fifteen

A bloodcurdling shriek sliced through the frosty air. Ben lifted his camera to his eye and peered through the lens, rotating the dial. He focused on the slope, newly reopened and heavily monitored, and snapped a cluster of images. The town council had discussed the recent events and decided to reopen the area, but with significant changes. Some changes would come into effect over the next year, and some were immediate, like the small portion of space designated as the vendor area. It redirected the traffic away from the residences.

The Sycamore and Martin families generously donated the funds for the project named the *Sycamore Skate and Sled Park*. A billboard displayed their future plans, which included a manufactured rink set in the organic outdoors to replace the pond skating, holiday music chiming from loudspeakers connected to the rink, and a variety of outdoor vendors. The town implemented a schedule for the park. The opening hours of nine in the morning until nine in the evening ensured the surrounding community had enough quiet.

The temporary changes seemed to satisfy Hank, who stood in line for a corn dog. Hank gave a nearby child a thumbs-up as they ran past. The old grouch had come a long way. The grinchiness of Hank softened as Emma took a page from Ben's mom's book and insisted on sitting down with the person who'd hurt her. Hank tried to avoid Emma, but she wouldn't let up. And when they finally got together, she was able to communicate in person what had already transpired in her heart. She forgave Hank.

In the end, Emma and Hank brought the idea of the Skate and Sled Park to the town council together. And as they told their story of a neighborhood fed up with the chaos, they also presented the solution: a creative reimagining of the landscape, enforced hours of operation and giving the locals a voice in the design.

Pop Up Food Vendors are a Hit with Locals. Ben mentally filed the potential headline.

Ben peered through the camera lens again, getting a clearer view of the kids. Oliver skated between his mom and his Uncle Jackson. As Ben focused the lens, it sharpened Jackson's features. The man was in love with Kim. It was evident to everybody. What was it going to take for them to see it? Oliver's feet slipped and slid, but Oliver remained upright. The couple cheered for his success.

"I do it! I do it!" Oliver's delight warmed Ben's insides.

Ben snapped another cluster of pictures.

On the far side of the park, Janelle Holmes shrieked. The Holmes family had a long way to go, but they were working with Family and Children Services. Janelle's parents were in counselling while Janelle lived with an aunt. They were committed to making better choices and earning back the privilege of raising their daughter.

A happy ending appeared as a possibility. Ben hoped they'd reach it. As he repacked his satchel, he mulled over his life choices.

Staying in Sycamore Hill no longer felt like settling for second best. He wasn't resigned to it. He chose it. The dream had been within reach, but he decided to reach for something else. Something better. Marrying Emma, raising a family, and supporting her as she ran her clinic.

"Uncle Ben!" Nico waved as he raced toward the hill. A long blue sled attached to a thin yellow rope bounced behind him.

And watching Nico grow up. Helping Claire. Being here for his aging parents. Becoming a dad.

"I thought I'd find you here." Emma lifted her face for his usual kiss, but he bypassed her freckled cheek and brushed her lips with his. The tension in his body evaporated, replaced with a settled peace.

"Where else would I be?"

Emma turned into his arms, and he briefly tightened his hold. She fit perfectly against him. His arms slipped from her waist, and he scooped up her hands. He tugged her toward the bench.

She snuggled into his side. "Are you done work yet?"

Even if he wasn't done, he wouldn't miss the chance to sit with his girl. They wouldn't be skating. Emma was still careful with her collarbone. It would take six to eight weeks to heal and at least the same period again to regain full use of it. He tucked his satchel into one of the cubbies built under the benches. "I'm all yours."

"We made it!" Meg huffed a bit as she and Eli joined Ben and Emma. "Are Owen and Gloria coming?"

"Any minute."

Meg and Eli swapped their boots for skates, and their banter filled Ben to overflowing. It was surreal to think he'd almost walked away from this. Gloria and Owen joined them. Ben and Emma laughed, watching their friends on the ice. They even tried their hand at crack the whip. Kathryn filmed from the edge of the rink. They'd probably show up on her Sycamore Hill at Sunrise show.

Jackson zoomed up behind Kim. He gestured to Oliver, and Kim nodded her consent. Jackson scooped up the boy from behind and tossed him into the air. Oliver shrieked with delight.

"Careful," Emma called out. "I don't want to have to get out my medical bag."

Jackson lowered Oliver until his blades grazed the ice's surface. He supported his weight, and they lapped his mother again.

"Do it again," Oliver giggled.

Ben's gaze returned to Emma. He couldn't wait to toss his children into the air. To skate and play and not be consumed with fear that there would be an accident.

Because accidents happened.

But his God reigned.

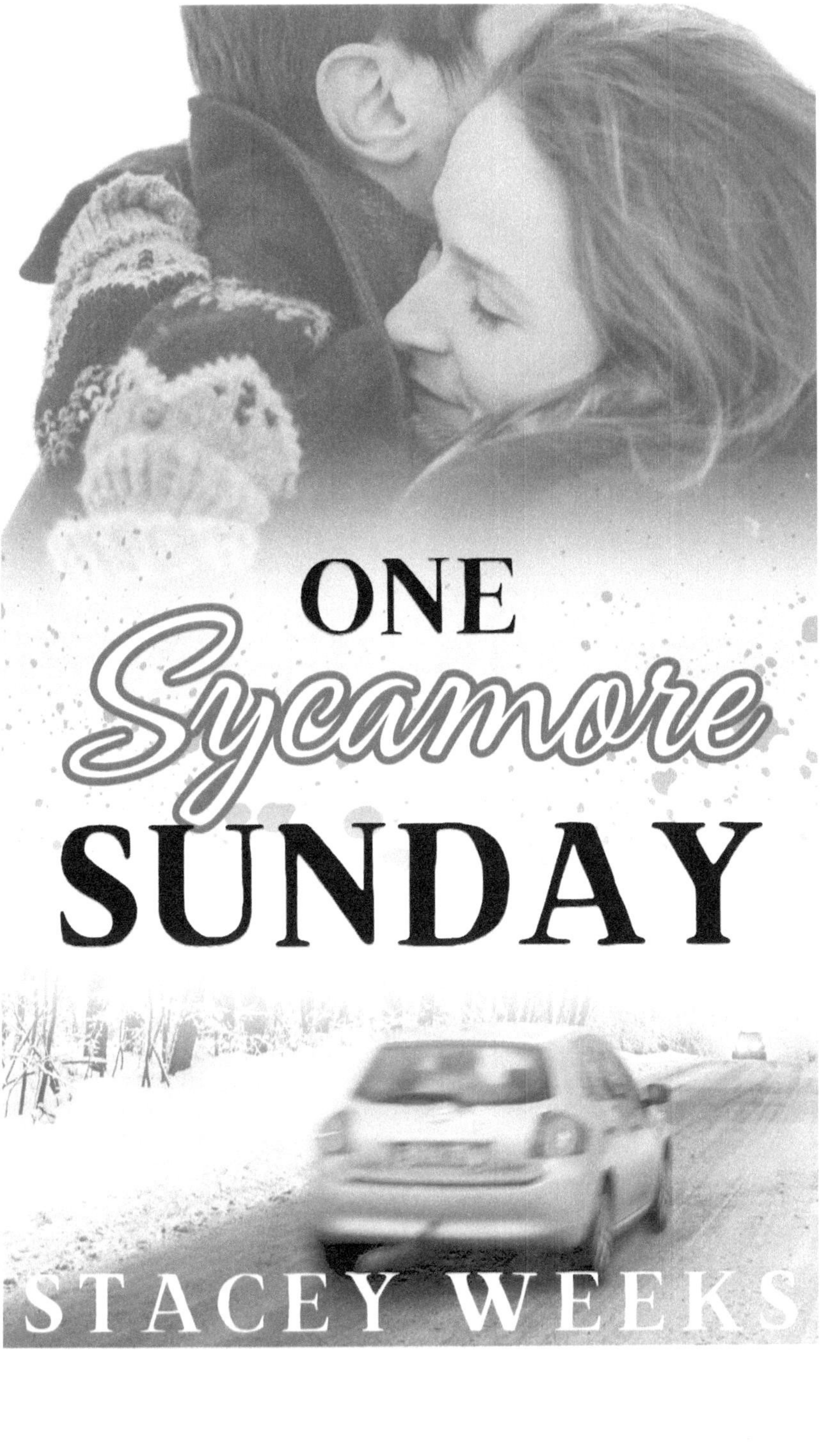

ONE
Sycamore
SUNDAY

STACEY WEEKS

One Sycamore Sunday

When a group of men abduct her son, Kim Jansen turns to the
only person she can trust—Jackson McGregor. Officer McGregor
would trade his life for the boy, but it's not McGregor the
kidnappers want. They want a woman Kim helped disappear, and
they've taken Kim's son as leverage. As McGregor races to save the
boy, Kim faces an impossible choice—protect her friend or save
her child.

One Sycamore Sunday is a high-stakes, fast-paced romance.

8:30 a.m.

❦

"Oliver!" Kim Jansen tapped her booted foot on the hardwood floor at the bottom of the short staircase. If he didn't hurry, they'd be late for church again. A crash and a thud sounded from inside his bedroom.

"I coming." His closed door muffled his reply.

Oliver was probably looking for something that he *just couldn't live without*. Her three-year-old came by his flair for the dramatic honestly. His father, Hayden, had always been a showman.

Bitterness filled her mouth, as it always did when she thought of Hayden. Kim swallowed the sourness and tightened her grip on the banister. Hayden wouldn't interfere again because Jackson, his twin brother, made sure of it.

The identical brothers shared the same rugged good looks, blond, wavy hair, and piercing blue eyes, but that's where the likeness stopped. Jackson was as good as Hayden was evil, proven when Jackson sacrificed his relationship with his twin to bring Oliver home. For that, she'd be forever in his debt.

But he didn't do it for her. He did it for Oliver.

She pressed two hands against her midsection as her insides flip-flopped. At least, that's what she told herself.

"Oli-verrrr!" Forced cheerfulness softened her tone. There had to be some sort of brother code that forbade a guy from dating his twin's ex.

Oliver's bedroom door opened. His soft curls bounced as he descended the stairs, dragging his stuffed bunny behind him. She'd given him the toy last month for his birthday, and he hadn't let go of it since. The rabbit's head thumped on each step.

"I coming."

When he reached the bottom, he stopped in front of her and lifted his face. She bent and kissed his cheek. "We need to motor, my little love." She ruffled his hair, her caress softening the urgency of her words. So, they arrived late for church. It was a small thing. When Oliver was gone, she would have given a life-time of last-to-arrive-at-church-Sundays to have her son back.

She shook loose the sad memories of their time apart. Hayden stole everything from her when he took Oliver, but letting her mind linger on that season of her life only birthed bitterness. And bitterness about the parental abduction that separated her from Oliver for fourteen months never led her to a good spiritual place.

Sucking in a breath through her nose, she lifted her chin. She'd forgiven Hayden, and she firmly believed the Lord would enable her to act accordingly despite his unrepentant heart. But forgive-ness wasn't the same as reconciliation. Grabbing her purse, she slung it over her shoulder, refusing to let guilt take root. She'd chosen to forgive, for her spiritual health, and had since discovered that forgiveness was more than a decision. The process took time.

"Do you have everything for Sunday school?"

Oliver attached the Velcro of his shoes and beamed at her. The sneakers were on the wrong feet. She should probably tell him to put on boots, but the fact he wore footwear at all was a win worth celebrating.

"Ready!" Oliver lifted his arms for her to pick him up.

"Not quite, buddy. You need a jacket." She handed him his puffy orange winter coat. The February chill had dropped below normal temperatures for their region, and their friendly groundhog had announced six more weeks of cold.

She helped his arms into his jacket and zipped up the front, ignoring the way he swatted her fingers because he wanted to do it himself. He wedged his bunny into his armpit and tugged on mittens and a hat.

The wind swirled the dusty snow and stung their cheeks as they trudged to the car. Frigid air made it hurt to breathe, and the cold seemed to make the scent of pine from the trees that lined the property stronger. It only took another five minutes to get Oliver buckled into his car seat and start toward the church. Eight-thirty. Not too bad.

She turned on the Christian radio station and hummed along to a familiar tune about God's goodness. Oliver chattered to himself. He held the bunny up to the window. "See Unca Jackson?"

"We'll see him at church."

"No working?"

"Not today."

Jackson worked for the Ontario Provincial Police, who provided a presence in Sycamore Hill. He worked every other Sunday, which meant either Constable Stuart James or Constable Noah Brown patrolled today. Kim still had to pinch herself to believe that Jackson had upended his career to move to Sycamore Hill to be part of Oliver's life.

The wind iced the fog as the tail end of nasty, blizzard-like conditions swirled. Forecasters predicted it would be clear by midday, in time for the Winter Carnival. Every year, the same travelling carnival set up camp on the outskirts of town. For one week each February, child-friendly tunes played on an endless loop, attracting children like sprinkles to a sugar cookie. At least the music didn't play on Sunday mornings.

"Rides?" Oliver cranked his neck as they passed the fairgrounds.

"Maybe after church." She'd ordered three tickets online last week, but she knew better than to tell Oliver about it this early in the day. He'd pester her all morning.

A small SUV emerged from the haziness behind her. It crept closer, so she tapped her brakes. Her stomach heaved at the lack of traction. The snow must have pressed into ice. She tapped her brakes again, but the guy didn't take the hint. He rode her backside like they were hitched. Clenching her jaw, she squinted in the rearview mirror. She didn't recognize the man and couldn't read his license plate, not that it would help. It wasn't like she could report him to Jackson for following too closely.

She flicked her gaze back to the road in front of her. Brake lights. She slammed the brake pedal. The wheels slid, and the antilock system kicked in and pumped the brakes. The back end swung left, then right. She cranked the steering wheel the opposite way. The arch got bigger and bigger as she tried to steer them out.

"Mommy!"

The vehicle spun three-hundred and sixty degrees and skidded across the center line. "No, no, no, no, no!"

By some minor miracle, there was no oncoming traffic. She stood on the brakes. The back tires spun as the front tires turned. When they finally gripped the road, she yanked left as hard as she could. She avoided hitting the vehicle that had stopped in front of her, but the car shuddered as they hit the ditch. Loose snow absorbed their arrival.

Oliver! She twisted.

Eyes spread wide. Pale skin. Bunny clutched in his fisted hand. But he was in one piece. *Thank you, Lord.*

"We're okay, honey." She rubbed his knee. A hum vibrated in her ears. She exhaled, and inch by inch, the tightness in her neck and shoulders lessened. They were okay.

A giant tear slid down Oliver's cheek.

They needed to get out.

The ditch wasn't deep, but the overnight snowfall had filled it. There was no way she'd be able to open Oliver's passenger side door, but she could open hers.

The other drivers had stopped, and three men hurried toward her. She forced herself to inhale slowly and deeply. They were okay, too.

"Are you all right?" The men reached the car and huddled around the driver's door.

"We're fine. Are you okay?" They appeared unharmed. She unbuckled and retrieved her purse, which had slid to the floor on the passenger side. "I'll call the police—"

The door jerked open, and her rescuer snatched her phone from her hands. Before she could speak, the man tossed it into the snowbank.

"What are you doing?" Wind stung her cheeks, and incomprehension blurred the edges of her vision. She thought the other men might intervene. But instead, they wrenched open the back door and fumbled with Oliver's buckles. Her mind denied what was unfolding. This wasn't real. It couldn't be real. Her ears roared.

"Mommy!"

Shock transformed into panic. She lunged toward Oliver, slapping the men's hands away. A growl erupted from deep within her. She'd kill them to protect her son.

A sharp pain split her cheek. The acrid tang of blood. What was happening? All she could see, smell, and hear was Oliver's fear. Her fear.

"Mommy!"

Cloudiness took over. Another blow landed, and it flung her into the passenger seat. Then came the sound of heavy feet and shouting.

Terror laced Oliver's words. "Don't hurt my mommy!"

She only caught bits and pieces. Oliver flailing his arms and legs. A rip. A wail. They pulled him from the car. She fought for consciousness. Oliver's cries were the only sounds that penetrated the roar in her ears.

The men were bigger and stronger. An angry bark emitted from one, and Oliver's wails faded. Kim struggled to right herself. She blinked rapidly but still couldn't see straight. Her cheek stung. Her body ached. She was wedged in a seat, her breathing shallow. Her heart beat in her forehead. The car was too quiet. It was a screaming silence that filled her mind and exploded from her lips.

And the radio played as if everything right in the world hadn't gone wrong. The artist crooned about a good God.

Kim fumbled with the door handle. Her panicked hands refused to work. Finally, she gave up and pounded the glass. "You're not good. You're not a good God. Not a good Father!" She pressed her forehead to the glass and wept. A keening. *Not again.* Hayden wouldn't do this to her. God wouldn't let it happen.

But Hayden had done it before, and God didn't stop it.

She had to think of Oliver.

Her mind cleared. She blinked. The hum of a thousand caffeinated drinks shot through her body. The passenger door wedged into the snowbank. That was why she couldn't open it. She clawed her way to the driver's side and out. A blast of cold hit like the arctic winter. Her boots sank into the snow past her ankles. Was Oliver on foot? He only wore shoes.

She should have made him wear his boots. Why didn't she insist?

She scrambled up the snowbank, her hands and knees burning with cold. Blowing snow filled the tracks from where the two SUVs had driven away. Minutes. Only a few minutes had passed.

They were gone. Oliver was gone.

Her legs gave way. *No.* Pushing herself up, she steadied her trembling arms. She needed to fight.

"Oliver!" A crawl morphed into a run. She sprinted toward a dark spot on the white bank. If she didn't stop moving, she'd find them. The toe of her boot jammed into an icy lip, and she lurched forward. Cold shot up her arms as her hands tunneled through the snow.

Oliver's bunny. A torn terrycloth ear dangled by threads. She clutched it against her chest. "Oliver!"

8:45 a.m.

〜

Jackson McGregor made all the appropriate sounds as he listened to his twin brother recap his latest adventure. He waved at Pastor Owen and Gloria as they crossed the foyer, pointing at the cell phone against his ear as the reason he didn't say good morning.

Owen nodded and pressed a hand to the small of Gloria's back. She was talking about flowers, her large gestures indicating these weren't just any flowers. The couple was probably discussing their wedding, which was only three months away.

Their friend group seemed to celebrate one engagement after the other lately. First, Eli and Meg. After a short spring engagement, they married in December. Owen and Gloria got engaged in September, and Ben and Emma right before Eli and Meg's wedding. It was like wedding fever had taken over the young adults. If the pattern held, Kathryn and Ethan would be next.

The pattern would skip him. He'd have to be satisfied with being Kim's friend and Oliver's uncle. A guy didn't marry his brother's ex. Not a good guy, anyway.

He glanced at his watch. The church service started in fifteen minutes. Kim should be here by now. Several families milled about, hanging up coats or swapping winter boots for inside shoes. He should be helping Oliver out of his winter gear, not chatting with his brother.

"I got another call. Can you wait a sec?" Jackson put his brother on hold to pick up Kim's call. "Did Oliver make you late again?"

"I need you." Ragged, short sentences. Clipped words. Heavy breathing.

Playfulness evaporated. He dug in the front pocket of his jeans for his car keys. "Where are you?"

"I'm on—" She sniffed with a snort-cry.

Pastor Owen paused at the side door that led to his office, and turned to look back at Jackson. His brows pulled together with a concerning look.

He mouthed to Owen. *Kim's in trouble.*

Kim would be on one of three roads. She'd stick to the plowed ones. He clutched his keys in his fist and scrunched his face, pressing his fist to his forehead. "Holiday Drive? Main? Sylvester? What road are you on?"

Pause, then a deep sucking sound. "Accident." Kim drew in another noisy breath. "Men. He's gone. Oliver's gone."

An acute sharpness tore through him. Men? Oliver? "Where are you?"

Owen's gaze followed Jackson. Curiosity colored Gloria's face. Jackson's hurried movements drew the attention of several families.

Meg and Eli approached. "Everything okay?"

Jackson shook his head, too focused on Kim to answer Eli.

"Oliver's gone. Gone." Each word from Kim came out shriller than the previous one.

"Kim! Where are you?" He needed a location, and he needed it now.

"H-H-H-oli-day Drive."

"I'm on my way."

Jackson bolted to the coat rack and grabbed his jacket from a hanger as he clicked back to Hayden. He'd only recently reconnected with his brother. Guilt had driven him to seek him out. For months, Jackson had fooled himself into believing the time he spent with Kim had just proved he was a good uncle. An invested family member. But somewhere, along the way, he'd fallen in love.

Even though Kim wasn't his to claim.

Sure, she and Hayden had never married, but they had a baby together. A child that deserved a mother and father. But Oliver would have no hope that they might reconcile if his uncle swooped in and captured his mother's heart.

"Keep us posted. We'll be praying!" Pastor Owen's words slipped out the church doors as they began to close behind Jackson.

The cold slapped Jackson's face as he raised the phone to his ear again. He ground his molars and pain shot down his jaw. Had Hayden sensed Jackson's feelings for Kim? Was this a pre-emptive strike? "What did you do?"

"Is everything okay?"

No, it wasn't. And Hayden had lost the right to ask years ago when he whisked Oliver overseas without Kim's consent, leaving the mess for Jackson to clean up.

"What's wrong?" Jackson could hear the familiar sound of knuckles popping in the background. Hayden's nervous response to stress.

"What did you do?"

"Nothing."

"Hayden—"

"Look, man. I'm not even there. Whatever happened, it's not on me."

Jackson unlocked his car and got in. He wasn't buying it. "Where's Oliver?" Impatience oozed through clenched teeth.

"Oliver's missing?" Hayden's pitch rose. Clear panic, but was it genuine?

"I don't have any details yet." Jackson's Bluetooth kicked in as he threw the vehicle in reverse and roared out of the parking lot. He wished he had the cruiser so he could light it up, sirens and everything. Jackson drummed his fingers on the steering wheel. If Oliver was really kidnapped, he'd have to call his Staff Sergeant.

"I'm on my way," Hayden said.

"Don't." Jackson wasn't sure he could trust him. Besides, Hayden lost any claim he had on Oliver years ago. He might sing a song of repentance regarding how he'd mistreated Kim, but that didn't mean he meant it. The guy was a chameleon. He became whoever he needed to get what he wanted. And right now, Jackson didn't have time to figure out Hayden's real agenda. He hung up on his brother. An officer could track Hayden down later and question him.

He redialed Kim. If she ditched the car, she could have lost consciousness. Did Oliver get out? Maybe he went for help? If they were lucky, the boy was knocking on some kind stranger's door, and the responsible adult would soon ring the police to report it.

But he wasn't banking Oliver's life on good luck. Or a kind stranger.

Kim picked up immediately. She sounded more in control. "What if this was Hayden?"

Jackson slowed for an intersection, looked both ways, and sped through. In less than a minute, he turned onto Holiday Drive. "Let's not make any leaps. I'm almost there."

"Hurry."

That was it. One word. One loaded, raw, painful request. "I am, Kim. I am."

She couldn't muffle her cries.

A rock lodged in his throat. Could Hayden be involved? Abductions by strangers made up less than one percent of kidnapped victims. Parents took ninety percent. Ninety-nine percent of kidnapped children returned alive. He clung to the statistics. He didn't want to it be Hayden, but if it was Hayden, at least he wouldn't hurt Oliver.

"I'm almost there." His knuckles whitened, and his fingertips tingled. He loosened his grip on the steering wheel. Would his brother do something like this? Was it fate that he was on the phone with Hayden or was that Hayden securing an alibi? He could have hired someone. Was this backlash for Jackson falling in love with Kim? What kind of man did that?

The kind who had done it before.

Jackson spied Kim's vehicle, and his chest lurched. "I'm here."

The back end of Kim's vehicle stuck from the snowbank. She stood to the side, shivering, and pressing her phone to her ear, hugging her body. When they locked eyes, heat surged through him. He pulled over and thrust the car into park.

Kim didn't wait for him to come to her. She barreled toward him with a guttural wail and threw herself into his arms.

Pressing his face into her hair, he inhaled her soft floral scent. He consoled her, but only for a minute. They didn't have the luxury of time for grief. Every second counted.

He eased her to arms' length so he could see her. Really see her. A laceration on her cheek wept red on her sweaty skin. Her hair, usually straight and smooth, was ratted and tangled. His temples and ears pounded. His vision tunneled. She was hurt. A faint shadowing darkened underneath her watery eyes. It promised to be a pretty shade of purple by tomorrow. Her gray complexion seemed more pale than usual against her dark hair. Almost translucent. Shock was setting in. He needed to get her warmed up.

He steeled himself. She needed a cop, not coddling. Get the facts. Make a plan. Treat it like any regular case.

Except it wasn't. It was Oliver.

He moved her slowly and deliberately toward the passenger side of the car. "Tell me everything that happened."

Kim's words wobbled. "A car riding my bumper distracted me."

"A car? What kind of car?"

"Not a car," she corrected. "A sport utility vehicle." Her exhalation shuddered. She sounded more confident. "It was definitely a SUV, and it was black."

"Okay, so this guy rides your tail. Then what?"

"I didn't see the other SUV in front of me. It was too late."

"A second one? Were they travelling together?"

"They took him, Jackson. They took him!" She pinched her waist and bent over, trying to suck in oxygen. "Right from the back seat. I tried to stop them. He hit me—"

His stomach clenched. He twisted her back into his arms and held tightly, squeezing his eyes closed. *Lord, please. Please.* It was all he had.

He opened the car door and helped Kim into the front passenger seat. "I need to call Emma."

Emma was the only medical professional in town. The nurse practitioner filled in as a paramedic several times in the past.

She fought his hands. "I don't care about me!" Her violent response momentarily stunned him. "They took Oliver!"

His gut cemented. This was bad. Really bad. "I'll call Stuart.

He's working today. And my Staff Sergeant. We're going to need help."

She nodded, tears soaking her face and dripping onto the burgundy scarf tucked into her coat collar. "Find him."

It killed him to have to turn away from her. Every cell in his body wanted to hold her and never let go, but he had to detach. It was their best chance.

He made several quick phone calls. Sycamore Hill wasn't equipped to deal with a kidnapping. He stumbled over the word, *kidnapped*. Just thinking about it made his stomach heave.

"Put out a BOLO notification to local police departments. I'll arrange for the detective and Missing Persons unit, the negotiator, and the IT officer." Every word Jackson's Staff said added a rock to Jackson's gut. This was real. Oliver was missing. "Stay with Kim until the team arrives."

"Yes, sir." They'd have to peel him off Kim if they tried to order him away.

Next, Jackson called Constable Stuart James, the on-duty OPP, and updated him.

"I'll get started on authorization for an Amber Alert," Stuart said. "I'll call in Noah, too."

Jackson finally called Emma. When they disconnected, Jackson didn't immediately turn around. He pinched his eyes shut. He was nowhere near clear-headed enough to do this. *Help me, Lord. I need to focus.*

Jackson knew the statistics. Of the one percent of stranger abductions, forty percent of the children died at the hands of their abductor. The first three hours were the most important.

Help me compartmentalize. Help me gather evidence so the team can hit the ground running when they get here. Don't let me feel anything. Please, oh please, God, please, lead me to Oliver in time.

He didn't say any of that to Kim. Statistics wouldn't help her. Letting her see his struggle to focus wouldn't help her. Only answers would. He turned and crouched in front of her. She sat in the vehicle, half in and half out, holding her head in her hands. He tentatively brushed his fingertips across her shoulder.

Her head jerked up. The skin around her red eyes bunched, and she fisted her hands.

"Let's warm you up. I asked Emma to bring Ben with her. He'll get your car to the garage. Give me your keys. I'll leave them under the mat." Emma had only recently returned to full-time work at her clinic, having just recovered from a serious shoulder injury.

Jackson despised needing to be so matter-of-fact. His stomach soured and threatened to expel his breakfast, but he swallowed it. He had to detach. He had to work the steps. It was the only thing keeping his head clear. Otherwise, he wouldn't have the mental strength to do what needed to be done. Oliver was counting on him. It'd been fifteen minutes since Kim called him. Thirty since the abduction. That left two and a half hours before they crossed a line that he wasn't willing to cross.

Please, Lord.

Kim nodded numbly and handed over her keys.

Emma wanted to know if she could share what happened with the church family.

Kim's heartbeat pulsed in her neck. She nodded permission, and he reached over her to crank the heat and reposition the vents to blow on her. He retrieved an emergency blanket from his trunk and wrapped it around her. He grabbed a water bottle from a case he kept in the back, twisted the lid off, and gave it to her. "Drink this." He fired off a quick text to get the prayer chain moving.

She took it, but didn't lift it to her lips. She stared vacantly at the set of tire tracks disappearing in the snow. Catatonic.

She needed him, but Oliver needed him more.

He forced eye contact. "I'm going over there." He pointed to her car in the ditch. "I need to look around."

She nodded, eyes glazed. She tugged the blanket tighter and rocked. Then the whimpering started.

He made himself walk away. He needed to work the case. He also needed to hold her and tell her he was going to find Oliver and bring him home. But he couldn't do both. Not by himself. And she needed him to be a cop more than a comforter. She just didn't know it. Finding Oliver was all that mattered.

Another phone call assured him the wheels were in motion. His Staff would get as many officers from nearby detachments as he could. Stuart was tracking Hayden down and sending local officers to pick him up, and Noah lived ten minutes out of town. He'd be there soon. Jackson crouched to study the tracks in the snow. It had stopped snowing, but the roads were a mess. It'd take Noah twenty to thirty minutes to get here. The Missing Persons unit was even further out. Two to three hours. Oliver didn't have that much time.

The harsh wind erased the crime scene and threatened to hold up their reinforcements. But if snowdrifts blocked the routes in, then they also blocked the roads out. That meant Oliver was still here.

Lord, please.

Oliver. His nephew. The son of the woman he loved.

9:15 a.m.

K im paced the short hallway in her house, sloshing hot coffee over her hand. The burn failed to register, but she felt the liquid drizzle over her wrist. She wiped the back of her hand on her thigh, and the spill absorbed into the denim. After changing from her church clothes into jeans and a sweater, she pulled her hair into a short ponytail. She numbly went through the motions of making coffee and putting out cream and sugar for Jackson and Stuart. It felt normal. How could life continue in its usual way when her son was missing? The world kept rotating and orbiting the sun when everything should have stopped. The universe should pause as they waited for news.

Any news.

Good news.

Please, Lord, bring good news.

Jackson was across her living room, leaning over Stuart's chair. They'd sent her to gather photographs of Oliver so they'd be ready for the Missing Persons unit coming from Orillia. Jackson had been avoiding her since they'd returned to her house. It was evident in the small things, like how he evaded her gaze and kept a room between them. He was pulling away, and the rejection pierced her soul.

Neither Jackson or Stuart looked up as she sighed. Kim sagged against a doorjamb, clutching her most recent picture of Oliver, running one fingertip over the image of Oliver's face. Over and over and over again.

Had she misjudged Jackson? If she couldn't count on him to be by her side at a time like this— Why wasn't he holding her? Why wasn't he promising everything would be okay? With Oliver's bunny wedged between her forearm and chest, she pushed through the doorway and set the photographs on the table. Jackson never looked up. She squeezed the bunny tighter. Since they returned to the house, she hadn't put the toy down. The idea of putting it down felt like admitting that Oliver was gone. It made little sense, but her heart accepted the flawed logic, even if her mind couldn't. She fingered the rabbit's torn ear. She needed to find her sewing kit. The rip would upset Oliver.

She yanked out the drawer in the end table. No sewing supplies. She moved to the bureau, opening and closing random drawers and cabinet doors. With each failure to secure her sewing kit, her heart wound tighter.

She started moving papers around on the table, moving closer and closer to Jackson. He continued to focus on whatever captured his attention. He'd pushed up his sleeves and leaned across the table, absorbed by the task in front of him.

Why didn't he realize she needed him?

His eyes flicked to the clock every thirty seconds. Each time, his body stiffened more. His withdrawal meant one thing. This would not end well. He knew Oliver was gone. Perhaps forever. And he couldn't look at her.

A tight lip press sent a bolt of pain streaking up her injured cheek, preventing her mind from pulling on that thread.

She retreated to the basement. She'd fix the bunny. Everything needed to be perfect for when Oliver returned. The cabinet beside the washer and dryer might have her sewing supplies. Her weight landed on each step with more stomp than necessary. Maybe that would get Jackson's attention. She yanked open the cabinet, retrieved her sewing kit, and slammed the door. The lack of a satisfying bang infuriated her as the soft-close hinges Jackson had installed functioned perfectly. She stomped up the staircase.

She pushed her way back into the living room, and her gaze collided with Meg's. Instantly, pressure built behind her eyes until the thought they might pop from her skull.

Meg's lifted eyebrows meant she'd heard Kim's clomping, and still, her friend didn't ask the pointless question everyone seemed to ask. Meg already knew that Kim wasn't okay. She would never be okay again. Meg threw her arms around Kim. "I'm so sorry."

Kim remained stiff-necked and rigid. If she gave way, if she yielded even one bit, she'd shatter into a million pieces.

Kim had met Meg when Meg applied to Life House. The women's shelter that Kim ran in Sycamore Hill provided counsel to battered women and helped them relaunch into a safer life. Kim had been in a counselling session with Meg, who'd run to Sycamore Hill to escape her ex, when she'd learned that Hayden took Oliver that first time. Their relationship had changed in that moment. Meg became the counsellor and Kim was the one in need of godly wisdom. It was the only time Kim blurred that ethical line and developed a friendship with a client.

A surge of gratitude rushed through her. Meg was God's gift to her. Meg, newly married and established in a good life, radiated hope. She was physical evidence of how God worked on behalf of His children. And Kim needed hope like never before.

Meg took the sewing kit from Kim's hands and led Kim to the couch. She placed the kit on the table.

"Jackson was at church when you called." Meg kept one arm looped through Kim's. They sat thigh to thigh on the sofa. "Emma updated Pastor Owen like you asked her to, and Pastor Owen updated the congregation. They've been praying ever since. I came as soon as I could."

Kim stared at the bunny positioned on her lap to face her. She stroked one velvety ear.

"Emma promised to keep her phone on her. When they find Oliver—" Meg's voice broke.

Kim loved she spoke with confidence. When. Not if. When.

Meg cleared her throat. "When they find him, she said to call her. She'll meet you wherever and whenever and make sure he's okay."

Emma pretty much said the same thing to her when she looked her over. The ridiculousness of being given a medical all-clear by Emma rang hollow. How could her physical body be fine when she was dying inside? Kim leaned into Meg, needing to feel her friend's presence. She swiped the tears that dripped from her chin. "What am I going to do?"

"Take it one moment at a time." Meg repeated the wisdom that Kim had shared with hundreds of women. "You're going to live in this moment and trust God. No good comes from borrowing tomorrow's fear." Meg wrapped an arm around her shoulder and gently rocked her. "You're going to believe that God loves Oliver, and He knows where He is. Oliver is not alone. The Spirit of God is with him."

Kim didn't know how to live in this moment. Not when the moment held such uncertainty. Not when it separated her from Oliver and undermined her confidence in God's care.

Meg's head pressed close to hers. Her friend's voice dropped to a whisper. "You're going to remember that Oliver is strong. Jackson is looking for him. I'm here as long as you need me. God is bigger than the storm."

Kim's gaze wound its way back to Jackson. Her gut tightened at his contorted expression. Hayden would not call. He didn't want money. He wanted to hurt Kim. Jackson remained unconvinced that Hayden had Oliver. But if it wasn't Hayden, if it was a stranger—

Her stomach cramped. She clutched the bunny to her gut and groaned.

Jackson lifted his head, and their gazes collided. Finally. His jaw tightened, and then he refocused on his work.

Her heart shrank. She was losing him, too.

A part of her had hoped she, Oliver, and Jackson might one day make a family that was more than uncle and nephew. She dreamed of marriage, but right now, he avoided her, failing to comfort her. He withdrew when she needed him the most, working professionally and detached. He'd drawn the lines around their relationship, and she saw them clearly. What if this meant his concern flowed from an uncle, not a potential lover? No. She wasn't thinking straight. Her mind was spinning in irrational circles. That was all.

Fear hit like a foot in the gut.

Her cell rang, and she jumped to her feet. She'd set it on the table, plugged into a power outlet, in case of a call. The vibration of the ring sent it drifting across the table's surface. She bounded into the room.

"It's a video call," Stuart said.

The ringtone sounded a second time. Her heart hammered her ribs as she reached for her phone. Jackson had changed the phone's settings, so they had several rings before the messaging system kicked in.

A third ring.

Her breath bottled in her throat. Her lungs screamed. What if they hung up?

"His video will be on," Jackson said. "Keep the screen centered on your face. Don't let him see us in the background."

She nodded. Her throat swelled. Black spots bounced in her peripheral vision. What if she couldn't speak?

A fourth ring.

What if she missed her chance to save Oliver? She paced in front of the table. What if—

Jackson readied his phone to record her phone screen. "Say what I told you to say."

Meg and Stuart hushed.

Kim pressed the button that allowed her to accept the video call. By the grace of God, the thickness in her throat decreased, and she squeaked out, "Hello?"

The phone screen lit up. Oliver sat at a table, stacking jumbo blocks. A juice box with a straw was open beside him. He was fine.

Kim clutched the phone. "Oliver!"

He didn't react.

Kim swayed, and Meg stepped behind her and supported her elbows.

Meg, not Jackson.

Oliver appeared unhurt. His skin blotchy from crying, clothing intact, no visible wounds.

"You can see he is safe, but he cannot see you or hear you." A mechanical voice filled her dining room. "Tell us where to find El, and Oliver will stay safe."

Kim's gaze zipped to Jackson's. She'd been prepared for Hayden. Maybe even a ransom demand. But not this.

Stuart held up a sheet of paper. *Who is El?*

"Why did you take Oliver?"

Jackson frowned. She flicked her gaze away.

"I don't have time for questions. Where's El?"

"El? I don't know an El."

Stuart held up another sheet of paper. *Short for Ellie?*

Elena? Jackson mouthed.

The blood drained from her head. Kim staggered. Meg's increased pressure on her elbows was the only reason Kim remained upright as fogginess crept at the edges of her vision. Kim clawed it back. She fell against Meg. Her head felt too heavy for her neck, ears roaring. All the moisture evaporated in her mouth.

"You remember her. That's good," the voice said. "You have until ten o'clock to give me her location." The caller hung up. Oliver's video feed disappeared.

"No—" Kim's head buzzed. This was about Elena Watters. She twisted into Meg's arms. Ten o'clock. Forty-five minutes.

"Who is El?" Meg's soft question brushed against her ear. It was as if she knew.

"Elena Watters checked into Life House yesterday," Kim whispered.

Meg's grip on Kim's arm tightened. Meg knew what it meant to run to a place like Life House. Months ago, Meg's ex had tracked her down to Sycamore Hill, and she'd had to face her greatest fear. Now, similar trouble followed Elena.

Jackson had arrested Meg's ex. Would he be able to stop Elena's?

Kim bent at the waist. Her breaths came in gasps. Elena had left a dangerous man. She had tried leaving him once before, and he found her and dragged her back. It took a positive pregnancy test for her to find the courage to leave him a second time. She'd die to protect her baby.

Elena came directly to Life House, thanks to the contact cards Kim had teams of people distributing all over the province. Kim had welcomed her and given her sanctuary, listening to her story and assuring her they would take the steps needed to protect her and her child. Instead of checking El into the residence house, Kim called Jackson, asking who he'd recommend to host Elena. Her gut told her the woman's ex wouldn't let her go easily, but she'd never guessed how far he'd go.

Spots danced in Kim's vision. Her thundering heart beat deep in her ears. This was her fault. She'd checked El in. She'd put her into protective housing. They'd taken Oliver because of her job.

9:30 a.m.

J ackson had years on the force. He knew what it was to be the official bearing bad news, the one searching for the lost, the one that longed to give innocent victims answers for their grief. But it had never been like this. He'd never been here. There was a reason officers recused themselves when they had a personal connection. It muddied the water.

Kim's entire body shook. She raised a trembling hand, but somewhere, partway up, it stopped and floated as if she'd forgotten what she was trying to do with it. She knew something. A piece of the puzzle had clicked, and the torment shredded her.

Her breath sounds shallowed, and when she straightened fully, her legs gave way. She collapsed against Meg, and her complexion faded to a sickly gray. She pressed her hand into her chest and clutched the fabric of her shirt.

Before he could insist she tell him what cut her legs from under her, Kim lunged toward the kitchen.

A dining room chair clattered to its side as she shoved it out of her way. A dish shattered on the ceramic tile. Kim moaned at a guttural level. She clawed at the laminate counter's edge and leaned over the sink and heaved.

And heaved.

And heaved.

Her body convulsed while she retched.

Meg beat him to Kim's side, but only by a hair. She slipped an arm around Kim's waist, held back Kim's hair, and did all the things Jackson burned to do but couldn't. The last time he let his emotions rule him at work, the bad guy won. He couldn't let that happen again. Not when it was Oliver's life on the line.

Kim gagged. With her head over the sink, she reached for the faucet. Still leaning over the basin, she rinsed the sink and her mouth.

Jackson hated that he couldn't comfort Kim, but this wasn't about his feelings. Jackson might not be Oliver's dad, but he felt like he was. Ever since he moved to Sycamore Hill, he'd filled the role that Hayden abandoned. Not because he had to, but because he wanted to. But right now, Oliver needed a cop, not an uncle or surrogate father.

He glanced at the clock's constantly moving digits. Stuart had reset the timer, so it counted down to the ten o'clock deadline like a bomb to detonation. When the higher-ups arrived, they'd boot him from the case. Jackson was too close. This was too personal. But until then, he was in. All in until Oliver came home.

Meg murmured soft words to Kim. The words he wanted to murmur. She rubbed small circles into Kim's back, and his palms itched with a need for physical contact. Meg promised Kim that she would get through this. Meg said Kim was strong.

The back of his throat ached. Meg was right. Kim was the strongest woman Jackson had ever met. She'd been through this before. Not exactly this, but close. When Hayden's parental abduction stretched over a year, Kim never stopped looking for her son. She never lost hope. And when Jackson reunited them, she did the hardest thing for a parent who'd lost her child. She shared him with Jackson and his parents, opening her heart to the family that had unwittingly contributed to her pain. Because that was what Oliver needed. She always put others first.

Lord, hour by hour, help her—help us—to walk in the strength of the Lord Jesus Christ, trusting Him for all we need and believing His Spirit is with us, strengthening us and upholding us, and comforting us.

Kim was strong, but God was stronger.

"Tell me more about El." Stuart broke the silence.

Kim stared into the sink. She didn't lift her head, or turn toward Stuart's voice, or acknowledge his question.

"Is El who you took to the farm?" Jackson's brief time in Sycamore Hill was long enough to meet the guys that'd have his back. A small police presence often called on the community in the initial crisis moments, and he made it his pattern to seek men of honor and cultivate relationships with them in every place he served. Moving here had been no different. So, when Kim called about a new client in need of a safe place, Jackson suggested Willow Creek Farms.

"Yes." She continued to stare into the sink.

Come on, baby, stay with me. Tell me what I need to know. Then she could fall apart because he'd carry it from there. "Is El still at the farm?"

Vacant eyes lifted to his. He saw how his tone hurt her, but he didn't have time to coddle her feelings. Not when that blasted clock lost a precious minute every sixty seconds.

Kim nodded.

Jackson locked gazes with Stuart. "She's at Willow Creek Farms. I gotta call Simon."

Matt Gaither, a local army man, had introduced Jackson to

Simon and Colleen Willow. Simon had served his country before retiring, and Colleen was no slouch. Used to running the farm alone when her husband was on leave, she'd fought off wild animals trying to feast on her chickens and even scared the occasional intruder away. They knew how to defend the defenseless.

Simon answered before the first ring completed, and Jackson updated him on the potential trouble coming his way.

Meg helped Kim to a chair at the kitchen table. She poured her another coffee. Both women avoided meeting his eyes.

"Stuart, do we have someone you can send to Life House?"

"Already on it." Stuart didn't look up from his phone. His thumbs pounded the keys in a text message. "I redirected Noah. If we're lucky, whoever has Oliver first searched Life House offices looking for Elena and left us some clues."

Lord willing, they'd have something to work with soon.

Jackson's gaze drilled into Kim's profile. She hadn't looked his way since his harsh questioning. She didn't understand he needed to shock her back to the present moment. Her urge to retreat was strong, but she needed to fight it and tell him what he needed to know. How much did God expect one woman to carry? Kim's experience with Hayden made her more sensitive to the trauma the women brought with them to Life House. Jackson loved her strength, but even the strongest person broke under the right pressure.

Lord, if it's possible, let this cup of suffering pass.

Jesus prayed that prayer, and God said no. Jesus took the ultimate cup for them. A famous pastor once said that Jesus bought endurance for His children through the cup poured out, the new covenant in His blood. And they needed endurance. Kim. Him. Oliver. They needed a strength they didn't have in themselves.

"Let's review the facts," Stuart said. "Whoever has Oliver wants to trade him for Elena Watters. Tell me about Elena."

Kim's glassy eyes stared past them.

"Kim," Jackson prompted. Her blinkless gaze tripped his heart. "Look at me." Jackson's need for sharpness shredded his soul.

Kim finally turned her face. She looked him dead in the eyes, and he nearly staggered. Her nostrils flared. Sweat beaded on her forehead. Her upper lip curled, exposing a slice of teeth.

He could work with angry. If she needed to hate him, so be it. He'd do whatever he had to, even though it churned his gut. "Tell Stuart about Elena."

Kim was spiraling fast, and Jackson needed her engaged and alert. Oliver needed her to be strong, stronger than she'd ever had to be. But he believed in her. God was with her. And that was what a mother did. They dug deep.

He ignored the judgement oozing from Meg. He didn't have time to explain the need for his methods. Not if the guy holding Oliver was Elena's ex-boyfriend. Jackson hadn't gone with Kim and Elena last night, but he documented his role in suggesting the farm and looked into Elena's ex, because if trouble was headed for Sycamore Hill, he wanted to be ready.

Kim licked her lips. Her eyes dulled to an acceptance that made his insides shrivel. "She was afraid her ex would follow her. He's obsessed with his baby."

Stuart nodded. "What else?"

Kim disconnected further. "He's dangerous. Connected with a gang in the city."

Reality slammed Jackson against the ropes. He and Kim might not recover from this fight. He'd seen it in other couples, in other cases. Tragedy and the tensions involved in kidnappings had ripped relationships more solid than theirs to shreds. But Oliver mattered more. Bringing Oliver home mattered more than comforting the woman he loved, grieving with her, praying with her, crying with her, no matter how much he wanted to pull her into his arms and promise her that everything was going to be okay. The reality hit him so hard it hurt to breathe. Indulging those emotions wasn't an option.

Jackson would comfort Kim tomorrow. He would fall apart and grieve for Oliver tomorrow. Tomorrow, he'd be everything Kim needed him to be. Today, he had to stuff his emotions to bring Oliver back, because anything less was unacceptable. Unthinkable. Not survivable.

Jackson forced his aching arms to stay at his side. Meg would hold Kim after he left. Meg would comfort her because Meg wasn't able to do the one thing Jackson could—bring Oliver home. He prayed Kim would understand why it had to be this way. "I think it's time I had a chat with Elena."

"You can't work the case."

Stuart's abrupt reminder made his steps hitch. Stuart was right. But not working on the case wasn't going to happen.

"I'll call our Staff again." Stuart picked up his cell. "We might need more than the Missing Persons unit. We might need Guns and Gangs."

El's ex was a notorious criminal with a long rap sheet. It complicated things. Oliver's chances of return grew slimmer by the second. The case snowballing downhill morphed into an avalanche that threatened to bury them. "I'll speak with Elena."

"Jackson—" Stuart pounded a fist on the table, jolting him. "You can't work the case."

"I can put information together for the Missing Persons unit."

Stuart held his gaze for a minute before giving a curt nod. "But that's it."

Jackson touched Kim's arm, and her head jerked. "I need to speak with Elena."

"She might not talk to you."

"Elena doesn't have a choice." Jackson notified Simon via text that he was on his way.

Thank the Lord for Meg. Meg's soft tone soothed Kim's bruises. Kim needed her community to be strong for her. God would work through His people.

Tension dialled up and pressure increased behind his eyes. He loved Kim and Oliver so much that it physically hurt. He bit his cheek until he tasted blood.

Stuart's hand landed heavily on Jackson's shoulder. "I just got off the phone with the Missing Persons detective assigned to the case."

"Who is it?"

"Burland."

Jackson nodded. Burland was good. They'd met at a conference once. Burland would maintain communication with Stuart and their Staff Sergeant as he and his team travelled, so everyone stayed updated.

"Guns and gangs will be here ASAP. But the weather and highway conditions mean we might be it for the next few hours."

The gang unit was just as far away as the kidnapping unit.

Jackson nodded. "We're gonna get this guy. We'll find Oliver and bring him home. This ends today."

Stuart ignored Jackson's use of the word we.

Kim's eyes shone, and Meg lifted her chin a notch. Jackson had finally done something right. He was going to rain hell on the man who'd hurt his family.

9:45 a.m.

❧

Kim pulled away from Meg. If Jackson was going to see Elena, so was she. "I'm coming with you."

He flattened his lips. "You're not. You can't."

"Your supervisor said I wasn't to be alone." She raised her chin, pushing her tongue against the back of her teeth as she weighed her options.

"You're not alone."

Swallowing the last trace of bitter bile, Kim shrugged, not needing his permission. "I can't find Oliver myself. I'm not able to stop this from unfolding, but I can, with absolute certainty, drive to where Elena is located." She levelled a look at him she reserved for Oliver's worst tantrums. He was not sidelining her. Not now. Not when it came to Oliver. She practically dared him to stop her.

From the corner of her eye, she caught Stuart sneaking glances their way, curious who would emerge the victor in this battle of wills.

The stiff lines on Jackson's face relaxed. He smiled like an adult indulging a child, or a superior tolerating a subordinate. It riled her so much she could have churned butter out of her ears.

"Your car is in the ditch on Holiday Drive. How do you plan to get there?"

Kim extended her palm toward Meg and without missing a beat said, "I'll take Meg's car."

Meg dashed for her purse and retrieved her keys. She plopped them into Kim's hand and raised her chin. It only wobbled a bit. "She'll use mine."

Meg's declaration lacked assurance. Her voice lifted on the last word like her statement was a question. Kim got it. She wasn't as confident as she pretended to be, either. Nothing about what went down today made her feel hopeful. But all that mattered was that she was going. There wasn't anything he could do about it.

"I could detain you for interfering with an investigation."

Except that. He could do that. Her empty stomach turned over. She pressed a hand against it and closed her eyes. "But you won't." At least she hoped he wouldn't. "We both know it." Kim stuffed her arms into her winter coat, grabbed her purse, and stomped to the front door. Every eye in the room followed her.

She lifted her chin. "I'm leaving. If you're heading in the same direction, I'd prefer to ride with you. But I'm going. End of discussion."

This was her olive branch. If Jackson didn't take it, they'd never recover. She needed to be part of the solution. And he needed to let her. If he kept shutting her out, if she stayed on the sidelines and something happened . . . She swallowed again. A mouthful of air bubbled in her gut.

"I'll stay with her," Stuart said. "You go. We'll be fine."

Kim swung her gaze to Stuart. "But—"

"No buts." Stuart's glare left no wiggle room. "You will not go. And the longer we argue, the less time we have to find Oliver."

He flicked his gaze to Jackson and tossed his keys to him. "I've got this covered. Take the cruiser."

Jackson caught the keys one-handed. The front door closed behind him. Kim fisted her hands at her side. She lifted her face, ready to rip into Stuart, but stopped short, thrown by the brokenness and compassion in his gaze.

"There isn't much Jackson can do. He's too close to this. Let him go. He loves Oliver, too."

Her mouth trembled.

"Soon, the Missing Persons detective will take over. The information Jackson is gathering can help the team, but he can't do it if you're with him."

She chewed her bottom lip. Her mind understood why it had to be this way, but her heart didn't. If she opened her mouth even the tiniest bit, she'd cry. And if she started crying, she would never stop.

Kim nodded. Her dry tongue bumped over her lips. She cleared her throat. "Can I use my phone? I want to see my notes on Elena."

A smile softened the hard lines of Stuart's face. He disconnected the phone from the power supply and handed it to Kim. "That's a good idea."

As Stuart returned his attention to his computer screen, Kim nudged Meg with her foot. "Distract him." She tipped her head in his direction. "I'm going after Jackson."

Meg's eyes widened.

"Give me a five-minute head start."

Meg mouthed, *no*, but Kim ignored her.

Kim slipped into her bedroom, grabbed an old jacket, and tiptoed to the back door. She winced as it creaked open. Once outside, she hurried to Meg's vehicle. In less than a minute, she was headed toward the farm. Elena owed her some answers.

She approached the last intersection before leaving the town limits, thankful the snow had stopped. The wind played with the accumulation like a cat tossing its prey, but at least it wouldn't get any deeper. The stoplight turned red, and her gaze connected with the driver in front of her via his rearview mirror. *Uh oh.*

The cruiser's lights swirled on and it pulled to the side of the road. Kim followed and lowered her window.

Jackson stormed toward her. His nostrils flared and white huffs of exhalations shot from them like steam. "Are you trying to get Oliver killed?"

Her head fuzzed. All she heard were the words *Oliver*, and *killed*.

"You can't be here. It goes against protocol."

Energy surged through her. "I don't care about protocol!"

Jackson pounded the vehicle's roof. "You have to go back."

"I can't be alone."

He shoved off the car, twisting away. His fingers dug into his hair.

"Jackson—" It came out all broken and distraught. He had to understand. She couldn't stay still as someone used Oliver to manipulate her. Not a second time.

"Promise to do exactly what I say." With his defenses lowered, she glimpsed his turmoil. He pressed both hands against the frame of the vehicle and leaned in, his vulnerability nearly undoing her. "I can't lose you, too."

Five gruff words gave her a peek at the heart beating behind the badge. He was still there. Somewhere under the shield was the man she loved, and it filled her with hope.

"Park in the bank's empty lot and get in with me."

She nodded and raised the window as he returned to the cruiser. She followed his instructions and locked Meg's vehicle. The rawness of their interaction reached places in her heart that she hadn't visited in a long time, and she melted a little. Not enough to follow protocol, but sufficient to climb into his passenger seat and lean across the console to press her palm against his unshaven cheek. She tipped her forehead against his. The bristles on his jawline scraped her soft skin, contrasting their God-ordained differences. It made her feel secure. Jackson would keep her safe.

"You won't lose me. You can't."

They lingered for less than a second before controlled detachment dropped back over Jackson's face. But this time, she saw it for what it was. Self-protection. Jackson was afraid.

And that terrified her on a whole new level.

Kim buckled her seatbelt and didn't say a word. She stared straight ahead, praying over and over the only words she could think. *Please, Jesus.*

He backed out of his parking spot and wound their way to the farm.

Please, Jesus.

Silence cranked the tension in the cab, broken only when Jackson announced, "We have a tail."

Kim rotated to look over her shoulder. "Who follows a cop?"

The muscle at the hinge of his jawline twitched. "Someone who just told you the price of Oliver's return."

They couldn't find El. Her plan worked. Her gut had been right to stash the woman somewhere safer than the Life House residence.

The SUV followed their turn. And the next.

Kim squinted, but her view was obscured. She'd promised El that her ex wouldn't locate her. But that was before he took Oliver. Before she understood the personal cost. "They wouldn't be stupid enough to grab El in front of a cop, would they?"

"No, but they'll make a plan to snatch her later while we are making a transfer. A person is most vulnerable then." Jackson stabbed the speaker on his phone and hit redial. The call connected to the vehicle's Bluetooth.

Jackson's world baffled Kim. He lived with dim statistics and constant heartbreak. Yet, he never hardened. He remained the kindest, noblest, most gentle man she'd ever known. They'd been practically co-parenting Oliver for over a year. She couldn't imagine a future without him. But he'd never kissed her beyond a chaste peck on the cheek or forehead. He never pushed for more than she was ready to give. Yet their connection seemed more intimate than friendship. Deeper. Rooted in the rich soil of shared faith and their love for a little boy.

The phone call connected. Kim recognized Simon's voice.

Jackson changed lanes and took a fast right. The back end fishtailed, but Jackson steered out of it. The cruisers were always winter ready, which was more than she could say for the vehicle following them. It hit the brakes too hard and arced. Each swing was bigger until they missed the turn.

Her breath shot out.

"Simon, I'm on my way to you. Elena's ex is trying to smoke her out. Stash her in the safe spot we talked about."

Kim snapped her eyes to Jackson. A new hideaway was news to her.

All the usual joviality in Simon's tone evaporated. He'd reverted to his army persona. "Yes, sir."

"Be there in ten. I need to make sure we lost the tail." Jackson disconnected. He glanced at her, his attention dropping to her white knuckles clutching the seatbelt.

"I've seen enough ditches today." She loosened her fingers.

"You should have stayed home." The muscle in his jaw twitched with the regularity of a pulse. "We could protect you there."

"When Oliver's in a safe place, I'll stay with him. Until then, you're stuck with me."

He chewed on his lip. A sharp whistle emitted from his nose. After a long, uncomfortable pause, he spoke. "I'm gonna drive a few more minutes. When I know it's clear, we'll double back in the right direction."

They rode in silence, each lost in their thoughts and fears until she broke the stillness. "What's the plan?"

She knew there wasn't a bone in Jackson's body that would sacrifice one vulnerable person for another. That meant he had an idea that was better than the horrible one simmering inside of her. Refining fires brought dross to the surface, and as the flames increased, the scum in her heart rose. Yesterday, she wouldn't have thought she'd ever consider betraying a client. Today, she not only considered it; she almost hoped it could be that easy to bring Oliver home.

And she hated herself for it.

"We aren't trading Elena. But we won't let Oliver die, either."

Pressure built behind her eyes. He hadn't really answered her question. Was it because the plan was confidential or because he didn't have one?

Please, Jesus.

She turned to the window, and the trees sped past. Oliver was nearby. But where? Was he crying? Hurt? Did he understand the danger?

She yanked her cuff over her fist and wiped her eyes.

Please, Jesus.

Jackson pulled into the laneway of Willow Creek farms. Simon was waiting on the porch. He bounded down the steps and met them at the car.

Kim fumbled with the door handle. Why wasn't he with Elena? Did something happen?

"El is gone," Simon blurted.

Kim's hurried movements froze.

"What do you mean, gone?" Jackson slammed the cruiser's door.

The men swirled in front of her. Kim's new goal became exiting the car. Remaining upright. Staying conscious. It took all her energy and focus. She opened the door.

Right behind those basic goals screamed the questions that never stopped. Did they take El? Did her ex beat them there? Was the tail a misdirect?

She climbed out of the cruiser. If Elena had fallen prey to the violent man, at least they wouldn't hurt her. Not until the baby was born. Light-headedness made her stumble. Her hands went numb as she twisted them. She moved toward Jackson, legs like tree trunks, propelled by a force impossible to resist. If they had Elena, what did that mean for Oliver?

Simon was speaking. His lips were moving. But Kim couldn't hear anything over the screaming inside her head.

9:57 a.m.

❧

Jackson's heart rattled against his ribs like a jailed man desperate to break free. 9:57. The kidnappers were calling in three minutes, and Elena was gone. He had no intention of handing her over, but he'd been counting on the woman's insight to navigate conversing with Oliver's abductors.

Simon's succinct update left little hope.

"She could still be here, right? On the farm?" Kim's gaze darted around the property. The hopefulness in her voice scrambled for a hold as her hands flapped in front of her body. She looked his way, but focused on something beyond him. Like it took all her strength and mental energy to remain engaged. She was grasping.

Jackson got it. It was all too fluid. Unstable.

9:58. Two minutes.

"I doubt it." Jackson squeezed the sides of his head. He paced a few steps away. Elena was hiding from a dangerous man, so she wouldn't stroll around a strange property. If she wasn't in her room, she was gone. His hands dropped to massage the tight knot in his neck. This threw in a wrench their engine didn't need. "Did she leave of her own volition?"

Less than two minutes. The clock never stopped ticking. One hundred and twenty seconds. It wasn't enough time. It howled in his ears.

Kim cradled her cell phone in her hands.

Watching.

Waiting.

"No signs of a struggle. I've searched the house and was going to start on the property when you pulled up. Brown's out searching the back woods. Elena's footprints led through the orchard."

"Noah?" Stuart had sent him to Life House.

"Constable James called when he realized Kim was gone." Simon's gaze flicked to Kim, who blushed. "He said Brown would approach from the south side. He's working his way across the property. I expect he'll reach the house in less than fifteen minutes."

Kim hugged herself as her head swivelled between Simon and Jackson. The snow crunched under her shifting weight. "What are we going to do?"

Jackson's skin prickled. She expected him to know. Stuart had pulled Noah. That was a good call. "We'll look at Elena's room. You'll stay with Colleen."

For once, she didn't argue.

But first, they had another phone call. Any minute now. Less than sixty seconds.

Simon's feet spread shoulder width apart. His arms hung loose at the sides, but the tension radiating from him belied his casual posture. Army men never changed. Like Kim, Simon looked to Jackson for direction, but he still didn't have any to offer.

"Elena rabbited." Simon said. "I don't know what spooked

her. When Colleen left her in her room, Elena said she was exhausted, so we gave her some space. I monitored the doors. She didn't leave through either of them."

They'd lost a woman. A pregnant woman. A woman who probably climbed out the bedroom window and hoofed it on foot without a jacket or winter clothing. If she didn't find warm shelter, her biggest concern wouldn't be the man chasing her. It would be the harsh elements.

Jackson bit back a roar. The cold burned his lungs. The alternative theory was that the kidnappers had found her. And if they had Elena, would they even call? Was Oliver already—

Don't go there.

9:59.

Kim's gaze ping-ponged between him and Simon. "What does this mean for Oliver?"

Simon was one of the good guys. There was no way someone hoodwinked him. Elena left of her own free will. But why?

"It means things just got harder." Jackson spoke through his teeth. A lot harder. He pinched his forehead, trying to force his thoughts to slow. "When they call, don't let on that Elena is gone."

"But if they have her, they'll know I'm lying."

"And if they don't have her, it'll buy Oliver time."

The phone rang. Jackson locked eyes with Kim. He placed both his hands over hers, covering the phone and muffling it. "You can do this. Blame me. Say the police moved her, and that you're trying to figure out where. If they say they've got her, play dumb."

Simon had his cell ready and started recording.

She was white-faced and desperate. Kim needed him to be strong, sure about their plan, not guessing at the last minute.

A noise gurgled in her throat.

"You can do this." He let go of her.

She tapped the phone's speaker option and moved it closer to Simon's device. "Hello?"

"Are you ready to give her up?"

Jackson's heart thumped. *Thank you, Lord!* They didn't have Elena. They didn't know she was missing.

A look almost akin to joy crossed Kim's face. *Hope.* Jackson's heart lurched. Hope was dangerous. Hope increased the devastation of a negative outcome. He leaned forward. *Come on, Kim. Sell it. You can do it.*

Kim jutted her chin. "The police moved her in the night. I don't know where."

The mechanical voice swore. "I said no cops!"

"No, you didn't!" Her outburst shocked everyone, including the caller.

Silence.

"But I'll find her." Kim squeezed the phone until Jackson thought it might break. "I just need a bit of time." Sobs now intermixed with her words. "Please don't hurt Oliver. Please don't hurt him."

Kim heaved. Jackson could barely understand her words. It was all too much. She was losing it.

"You have one hour, or your boy dies." The call disconnected.

Kim fell into Jackson's arms. She shook and buried her face in his shoulder, and it muffled her cries. Better people had broken under less. She'd handled it like a pro.

"I can't do this. I can't. I can't. I can't."

"You did good." Jackson rocked her. "You bought us an hour. It was good."

Jackson looked over her head at Simon. He needed Simon. The kidnapping unit was still too far out. Guns and gangs even further. Other OPP officers from nearby towns should roll in soon, but they weren't here yet.

Simon nodded, fully understanding the unspoken question. "We are getting her boy back."

Jackson's chest swelled. Hope was dangerous.

He tightened his arms around Kim and pressed his mouth to her hair. "Yes, we are."

Oliver was gone over a year when Hayden took him. Jackson would not let Kim lose Oliver a second time. Not even if it killed him.

Inside the farmhouse, Jackson kept Kim in his peripheral vision. Colleen placed a steaming mug in front of her. Kim wrapped her hands around it and pulled it forward. The steam drifted over her face. She never lifted the mug to her lips. She closed her puffy and red-rimmed eyes.

Colleen retreated to the kitchen, where she kept adding to a mountain of sandwiches. The men had to eat, she'd said, stuffing one into Jackson's hand.

It was a little past ten in the morning. The idea of food made his stomach roll, but Colleen was right. It could be hours before he'd get another chance to refuel. If he didn't eat, he might not have the strength he needed. He bit into the sandwich and chewed. Colleen made a good hoagie, but today it ground up like sawdust in his mouth. He forced himself to ingest the nutrition for Oliver.

Kim's meal sat untouched in front of her.

Jackson had called his Staff Sergeant and updated him on Elena's disappearance. The man wasn't happy that Kim tricked PC James and was now with Jackson, but there wasn't much he could do about it now. Jackson couldn't send her back to the house alone, especially when they considered the tail they had coming here.

Jackson emailed the phone call recording to his Staff. His Staff would update Detective Burland, who was still en route. Considering what they knew about Elena and her ex, she had to be the key. If they figured out her history, they'd figure out who she trusted and where she went.

Simon cleared his throat, and Jackson looked up.

Simon stood in the doorway, leaning a shoulder against the wall. He tipped his head toward the hallway, and Jackson pushed back from the table to join him.

"What do we know so far?" Simon kept his voice low so the women wouldn't be able to hear them.

Jackson darted a glance to Kim. She sat at the far end of the table with her feet hooked around the chair legs. Her vacant expression made him suspect she'd retreated to someplace safe in her mind.

Simon deserved more details than he got last night. The people who helped the residents of Life House walked a fine line of respecting the client's privacy and getting enough details to help them. When Kim dropped Elena off, she asked Simon to "keep watch." It was code for "trouble might come knocking."

On those nights, the man slept in a rocker by the window. From that position, he had a line of sight to his front and back doors, the laneway, and half the property. And he did it all covertly. The women were clueless about the sleep Simon lost for them. And Simon never asked for more information. But today, Simon's request for details was a fair one. They'd dumped a truckload of trouble on his land. He had a right to know what kind of missile was locked on its target.

Jackson leaned back in his chair. "Elena's dating a well-known gang leader in the city."

"Who's the leader?"

"Nathan Fieldstone."

"Why the fixation on Watters?"

"Nathan had a child with a former girlfriend. The child died in the crossfire of a gunfight with a rival gang. Then Nathan shot the mother for not protecting his kid. He's obsessed with ensuring this child lives to inherit his empire."

"El will never be free of him. A child binds you for life."

The men spun. How long had Kim been standing there listening? Judging from her expression, too long. Her eyes were heavy and her face pinched.

Jackson's gut clenched. Was that how she felt about Hayden? Bound forever? The truth hit below the belt. If Kim ever considered marriage, it should be to the father of her child, especially if Hayden had really changed, like he claimed. Jackson had been praying for years that his brother would repent. Could God be answering his prayers now? Would He do it like this? Was this God's way of reminding Jackson that he had no business hoping he'd ever be more than Oliver's uncle? But it might not matter. If he failed to bring Oliver home, Kim would blame him forever.

"Guys like Nathan don't stop coming." Simon folded his arms across his broad chest. "He wants his kid. She probably figured they'd track her here. But how? Why was she so certain they'd find where we hid her?"

"When the baby's born, he'll have no need for her," Kim said. "She knows what happened to the last woman."

"We have an hour." Jackson strode back into the dining room. "An hour to find her, and an hour to save Oliver."

Simon followed him. "What's Missing Persons' ETA?"

"They're en route. The soonest they'll get here is eleven o'clock this morning." Jackson looked out the window. The storm had cleared. Still, copious amounts of snow blocked many of the roads. "Unless the plows are out, it's going to be longer."

"This is on us." Simon's head bobbed, accepting the reality.

"It's on us," Jackson echoed.

Jackson trusted Simon to have his back. Noah would emerge from his search through the woods any minute, and they would make a plan together. These guys had battled evil before. They didn't scare easy, and they wouldn't back down. There wasn't a better team. But a bigger one would be nice.

10:30 a.m.

⌒◯

"El's phone." The sentence fragment popped out as Kim's brain moved faster than her mouth. Intake at Life House involved safety precautions. One thing Kim drilled into the women was to ditch their cell if they felt like they were in immediate danger. Many apps made locating a victim easy for a predator.

Simon frowned. "We never found it. I assumed she took it with her."

"If Elena brought her phone here, she would have known they could track her through it. She'd toss it if something spooked her." Fresh energy infused Kim. The device could hold information as to where she could have gone. "It's got to be close by."

Colleen entered from the kitchen and rubbed Simon's shoulders. "We searched the house."

"She might have held onto it for a while." Regardless of how deep Kim drilled that hole, the women she counselled refused to give up their devices until it became necessary. Elena would be no different.

Colleen gestured down the hall. "I can take you to her room."

Colleen led Kim down the corridor, and Jackson followed them. He didn't walk beside her, hold her hand, or offer any kind of comfort to her. He'd retreated again, and his physical and emotional withdrawal continued to sting. Jackson was doing everything he could to find Oliver. She believed it with her whole heart. Still, something between them had shifted. What if it never shifted back?

Her middle tightened, and the need to purge whatever remained in her stomach welled up in her throat. Kim wanted to rewind the morning. Oliver would spill his cereal at breakfast, and this time, she'd laugh. She'd tell him not to hurry while searching for his bunny. He'd zip his own jacket, and they'd be late for church. Kim fisted a hand against her mouth. She gulped a sob.

Colleen wrapped an arm around her shoulder and pulled her against her side. Colleen. Not Jackson. Kim teetered on the edge of losing the two people she loved the most.

They stopped at the last door. Colleen motioned for Kim to enter. The bedroom was a simple design. A single bed with a round bedside table, a desk, dresser, and closet. Kim recognized the duffle bag open on the foot of the mattress as one of the emergency go bags from Life House. Volunteers packed them with donated clothes and toiletries for cases like Elena's. There would be nothing personal in there. Still, Jackson rooted through it.

The window opened to the orchard, and all Kim could see were rows of dormant peach trees waving their snow-covered branches. Bush stretched behind the peach trees. The wind screamed around the corner of the house, verbalizing the howl Kim held back. Standing in the middle of the room, she rubbed her hands up and down her arms, and friction sent a shiver up her spine. Closing her eyes, she put herself into Elena's mind. She didn't need to know her well to get a feel for her character. Filling out the shelter's intake forms revealed a lot. The questions provided her with a bit of insight. Kim's lungs expanded. If she were Elena and trying to hide her phone to buy herself some time, she'd do her best to not implicate the family that sheltered her. Kim's eyes snapped open. "It won't be in the room."

"How do you know?" Jackson opened and closed empty dresser drawers. Elena hadn't even unpacked.

"She wouldn't lure the danger into Colleen's home."

Jackson's frown rubbed her frayed edges.

"She just wouldn't."

"Simon didn't see Elena leave, and he was by the front door. Nothing suggests she used the back one. That leaves the window." Jackson stood in front of the room's only window. He folded his arms across his chest.

"If Elena tossed the phone out there, it'd be buried by now." Kim rapped her knuckles against her forehead. *Come on, Lord. A little help!* Elena heard Kim's suggested precautions, so outside was the most logical place. But panicked people got confused. And the possibility remained that Elena's disappearance had nothing to do with being spooked by her ex's henchmen. She might have changed her mind. Elena wouldn't be the first battered woman to return to her abuser.

But she didn't strike Kim as the type to go back. She'd worked too hard to escape. And when a child entered the picture, women found reserves of strength. She'd seen it repeatedly. Elena didn't go back. But something made her feel unsafe.

The phone was their best shot.

"I'll call James and ask him to call the phone company's Corporate Securities department. They can provide the last known tower the phone pinged off." Jackson slipped into the hallway.

Kim opened the window. A rush of cold air cooled her hot skin.

Colleen peered over Kim's shoulder. "That's strange. These windows should have screens."

This was Elena's exit. Kim was sure of it.

Gripping the sill, Kim leaned outside. A rectangular outline was faintly visible. She'd bet her month's wages the window screen was buried underneath. A pattern of slight depressions in the snow led from the window. *Footprints!* They were nearly filled in, but the imprints were there. Kim hoisted herself onto the ledge and swung her feet over the sill.

"What are you doing?" Colleen fumbled for Kim's arm. She threw a frantic look in the direction Jackson had gone, but he'd wandered away.

"I'm finding that phone before the wind buries it until spring." The bedroom was on the first level. The drop wasn't far.

"Wait for Jackson."

Kim shook off Colleen's grip and dropped. The crusty top layer of snow crunched as she landed. There wasn't time to wait. Once the kidnappers figured out Elena was gone, they wouldn't need Oliver. Especially if Oliver saw their faces. Kim's stomach cramped. Elena's ex didn't seem to be the type of guy to leave witnesses, no matter how little or unreliable they might be.

"Jackson!" Colleen shouted.

Kim's cheeks numbed as the wind burned them. Leaving her jacket was a calculated choice that enabled her to avoid questions they didn't have time for. Drifting snow was filling in the footprints. Soon the trail would disappear.

"Wait for Jackson." Colleen shouted out the window.

Kim crouched, trying to get low enough to view the snow's surface at eye level. The subtle, sunken walking pattern led to the peach trees. Her heart quickened. Her breadcrumb path blew over and disappeared right before her eyes.

"I got a trail. I'm gonna see where it leads." Kim called up to Colleen as she pointed toward the trees. "Tell Jackson he can follow my tracks and catch up."

The further Kim got from the house, the louder the quiet sounded. There was a crispness in the wind. It had an edge and screamed winter wasn't finished with them yet. Ice cracked behind her.

Jackson.

Kim spun, a greeting on her lips, but only saw trees and white. The wind's whistle threatened to deafen her calls if she ran into trouble. Yeah, she should have waited for Jackson. Would'a, could'a, should'a, but didn't.

She hugged herself, unable to ward off the chill. How long until frostbite became a concern?

More footfalls.

Her ears strained. Animal or human? Her palms dampened. She retracted them into her sleeves. A rapidly swelling throat choked off any hope of calling for help.

What animals lived in the area? Which ones hibernated and which ones were cold and hungry? Should she call out? What if it was Nathan? Or one of his men? She should have waited.

A hand landed on her shoulder at the same time someone said her name.

Kim yelped and spun. She raked her nails down a body, but only pressed them into a winter jacket. Her vision tunneled. A badge.

"Ma'am, I'm Officer Noah Brown."

The cloudiness in her eyes cleared.

More heavy steps. Thrashing. Constable Brown shoved her behind him as Jackson burst through the trees with his gun drawn. His wildness softened when he recognized his co-worker. Chest heaving, he holstered his weapon, and Kim noted the intensity in his face.

"We don't have time to waste like this."

The correction stung.

"Let it go." Noah shrugged out of his jacket and threw it over Kim's shivering body. He squeezed her shoulders, the pressure grounding her. "You both love Oliver. Turning on each other won't help."

He was right. "I'm sorry. I was worried about losing the trail."

"In happier news, look what I found." Noah wiggled a phone.

"You got it!" Energy surged through Kim. "I knew it had to be out here."

"The cold has drained the battery. I was heading to the house for a charger when I saw you."

None of that mattered. They had El's phone. There'd be a lead on it. There had to be.

They hurried to the house. Jackson never spoke a word, but he didn't need to. His stony expression and stiff movements said enough. Even after warming up with two cups of coffee, something separated them.

"It's ready," Jackson said.

Kim joined the others crowding around the device, and Jackson powered it on. The home screen lit up. When face recognition didn't work, it reverted to its lock screen, which showed clips of the most recent messages.

"Who's Quinn?" Simon's forehead wrinkled.

Someone named Quinn had asked El for help. That was all they'd get until they unlocked the cell.

"Elena never mentioned a Quinn." Kim's shoulder brushed against Jackson's, and he stepped away.

"Quinn could be a short form, a nickname, code."

Making it even harder to find the person.

"How much of Elena's past did you cover during the intake?" Jackson still didn't look at her. Not really. Not the way she wanted him to.

"Our initial meeting wasn't going over history as much as it was implementing an emergency care plan. Gathering information comes later. After the crisis has passed."

Jackson massaged his jaw. "This could be Nathan trying to lure Elena out."

Kim wove her fingers from both hands into her hair and rubbed her scalp. If the phone didn't help, they had nothing. "I'll go through my file, but I'm sure I'd remember Quinn. It's an unusual enough name."

"Elena never mentioned Quinn to me, either." Colleen's forehead creased. "And I was asking questions about her friends and hometown."

"Stuart radioed to say the Missing Persons unit's ETA is fifteen minutes. Kim and I can take the phone to the house. The IT guy should be able to unlock it."

Jackson was already stuffing his arms into his coat. "And I want to search around here."

"Take Simon," Noah said. "I told him where to go."

Jackson's hurried movements paused. He and Constable Brown exchanged a look that made Kim's heart gallop.

"What aren't you telling me?"

Jackson diverted. "We only have thirty minutes before they call again. It's time to divide and conquer. Noah, can you take Kim to Life House so she can get her files on Elena and then get the phone to the Missing Persons unit? I'll stay here with Simon and follow up on Noah's lead."

Kim's head swivelled between them. They held something back. She felt it in her gut.

10:40 a.m.

❧

"What did Noah find?" As soon as Kim was out of earshot, Jackson zeroed in on Simon. Noah wouldn't have suggested they separate unless he found something he didn't want Kim to see. Something that would upset her. Jackson braced himself.

"It's outside."

Grabbing their winter coats, they set off on foot, trekking deeper into the orchard than before. Jackson's fingers started tingling in under a minute. His ears burned. They didn't have enough protection from the elements. They had a bit of time before frostbite became a risk. Enough to see what concerned Noah. Then regroup and make a plan.

They hiked for several minutes. The soundtrack of their booted feet breaking through the top layer of ice and crunching to the bottom played in a steady rhythm. Jackson kept one eye on the back of his friend and the other on the disappearing animal tracks. They were more likely to encounter deer than something danger-ous, but anything was possible.

Someone had travelled the path before them. The slender boot prints mixed with a few sets of wider and longer ones. Jackson snapped a few pictures on his phone. Were they Kim's? Elena's? These tracks went deeper, so they were fresh. Had Elena met someone? Who did she trust enough to share her location with? There were still more questions than answers.

His foggy exhalation puffed in a white vapor. Every step took them further away from the house. The kidnappers would call soon. Noah wouldn't send them on a meaningless hike, which meant this led somewhere. Somewhere important.

Deep breath in. Deep breath out.

They followed the broken twigs and trampled trail. The nearest branches lacked snow and the slick ground slowed them down. Twenty minutes until they called again.

"We're almost there." Simon pointed ahead.

If Jackson squinted, he could just make out a road cutting through the greenery. The wind raced across the small clearing. It molded the snow into sleek curves and peaks. The private road that Simon used for driving large equipment led here, to the end of the field. It dead-ended, so there was no reason for anyone else to take it. Yet the closer they got to the clearing, the more evident the importance of Noah's discovery became. Tire tracks compressed the snow. Several sets. Then he saw the dark patches.

No, no, no, no, no.

Jackson stopped. Walking, thinking, and breathing ceased. It was different when it was someone you loved. A harsh breath sawed against his throat. Detaching was impossible, making it harder and harder to do his job and bring Oliver home. Right now, all his energy channeled into the effort to stay impartial.

Blood. Diluted by the snow, partially covered by the blowing, but unmistakably identifiable. Stark red against a white canvas.

Sweat beaded on his upper lip. A painful rush whooshed deep

in his ears. Pain hit his chest. Tiny ice pellets battered his face. No wonder Noah took Kim home. It was too much. More than Jackson wanted to see.

Don't let it be Oliver's.

"Noah gave me a rapid blood type test kit. If you know Oliver's blood type, we can see if it's a potential match."

Disorientation and dizziness made it easy for the wind to push him forward. Jackson stumbled. He felt for his phone. *Just do the next thing.*

He called Stuart. Kim shouldn't be back yet, not if Noah stopped by Life House like they had planned, to grab the file she'd started on Elena. Jackson needed the Missing Persons detective to send someone to process the scene, preferably before Kim arrived, so she'd remain unaware.

Just do the next thing.

He called Emma. She didn't even say hello. "Did you find Oliver?"

"No, but I need his blood type. Do you have it on file? We're rapid testing a sample. If the type doesn't match Oliver's, Kim never has to know."

"I'll send it to your phone ASAP."

"Thanks. And can you keep this between us?" He wouldn't be able to handle Kim's hysterics. Not when he struggled to hold himself together.

"You bet."

Just do the next thing.

Jackson knocked away ice crystals that clung to his whiskers. He squatted, careful not to get too close. Contaminating the evidence helped no one. "Whose do you think it is?"

Simon stood off to the side, giving him time to process. Each retreated to a safe mental place and worked through the potential meanings. They could never unsee this scene. Unfeel these fears.

War exposed Simon to the worst of humanity. Jackson arrested men and women who'd committed unimaginable acts. But when it involved a child—it changed a man. This wasn't just any case; it was Oliver.

Deep breath in. Deep breath out.

Oliver, who laughed at all his jokes, cuddled on his lap, and begged for one more story. Oliver looked like Jackson, because Jackson and Hayden were identical. Strangers addressed Jackson as Oliver's father, and Jackson never corrected them. Deep down, that was what he wanted. He wanted the title, father. Oliver's dad. Kim's husband. And he never quite got over his rotten luck that Hayden met Kim first and screwed it all up.

And now Hayden wanted back in. He'd hinted on the phone that he wanted to make things right with Kim. But what did that mean? Did Hayden want to rekindle their romance? Did he want to apologize? Did he simply want to tell Kim that he was a different man now? If Hayden really was a changed man, he deserved a chance. But none of that would matter if the blood was Oliver's. If Oliver was dead, none of them would ever recover.

Please, Lord, don't let it be Oliver's.

Oliver lit up the room with his mischievous grin. He tested Jackson's patience with his endless questions. His boundless energy sent Jackson to bed exhausted.

A low moan grew from the bellows of his soul. Simon turned away. Jackson fell to his knees. One minute. He gave himself one minute to feel, then he stuffed it all into an emotional box and locked it. There'd be time for grief later. When they no longer had hope.

Jackson snorted, stood, and ground his teeth. He swallowed the rising pressure in the back of his throat. Could any pool of blood be victimless? It didn't need to be true, just plausible, so Jackson could continue to hope.

Simon offered a scenario. "If we're lucky, it's animal blood left from some poacher who scored big."

Poachers. Jackson could run with that. The orchards were full of deer.

"But if I had to guess—" Simon pointed at the bush. Tangled in the branches was one of those fabric ponytail holders that girls were always wearing. "Oliver doesn't wear scrunchies and neither do most hunters."

Jackson frowned. Would Kim remember if Elena's hair was up or down? Jackson studied the item's placement in the branches. The thick bush had a small, hollowed-out center. For the hair accessory to get tangled like this, whoever wore it had to have been hiding. He snapped a picture with his phone to show Kim later. "Was she hiding from a pursuer or hiding until a rescuer arrived?"

The tree rustled behind them, sounding more human than animal. The hairs on Jackson's neck prickled. His hand went to his weapon.

"I wouldn't do that if I were you." A coarse, raspy voice, the kind that comes from a heavy smoker, preceded swaying boughs dropping snow. The covering of white slid off the branches and to the ground. Two men decked out in winter camouflage emerged. They pointed their weapons to center mass. One gun levelled at Simon. One gun on Jackson. Jackson didn't like these odds, but then the shorter and stockier one lost his footing and fell to a knee.

"Get up, Damian." The larger man's lips drew back in a snarl.

Damian's pistol barrel slipped under the snow as he found his footing. When he lifted it, snow packed the barrel. That was good. Good for them, at least. Jackson jutted his chin toward Damian. Simon's head jerked. He'd seen it, too.

The gunmen herded Jackson and Simon closer and closer until Simon's back knocked against his. Not the best tactical position.

The big one plucked the scrunchie from the bushes. "She was told no cops. She's gonna pay for that."

They must have seen the cruiser at the house, since Jackson wasn't wearing a uniform. He raised his arms in surrender and took a step toward them. "No one said that. No one said no cops. Not once."

These two were thugs. The mastermind would have known the exact instructions. Even worse, they were amateurs, stumbling around the bush and not noticing a jammed gun barrel. Mistakes made them dangerous and unpredictable.

"I'm not a cop." Simon shifted into a crouch and lowered his voice. "Moving."

The military used terms like moving or cover to communicate tactical posture. Back-to-back was positionally dangerous. Only slightly better than open. Simon would want to get to cover. But before Simon could, Damian aimed the pistol at Simon's chest.

"Then you're no good to us." He pulled the trigger.

Instead of a clean shot, a gunshot combined with the sounds of fracturing metal echoed, drowning Damian's screams.

Simon dove, rolled, and bolted into the trees. Jackson darted in the opposite direction of Simon.

The shooter writhed on the ground. Shrapnel had to be embedded in his skin from the misfire. That made this fight one-to-one. Jackson liked those odds a lot better.

Thrashing behind Jackson confirmed he had the tail. Simon would circle back and contain the shooter. Jackson had to neutralize the thug after him. They'd end this. These two wouldn't hold up under questioning. They'd turn on Nathan.

A shot blasted, and a bullet slammed into a nearby tree. Jackson turtled into his coat as he ran.

Assuming he stayed alive.

11:00 a.m.

⁓

The hour was nearly up. Kim looked at the front door again. Jackson should be here by now. It was impossible not to read into his absence. He wouldn't miss the kidnappers' phone call unless it had been necessary. Her list of potential reasons for Jackson's delay churned her stomach. What if he found the kidnappers? Or worse, they found him? What if they hurt him? What if Elena returned and brought trouble with her?

Kim shook off the fear that Noah had uncovered something sinister. The list of possibilities was darker and longer than she could handle.

Kim had heard the undertones in their conversation at the farm. But curiosity didn't change that Jackson was right. Kim couldn't stay with him and get the phone to the detective. The detective needed her here, where they could record and analyze the calls. The team from Orillia arrived a little more than five minutes ago. They already set up the equipment. They were Oliver's best hope. That's why she'd gone with Noah without an argument.

"Where's Meg?"

"I ordered her to leave." Detective Marco Burland's mouth set in a hard line.

Stuart's complexion crimsoned.

Detective Burland and three others were at the house setting up when Kim and Noah returned. After introducing himself, Detective Burland introduced the team. Michael Cravey was the IT guy, and the rest were constables: Celeste Bentley, Tim Hibbs, and the negotiator, Ryan Eastwood.

"Meg had someone pick her up. She said something about going to the church, although considering the stunt you two pulled, I should have tossed her in jail." Stuart slapped some papers on the table. His nostrils flared.

Heat shot up the back of Kim's neck. She shifted her gaze to the case board the unit had set up in the living room, which was just a fancy white board that held pictures, notes, and a map. It reminded her of the murder board used on television shows. But no one called it a murder board. Not yet. Her stomach turned over. *Please, Lord, never.*

They just needed the kidnappers to contact them again.

11:01.

Her heart galloped. Each beat shoved her heart against her bones. The pressure forced the organ to ooze through the small spaces between each rib. "They've never been late before." She gnawed on a fingernail. She hadn't bitten her nails in decades. But between nervous picking and biting, there wasn't a single free edge or cuticle left. She fisted her hand and swung it to her side, bouncing it off her thigh.

"Don't panic." Detective Burland's clipped tone assured her that he'd been down this road before, and he knew how to play the game.

It'd been two and a half hours since they'd taken Oliver. The first three hours were crucial. She'd done her own research. Jackson thought he could keep the statistics from her and shroud everything in hope, but she'd been here before. A parental abduction was different. She hadn't feared for Oliver's life when Hayden had him. Still, the stats were the same. With each move of the second hand, Oliver's chances of a safe return diminished.

Why hadn't they called?

She practised mindfulness. Breathing in, two-three-four. Out, two-three-four. In, two-three-four. Out, two-three-four.

Her heart continued to fight against the boundaries of her ribs. Where was Jackson? Did the kidnappers grab Elena? Is that why they hadn't called? Or did Jackson stay away because he knew Detective Burland and his team had arrived and Burland would sideline him? Jackson couldn't be on the team. Even Kim understood that. He'd done what he had to do, and he'd done it with excellence. Now they expected him to do what was required in personal cases. Step aside and let an impartial officer take over. But if Jackson didn't return, they couldn't sideline him.

The phone rang.

Kim choked back a sob. Constable Eastwood looked to Burland, who lifted his hand in a gesture that meant wait. The two second delay dragged like hours. Burland barked at Constable Cravey, who was hurrying. His equipment intercepted phone calls and provided secure communications for the teams. He gave Detective Burland a thumbs up, and Burland pointed at Constable Eastwood to answer.

"This is Constable Ryan Eastwood. Who am I speaking with?"

"Where's Kim?"

"She's here. What will it take to get Oliver back?"

Kim gnawed on a fingernail.

"We left Kim a gift at the pond. Don't wait too long. The ice is pretty thin. She should come alone." They disconnected.

Kim's gaze zipped to the detective's. The game had morphed. Why didn't they ask for Elena? Why the pond? Was it Oliver's body? Was she going to find her baby's body because she protected Elena? Panic squeezed her throat. Black spots bounced in her vision.

Then, Officer Bentley was there. She squeezed her arms and forced eye contact. "Look at me. That's right. Breathe."

The blackness receded.

"You okay?"

Kim nodded, and Officer Bentley let her go.

"Why didn't they ask for anything?"

No one answered. Detective Burland unloaded a truckload of instructions, mobilizing Bentley and Hibbs to go to the pond.

"They said come alone." What if they saw the officers? What if it made them angry? But no one looked at her. Everybody knew what role they played in this production except her.

"Is it Oliver? Is Oliver the gift?" Her breaths shortened until light-headedness made her vision swim again. She grappled for a hold on the chair back. "Is Oliver dead?"

Everybody stopped. They saw her, finally remembering she was in the room.

"We don't know."

Kim found Detective Burland's lower register strangely calming. It grounded her like an anchor. "They said come alone."

"They always do, and they know you won't. Trust me. I've done this more times than I can count." Grey whiskers shadowed his chin and wrinkles deepened the corners of his blue eyes. He reached for her upper arm and gave her a reassuring squeeze. He didn't need her permission. Still, he waited for her to catch up.

What kind of person spent their life doing stuff like this? Her eyes dropped to his hand on her upper arm. His bare ring finger showed his life was a lonely one. The touch grounded her in reality. Was his single state intentional? Did the constant horror of his job sour him on marriage and parenthood? Did he fear bringing more people into their messed-up world? "What about Jackson?"

"Jackson can't be involved now we're here." His face took on a sympathetic look. "You can't go either. It's too dangerous. You're going to stay here with me. Officer Bentley"—the detective nodded to Celeste, who was pulling on Kim's winter coat—"will pretend to be you and pick up the package."

Before Kim could blink, officers Bentley and Hibbs were gone. Disobeying the kidnapper's direct order could backfire. She couldn't do this anymore. "I'm going to lie down for a bit."

Detective Burland narrowed his eyes. "I know what you did last time. I don't want to hear an engine start out there."

She bobbed her head.

Pulling the bedroom door closed, she balled her fists. Before she could even think through her actions, she slid out her bedroom window and sprinted across the backyard. Her cross-country skis were in the shed.

Adrenaline powered her. She yanked her ski jacket off a hook and pulled it on, clipped her boots into place, and glided down the back alley. If she stayed off the main roads, which were still bogged down with snowdrifts, and hugged the running trails, she'd beat the officers to the pond. She had the home court advantage.

She was already crossing the park when the officers pulled into the area earmarked for a new parking lot.

The parking lot sat opposite of the sledding hill. The town couldn't put down gravel until spring, but they plowed the area. Visitors parked on the frozen grass. It prevented congestion on the neighborhood streets.

Kim booked it across the abandoned park.

Bentley called her name, but Kim kept pushing forward.

The pond and the sledding hill were quiet. The storm might have scared off skaters and sledders. But it was more probable they gathered at the church. Even those who rarely attended church would pray for Oliver. Sycamore Hill banded together for the good of their neighbors. Hope infused her. Pastor Owen had checked in once already and assured her the church was bursting at the seams. Her community was fighting for her and Oliver on the unseen battleground where swords clashed, and God's kingdom forced back the darkness.

Kim glided past the billboard that illustrated the vision the town had for the sled and skate park. She'd granted the town permission to use a picture that Ben had taken of Oliver and Jackson. He'd captured Jackson's adoration for Oliver. He beamed at Oliver while supporting Oliver's weight. Oliver focused and poked his tongue out and scrunched his features while trying to skate. His expression of mixed determination, wonder, and delight undid her. The town council scheduled work to begin in the park in the summer. The hope was to have the recreation center completed before winter cycled around again. Would Oliver be here to see it? He'd been so excited to discover the plan included a hockey rink. This was to replace the danger of kids skating on ice that froze and thawed in a regular cycle as the winter temperature fluctuated in extremes.

Freezing air burned her lungs. On the surface of the pond lay hope: a tiny orange heap. The same orange as Oliver's coat.

Kim skidded to a stop. Her breath quickened as she unclipped her skis and darted across the pond without stopping to check the thickness of the ice. The potential danger didn't cross her mind until the voices yelling at her to wait registered. All she could see was the jacket. All she could hear was the kidnapper's command that she collect the gift.

Her. Not Officer Bentley.

She slid to her knees, and a cry rocketed from her. Relief that the coat wasn't covering a dead body and grief that it wasn't covering a live one battled. He wasn't here. She clutched the jacket to her chest and buried her face in the folds of it. Rocking back and forth, she moaned. She couldn't do this anymore. The cycle of hoping and losing hurt too much.

A brown paper envelope fell from the jacket pocket. She wiped her frozen cheeks, picked it up, and returned to land.

Officer Bentley glared at her. Wordlessly, she held out her hand for the coat and envelope.

Kim hadn't opened it. She could have. In those few moments alone on the ice, she could have torn it open and seen for herself whatever message the kidnappers had left for her. But she feared what might be inside.

Wearing gloves to protect the evidence, Officer Bentley opened the envelope. After flipping through pictures, she shifted so Kim could see them.

Kim reached to take them, and the constable pulled back. "Fingerprints."

Right. Kim squared her shoulders, steeling her insides. But nothing could have prepared her for images of Jackson, bruised and beaten.

His head lolled to the side. He slumped forward on a wooden chair with his hands tied behind his back. Blood trickled from the corner of his slack lips, exposing a bloodied mouth with missing teeth. One eye had swollen shut. A matted red mess clotted in his hair. She couldn't tell if he was dead or alive. She spun and retched, but there was nothing left for her body to expel.

Officer Hibbs positioned himself on Kim's other side. His gazed roamed the park. Was he looking for a shooter? Did he think they were watching?

Kim struggled to regain control. She wiped her lips with the back of her hand and gave Officer Bentley a curt nod. She was ready to hear the message that accompanied the photographs.

"We've got your kid. We've got your lover. Give us the girl or we go live online at noon and stream the cop's painful death. This is your last chance."

Both officers looked hard at her. "Lover?"

Kim fell to her knees. A keening deeper than she'd ever known ripped from her soul.

11:20 a.m.

⌖

Jackson parked the cruiser at the corner of Kim's street. "We'll have to walk from here."

Simon and Colleen followed him as he hurried to Kim's house. Walking was for later, after Oliver came home. Jackson would walk when he and Kim could each hold a little hand and swing Oliver between them. Until then, Jackson had one speed: double-time.

The kidnapper would have called by now. Jackson's gut panged like he'd downed a gallon of milk long past its expiry date. Sharp. Rolling. Explosive.

He eyed the unfamiliar vehicles parked in front of Kim's property. The vice grip squeezing his lungs lessened a little. Detective Burland was really good. Jackson straightened, and his lungs fully inflated for the first time since eight forty-five this morning. They had help.

Jackson took the porch stairs two at a time. Someone had swept the snow off them and sprinkled salt. He reached for the doorknob. It wouldn't be locked. The great room hummed with activity until he crossed the threshold. The buzz silenced. Jackson stopped, and Simon and Colleen stumbled behind him.

A female officer he didn't know questioned Kim. Tears dampened Kim's cheeks, her complexion all blotchy and red.

Sourness shot up his throat. All the hairs on his body jerked to attention. His skin prickled with cold sweat. They were too late. Oliver was dead.

He opened his mouth, but nothing came out. A squeezing in his throat pinched off the air. Sounds echoed, and the people blurred. He lurched toward the back of the nearest ı chair. Anything to help him stay upright. Oliver was dead, and he hadn't been here. *No, God. No.*

The constable looked up as he stumbled. Her face drained of color, and her eyebrows squished together. Her tight expression confused him. All she said was, "How?"

Detective Burland strode in from the kitchen and pulled up short. "Jackson?"

Kim's head snapped up. The room broke into a cheer and people started talking over one another. Kim let out a harsh breath. Then, with a snort-cry, she launched herself across the room. She flung her arms around his neck and buried her face in his shoulder. Her body heaved with effort, ragged breathing the only sound. For one glorious second, she pressed herself against him.

His body hummed. His hand dropped to her waist and wrapped around her to pull her closer as he buried his face in her hair. She belonged with him.

Her hands uncoiled from behind his neck, and she pulled back to arm's length. Her palms rested on his chest. With a tipped-back head, she dragged her gaze over his face. Then her fingertips skimmed his features, trailing his jawline, prodding his cheeks, caressing the rims of his ears. It was the gentlest and most intimate contact they'd ever shared. It was like she saw him through touch.

"How?"

The skin around Jackson's eyes tightened. Why was Kim acting this way? Her gaze remained fixed on his. He didn't hear a word of the chaos surrounding them. He only had eyes for her. He knew she saw him as more than Oliver's uncle. Every cell in her body communicated it.

Tears dripped from her chin. The warmth of her fingertips and the closeness of her body felt right. A long exhale lifted and lowered her chest. Her hands returned to his neck as she pressed her forehead to his. She locked her fingers behind his head, curling them into his hair. Then her mouth pressed against his. This wasn't the usual cheek peck they'd shared over the months prior. It was not an innocent greeting between family and friends. In the past, his mouth had found her cheek, forehead, and the top of her head, but not the lips. Never the lips. Not when Hayden remained between them.

His arms cinched her closer. Satisfaction grew as the last piece of himself snapped into place. Kim was his other half. The one bright spot in a devastating day. She made him believe he could do anything. He savored this. Her. The moment, as private as it could be with the Missing Persons unit watching with their mouths hanging open.

Kim pulled back to cup the back of his head with her hands. If she cared about their audience, she didn't show it. She rested her cheek on his shoulder. "I thought you were dead. All I could think was that I had never told you I love you."

She loved him. The declaration landed with the sweetness of a spring rain. She loved him! Then the rest of her sentence registered. "Wait. Dead?" He withdrew far enough to rotate. He looked at the makeshift case board leaning against the wall. Was that a picture of— His stomach heaved again.

"We got these." Detective Burland held out some photographs in a protective bag. The case board held enlarged copies. Burland didn't mention the embrace, but his mouth set in a hard line. Jackson could expect a lecture later for not disclosing the extent of his personal connection to the case. There were reasons cops didn't investigate cases that involved their family members. Reasons Jackson believed logical and necessary until today.

Jackson untangled himself from Kim. "It's Hayden. It has to be."

"Hayden?" Kim's hand flew to her throat, and her fingers splayed out. "Why is he here?"

"We were on the phone when you called." Jackson pushed the butt of one palm against his eyes. He sank onto the couch and clutched the photographs in his other hand. Was it just that morning that he considered sharing his feelings about Kim with his brother? "He's trying to help. He has to be."

Jackson's head spun like one of the theme park rides at the Winter Carnival. The Hayden he knew would never stand in for Jackson like this. Maybe there was something more to his brother's declaration of repentance. Right on the heels of hope played every memory of Hayden claiming to be sorry and begging for forgiveness. It replayed in his mind like an old movie reel. Hayden had sung this song before, but he'd never changed. Not for long.

"I told him not to come. He didn't listen." Disbelief transformed into anger. "He never listens."

Kim perched beside him like a bird ready to fly at the first sign of danger. She nibbled on her lip. "But how did they get Hayden? How did Hayden find Oliver when we can't? Why do they think

Hayden is you? What does that mean?" Kim asked question after question, but Jackson couldn't answer them. He put his head in his hands. Either Hayden was part of this and capable of horrors that sickened Jackson's soul, or Hayden was a victim, now at the mercy of whoever had Oliver. He didn't like either option. He wanted a third choice.

Simon spoke from the doorway where he and Colleen waited. "Could it have been Hayden in the truck that we passed on the road? Maybe the guys we saw nabbed him after we left?"

Simon's suggestion made sense. At least with that option, his brother wasn't evil. Just in the wrong place at the wrong time, trying to be what he should have been from day one—a father to Oliver. None of it added up. Hayden had never stepped up to own his responsibilities. He'd spent his life pushing them off onto Jackson. Why would he come back now unless God really did transform his life?

"They think Hayden is you because they don't know you have a twin." Simon ran his right thumb repeatedly over a scar on his left hand.

"You"—Burland pointed at Simon and Colleen—"can't be here."

The fist that had been squeezing Jackson's lungs since Kim first called him returned, juicing him until nothing but pulp remained. If anything happened to Hayden, it would be his fault.

After he and Simon had lost the gunmen in the woods, they hurried Colleen out of the house in case the men circled back to cause trouble. They passed a truck leaving, but Jackson never got a look at the driver.

"And you." Detective Burland gestured at Jackson with his thumb. "Back it up for me. Walk me through what happened."

"Simon is here because he needs to report his interaction with the kidnappers. We brought Colleen, his wife, because we wouldn't leave her alone at the house." Jackson gave Burland a summary of what happened at the farm.

"So, they know you're a cop."

Jackson nodded and jammed his hands in his pockets.

"But what led Hayden to the farm?" Colleen moved closer to Simon, slipping her arm through his.

"The more important question is, did Hayden arrive just as we escaped, and that's why they think they've captured me?" And his brother never corrected them. A spark of hope that his brother had moved from the kingdom of darkness into the kingdom of light relit. It would take a miracle, but God was in the business of miracles.

Burland handed Jackson the note from the pond. "The guy hunting Elena believes having a cop hostage gives him more leverage. Our only advantage is that they don't realize their error."

Kim briefly pinched the bridge of her nose before her fingers slipped down to press against her lips. "Why wouldn't Hayden correct them?"

"Maybe he did correct them, and they didn't believe him. How much traction could a twin theory get with strangers?"

Jackson refused to let Simon's practical response douse the flame. "Maybe it took the focus off Oliver? Maybe they didn't give him the chance." The possibilities rolled off Jackson's tongue. But Hayden didn't have a selfless bone in his body. He never did. Not even as kids. He'd throw Jackson under the bus to save his own skin every time.

Jackson wanted to roar. None of it made any sense. The weight crushed him. How was he supposed to cope without Hayden? Without his twin? How was he supposed to breathe?

The team's voices faded. Jackson retreated to his memories of Hayden and him as boys, playing in the woods, chasing the bad guys, and being the heroes. It looped to the soundtrack of his throbbing heart.

He reached for Kim. Slowly. Uncertain. The tables had turned. He slipped his large hand into her smaller one, welcoming her anchor. It was something solid to cling to before the pain of what-if and could-have-been swallowed him alive.

11:30 a.m.

K im squeezed Jackson's hand. His fingers twitched under hers. He was spiraling. Hayden might have been a lot of horrible things, and he may have made a lot of awful choices, but he was still Jackson's brother. His twin brother. The family Jackson turned his back on to prioritize Oliver. Jackson thought he had a lifetime to reconnect with Hayden, but Hayden now measured impending death in minutes. Not years or months. Not even hours. He only had minutes unless they found him.

Kim leaned into Jackson's side. He'd been her strength and anchor for so long. But he was only a man, and could only carry so much before the weight crushed him. It was her turn to be strong. She touched a hand to his heart.

"I got something." Officer Cravey clicked a few buttons on his laptop. All his tech ran through his computer. "I've been analyzing Kim's communications with the kidnappers. We've been focusing on what the kidnapper said. But there was something different in the background this time. Listen." He muted the voice and ran the background noise. Calypso-style music played.

Jackson pulled away from her, listening intently. "It's the carnival music! They're somewhere near the Winter Festival. On Sundays, the music doesn't start until church ends. That's why we didn't hear it earlier."

"Get me a list of everybody connected to that event." Burland set his palms flat on the table. "I want to know who Nathan spoke to."

"Already on it." Bentley spun her laptop around so Burland could see the screen. "I got a list of employees, and Nathan has a cousin running the Ferris Wheel. A Leo Carty."

"Do we know where cousin Leo is staying?"

"In the Sycamore Trailer Park. The entire crew is there."

Kim lifted a shaky hand to her forehead. It was all moving too quickly. In less than ten minutes, the team had mobilized. Before leaving, Officer Bentley paused in front of Kim and Jackson. She looked in Kim's eyes, and for the first time since the Missing Persons unit had arrived, Kim felt seen.

"I'll bring him home," Celeste promised. "My son is Oliver's age."

Kim nodded. She couldn't imagine doing Celeste's job with a small child at home.

Celeste and Jackson exchanged a look that seemed to satisfy Jackson. The team left. They'd be trekking through the back-woods that led to the trailer park any second.

Jackson paced. He repeatedly dragged a hand down his face. A thready muscle in his neck popped. He wanted to be with the team. Even she could see that.

"I should be there."

"We've been over this." Detective Burland didn't even look up from what he was doing. "You two are here with me and Cravey."

"Sorry I'm late." The front door opened, and a man stomped his feet on the mat. "I'm Constable Thurling from the Thames Creek detachment." He pulled off his hat, and a mop of dark hair spilled out. He looked like a teenager.

Jackson extended his hand. "Thanks for coming. The team just left to follow a lead."

"I stopped to help someone on the side of the road. The roads are nasty." Officer Thurling rubbed his hands together. Spying the coffee pot, he gestured to it. "Do you mind?"

"Help yourself." Jackson started pacing again with one hand gripping his other wrist behind his back.

Kim blocked his path. There wasn't anything she could say. She had nothing to offer except to be in this moment with him. This moment that might change everything for both of them. She reached for him. When he didn't resist, she threaded their fingers together. They stood toe to toe, and Jackson tipped his forehead until it pressed against hers. She didn't know why she'd waited so long to let Jackson know how she felt about him.

That wasn't true. She'd feared another error in judgment. Hayden pulled the wool over her eyes and pretended to be honorable when he wasn't. But Jackson was who he said he was. Her heart had known from day one. That first moment when she saw him in the airport security room when he'd brought Oliver back to her proved it. She felt it when he redirected Oliver to her for comfort in those first few highly charged moments. She saw it when he pulled up the tent pegs and moved to Sycamore Hill to be part of their lives. Jackson showed up. Every day. In a million little ways, he showed her he loved her, and she pretended she didn't see. He never pushed for more than she could give, but he accepted whatever affection she offered. Jackson was a good man. She was lucky to have him.

No, that wasn't right either. She was blessed.

Fluttering filled her stomach. That God had blessed her in the middle of this elaborate plan to rescue Oliver and Hayden slammed her. How did blessing and hardship coexist? Yet, here she was. Blessed beyond measure. Filled to overflowing. Trusting what she did not understand. Their eyes locked. Did he feel it too?

He moved to kiss her cheek.

Kim turned toward him. It was the smallest movement. He didn't pull away. Their noses grazed each other. He pressed his lips to hers. A firm connection. Soft. A warm promise. It was a kiss of hope. They were going to be a family.

Lord, please save Oliver. Save Hayden.

Her breath caught. Cold water splashed the moment. Their family included the person who'd hurt her more than anyone else. Her gaze drifted over Jackson's shoulder to the board holding Hayden's pictures. Kim hadn't been able to look at them when she thought they were Jackson. But it wasn't Jackson. That changed things.

Giving Jackson's hand a squeeze, she moved around him for a closer look. Officer Burland had taped the enlarged pictures up one after the other. Why didn't this version of Hayden exist earlier? Where was this self-sacrificing man when they were together? As she looked at the images, she realized she'd forgiven Hayden. Over the last year, she'd moved past the bitterness and found peace. She wanted good things for him and his future. She wanted his relationship with his brother repaired, even if it made her life uncomfortable.

"Don't look at them." Jackson tugged her arm.

She pulled away. "Is that corrugated metal?" Behind Hayden, a wall of sheet metal rippled like waves. It triggered a memory.

"We thought maybe it was the inside of a tractor trailer." Burland crossed the room and stood beside her as she studied the images. "Cravey is tracking shipments and looking for recent sales. Nathan's cousin might be in a trailer converted to a camper."

Warmth buzzed in her chest. Her hair swayed as she shook her head. "No, it's not a trailer. It's a shelter." Kim dragged her fingertips over the map tacked to the board. She knew this place. She knew where Hayden was, and it wasn't the fairgrounds. "Oliver and I were here when they took him." She pointed at a mark on the map at the abduction site. "We were going to church, which is here." She stuck a magnetic pin to the church's location.

Jackson tucked his hands under his armpits as he joined them. A furrow deepened between his eyebrows. "They'd have to be local to grab Hayden, take those pictures, and drop them at the pond."

"The pond is here." Kim pointed to a third location, marking it with another pin. "Add Willow Creek Farms." She pulled her bottom lip into her mouth. She was right. It was the only place that made sense.

"What are you thinking?" The side of Jackson's arm brushed against hers.

Her gazed roamed the map. She appreciated no one commented on the ticking clock. They waited, letting her think, letting her gather her thoughts. If she was wrong and they diverted officers from saving Oliver . . . But if she didn't suggest it, if she were right and Oliver or Hayden died because of it . . .

She couldn't finish that thought, either.

The tip of her tongue pushed against the back of her teeth. "It's only a guess. Maybe I'm crazy." She moved to her bookcases and ran the pad of her index finger along the spines of the novels and books she'd collected over the years. She pulled out a photo album. It was the old kind that had plastic sheets that you peeled back so you could tuck the photographs underneath. She flipped through the pages. "Is it just me, or does the wall behind Hayden look like this?"

The picture was of herself with her dad in front of a metal corrugated wall. It was identical to the wall behind Hayden, right down to the same scratch mark across the middle.

Jackson held the album against the picture of Hayden. "Where is this?"

"It's on the property my great-grandfather used to own. It's an old bomb shelter set back from the hiking trails, and it's near the fairgrounds." She stuck two pins onto the map. "Here's the shelter and the fairground."

"They're central to the other places."

"A bomb shelter?" Burland spun and slapped the table with both hands. "Why didn't anyone know about the bomb shelter?"

Thurling jumped, spilling his coffee, and Cravey pounded the laptop keys, pulling up information.

Kim hugged herself. "It's not common knowledge. My great-grandfather built it after the war. I only saw it once. It had fallen into such disrepair that it wasn't safe. Dad showed me when I was writing a paper in high school about the impact of the war on small towns. The area is so overgrown. I'm not even sure I could find it again."

"How much time do we have?" Officer Thurling looked at his watch.

"Twenty minutes."

Kim pressed a fist to her mouth. Twenty minutes. It wasn't enough time. "I should have looked sooner."

Jackson crushed her in an embrace. He squeezed her against his chest so hard she could barely breathe. His bristly cheek rubbed her temple. His lips warmed her ear. "You did it. You found him."

"I got information on the shelter." Cravey's fingers clicked on the keyboard. "Sending the location to your devices now."

"Jackson, you and Thurling head to the shelter. I need Bentley and Hibbs to stay on Oliver."

"Take this." Cravey handed Thurling an earpiece. "We'll keep you in the loop about the exchange."

"What about me?" Kim's mouth dried up.

"You're staying put. You and Officer Eastwood have a phone call to answer."

Kim swallowed. Right. The negotiator. She lifted her gaze to Jackson.

He cupped her hands with his and leaned in. "You can do this. We're going to get our family back."

Noon

Jackson swatted a low-hanging branch from his face.
Thurling had parked the cruiser a distance away, and now
they hiked in. Their winter camouflage helped them blend
into their surroundings.

"We've found the shelter." Thurling updated Burland through
his com.

Thurling had less experience than Jackson. He was greener
than the grass after a spring rain. Yet Thurling wore the com
because Jackson wasn't supposed to be working the case.

Thurling's brow furrowed as he focused on the voice in
his ear.

Jackson hated he didn't have an earpiece. He hated depending
on Thurling to relay updates. He got it. He understood why it was
this way. Still, he didn't like it.

Thurling signaled Jackson. "The exchange is going down. As
soon as they have Oliver, we'll breach."

This was it. It would be over in a few minutes. Jackson rolled
his shoulders. *Please, Lord. Please.*

Kim remained at the house with Burland and Eastwood. She had to be going crazy, but she'd be okay. She was strong. Jackson had first admired Kim's strength when he reunited her with Oliver a little more than a year ago. She'd shown great restraint in her movements. Despite aching with agony, wanting to hold Oliver, hug him, and cling to him and never let go, she held back. She'd suffered in ways most parents would never know, but she waited for Oliver's invitation. Putting her son's needs above her own, she waited until Oliver was ready.

Then she welcomed Jackson and his parents into her life. She accepted them, even after all Hayden had put her through and months of separation from Oliver and the agony of not knowing where her son was. And when she learned that Oliver's grandparents had him, she never blamed them. She accepted and believed that they didn't know Hayden had kidnapped his child. Her strength was beautiful.

She would do everything she could to save Oliver, except trade a soul for a soul. Not even to save her child. That took an uncommon strength. Supernatural strength. It came from a deep trust in God. *Lord, bless her desire to honor all life.*

Jackson's insides throbbed. His fingertips vibrated. Hayden and Oliver were close. The faint music from the carnival provided distant background noise. The shelter was underneath his feet. Nathan would be at the exchange. But he'd have left some muscle to guard Hayden.

"They're walking Bentley to the exchange point." Thurling cupped a hand over his ear, listening intently. "They see Oliver."

Jackson crept closer to the shelter's opening. According to Cravey's research, the shelter had two entrance points. It had a hatch in the top and a tunnel in the side of a hill. Kim confirmed only the tunnel was functional when she and her dad visited.

A figure with a bandaged hand emerged.

Jackson snorted. Damian. The misfired pistol hadn't taken the sloppy gunman out of commission.

The radio on Damian's hip buzzed. A second man wandered out, gesturing with his gun. Jackson's gut clenched. There was nothing blocking the barrel of that gun.

Whatever happens, Lord, save Oliver.

Thurling's expression contorted. Something had gone wrong with the exchange.

"We gotta breach. Go, go, go!" Thurling led, gun drawn. "This is the police. Put your weapon on the ground and your hands in the air."

The larger man spun, lifting his gun, and Thurling squeezed the trigger.

The man dropped.

Damian thrust his hands upward as Jackson approached. "Do you have a weapon?"

"A gun in my waistband."

"I got it." Thurling secured the first man, then lifted the back of Damian's jacket and removed the gun.

Jackson tossed Thurling his cuffs, keeping his weapon trained on Damian. Thurling secured him.

"You got him?"

Jackson nodded.

Thurling disappeared into the shelter. Seconds later, he emerged from the tunnel with an arm around Hayden.

"They have a second car hidden at the south entrance to the campgrounds." Dried blood covered Hayden's face. One eye had swollen so much only a slit remained. He was alive, and to Jackson, he'd never looked better. "Nathan was going to the backup vehicle if anything went wrong."

"We'll secure the prisoners and head to Sour Springs Road."

Thurling relayed their movements through his com. "Let's go." He nudged the cuffed men in the cruiser's direction.

"You'll never get there in time." An ugly laugh peeled from Damian.

Thurling prodded his back.

Hayden grabbed Jackson's shoulder. "They have snowmobiles. I saw where they put the keys."

Jackson met Thurling's eyes. "Plan B?"

Thurling's chin lifted. "Hayden, grab the keys. Jackson, you get the spike strip."

By the time Jackson grabbed the spike strip from the cruiser's trunk, Hayden had the snowmobile running. The twins faced each other. Jackson didn't like the rattle in his brother's chest.

"Go." Hayden's mouth twisted. It would have been a smile if his face hadn't pinched. He rubbed a bloodied hand across his jaw. "Get Oliver back."

"Lord willing, Officer Bentley already has him. She has a son the same age." That similarity would drive Bentley. Celeste would bring Oliver home or die trying.

Hayden blew out his cheeks and winced.

"Constable Thurling will bring you."

"I know."

Jackson secured the spike strip to the back of the snowmobile.

"I'll see you there." Hayden rubbed a hand over his chest and tapped his heart twice. It was the secret signal they used as kids.

"I love you, too." Jackson choked back emotion.

Seconds later, he flew over the fields. Avoiding the main roads saved significant time. He had to beat Nathan to Sour Springs Road.

Encouraged by the undisturbed snow, Jackson hopped off the snowmobile and grabbed the spike strip. He tossed it across the road just as the roar of an engine grew in volume.

A black SUV took the bend way too fast. Its back end slid. The vehicle hit the spikes. Jackson retracted the strip as the SUV skidded to an anticlimactic stop. All four doors opened, and several figures emerged like an exploded ant farm.

"Police. Put your hands up!" Jackson leveled his gun at the men.

Thurling's cruiser approached from the other side.

A streak screamed across the field.

Oliver!

Oliver's little legs pumped. He didn't have a jacket. Tears and dirt stained his cheeks. But he was alive.

"Gun!"

The gunman swung toward Thurling's roar, and Hayden launched himself toward Oliver.

Jackson swiveled to cover his brother. He didn't have a shot. "Get down!"

Thurling fired.

It wasn't supposed to go this way. This wasn't the plan.

Bodies and bullets spilled into the clearing. But all Jackson saw was the terrified boy running.

Take me instead, Lord.

Everything went too slow and too fast at the same time. The speeds battled in Jackson's brain for dominance. He just needed to reach Oliver. He had to get to Oliver.

But Hayden beat him.

Hayden dove and knocked Oliver to the ground with the cry of a warrior. He covered Oliver's body with his.

Jackson skidded to them and positioned himself on one knee. He held his gun over their cowering bodies and picked off armed men as they emerged like some warped game of Whack a Mole. Officers Bentley and Hibbs blocked the exit and joined the fight. Who would emerge as the victor was not the question. The good guys had this. The real question was how many casualties would such a victory cost?

Please, Lord.

Hayden and Oliver were too quiet.

Jackson reached for a pulse. Hayden turned to him. He opened his mouth as if he were about to speak as a shadow rose in front of them.

"Jackson!" Hayden charged like a bull on fire. He rammed the gunman at full tilt just as the gun went off. Both bodies hit the snow-covered ground and rolled.

Jackson pounced on the fallen man and wrenched his hands behind his back, making him howl. He bound his wrists to immobilize him.

Hayden rolled. Red bubbled through his fingers. A shot had pierced his shoulder.

"Looks like a through and through." Jackson put his hands over Hayden and pressed. "Keep pressure on it."

Oliver crawled toward them.

"I'm okay." Hayden's mouth fell open. The adrenaline that rushed through his veins would keep the pain at bay for a few seconds. Maybe minutes. Hayden curled an arm around Oliver and flattened him to the ground.

"Stay down." Chaos continued to abound, but the good guys were taking ground.

Officer Bentley made her way toward them, reached a hand out to Jackson, her eyes fixed on Oliver. A figure emerged behind her. A gunshot exploded as Hayden threw himself toward her, taking her down.

Jackson pulled his trigger and the gunman dropped, a red dot expanding on his chest. "Officer down!" Jackson lunged toward Bentley and Hayden.

Bentley rolled out from underneath Hayden. "I'm not hit."

Hayden's body jerked. A sudden stiffening posture. His eyes widened further, and then his features slackened. A stain seeped through his clothing near his heart. The surprised look in his eyes dulled.

"Hayden!" Jackson's chest constricted.

Everything faded as a wail grew. The wailing increased until it was all Jackson heard because it came from inside of him.

12:15 p.m.

⁓

Kim saw Emma first, and she ran to her friend. Before she could speak, Emma answered. "They're fine. Oliver and Jackson are fine."

Kim collapsed into Emma's arms, and Emma rocked her slowly. "I'll take you to them."

They threaded through the chaos. Kim could barely register the scene. Cloths covered three bodies. Dead, she assumed. People with badges and official uniforms of all kinds swarmed the area. Kim's gaze skimmed it all, finding none of what she was looking for.

"Mommy!"

Her heart lurched.

Oliver wiggled free from Constable Bentley and threw himself at her. Kim fell to her knees and opened her arms. She pulled Oliver close, pressed her nose to his sweaty head, and cried. Her chest swelled.

Oliver didn't have his coat. Officer Bentley had slung her larger jacket over his shoulders. He looked like a kid playing dress-up.

The cold registered as dampness seeped through Kim's jeans, but she stayed where she was. She didn't trust her legs to stand. Everywhere she looked magnified the cost of Oliver's rescue. Blood stained the snow.

"Kim?" Emma touched her shoulder. "Let me take Oliver."

Kim swung him out of reach and tightened her hold.

Emma crouched in front of her and looked her dead in the eyes. "Jackson needs you, and you don't want Oliver to see this." Emma tipped her head toward Jackson's direction.

Jackson and Matt hovered over a body prone on the ground. Matt crouched over the man, his army field training hard at work. Matt had performed emergency procedures while overseas. He'd know what to do while they waited for an ambulance from Grander. Matt pressed both hands over the chest wound, but thick red oozed between his fingers. "I'm losing him!"

"Not Unca Jackson," Oliver said. "Not Unca Jackson." His chant broke through the roar in Kim's ears.

Hayden.

"You're right. It's not Uncle Jackson." She stroked Oliver's silky hair, pushing it back off his forehead. He looked just like he had this morning. Perfect. Her tears dripped off her chin. She dragged her jacket sleeve across of her face. Her son. She had him back. He was okay. The impossibility of it made her bones quiver. She ran her hands down his arms and legs. She brushed her fingertips over his facial features. He was fine. She couldn't believe it. He was fine.

"I need to help Uncle Jackson. Can you stay with Emma? She'll stand close enough that you can see me the whole time."

Oliver peered into her eyes. "It's not Unca Jackson, Mommy. It's Unca Hayden."

Uncle Hayden? Why would Hayden tell Oliver that he was his uncle?

"Unca Hayden found me. He said I go home soon."

A sob swelled in her throat. Kim pulled Oliver into her arms and pressed his cheek against her shoulder. She stood and handed him to Emma. Jackson needed her.

The desperation in Matt's movements increased the pressure behind Kim's eyes. No matter what Hayden had done in the past, no matter how many ways and how many times he disappointed his brother, hurt her, or manipulated Oliver, he was still Jackson's brother. His only brother. His twin. The other half of him. You couldn't break that kind of bond. It couldn't end like this.

"Jackson?"

Jackson's lips moved, but his words didn't register. It was like she floated above the chaos, detached from the scene, watching it unfold from a safe distance. She saw Emma holding Oliver, his tear-streaked face pressed into her body and his tiny fingers clutching the fabric of her jacket. The other officers cuffed and hauled men to their feet. Jackson crouched on his knees, his face close to his brother's, lips moving, hands working. This wasn't the ending Kim would have scripted. But really, she didn't know how she'd write the end.

Her heart belonged to Jackson, but her body was one with Hayden. Two fleshes had joined. She didn't need her signature on a marriage certificate for that truth to hold weight in her soul. As broken as they were, Hayden was a part of her. He'd always be a part of her. God used Hayden to shape her into the woman she was today, to sand her edges, to make her more like Jesus.

But when Hayden traded himself for Oliver and Jackson, it was so out of character she didn't have a mental compartment for the action. She'd only known him to put himself first. Leaving him was the hardest thing she'd ever done. The scariest. It drove her to start Life House. It was why she came alongside people like Elena. She knew.

It took courage to stand up to a bully, and Kim knew what it cost to protect a child. She knew how it felt when someone took that child away, and she knew what it meant to only have God and to struggle to believe that He was good.

Red seeped from under Hayden's body and into the precipitation. It spread out in a ring underneath him. His eyes were open, staring into the sky as huge flakes of white clung to his eyebrows. The man who'd brought her unspeakable pain fought for each breath.

Kim dropped beside Jackson. The former chaos settled into a tense and screaming silence. The rescue hadn't gone as planned. Hayden had been shot.

"What were you thinking?" Jackson squeezed Hayden's hand.

Hayden turned toward Jackson's voice. They locked eyes. A lifetime replayed. Kim got the feeling that forgiveness had been asked for and granted without a word whispered.

Burland shoved medical pads under Matt's hands.

"I couldn't let her die." Hayden coughed. "She has a kid like Oliver. You said so. A kid needs his mother."

Hayden did this on purpose? Kim's head swirled.

"All the things you said . . ." Jackson's voice cracked as Matt pressed the pads over the wounds. "Your new faith, your desire to make amends . . ." Jackson choked, an anguished and tormented sound. "I'm sorry. I should have believed you. I do believe you."

The white absorbent pads turned red. Heat scorched the back of Kim's eyes. They were saying goodbye. *No, Lord. This is not how it ends.*

"I never gave you a reason to believe." Hayden coughed again. He turned his head to the side and spat out blood.

Burland spoke into the radio on his shoulder. Kim didn't hear his words, but she didn't need to hear them to understand his expression.

She glanced back at Emma and Oliver. A part of her wanted to walk away. It told her to scoop up her child and leave, giving the brothers this moment, but she couldn't. It was like cement had filled her limbs and she was stuck in this spot watching her past and her present collide with spectacular grief. Never in a million years did she ever think the three of them would find themselves in a circumstance where she'd be rooting for Hayden. Not when his presence threatened the future she wanted.

Yet, here they were. And with everything in her, she wanted him to live. She wanted him and Jackson to have time to make new memories. She wanted Oliver to know how Hayden showed up when it mattered. How the two men most connected to him in this world nearly gave their lives for his. She didn't just want Oliver to hear the story from her lips; she wanted him to hear the story told from them, healed and restored. Even if it meant she and Jackson could never be together. Even if it meant the consequence of her choices all those years ago was to trust the Lord with her future and with her heart. There was no fairytale end to this story. No happily-ever-after. It was too messy. Too many shades of grey. Too many layers of grief.

"You didn't have to do this." Jackson's mouth tightened. His lips turned white.

"It had to be me. Her kid needs her. And Oliver shouldn't lose his father." Hayden wheezed and coughed some more.

"You're Oliver's father."

"No." Hayden spoke so firmly that Matt's hands paused. Hayden's eyes cleared, and he held Jackson's gaze. "I'm the seed. You're the father."

Hayden's eyes clouded over again. They shifted and found her. Kim couldn't hold back her tears.

"I'm sorry." His face pinched as if every agonizing breath shredded his insides.

"I can't believe you came." She grazed her fingertips down his cheek.

"Of course, I came." His eyes squeezed closed. "It was you. It was Oliver."

Kim's breathing grew raspy. This couldn't be the end.

"Do you love him?"

She hiccupped a breath.

"Jackson. Do you love him?" Hayden repeated.

Jackson froze. Kim felt lightheaded. She didn't want to hurt Hayden, but she couldn't lie. "I do."

Hayden nodded. The movement was slight, like it cost him a lot to make it. "He's better than me. You have my blessing."

"You're going to be fine." Kim choked.

"I'm sorry for everything."

She'd heard those words a million times in the past. He was always sorry, but he never changed. He reverted to old patterns every time.

"I believe you." She pressed a gentle kiss to his forehead. "And I forgive you."

The tension left Hayden's face. As his features relaxed and the hardness in his body softened, Kim saw the man she'd loved years ago. She saw him for the choice he'd made in this moment—to put their child first no matter the personal cost. And she loved him for it.

It took hours to clean up the scene. More police officers arrived from other detachments, and Emma treated the wounded as best she could before the ambulances arrived from the city.

Kim sat with Oliver on her lap, fully believing that she would never let him go ever again. For now, he seemed content to let her hold him. Matt had done what he could for Hayden like he'd done for fellow soldiers in the war. After their brief interaction, Hayden passed out. Matt could not rouse him again. There was nothing left to do but pray.

Kim updated Pastor Owen and Gloria, who passed the information to the congregation. They'd been praying since nine o'clock in the morning, gathered in the church sanctuary doing battle on the unseen field. They promised to keep praying for Hayden's recovery.

The paramedics loaded Hayden into the ambulance. The medics didn't look optimistic as they slammed the ambulance's bay doors. Jackson pressed a kiss to Kim's forehead and another one on Oliver's cheek and went with his brother.

One question remained. It swirled in the aftermath's chaos—a mystery yet to be solved. Round and round it went in her head. She wanted it to stop. For the puzzle to be complete. But they were still missing a few pieces to the story. Where was Elena? And why did Hayden go to the farm in the first place?

March – One Month Later

Jackson couldn't take his eyes off Oliver. He played on the floor in Kim's now-cleaned up living room. No physical evidence of the former command center remained. Emotional evidence? That was a different story.

Oliver's footie pajamas stretched over his body like a second skin. His hair, damp from a bath, was combed off his face. His little lips puckered as he fit wooden train tracks together that spanned the length of the couch. He pushed a red train, making muffled noises. His cheeks puffed out with each chug of the engine, and Jackson's chest tightened. He wasn't sure if the stress in his body would ever fully release. They'd nearly lost him.

Beams from a vehicle's headlights arched through the picture window. The curtains were open despite darkness descending over an hour ago. Kim's neighbour backed her vehicle out of the driveway and drove down the street. To anyone peeking in from the outside, they looked like a family. A husband and wife puttering around the house. A fire glowing in the fireplace and the toddler playing on the carpet while the snow blew outside, frosting the windows. Dishes clanked in the kitchen, where Kim finished drying and putting away the plates Jackson had washed. To anyone looking in, they seemed normal. Typical. Functional.

Looks were deceiving on so many fronts.

Oliver, still clingy since his abduction, was restless after his bath. He insisted that someone sit in the living room with him. He was unsatisfied with playing in the kitchen and didn't want to wait for the dishes to be put away. He didn't want to be alone. Oliver didn't know what he wanted, but he knew what he didn't want. Kim nudged Jackson to go with Oliver, insisting that she would finish cleaning up.

"Play?" Oliver lifted a second train and handed it to Jackson. The tightness in Jackson's face lessened. He moved to the floor, sat on the opposite side of the train tracks as Oliver, and pushed the green engine down the rails. The magnets on the train cars were not strong enough for Jackson to pull the long train Oliver had clicked together. It separated in the middle.

He couldn't believe it had already been a month since Oliver's kidnapping. Hayden lingered on life support long enough for Jackson's parents to fly in and say goodbye. Jackson could have never guessed how one Sunday morning would change everything for everyone. Especially for Oliver, who drove his train along the track, unaware of the cataclysmic shifts that had occurred in his world.

Strangers assumed Oliver was Jackson's son. They shared the same skin tone and eye color. Their hair curled in the same backward wave that drove Jackson nuts. Their biological connection was obvious. But Oliver was Hayden's child. And now, Oliver would never know his birth father.

An ache unlike any other filled Jackson's soul like it did every time he thought of Hayden and his final sacrificial acts. Pressure built behind his eyes, and he scrubbed a hand down his face.

Oliver looked up, studied Jackson for a minute, and looked at the broken train. "I help." Oliver clicked the magnet on the front of his engine to the magnet on the abandoned cars. He chugged along behind Jackson. "All fixed."

Jackson's pulse throbbed in his throat. "Thanks, buddy."

Jackson couldn't excuse all the choices his brother had made in life. He couldn't pretend to be okay with the shady lifestyle he'd led or the way he flirted with the law and hurt the people who loved him. But that didn't mean Jackson wanted to lose him. It didn't make Hayden's death easier.

"I be a good helper."

"You're a great helper." When Hayden died, so did a part of Jackson. For a while, Jackson believed the part of him connected to his twin was gone forever. But he'd come to see that Oliver was a part of Hayden. Oliver was the piece that lived on and was the best part of his brother.

Kim coughed, and Jackson's head snapped up. She leaned a shoulder against the doorframe of the kitchen and watched them. Her eyes glazed, damp and gentle. "Coffee?"

"Yes, please."

She disappeared into the kitchen.

Jackson slipped his hand into his front pocket and fingered the family heirloom that begged to be slipped onto Kim's finger. He'd carried it with him all week, waiting for the perfect moment to make them everything they weren't yet: an actual family. "I'm going to sit on the couch." Jackson pushed himself off the floor. "Do you want to snuggle with me or play trains?"

"Trains." Oliver didn't even look up.

Jackson moved on the sofa so there was room for Kim. He rubbed a palm over his gut. Tension, he could do. Fear? All in a day's work. Horror? Not his favourite part of his job, but it came with the territory. Romance? Love? Making a relationship permanent? Becoming a dad? That was new.

Hayden had given his blessing before he died, shoving Jackson over the platonic line that had held him back all year. But how long was a guy who'd been waiting his whole life for a woman like Kim supposed to wait in a situation like this? Was there a grieving period?

His parents told him to go for it. His mom twisted grandma's ring off her finger and pressed it into Jackson's palm. If Hayden were here, he'd kick Jackson and say, get to it.

But this might not be an option if Hayden were here.

Jackson knew acutely that his shot at happiness with Kim came at the cost of Hayden's life. It was a lot to process. For him. For her. For everyone. Was she ready for it?

The sofa cushion sagged as Kim joined him and pressed a steaming mug into his hand. She cradled hers as she gazed at Oliver.

He hoped so. He was about to change their entire future if she said yes.

She'd say yes.

Oliver put his train down, pushed himself to his feet, gave Jackson's legs a hug, kissed Jackson's knee, repeated the gestures with his mom, and then returned to the toys. He'd been doing little things like that all month with Kim. Kim had asked Emma about it, and she'd insisted it was normal. Feeling overwhelmed and seeking his mom was a part of Oliver's processing. It made him feel safe again.

This was the first time he'd done it with Jackson.

He felt— Well, he didn't know how he felt. Knowing his presence made Oliver feel safe made his insides swell. A month ago, he wasn't sure what the next step was, but together, they'd grieved for what could have been, what should have been, but never would be. He and Kim faced the worst a couple could face and came out stronger. They belonged together.

There would be nights of dreams, tears, and terror as Oliver's young mind processed everything he endured. The body would force the trauma to the surface. Kim would process all she nearly lost, and all she did lose. But as they did, Jackson would be there to help. They'd do it together.

Jackson slung an arm around her shoulders, and she curled into his side. His body was exhausted, yet he doubted either of them would get much sleep, and it would have nothing to do with the caffeinated beverages they sipped.

Kim curled her legs underneath her and tugged a knitted throw blanket over her lower half. Oliver got up and stood in front of her on his tiptoes, trying to see into her mug. "Hot chocolate?"

"No." She covered the top of the mug with her hand. "Coffee." She made a funny face.

Oliver mimicked her expression and returned to his toys. "Coffee yucky."

Jackson enjoyed the normalcy of the moment. A tiredness that was more fulfilling than exhausting filled him. "Have you heard anymore from Burland?"

"Yes. He said Nathan's cousin got my cell number from my electronic ticket purchase to the Winter Festival. That's how they knew what number to video call."

"That makes sense." The puzzle pieces had filled in throughout the last four weeks. They even figured out why Hayden had gone to the farm.

After Meg lent her car to Kim, enabling Kim to follow him to Willow Creek Farm, Detective Burland had sent Meg home. Meg called Gloria for a ride to the church, so she could join the prayer meeting. As she waited for Gloria to pick her up, Hayden arrived. Meg thought Hayden was Jackson and started apologizing for interfering before Hayden could speak, and Hayden didn't correct her. She asked how it went at Willow Creek Farm, and he made up some excuse and left.

"Will you get to see Elena?"

Kim shook her head. "The police moved her into protective custody until after Nathan's hearing. She needs to testify, but Burland is passing my messages along."

"You really impressed him when you remembered that Elena wore a fitness watch and asked if he could ping it to track her down."

Kim lifted one shoulder in a shrug. "I used to watch a lot of crime shows."

Jackson laughed at her use of the past tense. The only programs they'd watched since Oliver's return were kids' shows or lighthearted comedies. They'd had enough crime for a lifetime. "I'm glad Elena is safe."

"And so is her baby. Nathan won't be able to touch them ever again. That's all that matters."

Elena was clever. Even Jackson had been impressed. She had run to a friend's house in Grander when Quinn messaged the code for trouble was coming. That Kim never forgot that in the middle of her nightmare with Oliver, another mother was fighting for her baby's life as well, made Jackson love her more.

Jackson took a long drink of coffee. The velvety liquid soothed his throat. "It kills me that Oliver will never know Hayden." Would Kim have given Hayden another chance so Oliver might know his dad? Did Hayden's death stain their relationship in a way that tarnished it forever?

Kim lowered her gaze to her cup. Her finger dragged along the rim. "I know." She lifted her face. "I know Hayden was changed because the Hayden I remembered would have never done the things he did for Celeste, Oliver, or for you."

Enough for her to grieve Hayden? Enough for her to need more time?

She repositioned herself.

This was it. His moment. His heart hammered in his chest.

She brought the mug to her lips again and waited. She lifted her eyebrows in a question. He couldn't tell what she was thinking, but her forehead crinkled in the most adorable way. They hadn't discussed her earlier declaration of love. They hadn't kissed again since the day Hayden had died. Did she regret it? Would she try to deny it or try to explain her reaction away? No matter what she did, she couldn't pretend she wasn't driven by love.

And not an extended-family kind of love. This was the love he'd been waiting for. It involved risk. Danger. It was costly. Knowing she loved him didn't guarantee that she'd accept his proposal. She'd already proven that she could make hard choices when necessary. She'd already shown her character. Obedience to God mattered more than desires.

He took a breath. *Lord, if this is Your will, if this is good for her, for us, help her see it and not feel guilt.*

He set his mug on the end table and slipped off the sofa and onto one knee.

Oliver stopped playing and looked up. Kim's hands trembled. Coffee sloshed onto the fabric of the sofa. Jackson took the mug from her and set it beside his. He wrapped both her unsteady hands in his. Unable to read her expression, he plowed forward anyway.

"I've loved you since the moment I met you. I love your love for God, your sense of justice, your selfless heart. There were a million reasons I couldn't ask you this question before, but none of those reasons remain."

Jackson slipped his hand into his pocket and pulled out the ring.

May - Two Months Later

"Oliver!" Kim tapped her heeled foot on the hardwood floor at the bottom of the short staircase. If he didn't hurry, they'd be late. The crash and thud that came from inside his bedroom made her smile. He was probably looking for his bunny. Her eyes prickled. She pressed her fingers against them until the pressure subsided. He got his dramatic flair from his father.

An ache swelled in her chest. She swallowed and tightened her grip on the banister. Hayden wouldn't be there today. Her midsection flip-flopped.

At her wedding.

"Oli-verrrr!"

Oliver popped through his bedroom doorway and into the hallway. She smiled as he bounded down the stairs.

She wiggled his bunny. "Look what I have."

He skidded to a stop in front of her and tugged the bunny to his chest with a squeal. The rabbit's ears flopped. Oliver lifted his face.

She bent and kissed his cheek, fingering the collar of his suit jacket. "You look sharp."

"I so sharp I could cut you." He puffed out his chest.

Jackson's parents followed Oliver down the stairs. "Sorry it took so long." Mr. McGregor ruffled his grandson's hair. "He's a squirmy little fella. That tie was tricky." The adoring look in their eyes made Kim think she might burst. Mr. and Mrs. McGregor were a special couple.

"Tricky." Oliver beamed at his grandfather.

"Are you ready?" Kim's mom came inside from the front porch. Her long skirt swirled around her ankles, and her eyes sparkled when they landed on Kim. "You look stunning."

Kim gave a little twirl. "I feel like a princess."

"Prettier than a princess." Her mom's fingertips moved lightly over her heart. "Your dad's in the van. He picked up Meg and Emma."

A gentle wind rocked the branches of the nearby Sycamore tree and kissed their cheeks as they trudged to the car. The scent of pine from the trees lining the property intensified. Emma hopped from the passenger side of the van and opened the door for Kim.

It took at least five minutes to tuck the layers and layers of tulle that made up her dress into the vehicle. Jackson's dad leaned forward to speak to Oliver through the open side door. They fist bumped. "Nana and I will follow in our car. See you there, champ." He nodded at Kim's dad, who was behind the wheel.

After much laughing, and ensuring Oliver was buckled properly, they were off. Twelve-thirty. Not too bad. The ceremony was supposed to start at one o'clock.

Dad turned on the Christian radio station. A familiar tune about God's ability to bring beauty from ashes made Kim's cheeks warm. Three months ago, she wouldn't have thought that even

God could redeem all that had gone wrong. But today— She blinked fast.

"If you cry, you'll ruin your makeup." Emma extended the tissue box.

Kim dabbed her eyes. "I'm fine. It's just a bit overwhelming."

Oliver chattered to himself. He held the bunny up to the window. "See Unca Jackson?"

"We'll see him at church."

Emma took a couple of tissues and stuffed them into her tiny clutch. "Are you ready? Gloria is at the church. She said Kathryn is all set up to capture our arrival on film."

Kim massaged the muscles in the back of her neck, then shook out her tingling hands. In a little more than an hour, she'd be Jackson's wife. "I'm ready."

"I ready, too!" Oliver chirped.

They arrived at the church, and with much laughter and fun, they made their way into the foyer. Kathryn snapped dozens of photographs before letting the camera drop and embracing Kim. "I'm so happy for you."

"Thank you." Kim sniffed back a tear and leaned into the embrace of her friend. It had taken so much to get to this moment with Jackson.

The double doors leading into the sanctuary were closed. Jackson was on the other side. Jackson waited at the end of the aisle for her to walk toward him and promise forever.

Mrs. Brisbane, Meg's neighbor, organized them into a line. She oohed and aahed over Kim as she ensured Kim's father stood on the proper side and that they were out of sight when the ushers opened the doors to escort her mom and Jackson's parents to their seats at the front.

This was it. The wedding party was next.

The exterior doors whooshed. A blushing guest dipped her

head with an apology. As she scurried past, Gloria gasped. "Tiffany?"

Mrs. Brisbane clucked her tongue and steered Tiffany by her elbow into the sanctuary.

Kim only knew of one Tiffany that could pull this kind of reaction from her friend. This was the former university roommate that tried to frame Gloria. The woman who jeopardized the Life House residents with some bogus drug study. Why on earth would she crash her wedding?

"We don't have time for this." Gloria smoothed her hands down the front of her dress. "We can deal with it later."

"But—"

"No buts." Mrs. Brisbane clapped her hands together upon her return. "That's your cue, ladies."

The doors to the sanctuary swung open. Oliver made a move, and Kim pulled him back. "Not yet."

The girls walked single file in a slow procession. A groomsman met each bridesmaid mid-aisle and escorted her the rest of the way. Now it was Oliver's turn. She squeezed his shoulders before releasing him. "Walk to Uncle Jackson."

"Look at me, Unca Jackson. I'm just like you!" Oliver gave a little spin before he raced down the aisle.

The guests laughed, and all eyes turned to Kim. It took all her self-control to not follow Oliver's lead and race toward the man she loved. But she was only doing this once, and she wanted to enjoy every second.

"Ready?" Her dad's question brushed against her ear. He held out his arm for her.

Kim threaded her hand through her father's arm. Unable to speak, she nodded.

"You made a good choice, sweetheart. Your mother and I are

very proud of you." He kissed her cheek and led her through the double doors.

Kim's gaze moved over their guests. Her community gave so much of themselves to support her and Oliver, especially these last few months, as they recovered from the trauma. Her freezer had enough prepared meals that it would be many months before Kim needed to cook a dinner. But more than the practical help, she'd never forget how they stood in the gap and prayed without ceasing for Oliver's return.

Tiffany blushed again when their eyes met, but Kim didn't have time to ponder her strange appearance. Her gaze found Jackson, and everything faded. On the arm of her dad, she began the slow march toward her future.

God is a good, good Father.

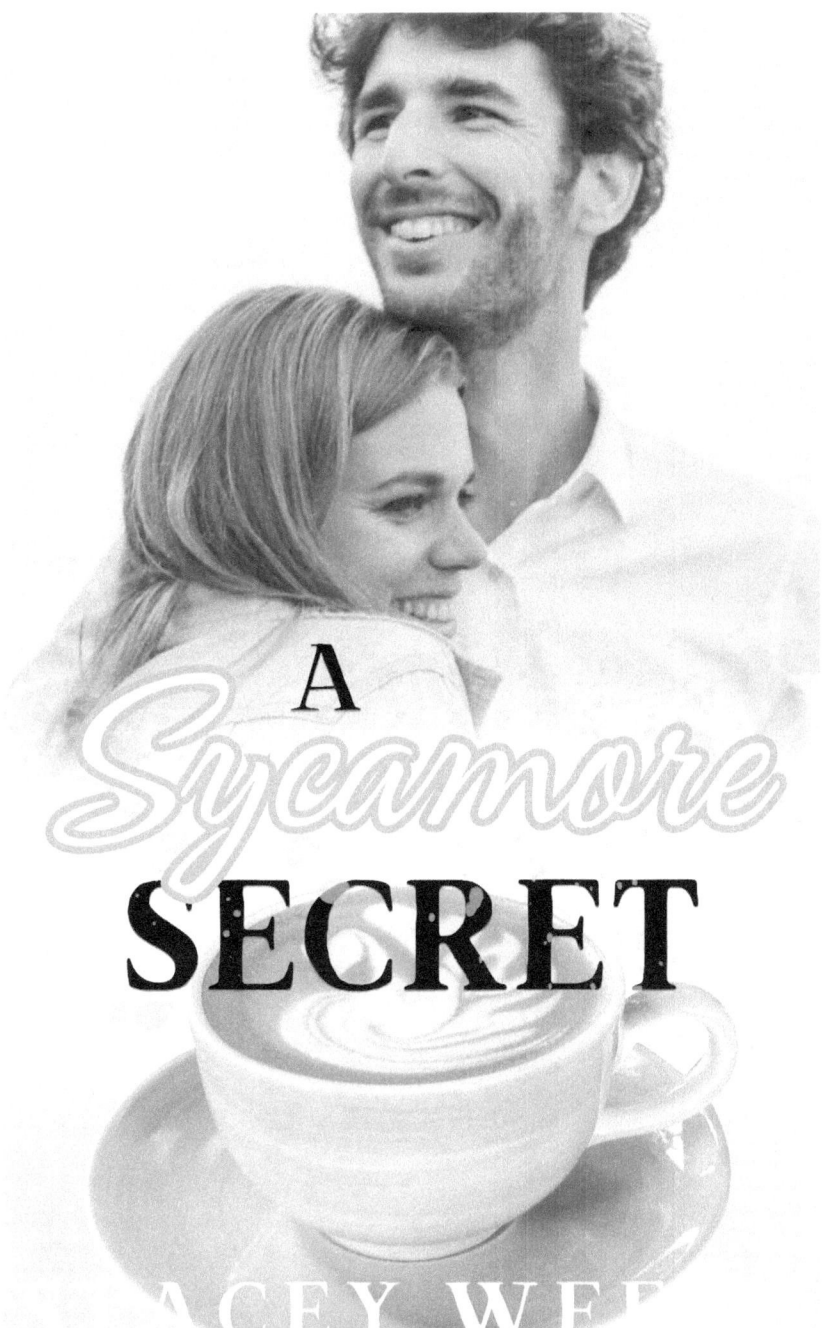

A
Sycamore
SECRET

TRACEY WEE

A Sycamore Secret

When the Audience Favorite Awards include Kathryn Withers's web show is a finalist, Kathryn livestreams daily, improving her chances of winning. But trending on social media backfires when the internet trolls connect the arrival of an unwelcome guest in Sycamore Hill to a shameful secret in Kathryn's past. A secret she'd do *almost* anything to keep hidden.

Ethan Roberts invested every penny in his bakery. When Kathryn streams from his location, the increased visibility boosts his confidence. Everything he has ever wanted is at his fingertips. But frenzied online comments and lingering paparazzi prove that mixing a tenacious morning show host, an entrepreneurial baker, and a decade-old secret only percolates trouble.

A Sycamore Secret is filled to the brim with small-town charm and a slow-roasted romance brewed to a sweet and smooth finish.

One

Some days, she had to confess the spotlight had lost its brilliance. Internet sensation Kathryn Withers mugged another smile in front of her boyfriend's bakery. "Did you get that?" She broke character, but she didn't move from where she stood in case Gloria hadn't captured the clip.

"I think so." Gloria scrunched her face and peered at the camera's digital screen. "Want to see?" She held out the device.

Releasing her sucked-in gut, Kathryn took the camera and reversed the footage. "I love the way you caught the sun glinting off the gilded sign for *The Muffin Man* and still managed to angle the shot so there's no glare on the front display window. And you kept me front and centre." Heat burned Kathryn's cheeks. She sounded vain. "You're really good at this. Ethan's going to love it."

Every so often, Kathryn gave her boyfriend's shop a shout-out on her show. A little free PR came with the territory of dating an influencer. Ethan was adding a coffee roasting lab to his bakery to set himself apart from the seemingly endless coffee chains opening store fronts in and around Sycamore Hill. The other businesses might have big bucks behind their brand, but *The Muffin Man* was the only artisan shop that roasted fresh beans onsite.

"I'll add it to my list of skills," Gloria quipped. "If the daycare reduces my hours anymore, I might need a side hustle."

"I'd offer you a job in a heartbeat. A volunteer job, of course." Kathryn gave her a sheepish grin. "Because internet TV doesn't pay beans, not even coffee beans."

Gloria tipped her head toward the bakery. "Wanna go inside? I'm starving."

"Absolutely. My treat." Buying her friend a cup of the best coffee blend in town was the least she could do, and considering she was heading into an evening of editing, coffee was practically a necessity.

Keeping her web show, *Sycamore Hill at Sunrise*, running required long hours and a heart devoted to the craft. It was the cost of fame, and being admired was all Kathryn ever wanted. However, after years producing the show, the thrill had lessened. Not that she'd admit that to anyone. To the rest of the world, she was Kathryn Withers, cookbook author, internet sensation, and social media influencer. But inside, she would always be Kathy, a little girl, looking for a place to fit in.

Gloria's phone chimed. Glancing at the screen, she said, "Meg's working today. She says she has news for us." With thumbs typing faster on the keypad than some people managed on a computer, Gloria replied to their friend's text message.

"Another good reason to call it a wrap. We can grab a coffee inside and hear her news." They had more than enough footage. Kathryn tended to over-record and then ruthlessly cut. She meticulously produced each minute of her show. That was the only way to ensure she delivered what her audience expected: a little self-deprecating humor, a pretty face, and up-to-date local news. Some called it gossip, but Kathryn disagreed. Gossip had a cruel bent, and what Kathryn did was harmless. She could never be unkind, having been on the receiving end of gossip too many times.

"Are you coming to the church potluck on Sunday?"

"Depends. Are you making sushi?"

An unladylike snort exploded from Gloria. "I learned my lesson. I'm sticking to noodles, cheese, and some sort of creamy condensed soup." Enough time had passed since Gloria's sushi disaster that she could laugh about it.

Kathryn admired her friend. Coming home to Sycamore Hill hadn't been easy, and finding her place in the community as Pastor Owen's bride had been even harder. But she'd persevered, and now she and Owen were happily married, and those troubles were a distant memory.

Kathryn folded her arms across her stomach. Was there a happily ever after for her? Her attention moved to the film equipment that needed packing. She loaded up the bag. Sure, she'd achieved what she'd always thought she wanted—the spotlight, admiration, and success. But she never expected it to be so exhausting or unfulfilling. It came with a lurking loneliness. A yearning that never felt fulfilled. From the outside, she looked like she had it all, but it was an illusion. One she was just as desperate to maintain as she was to shake free from its grasp.

Kathryn slung the packed camera bag over her shoulder and followed Gloria through the bakery door. A string of bells announced their arrival.

Meg looked up from behind the cash register. "Grab a table. I'll bring you coffees in a minute." She handed a customer his change.

Kathryn wove through the tiny tables for two and four people, choosing one with a clear line of sight into the kitchen. Ethan pulled a tray of muffins from the large industrial-sized oven. A hairnet tamed his dark mop. Kathryn loved the subtle wave in his hair and how he kept it just long enough that she could thread her fingers through it at the nape. Most customers came for the menu, but Kathryn came for her Muffin Man, who, incidentally, was rocking the apron she'd given him last Christmas. She'd silk-screened the question *Do you know the Muffin Man?* on the front of it. At first, she'd worried the apron had been a mistake since Ethan's dad used to tease him by dancing around him and singing that song. When Ethan had read the caption, she explained that the song needed new memories attached to it. And after only the tiniest hesitation, he'd pulled it over his head and whirled around, modelling it. He'd worn it every day since.

And her heart did somersaults every time.

Ethan's dad also called him Betty Crocker, but Kathryn hadn't yet come up with a clever gift idea to redeem that slight.

Meg clunked two mugs onto the table and poured coffee from the pot she carried in her other hand. "This is Ethan's latest blend. You'll appreciate its notes of vanilla and creamy body."

"Kathryn's appreciating a different kind of body." Gloria nudged Meg and looked pointedly toward the kitchen.

Meg snickered. "I see the lady prefers a full-bodied darker roast. Perhaps the title of Mrs. Muffin Man is in the near future?"

Kathryn lifted her mug to her lips to mask the scorching in her cheeks. Marriage looked good on her friends. Meg and her computer expert hubby Eli had married first. Then Gloria and Pastor Owen wed just last month in a beautiful May ceremony, beating their friends Kim and Officer Jackson to the altar by a week. Emma and Ben's wedding was this fall. One by one, all her friends had made their relationships permanent. It was like a real-life version of the old song, The Farmer in the Dell. Each man picked a wife.

Except hers.

That made her the cheese that stood alone.

Kathryn averted her gaze. She'd never felt pressure to tie the knot, but now that they were the only ones left unhitched . . . the coffee turned bitter in her mouth. It left an uncomfortably similar feeling to never being the chosen wife in the grade school version of the game. Every pot didn't find its lid. Even Scripture said there were all sorts of dishes and bowls in the kitchen. Some were made of precious metals, others of wood and clay. Some were saved for special occasions, others for ordinary use.

Ethan clattered in the kitchen, and his movements drew her attention like a meme from a video gone viral. When he noticed her watching him, his expression lit up, and Kathryn felt anything but ordinary. Her insides tap danced when he looked at her like that. Ethan dusted his hands on the front of his apron and hurried to their table. She tingled as he dropped a kiss on her forehead. "All done filming?"

"I think so." Kathryn smiled up at him, and her skin cracked. Cringing, she patted her dried-out, makeup- covered jawline. She always had to layer it on thick for filming. Tugging off her magnetic false eyelashes, she rooted around in her bag for a pre-moistened facial wipe. "I need to get this makeup off."

Ethan squeezed her shoulder. "You're gorgeous au natural."

Meg elbowed Gloria. "That's service with a smile."

"More than a smile," Gloria snorted.

Kathryn glared at her friends and swiped the cleansing tissue across her forehead. Even though she'd known Ethan since they were kids at summer camp, her middle still got all mushy when he touched her. It made her feel like the tastiest item on his menu. Maybe her man had a wife in mind after all?

"You might prefer me makeup free, but social media is a cruel and unforgiving employer."

"No kidding," Meg sniffed. "Did you hear about that writer complaining about how hard it is to maintain a healthy lifestyle while traveling?"

"Is that the guy from *Eating on the Road*?" Ethan leaned a hip against the table, in no hurry to get back to the kitchen. He folded his arms across his chest. His long-sleeved T-shirt did nothing to conceal the lean contours of his frame. She might have lovingly dubbed him her muffin man, but he was nothing like the tubby nursery rhyme character. Ethan was long limbed, broad shouldered, and all smiles, and knew—of course—who it was that Meg referenced. He followed a ton of foodies on social media.

Meg nodded. "He partnered with the nutritionist from *Killing Carbs*. They created easy recipes that only required the supplies found in a standard hotel room to cook."

Uh oh. Kathryn could just imagine how wrong that could go —an influencer's worse nightmare. Her gut flipped. She'd seen something in her news feed about steaming a chicken breast using a coffee maker.

Gloria giggled. "*#EatingRoadKill* is trending. People are posting images of the failed recipes."

Hijacked hashtags were the worst. There was no way for a content creator to control it once it went viral. Her friends didn't understand.

Both ridiculously huge missteps and small, poorly crafted posts could send brands trending for all the wrong reasons. There were no backsies on the internet. All publicity isn't good publicity, especially when your life's work is rebranded as *Eating Road Kill* by feverish followers. One negative connection like that could sink Kathryn, and everything she'd worked for would be gone.

"Kathryn?"

Ethan touched her arm, and she jerked. By her friends' stares, she realized she'd missed something.

"Are you okay?"

"Better than okay." Kathryn beamed the ray of artificial sunshine everyone expected from her. Anything less and she might as well axe her show herself. "But I'm afraid I missed what you said. My mind . . ." She flapped her hand.

Meg's hand dropped and rested protectively across her middle.

Kathryn's heart fluttered. "Are you?" Her gaze lowered to Meg's belly, then darted to Gloria, who was nodding, before landing back on Meg. "Are you pregnant?"

"Yes!" Meg squealed.

Kathryn shot to her feet and threw her arms around her friend. "That's wonderful!"

Outwardly, Kathryn did all the right things. She smiled, laughed, and wiped the corners of her damp eyes. But inside, another narrative played. If Meg was pregnant, it wouldn't be long before the others caught baby fever and their social circle moved from coffee shops to playgrounds. Her body quivered, but with none of the earlier delightful notes. This time, the sourness sank deep. Like the last kid waiting to be picked, dread clawed up her spine. The cheese stood alone, indeed.

The bells over the door jingled again, and Gloria's eyes bugged. Her gasp was sharper than the social media comments on Eating Road Kill.

Kathryn turned, and Tiffany Duthie gave an awkward wave.

Cringing, Kathryn's inner quaking morphed into waves. Tiff was part of a scandal that framed Gloria years ago. It involved a bogus drug study that was nearly approved for human trials on the residents of Life House, a local women's shelter their friend, Kim, ran. Meg lived at Life House for her first year in Sycamore Hill, and she took Tiff's reckless endangerment of the residents personally.

Tiff wasn't supposed to be here. Not yet. Not today.

A hesitant smile replaced Tiff's usual confident grin: a smile directed at Kathryn, not Gloria.

No, no, no, no, no.

Plausible reasons for her and Tiff knowing each other failed to gel. All Kathryn could think of was the truth, and the truth was not an option.

Meg stepped closer to Gloria and wrapped a protective arm around her quivering shoulders. "What do you want?"

Tiff's eyes widened and Kathryn gave her head a small shake.

Slumping ever-so-slightly, Tiff flicked her attention to Gloria. "Hi."

That was all she said. One word. And Kathryn's chest squeezed like she was hooked up to Ethan's juicer. She couldn't think. Couldn't breathe. She wasn't ready.

Tiff just showed up. That wasn't the plan. What good was a plan if a person didn't stick to it? Kathryn needed time. Tiff was supposed to give her a heads up. She was supposed to tell her when and where it would go down, not just *appear*.

Sure, Kathryn hadn't answered Tiff's message. But she didn't know how, and that didn't mean Tiff could just arrive.

Okay. *Messages*. Plural. There wasn't just one. And Kathryn did reply. She just hadn't answered the part about Tiff coming to Sycamore Hill, because that could ruin everything.

"I'm here to explain." Tiff jammed her hands into her front pockets. What she needed to explain didn't need clarifying. Everyone in Sycamore Hill knew Tiff Duthie's scheming had cost Gloria her university degree. Add that to the fact Meg was personally invested in the ministry of Life House, and Tiff was lucky this welcome wagon didn't run her down.

A muscle pulsed in Gloria's jaw.

Tiff's gaze darted to Kathryn and bounced back to Gloria, but not before Kathryn saw the disappointment in it. Tiff would never disclose how they knew each other. It would violate the code, which meant Kathryn's secret was safe.

For now.

Kathryn dampened her lips. How was she going to play this?

"I saw you sneak into Kim's wedding." Meg bought Kathryn more time to think. "I can't believe after everything you tried to do to Life House—to her—you crashed her wedding."

Tiff blinked rapidly and turned her face away. She swallowed. She needed support, that was clear. But that wasn't Kathryn's responsibility. There were tons of other people she could call on after she left The Muffin Man. It didn't have to be Kathryn. Pulling Kathryn into it had to be a conflict of interest.

"I didn't realize it was a wedding until it was too late." Tiff's lips folded in until they disappeared.

Tiff's eyes found Kathryn again. At least she thought they did. It felt like they did, but she wasn't about to lift her gaze and confirm it.

Hi-ho, the derry-o, Kathryn didn't want Tiff to choose her. So, she stared at Ethan's carefully constructed window display. She blinked until the pressure behind her eyes lessened. Helping Tiff wasn't optional. Kathryn knew that she'd help. But not until she figured out how to do it without destroying her life.

Kathryn squared her shoulders. "I should film the next segment."

Gloria perked, looking just as eager as Kathryn felt to get away. "Yes." Gloria slung her purse strap over her shoulder. "Let's go. I have nothing to say to that woman."

That woman. Gloria spat it as if even saying Tiff's name would sully her. Gloria's eagerness to escape and Tiff's devastated posture heaped guilt upon guilt. Gloria thought Kathryn was helping her leave with dignity, but Kathryn was using her. Kathryn was the one who needed to escape.

Kathryn threw a small smile to Ethan, who nodded encouragingly. He thought she was protecting Gloria, too. Shame heated her cheeks. She held her breath until the bells over the door jingled as it swung closed behind them. Guilt crushed her chest.

When a fellow addict reached out, you didn't walk away.

Two

"**D**o you want to talk about it?" Ethan flipped a bakery chair and rested its seat on the table so Kathryn could sweep the broom underneath. He'd locked the bakery doors a half hour ago, and when Kathryn showed up to help him close, he'd sent Meg home early. Meg was pursuing her Landscape Architect Degree and had a paper due tomorrow. She could use the extra time to work on her assignment.

Kathryn's expression pinched. She slogged through the evening routine with none of her usual joviality.

Ethan had debated all day on whether he should bring up Tiff's arrival. He'd noticed Kathryn's reaction to the woman. He'd almost convinced himself he'd imagined it, until Kathryn showed up with red-rimmed eyes. Tiff's reappearance had upset her.

"Talk about what?" Kathryn cocked her head with an expression of innocence. She'd pulled her hair into a ponytail and scrubbed of the heavy film makeup. He liked her better like this, clean and fresh like the girl he remembered from their summer camp days.

He kept flipping chairs, tracking her from the corner of his eye. She reminded him of the baby deer they'd befriended at camp. The poor thing was tangled in some fencing and didn't know it needed help. When they came at it directly, it fought them. It took them over thirty minutes to convince the deer that they were friendly. Finally, it stilled and let them free its legs, but the entire time its eyes stretched wide and afraid.

Just like Kathryn. A direct approach would make her bolt.

"We should talk about Tiffany." With no more chairs to flip, he puttered around, keeping her in his peripheral vision.

Kathryn puckered her lips and resumed sweeping with enough force that he was pretty sure he'd have to add a new broom to the weekly shopping list.

"Do you know her?" Ethan straightened the sugar canisters and the disposable stir sticks. Everything was in its place, just as it should be.

"We all know Tiff."

He frowned at her non-answer.

"I got her on film, crashing Kim's wedding. Remember? I spoke to her that day."

Kathryn had a strong reaction to Tiff then, as well. He'd seen the uncut wedding footage. When Tiff entered late, Kathryn's usual steady hand trembled.

He was about to challenge her when the bakery door rattled. The dead bolt held secure, but the string of bells resting against the top third of the glass bounced noisily. Ethan separated the slats in the blinds, and his mom grinned back at him.

Ethan unlocked the door and swung it open. "What are you doing here?" He pulled his mother into a hug. Looking over her shoulder, he grinned at his dad, who followed her into the bakery. His parents lived in Grander, and despite it only being a little more than thirty minutes away, they didn't visit often, and never unannounced. Ethan chalked it up to his dad's discomfort with Ethan's chosen profession. Dad liked his men to be men, and having a baker for a son was a tender spot. But Dad was trying.

"We were in the area," Mom said. "You've been gushing about the new coffee roaster, and we saw the lights were still on." She shrugged. "We took a chance."

"Hi, Mr. and Mrs. Roberts." Kathryn returned the broom to the cleaning closet and flipped down the bar stools that lined the counter separating the new coffee roaster from the dining area. Her stiff movements had relaxed now that their conversation about Tiff had been interrupted.

Mom hugged Kathryn, pulled back, slid her hands down Kathryn's arms, and squeezed Kathryn's fingers before letting go, not-so-subtly feeling Kathryn's empty ring finger.

Ethan glared at her, and she blew him an air kiss.

He kneaded the tight muscles in his shoulder. If Mom was any more obvious, Kathryn might notice her family heirloom ring was missing from her finger. Then he could kiss good-bye any chance of surprising her with a romantic, web-show worthy proposal.

Not that he had a romantic, web-show worthy proposal idea to implement. Kathryn was the creative one, and he could hardly ask her for ideas.

"That's an impressive piece of machinery." Dad's low whistle of appreciation shot confidence through Ethan.

Kathryn flicked on the recessed lights Ethan had installed above the roasting area. "The roaster was delivered last week. Ethan's been trying out recipes and blends ever since."

Ethan puffed like pastry under her praise. She really was the cream in his coffee. They were better together.

"Who'd have thought Betty Crocker would need experience as a machinist." Dad laughed at his own joke.

Mom smoothed a hand down the front of her shirt, but Ethan

noticed how it trembled. Despite saying for months that Dad really was proud of Ethan but didn't know how to connect with him, her involuntary reactions undermined her claims. Where was this effort that Mom spoke of? It certainly wasn't in calling him Betty Crocker.

Ethan deflated. Things were better with his dad than they used to be, but those little digs still hurt. His construction-working father never accepted that it took more than muscles and a refusal to cry to make a man.

Mom folded her hands in her lap and squared her shoulders. "We also stopped in to share some exciting news." She looked pointedly at Dad.

"Your mother and I invested in property in Northern Ontario."

"You're retiring?" A strange mixture of sadness and relief threw Ethan off balance.

"That's the dream."

Kathryn clasped her hands to her chest. "I've always wanted to see the Northern Lights."

Kathryn's enthusiasm bought Ethan a few extra minutes. She really was the soft creamy filling holding together two brittle wafers.

"We aren't moving there," Mom said. "At least, not yet. It'll be a vacation rental for now. There's a bit more paperwork to sign, but we wanted to tell you in person. And we wanted to see this." She gestured to the roaster. "It's quite the contraption. I love how it is right here, in the dining area." Mom's light, bubbly voice overcompensated for Dad's lack of enthusiasm. All the effort to connect came from Mom. Just like always.

"Ethan had to move the counter out a few extra feet to make room." Kathryn looped her arm through his. "Now he can host coffee tours, and it makes his business stand out from the chain stores popping up all over the place."

"You moved the counter out?" Dad checked out his work, seeming equally doubtful and impressed. Clearly it mattered little that Ethan had worked with his dad's construction company throughout most of high school.

"How does the roaster work?" Mom angled herself away from Dad.

"This is the drum." Ethan gestured to the machine's core, ignoring his dad's question. "The beans go in here, kind of like a front load washing machine. As the drum spins, the beans roast."

"It must smell heavenly in here."

Kathryn grinned. "Even the people who don't enjoy the taste of coffee have been drawn into the bakery. It's quite the magnet."

"The chaff comes out here." Ethan slid out the trap over a galvanized bucket.

"What are the probes?" Mom pointed to two metal rods.

"They track the roasting time. They're connected to my laptop, which runs an artisan software to track the first and second crack. Then, the beans cool in this spinner." Ethan pointed to the round basin that had an arm that spun to move the beans. It looked like a large mixing bowl.

"Cracks?" That was all his dad said. One word, lifted at the end to make it a question. Ethan should be thankful he was even listening.

"The first crack is when the moisture releases from the bean. If I stopped then, it would make a light roast. The second crack is when the cell structure breaks down. It creates a dark roast."

"I'm so proud of you." His mom fussed like always, but it wasn't enough.

For once, Ethan would like to make his dad proud. But things between them never shifted back to normal after Ethan announced his plans to attend culinary school and then apprentice under a local baker. His dad had assumed the kitchen was a phase, and Ethan would eventually work with him. When it finally sunk in that he'd never hand his business down to his son, Dad didn't speak to him for a month. But that was all in the past, according to Mom, the queen of excuses.

Dad was embarrassed. Ethan was determined. His mom was torn.

"Did you catch the game last night?" Dad addressed Kathryn. He'd stopped asking Ethan those kinds of questions years ago.

"Wouldn't miss it! That hit in the last inning—"

"I know. Incredible. He's only eighteen. Did you know that?"

And that was that. Ethan checked his watch. Dad was done with the bakery in less than five minutes. Four minutes longer than usual.

As Kathryn and Dad bantered, Ethan swallowed disappointment so bitter there wasn't a treat in the shop that could sweeten his gut. He loved that Kathryn could talk sports with his dad. The man needed someone to quip with over stats, hits, and scores. God must have been off his game when he gave a man that was all sports metaphors and muscle a son that was spices and frosting.

"You'll turn my boy into a man yet." Dad slugged Kathryn on the upper arm and bellowed at something she'd said.

Ethan looked away.

He was glad Kathryn and Dad got along. Really, he was.

His mom poked Dad hard.

He straightened and swung his gaze back to Ethan. "Looks like a big investment."

"Yeah." Ethan scratched the back of his neck. "I'm banking everything on it. Chain stores are crushing small businesses like me. I needed something to set me apart, and no one is roasting locally."

"The closest thing is the guy roasting beans in his garage and selling the fresh product to restaurants," Kathryn said. "But he's closer to Grander than Sycamore Hill."

"I went to his place to see about ordering local coffee," Ethan added, "and smelling the roasting beans firsthand convinced me. I didn't want to just sell local product; I wanted my customers to see and smell the process."

Mom's forehead wrinkled. "What does he think of your venture?"

Ethan shrugged. "I didn't meet him. He was out on a delivery. His girlfriend showed me around."

"Ethan's not infringing on his business," Kathryn clarified. "Ethan's not supplying restaurants. He's only roasting for his customers." She beamed at him. "He's going to offer coffee tastings, and we even discussed setting up a coffee delivery system where customers can order freshly roasted beans to be delivered weekly."

Ethan snagged a few baked goods from the front display and set them on the counter while Kathryn bragged on his marketing ideas.

His dad lifted his chin. "Out of all the things you could invest in, why coffee? Why not something more secure, like property?"

"You mean property in Northern Ontario?"

"Real estate is always a safe bet. It'll generate a nice passive income for your mother and me. Even Kathryn wants to see the Northern Lights. People will rent from us. You'll see."

"I think coffee is a secure, solid investment, and it makes sense for me. Nearly everybody drinks coffee, and nearly every food-based business sells it. Roasting it is the next logical step."

"It's brilliant." It was subtle, but Kathryn moved closer and stood with him. She tipped her face up and flashed that megawatt smile he loved. "He'll make a killing."

Dad grunted. "The boy could never kill anything. Remember when we went hunting that time?"

Ethan snorted. Mom could say all she wanted that Dad was proud, but pudding's missing ingredient was proof.

"Grant." His mom's tone carried a warning, and when her gaze shifted to Ethan's, it softened with an apology. "How are you going to beat the prices of the chain store?"

Ethan let his dad's barb go. It wasn't Mom's fault that he and Dad repelled each other like vanilla extract and mosquitoes. "I can't, so I'm not going to try. Real coffee lovers think of chain-store coffee like a fine chef thinks of fast food. I'm catering to a higher breed of coffee drinker."

"The coffee snobs?"

Kathryn lifted her chin. "We prefer to think of them as discerning customers that know a good product when they taste it."

His parents looked unconvinced. To them, Ethan would always be the little league dreamer picking dandelions in right field, oblivious to the game unfolding on the diamond. Pressure built behind his eyes until he could feel his heartbeat in his skull. When he looked at Kathryn, it intensified.

She put the pastries Ethan had retrieved on plates and handed each of his parents one, taking the pressure and focus off him. Then she changed the conversation. "Did you hear that my web show is up for a Fan Favourite Choice Award?"

Ethan's breath stalled. How didn't he know this? "You are?"

"I've never heard of that." Mom took a delicate bite of the pastry.

Kathryn's eyes danced. "My book agent confirmed it today, and I agreed to let my name stand." She looked at him. "I was planning on telling you tonight."

Ethan hugged her. "That's amazing!" He whispered the words into her hair. "Maybe this will lead to another cookbook deal."

Kathryn's eyes sparkled. "That's the hope."

"What exactly is this award?" Mom asked.

"It's a contest that takes place on social media. Fans vote for their favorite social media channel over the next few weeks. *Sycamore Hill at Sunrise* has a pretty good following, so I'm hopeful." Kathryn lifted a shoulder as if it were no big deal, except Ethan knew that it was.

He pressed another kiss to her temple. "Win or lose, you're always a winner to me."

"Good luck," Dad said.

"Sounds exciting," Mom added.

Except it wasn't. Kathryn hated popularity contests, and now she'd announced it to his parents, they'd be hounding her for updates. Their gazes tangled. She offered him a soft smile and the pressure that had been behind his eyes dropped to his chest and sucked the air out of him like a fallen soufflé. She'd thrown herself on the sword to save him, and he loved her for it.

Three

Kathryn stood between the diner's double doors in Grander and shook the rain out of her umbrella before folding it closed.

"Kathryn?"

Ethan's parents were leaving the diner as she entered. His mom gave her a quick hug.

"Grant, Shannon, what a surprise!" Kathryn looked past them to glance at the man standing behind them wearing an expensive looking business suit. He looked pointedly at his watch and bounced a briefcase off his shin.

Yeah, yeah, time is money. Kathryn ignored him.

Shannon squeezed her hands. "We just signed the papers for that investment property we told you about. What are you doing here?"

"I got a tip that Grander's mayor is making some sort of announcement that will impact Sycamore Hill. It's supposed to happen in front of the diner later this morning. I'm recording it for my show, you know"—she winked—"to drum up some votes."

The all-work-and-no-play suit gestured as if to usher them out the door.

"Wait." Kathryn dug into her purse for her phone. "Let me grab a snapshot of us. I have to post more content now that I'm in that contest." Kathryn flipped the camera into selfie mode and Ethan's parents huddled around her. She snapped the photo and quickly checked it. "It's perfect." She pointed to their business advisor in the background. "I'll blur you out," she promised.

"Thanks." As he dipped his head and looked at his watch again, a muscle in his jaw twitched. The suit was impatient.

They said goodbye, and Kathryn claimed a booth by the window as a waitress approached. The suit walked Mr. and Mrs. Roberts to their vehicle, despite the continuing drizzle of rain.

"I'll have a coffee, please." Kathryn dropped her gaze to the waitress's nameplate. "Thanks, Gabby."

Tiff Duthie slid onto the bench seat across from her. "And can I get a black coffee, please?"

"Sure thing." Gabby hurried off.

Tiff eyed the diner with a frown. "Any special reason we're meeting in Grander? I'm staying at the Sycamore Inn, and The Muffin Man is way nicer than this."

Gabby reappeared at the table with two thick ceramic mugs and a bowl of creamers.

Kathryn waited for the waitress to leave. Any special reason? Yeah. How about not wanting to be seen with the woman who'd hurt her friends. Wrapping her hands around the warm ceramic, Kathryn tugged the mug closer to her and let the wafting steam heat her face. Once Gabby left, she met Tiff's eyes. "Why'd you just show up at the bakery like that? The plan was to wait until I was ready."

"You'd been avoiding me. You were never going to be ready."

Kathryn sighed heavily and with exaggeration. "That's not what we agreed upon."

Tiff made a noise in her throat. "My sobriety is not about you. It's about me working the steps. This is my next step. And whether you're ready or not, I have to take it." Tiff's confident air lost its edge. She relaxed her posture and traced the rim of her mug with her fingertip. "But I was kind of hoping you'd act as my sponsor while I was in Sycamore Hill."

"Sponsor?" Kathryn sat back. Well, she didn't just sit back. She pressed against the vinyl-covered bench seat back as deeply as she could. She could not be Tiff's sponsor. Not in a million years. She bounced a curled knuckle against her thigh, her cheeks no longer comfortably warm but scorching.

"I have some apologies to make," Tiff continued, "and I don't expect them to be well received. But even if they aren't, trying will go a long way in keeping my relationship with God right."

That's when it hit Kathryn, hard enough she would have staggered had she been standing. *Tiff didn't know.* Her mouth dried up. Kathryn swallowed a gulp of coffee, yet the hot liquid failed to wet her whistle. "Nobody in Sycamore Hill knows about my past."

Tiff's mouth slackened.

Yup. Shocked.

Tiff rubbed absently at her arms. "You grew up in Sycamore Hill. How is that possible?"

Kathryn dumped a creamer into the coffee and studied its pleasant, swirling pattern. "You've heard my story. My drinking didn't get out of hand until I went away for university. My parents never told anyone."

Because they were ashamed.

Thankfully, her parents didn't live in Sycamore Hill anymore, having retired to their cottage years ago. Distance would spare them certain humiliation if Tiff's appearance outed the secret they'd worked so hard to keep hidden.

Kathryn was so familiar with feelings of shame, she could put it on like a favorite sweater. She kept her attention fixed on the pearly white cream trailing through the dark liquid.

Tiff studied her for a long, quiet moment. "I take the anonymous part seriously. I would never tell anyone about your addiction."

The weight on her chest lifted. Her secret was safe.

"But secrets can be triggers for relapse."

Who did Tiff think she was, lecturing her on sobriety? Kathryn had been clean years longer than Tiff. Besides, Tiff wasn't her sponsor. Kathryn didn't even have one anymore, and she was doing just fine. Before her last sponsor moved away, she'd told Kathryn it was the nudge Kathryn needed to shift from the meetings in Grander to the one in the Sycamore Hill Community Church basement. But Kathryn couldn't do it. She couldn't seem to make the leap from out-of-town-nobody to local-celeb-in-rehab. She knew she needed to. She even planned to. Someday. But who said someday had to be now?

"I was reading Luke 8:7 this morning."

Kathryn read no judgment in Tiff's expression. Only concern.

"Secrets will be brought into the open. Everything concealed will be brought to light and made known to all."

Kathryn's insides turned over, her stunned silence assuring Tiff the point had landed. Kathryn didn't want everyone to know. And if Tiff wasn't trying to draw Kathryn into her recovery, they'd never have to know. At least, not yet.

Tiff lifted her coffee mug and grimaced a bit of a know-it-all smile over the rim. "When you expose a secret, it loses its power. I should know."

Yes, she should. Kathryn had heard her story several times in support meetings. Tiff's secret addiction during her final university years is what started her descent. Before long, she was piling sin upon sin to feed her cravings. Accepting the pharmaceutical company's bribe to skew drug study results was the tipping point. Mostly because it implicated Gloria, her project partner. Guilt eventually led Tiff to rehab where she fought to get clean while Gloria fought to clear her name.

"I'm only staying in town long enough to make my apologies," Tiff said. "But knowing I could call on you when it gets rough would mean a lot."

When, not if.

Tiff accepted that it was going to be difficult, but she was doing the right thing anyway. Kathryn admired that about her. She could see why she and Gloria had once been good friends. When the girl was in, she was all in.

"Of course, you can call me." She said the right words but prayed she wouldn't have to live them out. Just the idea of it made her brain hurt.

Tiff grinned. "Thanks."

Kathryn knew the struggle Tiff faced. She'd followed the same path when she tracked down her university mates, the ones who exposed her drinking and arranged an intervention. Kathryn had said and done some awful things to them, and they had deserved to know that she'd turned her life around and that God eventually used their brave decision to change her.

But none of that happened within Sycamore Hill's town limits. No part of her old life followed her when she moved home, and she wasn't interested in revealing it now. Not when the entire community and internet world would be watching her and voting on whether they liked her. Social media was a fickle friend. People had been cancelled for less. But none of that was Tiff's fault. "I'll be here for you," Kathryn resolved, then looked at her watch. "Oh, it's almost time for the mayor's announcement. I need to get out there."

"You're recording yourself?"

"I connect my tablet to my phone's data to livestream and manage it with a remote."

"Let me help. It's the least I can do."

After throwing some cash on the table to cover the bill and tip, they set up out front. The rain had stopped, and the occasional ray of sunlight broke through the clouds. It was strange no one else gathered for the announcement. Kathryn opened the private message sent to her through her social media account. She double-checked the location and time. Maybe she'd get an exclusive? She tried to figure out the identity of the fan that sent the tip so she could thank them, but the account was under a pseudonym. She'd try again later.

Positioning herself so the light hit her from the front, Kathryn rotated her torso to a pleasing angle and beamed her high-wattage smile.

Tiff pointed at her from behind the lens to indicate they were rolling.

"Hello, Sycamore Hill. I'm live in Grander, waiting for the mayor, who is rumored to be making an announcement soon. This announcement is alleged to have a strong Sycamore Hill connection, and it looks like I've got the exclusive."

An engine roared behind her. Kathryn's scalp prickled, but years of training prevented her from turning until Tiff's steady hold on the tablet dipped just enough to reveal her huge, expand-ing, saucer-sized eyes. Kathryn shifted as a wall of cold wet hit her from behind. She shrieked.

Tiff pointed the tablet at the vehicle racing away, and then slowly turned back to a dripping Kathryn, who was now peeling her blouse from her skin with two fingers. Muddy streaks ran down her body. Her hair was plastered to the nape of her neck. Swiping a hand across her face, she pulled it away and looked at it. Black mascara. All captured live for her viewing audience. Her mouth sagged open, and for the first time in her entire career, she had no words. Nada. Zip.

Tiff turned the lens to face her. "That's all for now. This is Tiff Duthie, signing off for Kathryn Withers." She ended the video.

Kathryn rushed into the diner just as Gabby was coming out with a checkered tea towel. "I saw what that car did. Awful! It was like he aimed right for you." She handed the towel to Kathryn.

"Thanks." Kathryn twisted her hair to squeeze out the water. She mentally reviewed the items in the trunk of her car. She always had a change of clothes, but she wasn't sure she had time to reapply her make up. A slick, wet bun would have to do for her hair. "Do you know how long we have until the mayor makes his announcement?"

Gabby blinked several times. "What announcement? The mayor isn't scheduled to be here."

The ache in the back of her throat soured. She'd been set up. This was bad. So, so bad. The muffled ring spilling out of her purse intensified when she pulled it out. The cell displayed her agent's name. Kathryn's regular cooking segment produced such popular recipes that she'd landed an agent who sold her cookbook to a medium-sized publisher.

"Kathryn." Heather didn't wait. She started talking as soon as Kathryn answered. "I'm glad I caught you. I heard from the publisher. They agree that the contest is great press, not only for the cookbook, but also for the coffee book you pitched."

Kathryn put the phone on speaker and set it on the nearest table. She continued to wring out her hair. "That's great." A notification popped up on her screen. Someone had posted a video of her and tagged her.

Heather's prattle faded. Kathryn's fingers twitched as she tapped the notification and muted the video's sound. An anonymous account had already reposted the livestream just taken outside. It captured the vehicle deliberately veering to hit a puddle and drench her. The poster set the speed to slow motion, accentuating every micro-expression of Kathryn's.

She spun. Tiff.

No, she still spoke with Gabby.

Kathryn squinted and looked across the street.

Nothing lurked in the bushes. No one lingered.

The caption under the video read: *Small-town girl stages a fake event in the city.*

Fake?

"Kathryn? Are you there?"

Right, her agent. The book. "Yes, I am. Sorry, it's just a surprise. I figured the publisher wasn't interested in the coffee book."

"They weren't, at first. But when they heard about your nomination, they came up with a publicity plan that benefits everyone."

That pitch in Kathryn's heart twisted and stabbed. She replayed the video, muted, of course. Speaking of publicity . . .

"Imagine this: a camera follows you to capture the opening days of Ethan's roasting business. Viewers will see it all, the good, the bad, and the crazy. It'll give you more screen time, publicity for Ethan's business, and generate votes. Your gentle, self-deprecating humour has always been a hit."

Ethan needed the press. And it would solidify her next book, netting Heather a nice commission. It was a win for everyone.

Everyone but her. That fist always squeezing her lungs might as well rip them out of her chest. She'd never be able to breathe again if a camera followed her around 24/7.

Heather kept talking. "The other finalists have already started drumming up support on social media."

Had they also started their smear campaigns against competitors? Was that why she was here, dripping wet?

"Do you have someone that can film for you?"

"Yes," Kathryn answered automatically. Gloria would do it if she asked.

Heather babbled on about what a great opportunity this was and how all press was good press.

Kathryn snorted. Clearly, Heather hadn't seen the latest.

"Livestream is the best."

Kathryn jerked. "Live?"

"Yes, the unedited stuff is exploding online."

Impossible. Never in a million years. Not gonna happen.

Kathryn was really careful. She only let people see the parts of herself she wanted to share. If they saw the mess that existed outside the camera's frame, if they learned about her past, she'd not only kiss winning the contest good-bye, but also her show, and maybe even Ethan. She didn't doubt his love for her, but tons of girls had the hots for Ethan. Her followers were always dishing about him. And once he realized what a train wreck she was, he'd cut her loose. He had to. It was what any sane guy would do.

It wouldn't matter that her viewers called their reunion fate or referred to Ethan as the Ken to her Barbie or the peanut butter to her jelly. It wouldn't matter that she'd featured him on her show to make up for accidentally ruining a huge advertising campaign two Christmases ago. It wouldn't matter they'd been back together ever since.

"Did you hear me, Kathryn?"

"Yes, it's great. Thank you." Kathryn hung up. She'd send an apology email to Heather later. In all her Sunrise episodes and even in her short midday reels, people only saw the tiniest part of her. The perfect part. Because if her viewers saw the real her, they'd chew her up and spit her out faster than the flopped #EatingRoad-Kill disaster.

But what would be crueller, what she couldn't stomach, was the possibility that if she stopped being social media's sweetheart, Ethan might finally see the ugliest parts of her. And worse, reject her because of them.

Four

"Thanks for being my guinea pigs." Ethan rubbed his palms together as he stood behind the high counter in the bakery. Kathryn, Meg, her husband, Eli, and his business partner, Addison, sat on the barstools opposite the roaster. "I want to practice the tour before I start booking appointments."

"What exactly is a roasting tour?" Eli spun on his stool, ignoring the way Meg frowned at his childish action. Eli and Addison rented office space above the Muffin Man, where they engineered speciality computer software for various companies. They'd sold their most successful program to the town. It was a program they'd developed for Meg to use for a school project, but then they expanded the idea to streamline city permit applications of all kinds. The guys were more than happy to take a break and consume free coffee, and Eli loved any excuse to come down to the bakery and flirt with his wife.

The door rattled.

Ethan hurried to it and undid the deadbolt. "Sorry, we're not open yet."

"Your online hours say you are," the man huffed.

"Yes, we usually are, but I posted a notice that today we are filming a promotional clip and we'll open late." Ethan fished around in his front pocket and handed the man his card. "Come back later with this, and I'll give you a coffee on the house."

The man accepted the card with a grunt. He didn't appear placated. A bronze coffee mug pin on his lapel glinted in the light.

"I'll make it a punch card and give you five free coffees on me."

"Thanks for nothing." His grip on the door released.

Ethan double-checked that the sign he taped to the outside of the door was still there before rejoining his friends.

"When did you start offering a punch card?" Kathryn appeared genuinely surprised.

Ethan winked. "Just now."

"Ah," Addison cleared his throat, interrupting their exchange. "I came for the coffee, but I'm not too sure about the camera." He tipped his head toward the camera in Gloria's hands and frowned.

"The camera's your friend, Addison." Gloria lowered the lens and matched Addison frown for frown, but the corners of her lips twitched with playfulness. "Maybe Sarah will see it and decide she needs to be part of the Sycamore Hill social scene."

Ethan grinned as Addison's cheeks reddened. Addison met Sarah when he went to a tech conference in the city. Addison had visited her once in Glory River, but the official word was they were friends. Neither was ready to relocate for the other. Still, Ethan got the feeling the local girls paled in comparison for this guy.

"Since I can't get out of filming live," Kathryn explained to the group. "I appreciate your willingness to participate and take the pressure of me. Ignore Gloria as she films. I'll use the footage to drum up interest for Ethan's new venture."

"And generate votes for you for the contest." Gloria looked pointedly at Kathryn.

Kathryn waved off Gloria's comment. "Ethan will teach us about coffee, its history, and how to roast it. It's like a product tour. You'll know everything there is to know about coffee by the time we are done."

Kathryn gave them a few last-minute tips about acting natural, and when Gloria pointed the device their way, Kathryn transformed. She came alive like a second personality emerged. Her alter ego was confident, vibrant, and relaxed in a way core-Kathryn rarely presented. She even spoke differently, prolonging her vowel sounds. But as fun as camera-Kathryn was, Ethan loved the real Kathryn best.

"Hey friends." Kathryn batted her false eyelashes. "I have big news. Most of you know about my cookbook, *Move over, Betty, There's a New Crockpot in Town*, and I'm excited to tell you about my upcoming coffee roasting book! Part of my research involves trying out new flavors, understanding the roasting process, and immersing myself into coffee culture—which is a real thing. I mean, it's bigger than Barkitecture."

"Barkitecture?"

Gloria briefly panned to Addison to capture his confused expression.

"I did an entire Sunrise segment on the growing popularity of designing gorgeous indoor spaces for pets. Surely, you saw it?" Kathryn's slow drawl and cute gestures communicated that she didn't expect Addison to have seen the show. Her ability to downplay herself and her expectations on her audience was part of her charm.

Ethan snuck a glance at his phone, which he placed on the counter screen-side up, so he could track Kathryn's viewers. Every second, more people tuned in, and their comments floated up the side of his screen.

I love barkitecture!

Congrats on the book deal.

What's the title of the new book?

Fabulous episode. I transformed a closet for my dog.

Where did you buy your shirt?

"Let me introduce Ethan Roberts. Ethan, tell them a bit about yourself."

I've been to his bakery.

Last time I was there, some guy bumfuzzled the staff. Messed up my order.

Ethan flipped his phone so the comments wouldn't distract him while he addressed the camera. "I own an artisan bakery and coffee roasting business in Sycamore Hill called The Muffin Man."

Kathryn poked her head into the shot. "And ya'll know him as my better half." She winked before taking her seat at the counter. Kathryn typed a comment into her phone and left it, screen up, on the counter. It took all of Ethan's self-control not to let his attention drop to it.

Ethan placed four tiny mugs on the counter, one in front of each of them, while addressing the online audience. "I hope you'll come and enjoy the robust and fullbodied flavours coming your way from The Muffin Man."

"This is the only time I'm ever embracing a full body." Kathryn ran a hand down her slender side and clucked her tongue. "The camera adds too many pounds."

"Thankfully, I don't live on camera." Meg bantered perfectly. "Can I put cream in mine?"

Meg hadn't seen the online comment about the messed-up orders. That was the day Meg's volatile ex showed up to harass her. A few orders were delayed, a couple more mixed up. Ethan did what he could to make the customers happy, but Meg's safety had been the real priority.

Ethan set a little creamer on the counter in front of Meg. "Did you know that black coffee came from the Arab world? When Europeans wanted to be separate from the Arabs, they added milk to lighten the darkness." Ethan dribbled a trail of coffee beans across the counter as he spoke.

"Ahh, Ethan? Are these beans past their best before date?" Kathryn rolled a green bean between her index finger and thumb.

Gloria adjusted the camera angle.

He chuckled. "Coffee beans are supposed to be green. They are seeds that grow inside a cherry, which is a fruit."

"For real?" Ethan loved the way Eli leaned in with genuine interest.

"Each cherry has two seeds inside, and depending on where they grow, they can produce coffee beans with natural flavours of cinnamon, mango, or pecan."

Kathryn's screen lit up, and Ethan snuck a glance.

No way!

I didn't know that.

Kathryn had responded to the negative comment.

Bonus points for the word bumfuzzled. Impressive. *Shoot me a DM and I'll arrange a tour, on me.*

And that was it. The heart emojis were all over her response. But she wasn't done charming her audience. "The audience has some comments." Kathryn read from the screen. "*Brewlover* writes, Coffee's a fruit? That's the best news I've ever heard. *AllNatural* wonders if coffee can count toward our recommended daily servings of fruit? And *AllAboutTheKids* wants to know what makes for a fruitier flavor."

Kathryn's allure and Ethan's coffee knowledge reeled the viewers in. This was why he added the roasting business. People loved coffee, but they had no idea what was involved in making their favourite beverage. When they slowed down long enough and learned, it fascinated them. "Coffee is not exactly a serving of fruit," Ethan laughed. "I wish! Naturally processed beans have a far more fruity, earthy flavor than washed beans because the natural ones have been in contact with the cherry for longer."

Ethan lifted a premeasured amount of beans in his hands. He'd preheated the roaster, so all he had to do was pour the beans into the drum.

"What's the computer doing?" Addison pointed at the laptop connected to the roaster.

"It monitors the temperature and tracks the first and second crack." Ethan could almost see the wheels turning in Addison and Eli's mind. By the end of next week, they'd probably pitch some crazy upgrade to the program. The beans entered the browning phase, and a sweet, familiar aroma wrapped the room in a hug.

Kathryn's features eased into a dreamy and soft expression. "You all can't smell this, but I assure you, it's divine."

The scent transported Ethan back home. When he was a kid, he'd sneak downstairs and find his dad at the kitchen table with his steaming mug and newspaper. The smell of coffee made Ethan feel safe, how he always felt with his dad, until the day he realized his career choice was such a disappointment.

"What are you doing now?" Kathryn drew him back to the present.

Ethan gestured to the water tank behind him. "Better water produces better coffee. I use a filtration system that guarantees a lower mineral content." He poured coffee into their tiny mugs. "This brew has light notes of ripe fruit and a creamy body."

Kathryn wrinkled her nose adorably as she sniffed it. "Aren't we going to use the beans you're roasting right now?"

"No, those have to sit for a while before I can use them. I

prepared the ones for tasting last week." Ethan casually slipped his hand into his front pocket and clutched his mother's heirloom ring. As soon as Kathryn took her first sip, he was going to offer her the raw sugar and ask her to sweeten his coffee forever by marrying him.

Kathryn lifted the mug to her lips, pausing so Gloria could get the shot.

Ethan white-knuckled his grip on the sugar bowl.

But before she could sip, the bells over the door jingled.

Shoot. He must not have locked it after the guy left.

Tiff entered, and Kathryn fumbled. Coffee sloshed over the rim. She shot a panicked glance at the camera before dipping her head. Something was going on between Kathryn and Tiff, something Kathryn didn't want her viewing audience or her friends to see.

Ethan transferred the roasted beans to the cooling bin and turned it on. With his back to the camera, he regrouped. He wasn't about to share the most important moment of his life with a semi-famous troublemaker.

Before Tiff could speak, the blades in the cooling bin squawked like nails on a chalkboard. All eyes, camera included, swung back to the screaming machine. Eli and Addison hopped over the counter, knocking his phone to the floor.

"What's happening?"

Ethan could barely hear Kathryn over the scraping noise. He powered down the machine. Once the spinning arm stopped, he stuck his hands inside and felt around. He lifted out a pebble. "Stones."

Eli and Addison began picking through the beans, removing more and more stones.

"Who would do such a thing?" Meg rested a protective hand

over her belly as if the sabotage against Ethan's bakery was a threat to her baby.

Tiff bumped a chair, and it scraped the floor. Everyone turned as she backed up. "Clearly this is a bad time. I'll try later." The bells over the door jingled as Tiff hurried out the door.

Ethan retrieved his phone.

Coffee, $5. Metal scrapings? Free.

Coffee and a show.

Kathryn's audience had seen his failed launch. Great.

"That's enough for today," Kathryn spoke to the camera. "Tune in tomorrow for the answer to our very own Coffee Shop Mystery, titled, Who Stoned the Coffee Beans? Who knows, maybe my next book will be a cozy whodunit."

Gloria lowered the camera, and the group collectively sighed.

"That could have gone better," Eli said dryly, still picking stones from the cooling bin.

"I can't believe we just livestreamed that." Ethan collapsed onto a chair.

Kathryn stayed quiet. Too quiet. The spunky girl wooing the masses had evaporated. "I'm sorry."

She said it so softly the words took a minute to register. He met her gaze with a frown. "For what? It's not your fault."

She bit her lip in the way she always did when she was nervous. "It all got livestreamed. Another failed event I'm covering."

Ethan connected her dots. Just like what happened in Grander. But they couldn't be related. A competitor wouldn't destroy his life's work for a voting edge.

"If that was the plan, it backfired." Meg scanned her phone. "The comments are in your favor. Sure, there are a few cruel ones, but for the most part, people are hoping everyone is okay and wishing you well." Meg handed him the phone. "They even hashtagged themselves #CozyCoffeeSleuths and pledged to get to the bottom of it."

"Jump on the hashtag and ride the wave," Eli advised. "Let them figure out who did it for you."

Ethan's phone vibrated. He handed Meg her device back. "Hi, Mom."

Ethan expected her to launch into a million questions about the bakery, the stones, and what he was going to do, but she didn't.

"Our retirement plans have been pushed back. Your dad has one more job he needs to finish."

"K. Thanks for letting me know." Ethan didn't have the brain space to get into it right now. "Can I call you back later?"

"Sure."

They disconnected. His mom sounded off. He'd figure out why when he called back. Ethan ran his gaze over his damaged supplies. What was he going to do?

Addison poked around in the cooling bin, searching for stones as if a carnival game prize hung in the balance. "Did you have any trouble with the equipment?"

"None."

"Who else handled the beans?" Eli added a few more pebbles to the growing collection.

"Just me. The delivery guy left them at the back door because he got here about fifteen minutes early. He sent pic and a text message confirming the delivery. I brought them inside as soon as I arrived."

"Maybe we should loop in Jackson?" Having a friend in the police department sometimes gilded their gingerbread. "If someone added stones to your delivery, they only had a fifteen-minute window. There could be video surveillance in the alley."

Maybe. But Ethan wasn't holding his breath.

Five

Kathryn's online promotions sent a surge of new customers to The Muffin Man, forcing Kathryn and Gloria to take their coffee to a table near the back. Ethan only used paper cups when people ordered to-go, so they cradled ceramic mugs, dodging people and smiling as they went.

Kathryn caught a whisper of her name. Three girls huddled in the corner and not-so-subtly looked at their phones, her, then back to their phones. Great. She'd been recognized as *that Kathryn*. She cranked the wattage on her smile and hoped the dark circles under her eyes didn't show on any unauthorized recordings that hit the web.

She and Gloria snagged a table, and their white mugs clunked down, each one boasting a clever saying etched in black script. Kathryn added cream to her *Espresso yourself*, and Gloria lifted *Warning! I'm a caffeine addict* to her lips.

Kathryn's digestive tract coiled at the light-hearted use of the word *addict*.

Ambrosial hints of freshly baked goods and rich butter wafted from the kitchen. Meg hustled behind the counter, greeting customers and offering samples of Ethan's gourmet blends. Ethan hole-punched a coffee card and handed it back to a man. Based on the number of punches in the card, the man had been enjoying the coffee. Buzz, conversation, and clinking dishes played as a soft soundtrack.

The bustling scene released the pressure that had been steadily building in Kathryn's chest. Meg had been right about the coffee roaster incident. People were sympathetic toward Ethan's misfortune, just as sympathetic as they were toward her about her altercation with the vehicle and the mud puddle. Whoever was trying to discredit her was losing. Ethan's business held strong, and her popularity skyrocketed. In fact, both videos went viral, and they directed genuine coffee lovers who lived within the radius of Sycamore Hill to the Muffin Man— where she planned to livestream from the kitchen this afternoon with a famous internet foodie.

"Since we have a bit of time before we start," Gloria said, "I wanted to show you something." Gloria opened her laptop and spun it so Kathryn could see her screen. "I recorded some behind-the-scenes clips. I thought if I gathered enough, you might be able to turn the livestream off for a bit."

The knot in Kathryn's stomach that had been tightening since the contest began loosened. A day off sounded great. Impossible. Like magic. She dragged her finger over the trackpad and fast-forwarded through her friend's covert filming. Gloria had caught snapshots of her applying her film makeup, buying groceries, singing in church, laughing, and throwing popcorn at Ethan while the gang watched a movie. Gloria had captured beautiful B-reel film.

"When did you take this?" Kathryn pointed to the clip from church.

"I came in late because I was helping a fussy baby settle in the nursery. I saw you, and I thought it would be nice to show you just being you. You're so peaceful when you sing. But if filming in church crossed a line, you don't need to use it."

"Can I interest you ladies in a pastry?" Meg lowered a tray full of freshly baked goods and slices of apple pie with fragrant cloves and cinnamon spice. Under her breath, she added, "The girls at your nine o'clock are filming you."

Kathryn's mouth dried up, but she kept the smile on her face. "The pie, please."

Meg set a piece on the table in front of Kathryn. Gloria shook her head no, and Meg moved onto the girls, enticing them with the desserts and blocking their shot. "Recording someone without their permission might be legal, but posting it online can get you into a whole mess of trouble."

Kathryn tried not to smile as they ducked their heads and mumbled apologies.

"What do you think?" Gloria drew her attention back to the computer screen.

If she edited the clips right, she'd be able to offset the livestreaming with these bits and get a breather. "This is fabulous work."

Gloria ran her fingertip over the trackpad and clicked a few times. "I had a question."

Kathryn nodded and took a bite of the pie. Delicious.

"What's happening here?" Gloria played the now- famous video of Kathryn in Grander getting splashed. She paused it when Tiff turned the camera to herself and signed off for Kathryn.

Kathryn choked. She hacked apple pie chunks into her napkin and gulped scorching coffee to clear her throat. *Oh please, Lord, if anyone recorded me choking, strike their phone with a bolt of lightning.*

"How do you know her?" Gloria's mouth twisted on the word *her*. It was always *her* or *that girl*. Never Tiff.

Dabbing her mouth with the napkin, Kathryn cleared her throat. "I don't. Not really. I only know the parts of her she's shared with me." Shared in confidential AA meetings that Kathryn couldn't talk about, not even with Gloria.

"Come on, Kathryn."

"I can't say." Wouldn't even if she could. Because if she did, her secret would be out, too. The only way Kathryn could meet Tiff at an AA meeting was if she was in attendance herself.

Gloria's jaw moved back and forth, but the movement didn't hide her scowl. "I hope you know what you're doing. She wasn't just my roommate; she was my best friend. And she threw me under the bus to save herself, collecting a nice paycheck to boot. She only got a fine and court-ordered rehab because she agreed to help the prosecution build their case against Emergence Pharmaceuticals."

This was it. This was her window. She should tell Gloria that she met Tiff in rehab, because she wasn't breaking confidentiality if Gloria already knew she went, but her tongue stuck to the roof of her mouth.

"Like rehab actually rehabilitates," Gloria snorted. "It's only a matter of time before she relapses. She only went because it was a condition on her get-out-of-jail-free card. Do you know how much damage she could have done to the women of Life House if she wasn't exposed? If that drug trial had started—"

Kathryn tuned out. *Like rehab actually rehabilitates.* It landed like a punch. *It's only a matter of time before she relapses.* That's what Gloria thought about addicts. Kathryn channelled her fake smile that wooed the masses online. She carefully kept her body language relaxed and open.

Gloria wasn't the only one familiar with rejection. Kathryn

knew it so well that she once nearly killed herself trying to numb the pain. But this wasn't about her. Tiff was trying to do the right thing, and Kathryn had to help her work the steps of her sobriety.

Kathryn tried to moisten her lips, but all the saliva in her mouth had evaporated. "Forgiveness rarely feels deserved, and it is never easy." She reached for Gloria's hand. "But if you don't forgive, the bitterness will eat you alive."

Gloria turned away. A few minutes passed before she spoke again. "Forgiveness doesn't mean we trust someone who has proven to be untrustworthy. We are to be wise as serpents. It's in the Bible."

"And harmless as doves. That's the rest of that verse. Holding onto bitterness doesn't feel harmless."

Gloria flattened her lips. It wasn't a frown, but it wasn't a smile, either. "I'm trying, Kathryn. I really am."

"You ladies ready?"

Kathryn jumped at Ethan's interruption. She was so focused on Gloria, she hadn't noticed him standing beside the table.

Ethan's head swivelled from Kathryn to Gloria. "The food blogger arrived. He's in the kitchen."

Kathryn collected their dishes, and Gloria closed the computer. They stood.

"Have either of you seen a bakery key lying around? Addison and Eli lost one of theirs." Ethan chewed on his bottom lip.

"No, but we'll keep an eye out," Gloria promised.

They followed Ethan to the back. Last night, Ethan had set out premeasured ingredients and the small appliances they needed on the back prep counter. An up-and- coming food blogger from TasteBud Explosions was going to try the results of their short baking segment. They got the shot in one take, which was amazing. Kathryn channelled all her tension into charm, and within minutes, she had Mr. TasteBud in stitches.

She was ready to prematurely call the segment a victory when Mr. TasteBud lifted their scrumptious looking creation to his lips. He took a bite—a big one.

Gloria zoomed in for his reaction as all the wonderful gooey goodness slid down his throat.

Instead of smiling, he exploded in gags and spit into a napkin. There might have even been a bit of dry heaving, all live on internet TV.

"That's awful!" He furiously wiped his mouth. "It's loaded with salt." He downed an entire water bottle in one swig.

"I measured these myself." Ethan swiped a finger in the now empty sugar bowl and licked. His mouth puckered. "Salt."

Kathryn looked directly into the camera, still broad- casting. "Our coffee shop saboteur strikes again."

Six

Ethan looked at his watch for what must have been the tenth time in as many minutes. He peered through the window on the bakery door. Ben should be here. His friend never said what the urgency was, but Ethan figured he was writing some sort of article for the paper about the recent mysterious happenings at The Muffin Man.

His leg bounced. The last week had been a flurry of activity. Despite several setbacks, the promo Kathryn generated drew in a crowd. Everyone wanted to know who was targeting The Muffin Man, and ideas abounded that were crazier than the fake moon landing and flat earth theories. Ethan was supposed to open in an hour, and if the trend continued, he'd need every second to prepare. He tried telling Ben that, but Ben insisted they meet.

Today.

This morning.

Before opening.

Ethan looked at his watch.

He unlocked the bakery door and stared down the
street. Through the foggy morning haze, two figures emerged.
Finally!

Ben hurried up the sidewalk with his wife, Emma. Ethan
ushered them inside before locking the door again.

Ben didn't even say hello. He thrust a newspaper toward
Ethan. "Did you see this?"

After motioning for them to take a seat at the small bistro
table nearest to the kitchen, Ethan took the paper from Ben. Two
coffees waited for them, along with a small pitcher filled with
cream and a bowl of raw sugar packets. "I made you a coffee. It's a
new blend I'm trying."

Ben pulled out a chair for Emma, and Ethan turned around
the chair across from them and straddled it. He unfolded the
paper.

Neither Ben nor Emma touched the coffee.

Pressure built in Ethan's chest as he processed the local headline. His gut heaved. *Local Bakery Brews Controversial Kopi-
Luwak Coffee. Should Citizens Be Concerned?*

"You've got to be kidding." He'd only just recovered from the
stone incident. Then the disastrous baking segment spoiled his
publicity idea and his new plan to propose to Kathryn. After the
food blogger had raved about his delicious treat, Ethan intended
to drop to one knee and offer to be Kathryn's personal chef for
life. But nothing about yesterday panned out the way he'd hoped.

He tightened his grip on the paper. And it never would, if the
press had its way.

Ben made a face. "If I'd seen it, I would have killed it. I'm
sorry."

A bolt of pain shot through Ethan's jaw, and he scrubbed a
hand down his chin. "Someone has it out for my business."

Ben's nostrils flared. "That's what I was thinking."

"Do you think it's someone local?" Ethan tossed the paper on the table. He couldn't imagine any of his direct competitors stooping to this level, but the economy was tough, and desperate people did desperate things.

"I don't know, but I'm gonna look into it," Ben promised.

Ethan pushed his sleeves up and pulled at his collar. Everything suddenly felt tight. Too constricting. It made it hard to breathe. Whoever said there was no such thing as bad press was never accused of serving coffee made from pooped-out coffee cherries. Ethan's stomach flipped as another realization struck him. *It's Grander's paper.* "My dad's gonna see this."

"He won't believe it." Emma shook her head. She gave his dad too much credit. Except Dad had been watching him lately. He even followed The Muffin Man online. Maybe Dad was trying?

Ethan lurched to his feet. The chair skidded a few inches. He paced a semi-circle around the table. "I can't control what anyone believes." He understood that logically, but that didn't help the churning in his gut. If Dad really was trying to connect, this would only give him another reason to criticize his career. Another reason to try and convince him to hang up his apron and pick up a nail gun like Dad always wanted. Except—Dad hadn't asked in a while. In fact, Ethan couldn't remember the last time Dad had asked him to consider a career change. Maybe there was something to Mom's claims, after all?

The oven beeped. Ethan trudged to the kitchen and removed a tray of muffins. He placed it on a counter already filled with dozens and dozens of cooling baked goods. The urgency to open had vanished.

"It's not true, is it?" Emma's cringe was unmistakeable, even from the kitchen. It sank what was left of his hope. Was that why his friends left their coffee untouched? If they had to ask, strangers would just run with the rumor. It was the ice cream topping on today's mud pie.

"Of course, it's not." He yanked off his oven mitts and chucked them on the counter.

A faint blush shaded Emma's cheeks, and he instantly felt guilty. It took a tremendous amount of self-control to not stomp back to the table, but he managed to rejoin them without throwing the tantrum brewing in his soul. He spun the chair so it faced them and slumped into it.

"Is it really made from partially digested coffee berries?"

Ethan blew out a sigh. "Yes. Kopi-Luwak comes from coffee cherries that are eaten and defecated." Ethan might as well say it. Everyone would be wondering about it. Thinking it. "But I don't serve it."

His attention drifted to the front window. The sun was rising and soon, the street would fill with shoppers. But he'd probably have more protestors than customers.

"Hey"—Ben reeled him back in—"I've seen this type of story before. The best thing you can do is be proactive. Show people that your business practices are ethical." Ben opened the paper to the full-page spread. It featured Kopi Luwak's popularity with high-end roasters and images of the poor Asian Palm Civets caged at unethical farms.

Ethan blinked, too stunned to respond. This smear took the cake. Or, more accurately, the muffins.

"The paper takes false reporting seriously, and since this is untrue"—Ben stabbed the article with his index finger—"whoever wrote it is going to be in big trouble. I'll push for a retraction."

"Thanks." But the damage was done. People couldn't unread a headline. It might be impossible to unscramble this omelette.

Ethan dug his fingers into his hair, tangling them in the hairnet he forgot he wore. He tugged it off his head.

"You survived the other things. You'll survive this." Emma's promise sounded nice, but the fact she still hadn't sipped her coffee undermined her good intentions.

His cell phone rang, and the call display lit up his mom's name. Lately, she seemed to have a knack for phoning moments after a disaster. He sent her to voicemail, only feeling the tiniest twinge of guilt. He didn't have the emotional bandwidth for his parents right now.

"My dad's always wanted me to take over his business. I've spent more money than I have to buy the roaster. Maybe it's time to hang up my apron."

The shrill of his cell cut him off.

His mom.

Again.

He might as well get it over with. "Hey, Mom."

"We'll go," Ben whispered. "I'll write the follow-up story, so you don't need to worry about the content. We'll get to the bottom of this."

Ethan nodded absentmindedly, followed them to the door, and locked it after they left.

"Dad's in the hospital," Mom blurted.

His chest seized.

In the background, Dad scolded her. "I told you not to call him."

If Dad was talking, he had to be okay. "What happened?"

Ethan tugged a paper napkin from the dispenser and wiped the back of his neck. He might feel conflicted about his relationship with his dad, but he wasn't ready to say good-bye to him.

"He fell off a ladder on a job."

"Dad needs to stop doing this kind of work." He was getting

too old to shinny up ladders and walk across rooftops, but no matter how much he encouraged his father to retire, Dad pushed back. Clearly, Ethan's hope that their rental property in the north was the start of a retirement plan was premature.

"Shannon," his dad warned.

"Why was Dad on the ladder? Why wasn't Joel up there instead?" Dad's foreman was supposed to do the roof work so Dad could stay on the ground.

"Joel and Shelley had a wedding today, and we needed to finish the job."

"The job can wait."

"We need the payment, and your dad can't bill the customer until the job is done."

"Are you having money problems?" Had his parents stretched themselves too thinly buying the rental?

"Our too good to be true deal was too good to be true," Mom blurted.

"Let me talk to him." His father didn't sound injured. At least not physically. There was some muffled shuffling, and then Dad took the phone. "It was a real estate scam. I'm trying to get our money back, but until I do, I have to take a few more jobs."

Ethan stretched the skin between his eyebrows with his thumb and index finger. His dad couldn't stop working. "Why didn't you tell me?"

His gruff father wheezed, and the formidable man sounded surprisingly vulnerable. "I was embarrassed. What kind of man loses his life's savings at this stage of the game?"

"How long until you get it back?"

Pause.

"Dad?"

Another shuffling sound and muffled words, then Mom was

back on the phone. "We tried to sell it right away, but—it's complicated."

He knew all about complicated.

"We found a company that promised to resell our share. They required an upfront fee."

Ethan's stomach pitched again. That sounded like a refund and recovery scammer.

"We never heard from them after paying. Now we're getting calls from other people, and for another fee, they promise to get our money back."

"Don't pay anything!" His parents were on a sucker list, which meant every cheater in the province was about to descend.

Silence.

"You already did, didn't you?" The bakery door rattled against the deadbolt. Ethan held the phone with one hand and peeked through the blinds. Kathryn.

"We didn't know—" Mom cut off. More muffled sounds in the background. When she spoke again, her forced cheeriness made his eyes gummy. "It's almost time for you to open. We can chat later."

"I'll come as soon as I can." He swallowed, and a painful lump moved down his throat. He rubbed the butt of his palm in circles on his chest. Even his lungs hurt.

"I know you will." They disconnected.

Ethan opened the door, and Kathryn practically fell inside. Her white face and trembling lips heaped more weight on him. He struggled to breathe. *Lord, I don't know how much more I can take.*

"I don't know how it happened," she prattled. Kathryn never prattled. "But someone posted a picture of me drinking coffee here and said fans had no business supporting a woman that thumbed her nose at animal rights. A gourmet cup of coffee wasn't worth caging Asian Palm Civets. It linked to an awful article—"

Ethan crushed her against his chest. "I know. Ben and Emma were already here. It's not your fault. A freelancer sent the story to Grander."

Kathryn mumbled into his shoulder. "If only I wasn't in this stupid contest."

"It's not your fault."

"How can you say that? I'm the target. You're collateral damage."

Ethan didn't like the way she owned it. This contest had wound her tighter than a coiled whisk. No, that wasn't quite right. She started acting like she was a few eggs short of a dozen when Tiff arrived, and the few eggs she had were cracked.

Kathryn pulled away from him and tilted her head back so she could look into his eyes. "If I hadn't been filming here or working on a coffee book, none of this would have happened."

Ethan shook his head. "If you hadn't been filming here, I wouldn't have had my best week since adding the roaster."

Her eyes widened. "Really?"

He nodded. "The stones drummed up sympathy for me. This will turn out to be good as well. You'll see." Ethan didn't feel half as confident as he pretended, but he was clinging to God's promise to use all things for good in the lives of his children. Even if God might define good differently than he did.

Kathryn bit down on the corner of her lower lip in the way she often did when she was thinking. "What if I used my social media fan base to get out ahead of any more negative stories?"

"How?"

"Blogs, videos with customer testimonials, public appearances —anything that might help build trust in your brand again and reassure customers that there is no truth to any of this nonsense.

We could create a certification label for your coffee that guarantees it is ethically sourced."

"If I provided a certificate guaranteeing my coffee's ethical origins, customers would know they can trust that it's not from the kinds of places that mistreat animals." He liked this. He liked it a lot.

Ideas spilled from Kathryn. "You should create a blog post or video apart from me, explaining why you don't source Kopi Luwak beans. I'll cross post it on all my social media feeds, and ask my followers open-ended questions to get a dialogue flowing."

"We could expand it. Talk about why I don't use any unethical products."

"It might also be helpful for you to highlight the steps you take when sourcing fair trade coffee beans so customers can have full confidence in the quality of your product. You know, like you did on our coffee tour."

Ethan smiled. It was a great idea. He and Kathryn would tackle this problem head on. They'd do it together because they'd always been better together, like a perfect salty and sweet combination. His gaze flicked to the cupboard where he'd stashed the engagement ring. Maybe he didn't need to wait for the perfect moment. Maybe the moment was now?

Kathryn turned into his arms. "I believe in you." Her warm breath sent a shiver down his back. "We can do this."

No, not now. It was nearly time to open, and he didn't want to propose and have to shove her out the door. Besides, since the cooking disaster, he'd reconsidered his plans. He wasn't sure he wanted to share the most important decision of their lives with customers or fans. He'd keep the ring on him and wait for the perfect moment and just ask. That was the new plan.

Ethan pressed his lips to Kathryn's forehead and framed his strategy to earn back the trust of his customers. He'd create content for the bakery's social media platforms and send an email campaign with customer testimonials and positive stories about his business. He'd turn this ship around. And if Kathryn worked her magic behind the scenes by helping him spread the word, they both might get everything they wanted.

His watch vibrated on his wrist. Eight o'clock. With one arm around Kathryn, he unlocked the deadbolt to The Muffin Man. There wasn't a customer in sight.

Seven

The phone trembled in Kathryn's hand. It vibrated with another notification. Someone had commented on or liked the post. Not her post. Not the fun reel she'd put up earlier this morning. The action wasn't happening on Ethan's feed either. He'd uploaded a video in response to the smear article. Kathryn commented on it, sharing his outrage over the false claims. Both of those threads were suspiciously quiet. She'd checked.

Then double-checked.

The reel gaining traction originated with some internet troll that tagged Kathryn in a montage of photographs from her university days. Not just any pictures of her, but the intoxicated, hard-partying her. The her she hadn't been for years and, with the Lord's help, would never be again. Swiping with her thumb, she flipped through the images. Revulsion shot up her throat. The snapshots hijacked her brain and transported her into the past.

Her mouth watered at the sight of a bottle against her lips. It was like someone had rewired her pleasure circuits in a blink. She could almost feel the cool, smooth glass. The pressure of the bottle. The burn in her throat. She ground her teeth. Just because her body reacted with a longing she'd hoped she'd killed years ago didn't mean she had to give into the urge to indulge.

She wouldn't indulge. Not even mentally.

She forced herself to detach. To think logically. To investigate. The poster had to have dug deep into her history to get his hands on these pictures. That meant taking her down wasn't an impulsive decision. He'd invested in her. Looked for the people willing to share. This was premeditated sabotage, and if it came from the same person targeting Ethan, it was proof she'd pulled the bakery into her damaged orbit.

She was the rat in Ethan's kitchen.

Her device dinged again. Another comment.

The knots in her stomach tightened. The brutal thread of responses attached to the post was even more humiliating than the photos. Her phone kept chiming as the world interpreted what they saw. She turned the device face down on the table and gagged on the sob rising in her throat.

She lurched to the nearest window and pulled the cord for the blinds, cutting off the sunlight. In the living room, she tugged her fabric curtain panels closed, dropped onto the sofa, and cradled her pounding head. She had worked too hard for it to end like this. Yet, her dirty laundry flapped in the online breeze for everyone to see.

To comment on.

There were too many opinions about the stability of recovering addicts.

She lunged to the kitchen and vomited in the garbage can. After rinsing her mouth, she dragged a sleeve across her lips and slid to the floor. She should have never agreed to let her name stand on the contest. Her pride did this. Her misguided need to be chosen might undo all her progress in life. Her chest heaved even as her breaths shallowed. The room swayed. She forced her head between her knees and inhaled deeply. It took a few seconds for her heart to slow and her vision to clear. As soon as it did, she snagged her phone off the table and scrolled. It was like driving past a car wreck. She knew she shouldn't look, but she couldn't help it. Her gut flipped again.

Most of the comments were negative. The web thrived on a good scandal, and the trolls loved nothing better than shaming a person who claimed to love Jesus. It didn't matter if the story was true. All that mattered was the juice oozing from the details.

The smattering of kind comments that contained under-standing were not loud enough to turn down the negative. Anything good was buried in cynicism within seconds of appearing.

Ding.

Fair or not, the secret was out. Kathryn was a drunk. Is a drunk. According to rehab will always be a drunk. At best, she could strive to live her life publicly as a sober alcoholic that never forgot sobriety was achieved and maintained one day at a time.

Ding.

She pushed her fingertips into her forehead and stretched the skin. The tightness felt good. Like a mini endorphin release. Was it so bad they knew?

Maybe not, except that her competition was using it as a reason people shouldn't vote for her. As a reason for people to boycott The Muffin Man.

The headlines taunted.

Small town girl hides big time secret.

Who is the real Kathryn Withers?

Not role model material.

And when Ethan saw it, he'd never look at her the

same way again.

Tiff's name popped up on her phone screen. *Are you okay?*

Yeah.

Do you need company?

Code for, are you tempted to drink? Do you need a chaperone? Do you have access to booze?

No.

I'm here if you change your mind.

Kathryn gave it a thumbs up. She didn't believe Tiff was involved even if her modus operandi was public humiliation. Tiff was the only one who reached out. Fresh pressure climbed up her throat. Where were her friends? Why weren't they texting? Had Ethan seen it yet?

Her doorbell rang.

Kathryn pushed to her feet and padded to the door. She lifted onto her toes to peek through the peephole.

Gloria. Owen stood just behind her.

Kathryn melted a little. Gloria didn't call because she came. Kathryn pressed her forehead against the door. *Lord, I know I asked where they were, but I'm not sure I'm ready.*

"I can see your shadow," Gloria said. "Please, let us in."

Kathryn opened the door. She wasn't sure what she expected, but whatever it was, it wasn't what happened. Gloria flung her arms around her and hugged her tightly.

Kathryn stumbled back a few steps, but Gloria held firm. Hope bubbled up from that deep place inside that had been afraid her friends wouldn't stand by her.

Of course, Gloria came.

Owen closed the door behind them.

After what felt like forever, Gloria finally released her. "I saw the awful things they wrote. And those pictures! They have to be photoshopped. Why would someone do that?"

Kathryn's mouth dried up. She tried to dampen her lips, but couldn't. She jerked her gaze to Owen, who nodded. He'd already connected the dots Gloria refused to consider.

Kathryn squared her shoulders. It was time. She settled her eyes on Gloria. "They did it because it's true."

Gloria's mouth slackened. In fact, the intensity in her entire posture diminished. She stared with such a mix of disbelief and confusion that Owen slipped an arm around her. But to her credit, she stayed calm.

"Why don't we sit down," Owen suggested.

Kathryn's apartment was a modest one bedroom. The living room held a sofa and one occasional chair. Kathryn took the chair.

"Can you explain it to us?" Owen's question held no judgment and his posture no rigidity. Owen was just Owen, her friend and her pastor.

Kathryn tucked a strand of hair behind her ear and sucked in a breath. She held it a moment, waiting for the thickness in it to subside. She might as well get used to answering questions. She'd be telling her story a lot over the next few days.

Here I go, Lord. For better or worse.

Her cheeks tingled hotly. "I'm a sober alcoholic. I've been sober for years now, but my story is not something I've ever shared with anyone except my sponsor and the others in recovery meetings."

"When did it start?"

"High school." Kathryn averted her eyes. She'd told her story so many times in so many church basements that it rolled from her lips as naturally as breathing. But reactions didn't matter as much in those settings. This was different. This was with people she cared about.

"I was at a party when someone twisted off the top of a beer and handed it to me. I drank it to fit in. I didn't even like it, but it took the edge off."

"The edge of what?" Gloria interjected. Fair question.

She shrugged. "High expectations. Teachers, parents, my friends. Everyone thought they knew who I should be, but no one ever asked me what I wanted. Eventually, I liked how I felt when I drank even if I didn't like the taste."

"High school." Gloria echoed, stuck on the timeline. Her brow furrowed. "I was in high school with you. How come I didn't know this?"

"I was a few years ahead of you. We ran in different circles. And really, it didn't become an issue until university. Until then, I was a social drinker."

Gloria reached across the tiny coffee table separating them. She extended her hand and waited.

Kathryn's gaze dropped to the offering. She lifted her hand slowly. Unsure.

Gloria clasped it and squeezed. "I feel like I should have been there for you."

Kathryn swallowed. Letting Gloria work through misplaced guilt was part of the process. But there was more. What was the saying? In for a penny, in for a pound? She tugged her hand free and folded it in her lap. "Everyone seemed to juggle expectations better than me. I turned to booze more and more. By the time I got to university, I was depending on it just to make it through the day. When I came to class with it on my breath, my roommate gave me an ultimatum—tell someone I had a problem or she would. My parents put me in rehab, and I cleaned up and graduated only a half year after my friends."

"Why didn't you tell us?"

"Have *you* told everyone the things in your past that you are the most ashamed about?" Kathryn snapped.

Gloria grunted. "I didn't need to. The minute I returned to town, the local gossip chain did it for me."

"And you hated it," Kathryn said. Gloria might know what it was like to crave acceptance from people unwilling to look past your faults, but their experiences were like comparing apples and oranges. Sure, both were fruit, but they were fundamentally different at their core. Gloria's scandal was based on misunderstandings. Kathryn deserved what she got. Her gaze fell to her hands on her lap. When would her debt be paid? When would she stop reaping the consequence of her choices? She tucked her hands under her thighs to stop her fidgeting.

Owen gently cut in. "Where have you been attending meetings?"

Of course, Owen knew she didn't attend local meetings because they were held in the church basement.

"Grander. Not as many people know me there."

"Is that where you met Tiff?" Gloria finally pieced the puzzle together. It was no secret that Tiff blamed addiction for her questionable decisions.

"Yes."

"We're here for you, Kathryn. Whatever you need. This," Owen pointed at the phone, still humming with comments, "is not who you are."

She snorted. Wasn't it? She'd hid her real self from her best friends. When Tiff needed her, she backed away. Alcoholics perpetually put themselves first, sacrificing others on the altar of their desire. She pulled her knees into her chest and made herself as small as possible. It was the story of her life, but she desperately wanted this telling to have a different ending. "It doesn't matter. It's who they think I am. That'll be enough for the publisher to pull the book deal. Enough to tank my show."

She was going to lose it all.

"Look at me." Owen waited until she did. "You are a new creation in Christ. And when Jesus took your sins, he also gave you His holiness. You were saved, are saved, will be saved by a Savior who was, is, and is to come. This"—he pointed at the phone—"doesn't define you." He pointed up. "He does."

Were saved, are saved, will be saved. Was an addict, is an addict, will always be an addict. She looked away. She felt stupid. How could something so massive catch her off guard? It was just like addiction. It happened when a person wasn't looking, and by the time they realized the risk, it was done.

The phone hummed again, and Gloria picked it up. "Your trolls are really throwing gasoline on this fire."

"That's because alcohol addiction is still heavily stigmatized," Owen said. "People think they can't trust or respect someone who has ever struggled with substance abuse."

Gloria plucked her bottom lip. "Do you think Tiff tipped them off?"

All the warmth growing in Kathryn's chest froze. "That's a perfect example of what Owen just said. You don't trust Tiff. Even though she has tried to explain what she did was because of her addiction. Even though she is different now, has tried to make amends—"

"—make excuses."

"We're not here to argue about Tiff," Owen cut in. "We're here for you, Kathryn. And you're the same person you were yesterday, only now you've got this public victory under your belt."

Kathryn shifted her gaze from Gloria to Owen and then back to Gloria.

"That's something worth celebrating," Gloria said softly. Almost apologetically.

"And maybe even something worth posting about online," Owen added.

Kathryn froze. "Posting?"

"Take control of the narrative. Sobriety isn't something to be ashamed of; it's a hard-won victory in your life that doesn't disqualify you from God's family. It's part of what God used to draw you *into* the family. So, stand up. Own your past. Share your story. Refuse to worry about what people might think of you or how they might judge you because it's about more than you. It's about what God has done in you, and what He can do for others if they are willing to trust Him."

Kathryn didn't answer. She couldn't. It was more complicated than Owen knew. She didn't want to be the poster girl for sobriety. She didn't build a public life around the most shameful choices she'd made. She built a public life to . . . to . . .

Why did she build a public life?

To prove to herself she was worthy of admiration? To show all those people who rejected her that she'd made it? What was she trying to prove? Who was she trying to prove it to? She glanced at her phone still in Gloria's hand. Why hadn't Ethan reached out? Why wasn't he the one knocking on her door?

The phone buzzed. Kathryn extended her hand palm up, and Gloria handed the device over. Kathryn didn't bother reading the message. She just powered it down. If Ethan rejected her because of this, she wouldn't survive.

Eight

It was hours before sunrise when Ethan stabbed his key into The Muffin Man's deadbolt. Yesterday had been a disaster. The longest twenty-four hours of his life. The majority of the customers through his door had used the hashtag #CozyCoffeeSleuths, and without ordering a single item, they spent the day posting online and peppering him with questions about coffee and Kopi-Luwak and health code violations. To add insult to injury, he learned about Kathryn's crisis second-hand. While trying to keep up with the comments on his public response, someone mentioned Kathryn's addiction, and it sent him down a rabbit hole.

The cherry on that sundae was a trip to the hospital to see his dad and look over the real estate paperwork his parents signed. Then, he grieved with them over what it all meant. They could lose everything. The only good thing to come from it was when Dad had said how he should have done his research like Ethan did before investing in coffee. It was almost a compliment. Ethan tried reaching out to Kathryn to loop her in regarding his parents, but it went straight to voice mail. He sent off several text messages telling her that he wished he could be with her. He anticipated a typical sassy comeback or at least a compassionate word for his folks, but he got nothing but crickets.

Crickets from her, nosiness from others.

He'd been just about to ask Jackson to do a welfare check when Owen connected. Kathryn was fine. She'd turned off her phone. She didn't want to talk.

After putting out his own fires, he got it. At least he tried to get it. Talking about it while you were dealing with it was overwhelming. Owen encouraged him to take care of his parents, address the business issues, and keep them updated. Owen assured him that he and Gloria would stay with Kathryn, and they'd let her know why Ethan wasn't there.

Owen managed the crisis, not Ethan. Gloria comforted Kathryn, not him. If anyone should be with Kathryn, it was him, but he was the one she pushed away, and for the life of him, he couldn't figure out why. If they had any hope of having the future that he wanted them to have, they needed to be a couple. They needed to be there for each other. That meant Kathryn should have been at the hospital with him, but she wasn't. He should be at her place right now, but he wasn't. And the implications of those facts made his heart hurt.

Ethan flipped the bakery lights and locked the door behind him as a small crash sounded in the backroom.

"Eli? Addison?" He moved toward the noise. Eli and Addison had eventually located the lost bakery key. Or, to be more accurate, a customer had found it stuck behind the napkin dispenser and turned it in. Sometimes he could hear the guys in their shared hallway, but hardly ever at five o'clock in the morning.

Another rustle. This time closer.

Ethan's heart thumped. He slowed to a crawl, advancing toward the kitchen flicking on lights as he went. As he neared the coffee roaster, a shadow leapt over the counter and shoved him aside.

Ethan fumbled for the nearest barstool, toppling it on his way down. His head bounced off the vinyl flooring. Rebounding quickly wasn't fast enough. By the time his eyeballs stopped vibrating in his skull, the shadow had disappeared out the back door.

Ethan rubbed the back of his head, and his hand came back sticky. He swayed, catching himself against the counter and smearing blood along the edge. The police. He had to call Jackson.

Stuffing his hand in to his pocket, he retrieved his phone, fumbling through his contacts to find his friend's number.

"I'll be right there," Jackson promised. "I'll call Emma."

Ethan sank to the ground. *What else, Lord? Hasn't it been enough?*

"Can you stop by the shop? Someone broke into the bakery." Ethan massaged his pounding head. At least Kathryn finally answered his call. A part of him had expected her to send him to voicemail.

"Are you okay?" Kathryn's voice wobbled.

Ethan dragged a hand through his hair, brushed against the bruised spot, and winced. No, everything wasn't okay. Not for a million reasons. But he couldn't get into any of that. Not yet. She might not come. He deflected. "Everyone's here except you and Gloria."

"Gloria's with me. She spent the night."

"Eli and Addison are going to try to fix the busted computer, but if I can't get the roasting program running, it'll be out of commission indefinitely."

"We'll be there as soon as we can."

"See you soon." Ethan rubbed his forehead. The strong prescription Emma had filled for him hardly took the edge off. His wound didn't need stitches, thank the Lord, but it was ridiculously tender.

He decided to close the bakery for the day and posted a sign on the door that apologized for the disruption. He updated his social media accounts, and theorists pounced, surmising he couldn't take the scrutiny on his brewing practices. If he couldn't take the heat, they'd said, he should get out of the kitchen. Ethan didn't dignify the comments with a response. He wasn't even sure he cared anymore.

While online, he'd checked Kathryn's web station. Sycamore Hill at Sunrise ran a repeat.

"She's on her way." Ethan turned to his friends seated around the largest table in his dining area. Eli and Meg, Jackson and Kim, Ben and Emma, and Owen were here. Kathryn had withdrawn from them all, and the girls insisted they do something to show her their unwavering support. Ethan's break-in provided the perfect opportunity.

Ethan wasn't sure. It gave off *intervention vibes*, and Kathryn didn't need one. Owen insisted she was managing fine, but the girls were adamant. Ethan rubbed his midsection. His gut roiled more than the time he'd used outdated milk in a muffin recipe.

Within fifteen minutes, the bell above the door tinkled. Kathryn hurried inside, her face drawn into a worried frown as she scanned the room for Ethan.

Gloria followed.

Kathryn shrugged out of her light jacket and hung it on the hook by the door. "What's the plan?"

He moved toward her, but before he could speak, her eyes widened. All the color drained from her face. Her hand trembled as she gently brushed the backs of her fingertips against his cheek. "You're hurt."

He covered her hand with his, turning into her palm. "You're hurt, too."

She jerked her hand free and stepped back.

"Please sit." Meg motioned to a chair.

Kathryn didn't move, so Ethan nudged her toward the empty chair beside Kim. Kathryn narrowed her eyes but obediently sat down. "What's going on?"

Kim scooped up Kathryn's hand and squeezed it briefly before letting go. "We want you to know that we're here for you."

Kathryn snapped her gaze to Ethan's. Confusion colored her face.

"Someone broke into the shop." He backpedaled. "That's why everyone came here." He knew their focus on Kathryn was a bad idea.

"He called me to report it," Jackson said. "I brought Emma to treat him, and Kim tagged along."

"Where's Oliver?"

"My parents are in town," Kim answered.

"I showed up for work," Meg said. "That's how I heard about it."

"And we were in the office upstairs." Eli answered for him and Addison.

"After I made the report," Jackson said, "we started talking about you."

"Me?" Kathryn echoed. She blinked rapidly and clenched her fists in her lap. "He's been hurt. Someone broke into his business, probably the same someone who has been trying to sabotage him for days, and you talked about me?"

Ethan scooted a chair closer to Kathryn and sat in front of her. "We've seen the online comments. We love you, and we want to be here for you. Tell us how."

Kathryn's phone rang. The muffled sound from inside her purse crackled in the hostile air. Kathryn pushed to her feet, walked a few steps away, and turned her back on the group. "Hello?"

Ethan skimmed his gaze over each of his friends. This wasn't how it was supposed to go, and they looked just as flustered as he felt. Kathryn's clipped responses to whomever was on the other side of her call only cranked the tension dial in the room.

Kathryn disconnected, but she didn't turn to face them.

"What's wrong?"

Nothing.

His chair scraped against the floor as he stood. He gently laid his hand against her shoulder, and she spun. The flash in her eyes stole his breath.

"The publisher cancelled the coffee book deal. I've had too much bad press. But you all know about my bad press. It's why we're here, isn't it?"

Her reaction sent equal shots of defensiveness and thrill through him. He hadn't seen Kathryn so passionate, so human in years. This was the woman behind the mask. The woman he'd caught glimpses of, the one he remembered from camp but had since been hiding behind layers of film makeup. This was the Kathryn he fell in love with, and she wasn't the people-pleasing, self- deprecating public pushover she'd somehow morphed into over the years. And she was just getting started.

"You want to know why I haven't opened up? This is why. Here." She swept her arm across her body in a massive gesture. "I haven't changed. I'm still the same person I was last week and the week before that. The only thing that is different is that you all know I attend recovery meetings." She dragged her gaze over each one of them. "Ethan is the one in crisis, but you're all here to talk about my resolved past. None of this"—she gestured with both hands now, swirling them in front of her body as if she was waxing the floor—"is necessary. And it is exactly why I never told anyone."

Ethan didn't know whether to correct her or cheer. He went with correction. "They were here for me. They came right away."

She gave him a bitter smile. "But you didn't call me. Not until after."

And there it was. The reason for her pain. He could say it was because she shut him out yesterday. He could blame it on a lot of things. They had equal amounts of skin in this crime, but now wasn't the time to divide responsibility. He'd been so consumed with how her withdrawal yesterday had hurt him that he'd turned around and hurt her.

Kathryn strode to the coat hooks and snatched her jacket from the rack.

Ethan trailed her. "I should have come over yesterday. I should have insisted you let me. Then, I could have told you about my dad. You'd have been my first call today—"

"What about your dad?" Her knuckles whitened where they clutched her jacket.

Ethan briefly recapped his parents' ordeal, starting with the work accident and ending with bleak financial outlook.

"Let me look into it," Jackson interjected. "Crimes targeting seniors are on the rise, and I can pass this along to the cop heading up the division in Grander. Maybe they've heard of the scheme."

"Wait." Kathryn opened her photos on her phone. "I saw them in Grander. I have a picture of the guy who sold them the property. He was at the diner with your parents the day I was there." She found the image and held it up for Jackson and Ethan to see the image.

Jackson squinted. "Can you send me that? I think this is the guy the division has been watching. I'll forward it to him to confirm."

She tapped a few buttons. "Done." Kathryn shrugged into her coat and looked at Ethan. "I still need to go." But she said it gentler. Less angry. And she didn't move away when Ethan swayed close enough that his lips brushed against her hair.

"I'm sorry."

She lifted her face. Her wet eyes and rosy round spots high on her cheeks compounded his guilt.

"You can't fix this for me, Ethan." Her voice cracked. "You can't fix me. I need time to figure things out. Time to decide on my next steps."

Rejection sliced through him.

"I'm sorry." She slipped out the door without a kiss goodbye.

"We shouldn't have done it this way." Emma paced.

"I should have called her into the office and spoken with her alone."

"We shouldn't have done it at all," Ethan corrected her. "We should have trusted that Kathryn is a responsible woman who would have reached out if she needed us." Another awkward silence descended, but Ethan didn't feel the need to smooth this one over.

"I'd better file the report on your break-in," Jackson said.

"If I can take the computer, I might be able to create a patch that allows the program to run despite the trouble." Eli stood up as well.

"Go ahead." Ethan didn't care about his program anymore. His mind went with Kathryn.

The girls launched into a discussion. They proposed different strategies, such as creating an accountability system with one of them sending reminders if Kathryn started slipping back into unhealthy habits, creating goals that would keep her motivated and feeling successful.

Ethan didn't engage. They were treating her as if she had relapsed. She deserved better from them. From him. He felt desperate to make things right but wasn't sure that was even possible.

Nine

Kathryn turned off the main road and onto a side street. She rode with Gloria to the bakery, but now she wished she'd driven herself. The park was to her right, a school to her left, and her apartment a few more blocks away. She stomped instead of walked, not even aware of the force with which her feet hit the pavement until her shins began to ache. She slowed her pace, but her racing heart refused to decelerate.

There were a few people on park benches. A handful of cars drove by, and the schoolyard was empty. The morning sun hid behind the clouds and the grey pallor covering the neighbourhood matched her blackened mood. She tucked her hands into her pockets, kept her head down, and avoided eye contact, ignoring the weighty threats of the continually darkening sky. She needed to get home before someone recognized her, and the morning commuters would tumble from their houses any minute.

Shadows played peek-a-boo with the trees and shrubbery, but the shade didn't scare her. She'd survived worse darkness than a mid-summer morning storm, and she'd survive this.

Just breathe.

She inhaled the sweet, pungent, pre-gale aroma.

Listen.

The breeze intensified and rustled the branches. Leaves sanded against each other in a crispy spring symphony. Nature came alive with anticipation.

Feel.

Trepidation reverberated in her soul, increasing the pressure in her chest. But she was used to this. Unease. Indecision. Wanting to belong but learning you didn't quite fit. She was different, the girl not quite like the others. The familiarity of it was strangely comforting. Rejection felt safe. Recognizable. Like waters she could navigate because she had been swimming them her entire life. Even if the winds stirred into a funnel, ripped branches from the trees, and huffed and puffed their threats of violence, she was safe from the most dangerous threats. No one could hurt her if she didn't let them in.

Kathryn hitched her shoulders until the collar of her jacket covered her ears. She'd been sober for years. She'd made it through worse days without a drink, and she'd make it through today. It didn't matter that her fans had turned on her. It didn't matter that she'd lost the book deal. It didn't even matter that her friends thought she was vulnerable. She knew who she was, and that was enough.

But if it was enough, why did she devote her life to presenting a perfect Kathryn? Why did she set herself up to need the approval of others to succeed? Why wasn't what God said about her enough? *Was saved, is saved, will be saved* was far more powerful than *was an addict, is an addict, will always be an addict.*

A teardrop slid down her cheek, and she swiped it with the back of her hand. What went down at The Muffin Man felt like the intervention her university friends once staged. Her ego couldn't take it, wriggling and writhing like bolts of energy seeking ground. Her friends had good intentions, but their sincere concern landed on her already-wounded pride. Truth was catching up with her, and she couldn't outrun it anymore. *Lord, forgive me.* If she could just get to her apartment. Get inside before the sky opened and everything she'd been fighting to keep contained poured from the heavens.

The clouds moved and shrouded the earth under a blanket. Instantly, the neighborhood darkened. It was as if the forecasted storm heard her goal and received it as a personal challenge to beat. Sheet lightening flashed a megawatt grin, but the following thunder never came. The sense of urgency lifted. The heavens could play with the dimmer switch all it wanted, and the clouds could keep blowing smoke, but until the storm gave a thunderous war cry, it remained miles away.

"Kathryn?"

She jumped. She could just make out the figure of a person sitting on the park bench. A woman, judging from her shape, with a grip on a bottle wrapped in a plain brown paper bag that rested on the bench beside her.

"It's Tiff." The shadow sniffed and dragged a forearm across her face. A bright flash briefly illuminated Tiff's face; this time followed by a faint rumble in the distance. The storm inched closer.

"Are you okay?" Kathryn perched on the bench beside Tiff, the bottle of alcohol sandwiched between them. Now she was closer she could see her blotchy skin and puffy eyes. But the puffy eyes were clear, thank God.

Tiff's eyes dropped to the unopened booze and lingered. After a few quiet seconds she lifted them back to Kathryn's. "No."

"Then I'll sit with you until you are." Kathryn leaned back on the bench and stuffed her hands into her pockets. The wind picked up, snatching tendrils of her hair and stretching them out. Kathryn couldn't solve Tiff's addiction, but a powerful God could use her presence. Tiff didn't need Kathryn to say anything. Kathryn didn't need to pry. She just needed to stay.

Staying affirmed the gravity of this moment. Kathryn's gift was proximity. She was here, and she would not leave. Not even if the heavens opened and pounded their souls.

Kathryn patterned her response after the One perfect at the ministry of presence. Not just being passively present but being actively present. Compassion always moved Jesus to act. She moved the bottle from between them on the bench to her other side. She'd do whatever it took to stop a fellow sinner from taking a drink or popping a pill, and she'd do so while displaying the gentleness of her Savior.

If she could fill this gap for someone else, why did she bristle when her friends tried to fill it for her? She pushed her arrogance aside.

They sat quietly. The temperature dipped with each minute. Without a word being exchanged, Kathryn gave Tiff's hand a gentle squeeze. The warmth radiating from Tiff filled some of the emptiness inside Kathryn. They sat for what felt like an eternity.

Finally, Tiff broke the silence. "I didn't think it would be this hard."

"Gloria and Kim still won't hear you out?"

The first fat drops began to fall. "I made a counselling appointment with Kim, so I was able to speak with her."

"Sneaky." Kathryn leaned and bumped Tiff's shoulder with hers. She didn't know whether to be impressed or not.

A tiny smile broke Tiff's hard features. She tipped her head back and closed her eyes. The rain landed sporadically. One drop on the shoulder wicked away by the fabric of her shirt. Another on her head. A cold pellet landed on Kathryn's cheek and dripped like a tear. She wiped it away.

"After about twenty minutes," Tiff said, "Kim finally relaxed and engaged. We'll never be friends, and she'll never trust me, but she forgave me."

A bit of the weight compressing Kathryn's lungs lifted. She didn't squeeze Tiff's hand or even tug up her hood. The moment felt too fragile to move. "So why the purchase?" She lifted her chin toward the bottle.

Tiff's mouth twitched. "I went straight to Gloria's after meeting Kim. Well, straight to her parents. I apologized to them first."

"And?"

"And they heard me out. They said all the right things, but I didn't feel forgiven."

"Forgiveness is a decision," Kathryn said. "If they said they forgave you, believe them. Their feelings will come as they live out the reality of having forgiven." Kathryn hadn't known the Sycamores to be anything except honest and sincere. "Take today's victory. I hear that two people forgave you. That's a massive win."

"Maybe."

"So why the bottle?" she pressed.

"I couldn't reach Gloria, and it suddenly felt impossible to try."

"That might be my fault." Kathryn wasn't surprised Gloria refused to take Tiff's call. Her friend was still deeply hurt by Tiff's betrayal. But the real reason for Gloria's rejection was simpler than Tiff knew. "Gloria was with me. I lost the book deal. My fan base has tanked. And my friends just held an intervention of sorts."

Tiff's eyes snapped to Kathryn's. "Are you drinking again?"

"No. But everyone just found out about my past. They're working through the discovery."

"How did that make you feel?"

She shrugged and averted her eyes. "Like I let everyone down. Like I'm the same screw-up that nearly threw away my life." Kathryn picked up the paper bag and pulled out the bottle. Her gaze dropped to the label. "I feel like I'll never get my act together, even though I've been sober for years. Even though I can hold this bottle right now and not want to drink."

They both stared at it. It was amazing that such a tiny object held the power to destroy lives.

"My morning devotion was on Psalm 69," Kathryn said. "In it, the waters came up to the psalmist's neck. He's sinking. There's no foothold. He's weary. He's waiting on God." Her voice cracked. Why could she apply all the right things to Tiff but not know them for herself? "'Answer me,' the psalmist says. Not because he deserves it. Not because he has earned it, but because the steadfast love of the Lord is good."

"I'm familiar with it," Tiff nodded. "I might not be able to quote the psalm, but I know it ends with an expectation of deliverance."

"Deliverance from this?" Kathryn lifted the bottle between them as the distinct click of a camera sounded in the bushes. She froze. "Who's there?"

A rustle. Then a figure darted out. Kathryn jumped to her feet, but Tiff grabbed her arm. "Let it go."

The figure ran off, disappearing into the neighborhood. Kathryn glared at Tiff. "I could have caught him!"

"To what end? We don't know who that was or what they were doing here, but we both know how easy it is for things to turn ugly if we give into our anger or our pain."

Kathryn closed her eyes. An image of tomorrow's potential headlines flashed before her. *Two misfits drown their sorrows in Sycamore Park.* That would convince her friends she was fine.

Kathryn gripped the skinny neck of the bottle. Every muscle in her body tensed. Even though it was only a few seconds, it felt like an eternity before she made up her mind. "We don't need this." She unscrewed the cap and emptied it on the ground.

Tiff nodded approvingly, but she bit her bottom lip as the bottle drained.

Kathryn slid the now empty container back into the damp paper sleeve. "Everything will be all right. No matter what happens, everything will be fine because there's light at the end of every tunnel."

"What if that light's a train?"

"What if it's hope?"

Tiff's gaze dropped.

"Maybe it doesn't matter if it's a train as long as you're not standing on the tracks when it comes through."

Tiff stuffed her hands into her pockets. "I don't know what I would have done today. Thanks for stopping. For caring."

Kathryn got it. It didn't matter how many years had passed, and it didn't matter that the cravings themselves had weakened. Her body remembered the warm burn of alcohol and its promise to help her forget.

"You need a distraction. Why don't you film for me today?"

"I thought Gloria was filming?"

"She was, but she and Owen have hospital visitations in Grander." Besides, Kathryn wanted a bit more space from her friends. She needed to figure out her next move now that the book deal was gone. And since she would most certainly lose the fan competition, she had to decide if salvaging her career was something she even wanted.

"Thanks."

Kathryn nodded. "Anytime." Because it was about more than her. She finally saw that.

Ten

Eli than strode down the sidewalk. Streetlamps illuminated the early dusk. He'd spent the day chewing on everything that had happened. After Jackson filed the report of the break in, Ethan sent Meg home, because he decided to keep the shop closed until he could be sure his unwanted visitor hadn't sabotaged anything else on his visit.

Ethan checked in with his parents. His dad was recovering from his fall, and surprisingly had little to say about Ethan's predicament. The retirement scam had served his dad a huge helping of humble pie, and Dad kept his business advice to himself.

Still, Ethan knew if this roasting thing was ever going to cut the mustard, he had to expose his tormentor. So much had occurred in the last few days that his mind spun, and since he processed best in the kitchen, that's where he was headed. He'd given Kathryn the space she'd asked for and kept his distance all day. But how long was enough? He itched to seek her out, to let her know that he loved her no matter what, but the velvet box that would prove his love was still tucked inside the cupboard at the bakery.

Mom had asked him why he hadn't given Kathryn the ring, and she didn't agree that he needed to make the proposal *an experience*. She kept saying he should just propose, but he couldn't. It had to be perfect. Kathryn lived online, and this had to be social media worthy. Besides, Kathryn was the one life choice his dad approved of.

No, that wasn't quite right. Dad had said he was proud of how Ethan researched the coffee business before investing. If their relationship was ever going to improve, Ethan needed to start taking his dad at his word and believe him.

Thunder rolled. The stormy day had spilled into the evening, and it suited his mood. Dark, black, and angry. Angry at the people harassing Kathryn online. Angry at the people messing with his bakery. Angry at, well, everything. Nothing had gone according to plan. He couldn't stop what was happening to Kathryn. He couldn't fix his relationship with his dad. He couldn't repair the broken software or stop whoever had targeted his shop. But he could keep things simple and do one thing right. What could be simpler or more right than the Muffin Man proposing by hiding the ring inside a muffin?

Ethan unlocked the bakery door and went directly to the cupboard. He removed the ring and slipped it into his front pocket. Another stormy rumble vibrated in his chest. If Ethan didn't know for certain that Addison and Eli had also worked from home today, he'd have thought they were dragging their office furniture around upstairs.

Ethan patted his pocket as he strode to the kitchen to set the oven to preheat. As he collected ingredients, a sense of unease settled over him. Something was wrong. The early aroma of freshly roasting beans wafted in the air. His gaze zipped to the lit green light on the coffee roaster. Why was it on? He wasn't roasting anything. He fumbled the muffin cups and dropped them. As he bent over to retrieve them, a deafening roar exploded. The sharp sting of a blast radiated through his body. It knocked Ethan off balance and threw him down. Pain and shock hit like a wall. His ears rang. His chest ached, and a thick fog clouded his vision. Everything moved in a hazy, slow motion.

An eerie silence descended, contrasted only by the roar in his head.

Ethan didn't know how long he lay there. There was no pain. The counter he'd been crouched behind somewhat protected him. A penetrating chill numbed him when he should feel heat. He was unable to move— unable to think—until the throbbing of his heart shifted from his chest to his ears. And then another sound— the shrill squealing of an alarm. He rolled to his side and gagged. A sickening scent swirled. The wind tugged his hair.

Wind inside the bakery?

A face appeared. Sudden light. The warmth of hands felt good as they prodded his body. "Ethan!" someone repeated.

It seemed far away, but the feet were right in front of him. *Why was he eye level with feet?*

Jackson's face came into focus. His lips moved.

Jackson had said something, but with his ears ringing, Ethan couldn't understand. He blinked. He pushed himself up.

Jackson grasped him under his arms and helped him. "We gotta get you out of here."

Ethan pieced it together from, "We gotta . . . out . . . here . . ."

Finally upright, Ethan staggered. The roaster had literally exploded. Tables were overturned and hunks of machinery had wedged into the counter he'd been behind. He could have died. Or Meg. Or Eli and Addison. If he'd been open—

He swayed and pressed the butt of his palm to his forehead. *Lord, thank you for protecting us.*

"Is anyone else in here?" Jackson yelled.

Ethan shook his head.

Jackson guided him through the door that wasn't. The blast had blown the glass into pieces. Ethan hobbled across the street. People had started to gather. Emma waited under the covered patio of the restaurant across the street, her black medical bag clutched in her hands. Someone had pulled the tables apart to make space for an examination. "Sit him here."

Ethan couldn't do anything but obey.

"Can you hear me?"

He shook his head. That hurt. He winced. That also hurt. "Not well."

Jackson hovered as Emma's hands moved over Ethan's limbs, periodically asking with exaggerated enunciation if her touch was painful. Between reading her lips, and the few words that waded through the hum in his ears, Ethan was able to follow the conversation. "You don't appear to have any broken bones, and everything else seems in working order, although you're going to have some impressive bruising tomorrow."

Jackson sagged at Emma's assessment and his eyes briefly closed. "I'm gonna see what I can learn. You're lucky I was here. Someone had called to report a potential break-in at the bakery, and I had just pulled up when the place exploded."

Ethan only caught the odd word. *Lucky* was one of them. He nodded, although it wasn't a word he'd have chosen.

The Lord gives and the Lord takes away. There was nothing in there about luck.

It could have been much worse. They could have been open and serving customers.

Ethan tried to stand, but Emma held him down. "Not until

I'm finished." She flicked a pen light into his eyes before slipping it into her chest pocket. Then she held out her hands. "Can you squeeze them?"

He wasn't sure what she was assessing, but she seemed pleased, so he must have passed the test.

She crouched at his feet and slipped her hands under his shoes. "Can you press down like you're pushing on two pedals?"

He did.

"Now walk to the edge of the patio and back." She motioned the desired pathway with her hands.

He felt her stare drilling into him with every step.

Seemingly satisfied, she helped him sit back down. After popping the earpieces to her stethoscope into her ears, she pressed the disc against his chest. She listened intently. How she heard anything over the growing crowd and the sirens was beyond him. She looped the scope around her neck and smiled. Her first smile.

Relief rocketed through him. He was going to be okay. "How did you get here so fast?"

"Ben listens to the police scanner. He heard the report about the break-in. We were coming to check it out."

We. Ethan looked around. Ben was snapping pictures.

A spectacular flash lit the sky, and a thunderclap made Emma jump. The crowd pushed closer despite the sudden downpour unleashed by heaven. Constable Stuart James had arrived and beat the growing crowd of spectators back with a scowl that should have terrified them. It softened only when he looked at Ethan.

"Can I follow Jackson?" Ethan asked Emma.

She nodded her consent. "But we're going to the hospital as soon as the ambulance arrives."

Ethan followed Jackson's path. The exterior walls still stood, but much of the glass was gone. The dining room damage looked mostly cosmetic. Tables and chairs were overturned, but nothing was charred. The sprinklers never even came on. The mess radiated from where the coffee roaster had stood. As if on autopilot, he catalogued the damage. Twisted metal was strewn haphazardly in the room. An acrid smell lingered. The kitchen was okay. The counter he'd been crouched behind had moved at least a few inches. Canisters of flour, chocolate chips, and sugar rolled on the floor. He rubbed his chest.

Jackson frowned, and it made his chest hurt more. "Could have been gunpowder in the roaster."

"Gunpowder?" He had to have misheard him. He tugged his earlobe.

"If I'm right," Jackson said, "when the roaster was turned on, the heat caused the gas to expand, causing the explosion."

"Ethan? Ethan?" Kathryn's panicked cry cut through the static in his ears. Kathryn threw her arms around his neck. "Emma called me." She raked her gaze over him. "She said you're okay."

"I am." He burrowed his face into her hair.

"But your bakery—"

He crushed her to his chest. "I know."

Eleven

Kathryn wiped her face on Ethan's shoulder and thanked the Lord for the millionth time that he was okay. When she had rounded the corner and first seen the bakery's damage, her legs buckled. Tiff had practically carried her to Emma, who pointed out Ethan and Jackson inside the bakery.

"I can't do this," Kathryn had said to Emma. Her heart raced. She was having a heart attack. That had to be it.

Emma did a quick assessment, then squeezed Kathryn's upper arms and looked into her eyes, nodding affirmatively as she spoke. "You can. Just take the next step. Do the next thing."

Kathryn mirrored her friend's nodding and then looked at Ethan picking through the wreckage. He was the next thing. Being there for him. Making sure he was okay.

And he was, but the bakery wasn't as lucky.

Kathryn gently touched Ethan's cheek. "Should I call your parents? Someone should watch you through the night and ensure you're really okay."

"He's going to the hospital when the ambulance gets here." Emma had followed Kathryn across the street. She watched them so closely Kathryn briefly wondered if she was withholding a medical concern, but immediately discarded the notion. That would be unethical, and however difficult, Emma always made the ethical choice.

"Good. That's good he's going to the hospital." Kathryn echoed. "I'll call your parents from there. There's no need from them to come to Sycamore Hill to only turn around and go back to Grander's hospital."

"Kathryn? Ethan?" Gloria shouted from the perimeter Stuart had set up. Owen stood behind her with a hand on her shoulder. It was impossible to miss how Gloria frowned at Tiff, who had stayed on the scene but stood off to the side in the rain.

The winch in Kathryn's stomach cranked. Even here, in the wreckage of Ethan's life, Gloria struggled with Tiff's presence. The air practically crackled.

Kim joined Gloria at the barricade, also grimacing in Tiff's direction. Her friends didn't even try to hide their feelings. They probably thought they were being supportive, even protective of Kathryn, but it roused an unexplainable disappointment in her.

"I need you"—Jackson jutted his chin toward Emma —"and you"—he turned to Jackson and included Kathryn in his stare— "to leave. This isn't a tourist attraction. It's a crime scene."

"Crime?" Kathryn repeated. "It wasn't an accident?" The winch cinched tighter.

"Out." Jackson pointed.

"I came as soon as I heard," Kim said as they approached.

"We were just getting back from Grander. What happened? We heard something like an explosion," Owen said.

Ethan ruffled his already mussed hair. "I'm not sure. I was

going to bake muffins when I noticed the roaster was on. That's the last thing I remember."

"You didn't turn it on?"

Ethan shook his head.

The rain failed to deter onlookers, and the sidewalk and people holding umbrellas of all shapes and sizes soon sprinkled the area like imperfect candy sprinkles on a sugar cookie.

Officer Stuart lifted the crime scene tape and allowed their group to stay on the bakery-side of the boundary. The flimsy barricade was the only thing preventing the crowd from descending on Ethan.

Tiff was on the other side.

Their gazes met. Kathryn nodded in response to her unspoken question. Tiff's chin lifted, and she stepped back, letting the outraged crowd swallow her. Kathryn caught bits and pieces.

"I heard it was premeditated."

"Who would do this?"

"It sounded like gunshots."

"It has to be someone we know."

Ben wove through the throng, gathering quotes for the newspaper, reminding Kathryn that she should have been recording. It was her job. But the idea of capitalizing on Ethan's devastation made her stomach heave, followed by a nauseating thought that was almost as distressing as the destruction. *Was that how her friends felt when she recorded them for the news?*

Kathryn had covered the drug scandal that smeared Gloria's name. She filmed Meg holding the protest sign in front of a heritage tree with Eli chanting beside her. When the town divided over the sledding hill, Kathryn was there with her camera, even catching on film the horrid moment when Emma broke her collarbone. And most recently, she'd covered the story of Oliver's kidnapping and return. Her stomach pitched, and she hugged her waist.

As if he sensed her distress, Ethan pulled her into his arms again. She turned into him and couldn't stop the tears, not when he pressed his lips to her temple. Not even when he whispered that it was going to be okay. She was supposed to be consoling him, but everything had flipped.

Emma leaned in to whisper, "This is the next thing. Grief. It's okay."

Kathryn mourned Ethan's loss and her own insensitivity, and sobbed in relief that every one of her friends were standing here beside her, safe and unharmed.

Jackson exited the bakery and tacked crime scene tape over the door's frame before addressing the growing crowd. "If anyone saw anything, or knows anything, please come and speak to me before leaving."

Clara Brisbane flapped her arms from the front of the pack. "There was a man," she said, in partial hysterics. "I called about the break-in."

Jackson lifted the perimeter tape so Clara could come closer.

"He was wearing dark jeans. I saw him through the bakery's window and then on the street right after the explosion." Clara wrung her hands in front of her thick middle. "Are you all okay?" Her worried gaze dragged over each one of them, lingering on Meg.

Of course, Clara was concerned about Meg and the baby. They'd forged a deep, almost familial bond over the last year.

"We're okay. I wasn't here when it happened." Meg rested her hand over her midsection.

Clara's fidgeting relaxed.

"Did this man say anything?" Jackson drew Clara's focus back.

Mrs. Brisbane shook her head. "No, but he was watching the bakery. He came out from the alley as Ethan went in from the front. It was like he knew it was going to happen any second. When Ethan turned on the lights, he started to cross the street like he was going to knock on the door, but then the windows blew out." Her gaze bounced between Jackson and Ethan. "I've never seen him before."

If Clara didn't recognize the man, that meant he wasn't a local. Clara knew everyone.

"We need to find this guy," Jackson said. "If he's not involved, he may be able to tell us what happened." Jackson pointed her toward Stuart and waved to get the man's attention. "Can you get her full statement?"

Stuart gave a two-fingered salute.

A horn beeped, and the crowd parted to let the ambulance from Grander through. "It's time," Emma said.

"I'll go with you." Kathryn followed Ethan to the ambulance.

Emma shared her assessment on Ethan with the medic opening the bay doors and helped Ethan inside. Her report sent a million and one waves of gratefulness through Kathryn. It could have been so much worse.

Kathryn joined Ethan in the ambulance once they got him sitting on the gurney and Emma had exited. Emma reached back and squeezed Kathryn's hand. "I'm praying."

"Thank you."

Emma left.

"I'm Simon," the medic said. "I'll be with you the whole way to Grander. This is my partner, Cassie. She's driving."

Cassie appeared at the back of the open bay doors and gave a little wave.

Kathryn bit the inside of her cheek. Simon's laid-back tone

was a touch too mellow. Shouldn't Cassie be behind the wheel with the sirens screaming, racing them to the hospital? Shouldn't Simon be doing something more? But she didn't voice any of that. Instead, she said, "Hi."

Simon maintained strong eye contact with her, and she realized he was doing something. He was trying to assess whether or not he'd have two patients to treat. After a few more uncomfortable seconds, he shifted his full attention to Ethan. "Can you hold your arms out horizontally, palms up?"

Ethan did.

"Good. Now close your eyes."

It seemed like a preschool game. *Simon says hold out your arms. Simon says close your eyes.*

Simon tapped Ethan's shoulder.

Ethan opened his eyes, and his gaze immediately found hers. "It's not your fault," he said.

Her chin quivered. "Ever since I let my name stand in the contest—"

"Not your fault," he repeated.

"Lay on your back." Simon helped Ethan into a supine position and bent his knees to thirty degrees. He flexed both of Ethan's knees and rested one on the gurney. He extended the other and allowed it to drop. Then he repeated the steps with the other leg. He continued with his evaluation as Cassie handed him instruments and added the occasional comment.

"Is he okay?" Kathryn asked.

"I think so," Cassie answered. "We need to take him to the hospital for further testing. Would you like to ride in the front with me?"

"Okay." She gently pressed her lips to Ethan's. "I'll see you when we get there."

Kathryn buckled into the front passenger seat as Cassie put the ambulance in gear. She didn't turn on the sirens. That had to be a good sign.

The ride to Grander was awkward despite the easy-going attitude of Simon's partner. Cassie had fallen silent when it became clear Kathryn didn't want to chat. All Kathryn wanted was a promise that Ethan would be okay, but she knew the woman couldn't give her that. So, there was nothing to say.

They drove out of the storm. Eventually, even the pinging of raindrops ceased. The clouds kept rolling and an occasional thunderclap rumbled, but it sounded more and more distant each time.

The ambulance rocked as Cassie stopped in front of the hospital's emergency entrance.

Kathryn hopped out. She immediately grabbed hold of Ethan's hand and walked alongside the gurney as they entered the hospital. A doctor joined the team, and Simon updated him.

"I want a CT head and chest X-ray," the doctor said.

Ethan tightened his grip on her hand.

They aimed the gurney toward double doors, and a nurse stopped Kathryn. She lost her hold on Ethan, and before she could react, he was gone.

"It'll take about thirty minutes for the test, and then the doctor will need to review the results. You can wait there." The nurse pointed to the waiting room they'd breezed past. "Or, the cafeteria is open."

Kathryn's chest was too tight to answer. She watched through the window in the door until Ethan disappeared around the corner. Then she made her way to the cafeteria. After buying a coffee, she chose a table in the back. With her elbows on the table, she pressed her forehead into the butt of her palms.

"It'll be okay." Kathryn had to believe Ethan would be fine and his business would recover. They couldn't give up on The

Muffin Man. Ethan came alive in his bakery in a way that Kathryn could only hope to imitate one day. She enjoyed her job. She did good work. But she didn't thrive in it like Ethan. When he interacted with customers, created new recipes, or catered custom orders for events, she knew she witnessed the fulfillment of 1 Corinthians 10:31. *Whether you eat or drink or whatever you do, do all to the glory of God.* Ethan baked to the glory of God. His business was his platform for serving others. It was never just about him. He paused and prayed with staff and customers, he generously sponsored a children's soccer team, and he hosted game nights for Sycamore Hill Community Church's youth group. The bakery had to be salvageable. The town needed it.

Just do the next thing. Kathryn sucked in a breath. The next thing was hard.

She called Ethan's parents and looped them in. She didn't know how long she sat there staring at the coffee she never drank, but when her phone dinged, she assumed it was Shannon and Grant. They were probably here and looking for her. When she glanced at the screen, her heart seized.

Distasteful social media comments were creating an explosion bigger than the one that took out The Muffin Man. One person even posted song lyrics in the past tense. *Did you know the muffin man, the muffin man, the muffin man?* She tossed her phone on the table and pulled up her shirt collar to cover her chin and nose. A bitter tang filled her mouth. How were these sorts of comments the fruit of her labor? What was she giving her life to? How did 1 Corinthians 10:31 play out in her world?

"Kathryn?"

Her head snapped up. "Mr. and Mrs. Roberts." She stood. "They took Ethan for some tests. He should be back anytime."

"He's already back. We spoke with the doctor."

Already back? How long had she been sitting here?

"They're releasing him. He has to follow up with an ears, nose, and throat specialist and the family doctor in a week."

She sagged. *Thank you, Lord, for one million and two reasons.*

Shannon wrapped an arm around Kathryn's shoulder and guided her out of the cafeteria. "This has been a long day already. Why don't you come home with us? It's almost dinner time, and you shouldn't be alone, and Ethan's staying with us for a few days so we can watch him."

In less than thirty minutes, they were in Shannon and Grant's living room, drinking hot beverages. Gloria promised to pack an overnight bag for Kathryn and drop it off later. In the meantime, Kathryn had changed into a borrowed pair of jogging pants and a hoodie. Everyone looked exhausted. Shannon and Grant peppered Ethan with questions, but Kathryn couldn't live through the telling another time. "Why don't I make us something to eat?" She stood. "How do omelettes sound?" Kathryn had been in the Roberts' home enough times to feel comfortable making the offer.

"That would be lovely, thank you." Shannon smiled at her.

Kathryn went into the kitchen, pulled out a small cutting board, and started chopping an onion and a few small peppers for omelettes. She opened the fridge and rummaged around, looking for the salsa. She knocked over a corked bottle of wine, and the chaos in her mind screamed to a halt. Desire hit like a wave. It happened like this sometimes. Coming from nowhere and stealing the breath from her lungs. Her fingers tingled at the memory of dumping the cheap wine with the twist-off cap in the park. She felt a sharp pang of regret, the kind she hadn't felt in a very long time.

Kathryn slammed the fridge. Now working quickly, she sliced through the vegetables until they were finely diced. More than finely diced. Minced would be more accurate. Anything to keep her mind off the smooth feel of the glass bottle, the crackle of the paper encasing it, the sweet scent of its contents gushing over the rim as she dumped it.

"It's not going to help." She had to convince her betraying senses. "One drink *can* hurt me. It *will* hurt me."

Her hands trembled. The bottle pulled like clickbait.

Twelve

An ache tightened the back of Ethan's throat. When he left his parents in the living room to check on Kathryn, he didn't expect to find her like this. Harsh fluorescent lights illuminated her pale skin, and a single bottle of booze sat on the table in front of her. She wasn't touching it. The cork was in place. But she was fixated on it. Tension thickened the air. He didn't know anything about addiction, but he knew in his gut this moment mattered. What he said and did next would impact their relationship forever.

Ethan moved as if he were approaching a frightened animal. He knelt on the floor by her chair. He didn't touch her. He kept his voice gentle and low. "Kathryn?"

Her gaze zipped to his. The cord in her neck throbbed with a pulse. Her hands—that had been clasped in her lap, writhing and twisting—stilled. She looked terrified.

If Ethan had one wish, it would be to melt the fear from her face and the anxiety from her body and replace it with confidence and joy. His single wish would be for her, not his destroyed business. He knew enough about addiction to understand he couldn't fight it for her, but he could stand with her. He would do everything within his power to ensure that she knew she would never again stand alone.

Kathryn's eyes brimmed, but determination shone through as well. She dampened her lips and nodded slowly, as if coming to some kind of understanding in her head. With her chin high, she inhaled hard. "I saw this in the fridge."

He remained quiet.

"I wouldn't be able to sleep here knowing this bottle was here. So, I took it out."

He reached for her hand. She didn't pull away, and he counted that as a win.

"Then I realized it wasn't mine. Not mine to drink. Not mine to dump." She shrugged, snorted, and let out a raw laugh all at once. "Then I didn't know what to do."

He swallowed the lump wedged in his throat. "Thank you for sharing that. I imagine it's not easy."

She pressed her lips together until they became a thin, white line. Pinching her eyes closed, she took another breath before shaking free of his hold. She pushed back from the table and stood. She didn't reach for the bottle, but Ethan could see the struggle.

After a shaky step backward, she strode to the counter. She leaned her hip against it and folded her arms across her chest. "I've ruined everything." Her voice wobbled. "Maybe you'd be better off without me."

Ethan's heart jolted. He couldn't imagine life without Kathryn. He moved in front of her. The energy humming between them could have powered the house. He looked into her eyes, trying to convey love and strength. "Never," he said softly.

"I'd never be better without you. If I had to pick between the shop and you, I choose you. Every time and in every way."

A sad smile curled her lips. "I've spent my whole life believing no one would ever choose me."

His head swayed in disagreement. "Not true. Tiff chose you. Your friends chose you. And most importantly, God chooses you. Every drink. Every poor decision. Every sin. It's been nailed to the cross because He chose you."

Kathryn caught her lower lip between her teeth. Her features softened, and the tears she'd been blinking back rolled down her cheeks.

"He knows you fully." Ethan spoke as he approached slowly. "Every thought, every desire, every action, and every failure. He loves you anyway." Ethan snagged her hand and tugged gently, giving her enough time to pull away if she desired. When she didn't resist him, he wrapped his arms around her. *Lord, help me to love her well.*

She buried her face into his chest. They stood like that, quietly and contentedly, until she whispered into his shirt, "What if I never fully recover? What if every crisis brings it back?"

She didn't have to define *it*. It was the secret she'd carried for far too long. It was the thing she'd allowed to define her. The thing she wanted no one to know but now everyone knew. He tipped his head and spoke into her hair. "Then we face it together."

He wanted to say something more, but words failed him. He wanted to tell her he understood her pain, that he'd take it away if he could. Overwhelmed by a sense of responsibility to protect and guide and love her no matter what, he tightened his arms and let his presence be his offering. Ethan rubbed small circles on her back as she wept, crying so hard he wondered if this was the first time she'd ever let herself grieve.

"Thank you for not leaving," she whispered. "For not believing the worst."

He cupped her chin in his palm and lifted her face. "You don't have to thank me." He tucked a strand of hair around her ear with his other hand. "I love you."

She wiped away the last drop of dampness from her cheeks and straightened up just as someone cleared their throat in the doorway.

His father stood frozen in place. His face lit with worry but also filled with awe. He'd held back Ethan's mother, who seemed about to burst. When Dad let her go, Mom rushed to Kathryn, but Dad held his gaze with a look Ethan couldn't quite identify. "You're a good man, Ethan. I'm proud of you."

Ethan couldn't breathe. He didn't realize how desperately he'd wanted to hear those words from his father until an invisible weight lifted from his chest. *His dad was proud of him.* Not for swinging a hammer or for fixing a car, but for loving Kathryn well. Mom had been right all along.

Mom fussed over Kathryn as Dad quietly and unobtrusively uncorked the wine and dumped it down the sink. Ethan's entire body relaxed. His parents chose Kathryn, too.

"Do you want to talk about it?" His mom led Kathryn back to the table and offered her a seat. Dad put on the kettle and removed hot chocolate and several varieties of tea from the cupboard. It was the most domestic action Ethan had ever seen his dad take.

Kathryn explained everything—the pranks pulled on her during the contest, the bullying online, the cancelation of her book, and Tiff showing up and complicating her life. She said things Ethan didn't even know. It was as if now that the secret was out, it all had to come out.

Once Kathryn finished, she smiled. Really smiled. Her eyes

looked lighter and her countenance brighter. "I had no idea how heavy that was to carry alone. I'd gotten used to it."

"We aren't meant to do life alone," Dad said. "We need each other."

Ethan's mouth dropped. Who was this man? His dad never spoke of community or needing others unless it was to fill the roster of a ball team.

"Considering everything that's happened at the bakery," Dad continued, "do you think the police should know about the online harassment? It seems small when we consider it in isolation, but altogether—" Dad shook his head. "I don't believe in coincidences."

"The timing is suspicious," Kathryn agreed, "but the person did nothing illegal."

Ethan's cell phone rang. "It's Jackson." After a quick conversation, they disconnected. "He wants us to come back to the bakery in the morning."

"We can drop you off, or if you prefer, we can drive to Sycamore Hill tonight to pick up one of your vehicles."

"All of us," Ethan clarified. "Jackson wants to see all of us."

Thirteen

T he time it took for Ethan's dad to find a parking spot gave Kathryn a few extra minutes to settle the butterflies in her stomach. They had to park two blocks over from the bakery, which didn't make sense. The road should have been cleared by now.

"Look at the people." Shannon's mouth gaped. "This can't be because of the bakery. Not still."

"I think it is." Kathryn pointed to the crime tape that still barricaded a section of sidewalk. The street was clear, however, traffic slowed as gawkers crept by.

As they hurried down the sidewalk, the persistent scent of dust clung to the back of Kathryn's throat. It was faint, like the lingering aroma of a campfire. Even the air felt too warm for a late spring day, despite a weak breeze coming from the direction of the pond.

Kathryn snuck a glance at Ethan. He remained quiet. But the closer they got to the bakery, the tighter he squeezed her hand. It felt good to be needed. To be the person giving something rather than being the one always taking it.

Any doubts about Ethan's commitment to her had vanished yesterday, wiped away by his gentleness and love. But alongside that certainty came conviction. Kathryn should never have doubted him or her friends. She'd allowed the enemy a foothold in her mind, and he'd thrown a party. Her cheeks burned just thinking of how she sat in front of the bottle debating, wondering, desiring, and hating herself. The enemy condemned God's children, but Kathryn was learning there was a massive difference between conviction and condemnation. If she'd learned anything in her battle for sobriety, it was that the Lord convicted his children to prompt repentance and change. His lovingkindness led to a repentance that removed guilt, not heaped it on.

Jackson, Stuart, Ben, and Tiff waited outside the bakery on the sidewalk. As soon as he saw them approaching, Stuart met them at the boundary and pulled the crime scene tape aside to let them into the inner sanctum. Someone had knocked out the remaining shards of glass that clung to the window frame, leaving just the rectangular opening. Someone had also cleared the glass that had spilled onto the street. Several people moved about inside. Tiff held a camera.

Ben pointed at it. "She might have video of the guy Clara Brisbane mentioned."

"I called Clara over as well." Jackson looked at his watch. "She'll be here any minute."

"You were filming?" Kathryn blinked several times. She hadn't asked Tiff to record anything.

"I hope you don't mind that I recorded for you. I wasn't sure what you might need for your show."

"It gets better." Ben leaned forward, eagerness spilling out. "Tell them the rest."

At Ben's encouraging nod, Tiff grew more animated and confident. "After we met in Grander at the coffee shop, I secretly set up a nighttime camera to catch you coming and going from the bakery."

Kathryn gasped. "You never told me that."

Tiff's cheeks reddened. "I was only going to tell you if I caught something worthwhile for your show." She lifted her shoulders sweetly. "I didn't know I couldn't record audio."

"Either way, her ignorance might have broken the case," Jackson said.

Tiff cast a quick look in Jackson's direction. "I didn't realize the potential legal implications until Jackson told me." She shrugged. "Reality TV shows do it all the time."

"With consent," Stuart said.

Tiff tugged her lips between her teeth. Jackson took the camera from her and began scrolling through the feed.

"Officer McGregor!" Clara waved her hand from outside the crime scene tape.

"I'll get her." Stuart let Clara in and escorted her to their group.

"Is this who you saw?" Jackson turned the screen to Clara.

"Yes!" Clara's sausage log of a forehead curl bounced with her head bobbing.

"Do you recognize him?" Jackson turned the screen so Kathryn and Ethan could see it.

The hope that had been building in Kathryn's chest plummeted. "No, I don't."

"I might." Ethan squinted. "Can you zoom in on his collar?"

Jackson rotated the camera to Tiff, who zoomed in for him.

Ethan jabbed his finger at the screen. "He's wearing the same pin on his collar."

"Who?" Kathryn asked.

"He came to The Muffin Man the day we found those stones mixed in with the coffee beans. He said he was there to buy a coffee."

Kathryn's jaw loosened. "I remember him. He tried to push in when you said you were closed."

Ethan took a step away and spun on his heel. After a few seconds, he faced them again. "Why would he target me?"

"Maybe he showed up to watch the fallout of his handiwork, and when you closed the shop to livestream for my channel, you robbed him of that?"

"Do you know who he is?" Shannon asked.

Shannon and Grant had been so quiet that Kathryn had forgotten they were there.

"No, but his information is on the shop's computer. I appeased the guy with a punch card for free coffee, so when he came in to claim the first one, he had to register. He's been back several times."

"Where's the computer now?" Grant looked dubiously at the shop.

"Addison and Eli took it home to try and fix the program."

Kathryn's gaze collided with Ethan's and held. His whole demeanor changed as understanding and then relief flooded his frame. "They took it home. They'll be able to recover the information. We got him."

"It's unlikely he registered with the real name." Jackson frowned.

"Why would he do this?" Ethan blew out a frustrated sound and Kathryn threaded her fingers with his. A small part of her still feared the bakery misfortune was connected to the contest.

Ben's gaze drilled into her. "I interviewed this guy. He runs the wholesale coffee bean business, Cool Beans. I should have noticed something was off."

Ethan jerked at the company's name. "I went there. I had considered ordering my beans from him before I decided to invest in a roaster."

"Tell me more about this place." Jackson jotted down the company name.

"I didn't meet this guy. I spoke with a woman. Cool Beans is a little more than halfway between Grander and here. It's a small business. They roast beans in the garage and ship their product locally."

"And I was promoting your marketing plan to ship coffee bean orders directly to customers," Kathryn finished. It was all starting to make sense.

"I got the feeling he'd been watching Ethan for a while," Ben said. "Worried some of his marketing strategies were going to over-shadow him."

"But I wasn't a threat to him. I wasn't moving into the whole-sale market. I was targeting customers, not businesses."

"There is no way he could have known that," said Kathryn.

Ben's mouth tightened. "I should have seen this coming."

"It's not your fault," Ethan told him.

"That's what I keep saying." Emma looped her arm through Ben's. Gloria, Owen, and Kim had exited the bakery behind her. It was almost comical, the way they filed through the doorway despite the huge opening where the window used to be.

"That's enough for me to track him down and bring him in for questioning."

Tiff's mouth tightened as they neared. But, instead of pushing Tiff out, the group widened the circle and let her in.

Kathryn welled up. There was something different about her friends. Something that felt helpful and not judgmental. But she couldn't put her finger on what had changed. They were acting like they always did. Maybe the person who changed was her?

Maybe what she previously saw as judgemental and harsh was her looking at her friends through the wrong lens?

"What is everyone doing here?" Ethan's eyebrows shot up. He looked at Jackson. "I thought the crime scene tape meant you were still investigating."

"No, we're done, but your dad asked us to leave it up for a bit. At least until the new window goes in."

"My dad?" Ethan echoed.

"I'm probably needed inside." Grant's mysterious smile revealed nothing as he turned to slip into the store, but Shannon's shiny cheeks and twinkling eyes looked more mischievous than a toddler sneaking a cookie.

"Hold up." Jackson stopped them. "I have something for you as well."

Grant stuffed his hands into his front pockets and rolled onto his toes and then back onto his heels. Kathryn noted how he avoided looking at Ethan. Something was afoot.

"Thanks to the picture Kathryn took that morning at the diner in Grander, we caught the guy who scammed you."

Shannon gasped and grabbed onto Grant's arm.

Jackson grinned. "I contacted the fraud unit, and they had a lead on the guy. They caught up with him. The judge will likely suspend the sentence if he repays everybody, and guys like this usually do to avoid jail.

Thankfully, he hasn't spent the funds yet, so you'll likely get it all back."

Mom threw her hands into the air. "Hallelujah! Thank you, Jackson!"

Jackson grinned. "Don't thank me, thank Kathryn. Without her photograph, we wouldn't have found him. The name he gave you was bogus, and his business front has been deserted."

Shannon threw her arms around Kathryn, laughing and crying.

Kathryn met Jackson's eyes over Shannon's shoulder. He smiled as he said, "I thought you all might be ready for some good news."

Thank you, she mouthed.

"Thank you." Grant vigorously shook Jackson's hand, clasping his arm, then repeated the action with Stuart. He wiped his eyes. Kathryn thought he even stood a little taller.

"Not to put a damper on the celebration," Gloria interrupted, twisting her lips into a frown. "But has anyone been online?" She wiggled her cell.

Kathryn's stomach twisted. They were announcing the winner of the Fan Favorite Choice Award today. She'd hoped her friends would forget. "It wasn't me, was it?"

"What wasn't you?" Shannon pulled a tissue from her purse and wiped her eyes.

Gloria shook her head. "I'm sorry. You didn't win." Ethan touched her arm. "I'm sorry, too."

Kathryn waited for disappointment to fall. And waited some more. She must be numb. "How bad is it?"

"Someone posted a picture of you holding a bottle in the park with Tiffany. The comments are awful."

Tiff gulped. "I'm sorry, Kathryn. That's my fault."

Kathryn's heart dipped, not over losing the contest, but over the idea that Tiff might add this to the burden she carried. She squared her shoulders. "So what if I lost the contest? So what if perfect strangers draw the wrong conclusions about what was a huge victory for us. We have what really matters." Kathryn looped her arms through Gloria and Kim's. "Friends that care, and friends that we care about." She held Tiff's watery gaze. "That includes you."

Tiff gave the tiniest nod.

"Why don't you tell them, Tiff?" Gloria nodded at Tiff.

Kathryn caught her breath. Gloria had called her *Tiff*. Not *that girl*.

Tiff's smile faltered, but only for a second. "You guys need to come inside."

Ethan's arm circled her waist. "Why? What are you all doing here, and why did Dad ask to leave the crime scene tape up?"

"We have a surprise." Emma's gesture indicated that Kathryn and Ethan should follow them.

The interior had been swept clean. Tables and chairs were stacked neatly in the back. But the immediate area surrounding the roaster still showed scars. Holes of various sizes perforated the counter separating it from the kitchen. Bits of cupcakes and pies even splattered the ceiling. Flour and cookie crumbs dusted every surface like drywall dust. Ethan wrapped a hand around the back of his neck.

"How did you walk away from this?" Shannon's eyes were huge. She hadn't seen the scene until now, and the reality that Ethan could have been killed nearly buckled her.

"I was behind the counter."

The destroyed counter. Kathryn's stomach heaved. Grant cleared his throat, and the horror on Shannon's face was quickly replaced with suppressed excitement. Something was up. Shannon nodded encouragingly at Grant.

"You know that your mom and I had been looking for passive income to help in our retirement years." Grant addressed Ethan. "We had decided that if Jackson was able to recover any of our money, we wanted to invest it in your coffee business."

Ethan's mouth gaped, and Kathryn slipped her arm through his.

Grant introduced his foreman, Joel. Both of them had huge

smiles splitting their faces, and a small crew of men fell in behind them. "Nobody deserves to have their life's work taken from them like this." Grant gestured to the now mostly emptied space. "We're going to rebuild The Muffin Man even better than before."

Ethan screwed up his eyes. Considering all the ways his father had tried to lure Ethan away from a career as a baker, Kathryn got it. Logic dictated Grant should be dancing on The Muffin Man's grave, but instead, he grieved with his son.

"But you didn't know about the money until just now." Carving a hand through his hair, Ethan held it back and then released it. He eyeballed his dad.

"Once we decided to invest, we also decided it didn't matter if we got the money back or not. We were all in. You are our safest bet. We believe in you, and if you believe in The Muffin Man, then so do we."

Ethan's mouth slackened. When he didn't move, Kathryn nudged him. "Go hug your father."

Ethan stumbled forward, and his dad met him halfway. The two men embraced. "You turned out great in spite of me." Grant's muffled words warmed Kathryn's heart.

They pulled apart, and Grant swiped a backhand across his eyes. "Joel assembled the crew last night, and with Jackson's permission to be on the scene, they've been working non-stop."

"How'd you find a crew?"

"Pastor Owen called some young men at the church, and it turns out there are a few guys looking to apprentice. Once Joel fills out the government forms, we'll have enough workers." His cheeks flushed.

"What about retirement?"

Grant snorted. "There wouldn't be a retirement without you and Kathryn. I'm sorry it took something like this to bring me around."

"And I'm here to make sure he stays off the ladders." Joel winked.

Mom threaded her arm through Grant's. "We're starting the paperwork so Joel can eventually take over the business and the apprentices. But all this is only if you want it. You don't have to partner with us. What do you want to do, Ethan?"

Kathryn held her breath, and Ethan held his dad's gaze.

"I'm done telling you what you should do," Grant said.

Ethan was positively gobsmacked, and it made Kathryn feel lighter and happier than she ever thought possible. Tears prickled, and Kathryn squeezed Ethan's arm. "What do you think?"

Ethan surveyed the space. His grin started small but soon mirrored his father's. He thrust a fist into the air. "We rebuild!"

Everyone cheered.

One Week Later

"C an you believe my dad?" Ethan pointed across what used to be the bakery's dining area to where his dad ordered around his construction crew. Light-headedness scrambled his brain. He still couldn't believe all that had unfolded.

"It's kind of mind-blowing," Kathryn agreed.

Dad wasn't the only one blowing Ethan's mind. Kathryn hadn't been online since the night they'd announced she'd lost the contest. She hadn't responded to a single comment or question. In fact, she'd deleted the apps from her phone. She blamed the remodel, but they both knew a full schedule had never stopped her before. She had chosen to pull back to gain perspective, and he hadn't seen her happier or healthier despite the disturbing details trickling in as Jackson and Stuart continued to fit the puzzle pieces together.

Shawn—the guy who'd targeted Ethan—had been watching him for a while, waiting for the opportunity to swap out a premixed bag of beans and pebbles with the ones left by his delivery man near the alley door. Even worse, while Shawn was in claiming his free coffees, he lifted a key from Addison, had a new key cut, then returned Addison's key to be "found" in the bakery. Shawn had the freedom to enter and exit at will, swapping salt for sugar to bomb the cooking show, damage the computer, and add gunpowder to the roaster. The unbelievable details could have filled a crime show episode, yet Kathryn didn't report on a single one.

She'd stayed by his side, swinging a hammer, hanging drywall, and laughing full belly laughs like when they were kids. It was odd; in a crazy way, despite all the losses, this had been the best week of Ethan's life.

Dad's crew had gutted the space in a single day, and the trades had already been in to update the wiring and plumbing. And now, Dad stood over a folding table and studied plans—plans Ethan had drawn up years ago when he'd been dreaming about what he'd do to the bakery if he ever had the time and money to renovate.

Just a few months ago, Ethan would have never thought this moment was possible. Back then, his dad was more likely to tease him about his work than encourage him. Now, here they were, in the ruins of The Muffin Man, making his dreams come true. The difficulty of the last few weeks had really been an opportunity in disguise—an opportunity to work with his dad and craft something that reflected the best of both of them. This was something they would both be proud of.

"The only shock bigger than seeing your dad here is seeing them together." Kathryn pointed her chin in Tiff and Gloria's direction.

All his friends had been showing up daily to do whatever labor they could. Gloria, in her collared shirt and khaki pants, and Tiff in a pair of dark jeans and a graphic t-shirt, chatted as they measured and cut drywall. The women couldn't be more different. When Gloria placed her hand over Tiff's and they bowed their heads as if to pray, Kathryn tightened her hold on Ethan's hand.

Ethan planted a kiss on her temple. "It's not fair," he said softly. "Everyone is getting what they wanted but you."

Kathryn lifted onto her tiptoes and lightly brushed her lips against his. "That's not true."

Before she could elaborate, a police cruiser parked out front, and Jackson approached with a somber expression. "Can I grab you two for a minute?"

They followed Jackson outside.

"We have some news about the threats and bullying Kathryn received online."

Kathryn stiffened. "I didn't know you were still looking into that."

"I know you were very concerned that your participation in the contest was somehow to blame for Ethan's misfortune. I can tell you with one hundred percent assurance that concern is unfounded."

Any rigidity left in Kathryn's posture evaporated, and Ethan relaxed. Fully relaxed. She was going to be okay.

"I never believed it was connected," Ethan said.

"I wouldn't say they were disconnected," Jackson corrected him. "The events are connected, just not in the way that you thought."

A chill swept over Ethan. He bit the inside of his cheek.

"I poked around on several social media platforms, and I found your bully." Jackson looked Kathryn in the eyes. "She and Ethan's saboteur are in a relationship." Jackson showed Kathryn and Ethan a picture of the girl.

Ethan shuffled back a step. "That's the woman I spoke with at Cool Beans." The implications of this discovery hit like an anvil. *It was his fault.* "My misfortune wasn't connected to your contest." He looked at Kathryn. "Your misfortune was connected to me."

Jackson nodded. "They cooked up this idea when you announced your plans to start a coffee bean subscription service. They thought if they could discredit Kathryn while she was trying to promote you, they'd also discredit you, and no one would make the connection back to them."

"I can't believe it." Ethan felt dizzy. "I'm so sorry."

"I don't know if this helps," Jackson said, "but they didn't know you'd be in the bakery when the roaster exploded. When Shawn saw the announcement that you were closing for the day due to the break in, he used his key to let himself back in. He even waited until the adjacent businesses closed. They didn't plan to hurt anyone."

"Was he there when Ethan arrived?"

Jackson nodded.

So he *had* heard someone moving around! Ethan had assumed it was thunder.

"Shawn put in the gunpowder, turned on the roaster, and hurried out the back door."

"And he had no idea I'd come in the front door," Ethan murmured.

"That's why he was there in the aftermath. He blended in with the crowd because he needed to see that you were okay."

"And that's why Clara saw him." Kathryn finished with a snort. "How could anyone be dumb enough to think heating gunpowder wouldn't hurt anyone?"

"Gunpowder burns very quickly because the potassium nitrate supplies oxygen to the charcoal and sulfur, accelerating the burn rate. This combustion creates a gas more dangerous than the actual gunpowder. Had they heated it in the open air, the gas would have just expanded into the air," Jackson explained.

"But since it was trapped in the roaster—" Ethan started.

"It forced its way out with an explosion much bigger than they anticipated," Jackson finished.

They all looked at the bakery in silence.

Jackson shifted gears. "I got in touch with the awards coordinator, and after updating them on virtual stalking and harassment laws, they announced a plan to reorganize before next year's contest. But it doesn't change anything for you this year, Kathryn."

"That's okay." Kathryn said it in a way that Ethan really believed her. It really was okay.

"Let me know if you need anything else," Jackson said, before leaving.

"Are you really okay with this?" Ethan needed to hear it again.

Kathryn hugged her middle and surveyed the storefront. "I am. You know, great things have come from this. Things that might not have been had the details unfolded any other way. How can I be anything but thankful? God took what the enemy meant for evil and turned it around and used it for good."

On the other side of Ethan's newly installed window, Gloria and Tiff chatted. Gloria threw her head back and laughed as Tiff gestured animatedly. His dad stuffed a drill in the appropriate holster on his tool belt, as Eli and Addison, with Ethan's computer tucked under his arm, descended the stairs. It was working out for everybody but Kathryn. Ethan wanted good for her as well. "You amaze me."

She turned into his arms and leaned her cheek against his chest. Maybe his problem was he was trying to define what good meant. Maybe he needed to let God define it? He breathed in the familiar scent of her shampoo. The sun glinted off the gilded Muffin Man sign that someone had scrubbed clean and rehung. As their friends worked inside, the occasional shout of laughter trickled out. For one blazing moment, everything was perfect.

Ethan motioned for Kathryn to go into the bakery ahead of him. They walked through the newly installed door that was even nicer than the previous one. As they approached his father, Ethan slapped a hand on his back. "Let me see these kitchen plans."

Dad tucked a pencil behind his ear. "I was thinking, why not expand a bit more?" He pointed at the space between the wall of ovens and the sink. "If we pushed this wall back and widened this gap, you could add a nice-sized prep counter in the middle."

Ethan's throat squeezed. His dad was not only helping him rebuild, but was designing the space with Ethan's needs in mind. It really was a miracle. "I'm not sure I can afford it. The insurance came through, but I'm pinching pennies already."

"When we get our money back, your mother and I are putting it into the bakery."

Ethan's father unfolded an updated design. It had all the details of Ethan's original dream, but expanded. Ethan's lungs compressed.

"If we move the cafe area near the back"—Dad pointed to the drawings—"we can include a wall of built-ins that hold board games and a mini library or bookstore. Customers can grab coffee or lunch and linger."

Kathryn's eyes sparkled. "And what about evening events? That's typically the slowest time of day, but if you did that, you'd have space to host things like art classes, poetry reading, open mic nights. You'd be the hub of activity for local artists. You could even host recovery meetings here after hours instead of in the church basement."

"All subject to your approval, of course," Dad said.

"I think it sounds wonderful," Ethan said. "More than wonderful. It's amazing."

Kathryn beamed her first high-wattage smile that wasn't aimed at a camera. The Muffin Man wasn't just becoming his dream business, it was becoming theirs. His dad smiled proudly, as if he'd known from day one things were going to be this way—him redesigning the bakery, Kathryn providing insights, Ethan living his best life. The bells above the door jingled, and everyone lifted their faces.

Meg's cheeks flushed as she balanced on the top of a small stepladder. "It didn't feel right to not hear the bells."

Ethan thought he might burst. This was his family. It was more than those related by blood but included those connected together through friendship—he gazed at Kathryn—and love.

Two Months Later

Tiff gave Kathryn a thumbs up, and Kathryn looked at the camera, dead centre. "It's been a few months since I've been online, and it's finally time I addressed the crazy comments. No, I did not check into rehab. No, my relationship with Ethan didn't end. I pulled back to give the trolls time to move on. I pulled back to gain some much-needed distance so I could gain some much-needed perspective. I was in front of the camera so often that I had forgotten who I really was, and it had impacted my mental health negatively. You've never seen me like this before, makeup free, no filter, just plain Kathryn. I decided my last episode had to be this way for a specific reason."

Ethan approached from behind Tiff, and Kathryn looked past the camera to catch his eye. His beaming smile of approval gave her all the courage she needed.

"Many of us, me included, present an online personality that is disconnected from reality. We only show the perfect us. The filtered us. The us we wish we could be. But no one is perfect. In my attempt to livestream during the Fan Favourite Choice Awards, you saw my flaws. You saw parts of me that I didn't want anybody to see. But God used that exposure to do a work in my heart. He used it to rebuild me."

Kathryn lifted her phone so it was in the frame and paused to read the screen. "Yes, the contest impacted Ethan's bakery. Yes, he has to rebuild from scratch."

She flicked her gaze back to the camera. "I'm reading your comments as my friend films so we can dialogue. I appreciate your concern for Ethan's bakery and for what happened to me, but the hate toward the culprit is not necessary. It needs to stop. *Name and shame* is not a trend I want on my feed, so all posts with that feel have been and will be deleted."

She read a few more comments. A smile softened her face. "No, I won't DM anyone the details so you can take care of it for me."

More comments popped up on the phone newsfeed.

We love you, Kathryn.

I knew you could never relapse.

I missed your channel.

And then finally, one she had been hoping for.

Praying for. The reason she was making the change to speak more openly about addiction, mental health, and the daily struggle to live clean. Someone named StillFalling wrote:

I've followed your channel for years, and as I saw your story unfold, I felt hope for the first time. If you can get your life back together after addiction, maybe I can too.

Pressure grew behind her eyes. "StillFalling, whoever you are, if not for the grace of God we'd all stand before Him ashamed and condemned. I wore the labels alcoholic, bad friend, gossip, and sinner. But now, I wear the robes of righteousness bought by

Christ's blood. He superimposes the reality that I was saved, am saved, and am being saved over the fact that I was an addict, am an addict, and will always be an addict. My addiction doesn't get to define me. He does."

StillFalling responded, *You've overcome a lot.*

"Jesus overcame a lot," she corrected.

You're an inspiration.

"Praise the Lord, this time I will inspire others for Him."

Are you changing things?

"Everything changed when I realized it didn't matter if I won or lost the Fan Favorite Choice Award. It didn't matter if no one picked me because God had chosen me, and because of that, I will never be alone."

Something that had been more important to her than anything else ceased to matter because the Lord mattered more. The weight of a million pounds lifted.

Approval no longer defined her.

"Yes, things are changing," Kathryn replied. "My media channels will remain active, but I'm no longer covering the daily news. I'm not jumping back into the grind to produce live clips. I'll pop in and out with pre-recorded videos to keep you updated on things like—" Kathryn gestured to Tiff to pan the bakery. "Ethan's shop reopening tomorrow! I'm so proud of his hard work." She trailed her fingers along the countertop. "I recorded some before and after videos and I'll post those at a later date." A much later date, because she was learning about the balance and boundaries she needed to keep in place to stay healthy.

"This is Kathryn Withers—" Kathryn swallowed. Wait—

Her mom's name popped up her feed. *We are so very proud of you.*

Everything stopped. Her parents were watching? And they

were proud? After everything she put them through, they were proud? Kathryn's throat swelled. The pressure behind her eyes threatened to spill onto her cheeks.

You are brave, strong, and inspiring. We always believed in you.

Viewers were hearting her mom's comment faster than Kathryn could count. Her head fuzzed. Was it possible that the shame and denial she'd attributed to her parents was actually a reflection of her own guilt?

Tiff waved like a wild woman. She spun the camera to face her. "Hey everybody, I'm Tiff, and before Kathryn signs off, Ethan has something to say."

Ethan stepped into the frame and dropped to a knee, holding out a tiny black box.

Kathryn gasped. The tears she'd been fighting fell. Her heart thumped wildly as Ethan opened the velvety lid. Inside, a delicate ring sparkled.

This wasn't happening. It couldn't be happening. Kathryn didn't know what to do or say. Shock had stolen her voice and her thoughts.

"Kathryn Withers, I wavered on whether I should do this privately or publicly. In the end, I decided to do this online because I want the whole world to know you have changed my life for the better. Ever since we first met at summer camp when we were kids"—his words were hoarse and laced with emotion—"you've been an amazing friend and confidante. I can't imagine living another day without you in my life."

Kathryn lifted her gaze from the ring to his eyes.

"I've known you were the one since we were eight years old, and we spent afternoons catching insects. You'd catch them, set them free, and mumble something about all God's creation deserving to live."

Kathryn laughed. During these past few joy-filled months, she rediscovered that simple eight-year-old who loved to dig in the dirt.

"We belong together," Ethan said.

Her mouth twitched. "Like pork 'n' beans?"

"Like Barbie 'n' Ken." His lips turned up.

"Like peanut butter and jelly." She swayed closer and arched a brow in a challenge.

He accepted. "Like break 'n' enter."

Was he remembering the night he broke into her house to retrieve his grandmother's recipe? That was the night they got back together. The night they filmed in her kitchen a Sycamore Sunrise episode that prompted his dad to reach out and begin mending the rift between them.

"Salt 'n' pepper."

"Coffee 'n' cream."

"Ah, guys," Tiff interrupted. "You have a few online comments to address."

Ethan took Kathryn's phone from her hand and laughed as he read them out loud. "Just ask her already. Kiss her." Ethan's voice caught. "Your parents gave their blessing and my dad says, you're a keeper, just like my mom."

Kathryn's heart felt full.

"One guy says if I don't ask, he will." Ethan looked up and caught her gaze. "I can't have that."

Ethan picked up her hand. Kathryn's breath caught. Her lungs expanded until she thought they might burst.

"Kathryn Withers, will you make me the happiest man on earth and be the cheese to my macaroni?"

She burst out laughing. The cheese wasn't destined to stand alone after all.

"I mean, will you be my wife?"

She nodded almost imperceptibly before finally managing to whisper, "Yes!"

Ethan rose to his feet and embraced her tightly amid swelling cries from their friends, who had gathered behind. Kathryn laid her head on the chest of the man she'd always loved. They fit together perfectly. Like love and marriage.

Fatal Homecoming

ROMANTIC SUSPENSE

In the crosshairs of a killer...

Travel writer, Jessie Berns, returns to her hometown to find answers about her brother's suspicious death. With the help of an old friend, Detective Rick Chandler, they pursue a truth that someone is willing to do anything to keep hidden—even kill again. They uncover decades-old secrets that expose hidden sins and threaten the lifestyles of high-powered people in their small community. As they close in on the devious mastermind manipulating the town, it becomes frighteningly clear to Rick that Jessie is not the one calling the shots in her private investigation. She is the killer's new target.

Praise for Fatal Homecoming

If you are looking for a great read, encompassing Christian values, that will keep you spell bound from beginning to end, this is the book for you! It has a riveting plot that will keep you on the edge of your seat, with your heart pounding!! My attention was grabbed on the first page and I just could not put this book down. This book is packed full of suspense.

A great novel packed full of romance and suspense! Don't miss it!

— ~KARLA / BOOK REVIEWER / 5 STARS

Wow - You are not going to put this one down until you are finished! If you enjoyed those Nancy Drew and Hardy Boy style books, this one is for you.

After many years away from the small town she grew up in, Jessie returns for the funeral of her brother. What happens after she arrives is nonstop action until the murderer or perhaps murderers are caught. I must admit, there were several characters that I suspected, but I certainly was way off base. The author has done a fabulous job of keeping the reader in the dark right up to the end. The lesson learned from the pile of rocks was important for all generations.

— ~BETTY / BOOK REVIEWER / 5 STARS

Fatal Homecoming is a fast-paced suspense with more than enough action and danger to keep even the most avid suspense fan glued to its pages. I really enjoyed reading about the Royal Canadian Mounted Police for a change of pace.

Well rounded characters and a riveting plot keep me reading until the end. I also liked the way the author managed to weave a strong spiritual message into the story through conversations between the primary characters who found that depending on God was all that would get them through the increasing threats to their lives.

— ~ PAM / DAYLONG REFLECTIONS / 5 STARS

Acknowledgments

Writing is never a one-person adventure. Despite the hours I live inside my head working on a story or book, countless others invest in the project. I would have never created Sycamore Hill without the encouragement of my writing friends in the Brantford Writers Group. Thank you, Karen, Sandy, Heather, Tara, and Deirdre for your enthusiasm and belief in me. You believed these characters had more to their stories.

Thank you to an extraordinary editor, Olivia, from LivEdits. You helped tie the threads of this story together.

And thank you to my family for always believing in the stories I want to tell.

You Can Make a Difference

REVIEW RETURN TO SYCAMORE HILL

Did you enjoy this book? You can make a difference. Honest reviews of books bring them to the attention of other readers. If you enjoyed this book, I would be grateful if you could take a few minutes to leave an online review or star rating where you purchased the book. You can also post reviews and star ratings on Goodreads and Bookbub.

About the Author

Stacey Weeks writes contemporary romance and romantic suspense filled with strong women, honorable men, and just enough heart-pounding sweetness to keep you turning pages. Her stories are rooted in hope and grace.

She's also the author of non-fiction titles like *Glorious Surrender*, *Chasing Holiness*, *Season of Wonder*, and *Unceasing Prayer*. A ministry wife and homeschooling mom of three, Stacey holds graduate certificates in Women's Ministry and Biblical Counselling from Heritage College and Seminary.

When she's not writing or speaking, you'll find her with a cup of tea and an open Bible, sharing hope (and laughs) with women. She a child of the "play until the streetlights turn on" generation, she loves fixing old things, and above all, she follows Jesus, her greatest joy and deepest hope.

facebook.com/writerSWeeks

x.com/writerSWeeks

instagram.com/writerSWeeks